HATCHED

ROBERT F. BARSKY

Mechanicsburg, PA USA

Published by Sunbury Press, Inc.
105 South Market Street
Mechanicsburg, Pennsylvania 17055

www.sunburypress.com

For information about special discounts for bulk purchases, please contact Sunbury Press Orders Dept. at (855) 338-8359 or orders@sunburypress.com.

To request one of our authors for speaking engagements or book signings, please contact Sunbury Press Publicity Dept. at publicity@sunburypress.com.

ISBN: 978-1-62006-740-6 (Trade Paperback)
ISBN: 978-1-62006-741-3 (Mobipocket)

Library of Congress Control Number: 2016944956

FIRST SUNBURY PRESS EDITION: August 2016

Product of the United States of America
0 1 1 2 3 5 8 13 21 34 55

Set in Bookman Old Style
Designed by Crystal Devine
Cover by Amber Rendon
Edited by Janice Rhayem

Continue the Enlightenment!

All of the events in this story are fictional.

That is, all of the events recounted in this story were like eggs,
and all of these eggs were incubated under conditions sufficiently
    ideal
as to lead them to hatch, and then once hatched,
they were placed in a cauldron lined with warm butter,
and then they were combined, seasoned, heated, and, finally,
    served.
To you.

The resulting eggy mixtures are artifices of truth,
they are snippets, lifted from known sources and then distorted,
they are fake fantasies, incorrectly recalled, and then transcribed,
and they are not, really, real.
But like all fictional, partial reminiscences that have been
    aesthetically rendered,
and like all of those sensations that emerge from our imbibing
    concocted recipes,
they are delicious.

And they are all also true.

CHAPTER 1

Immaculate imperfection. Silent to the touch, but teeming with all of the potential that can be excited by fertile stimulation. From up close, it seems painted with an imperfectly mixed, white gouache upon an uneven surface; from further back, it is an oblong globe, steadied from the center to the periphery to withstand the gentle swaying of the nest, the wind, the rain. The shell is solid, protective, and yet, always, and secretly, vulnerable. It's hardy and well-insulated inside, but once expelled into the world of knocks and piercings, the yolk suffers and thereby reveals the single weakness of a shell pervious to rigid surfaces, its soft and mottled form suddenly blistered, cracked, dented, revealing tender, white flesh within, but concealing a core, an essence, a willing soul now and forever unfulfilled. Never to consume, the yolk now settles, haughtily, awaiting the fate of consumption. . . .

Suddenly, its very essence is reminiscent of Sunday morning, when Dad would for once sleep in and, that accomplished, would awaken the household with 'Rise and shine!,' accompanied by the sizzling sound of butter caressing and then solidifying the gooey translucence into white, the bulbous yellow to a globe and a world unto itself. The buttery pan, once heated, makes golden magic of this bulging, yellow world, now perched atop a gooey throne that, from the end towards the center, grows into a plastic base. The battered shells now ruthlessly discarded reveal untarnished and impeccable interiors, smooth walls now dripping with the liquid white remains, having for their trouble preserved the yellow center of the world, bulging, nearly heaving, now intact, defying gravity's pull and begging. . . .

"Would you like another one?"

"What? Oh!" Jude, startled into submission and then into feigned aggression, looked up, almost violently, and was thus transported from a state of transfixion to one of planned aggression, and then bewitchment. Vulnerable through his heightened senses, he was shocked into the world by eyes, green, oscillating side to side, shining. Suddenly still, they drew him in, glistening.

He blinks.

Sparkles of light now capture his gaze, a regard that had been so long focused upon the paper in front of him, and, moreover, on the shining, white egg in his hand, and, intermittently, upon the shards of a second eggshell that was splattered out before him.

It took him a moment to realize that she was speaking to him, and he let his eyes drift down to her lips. Now they were frozen in a kind of grimace. They had been stilled by his silence.

"I'm sorry . . .?"

"Did you want another egg? I don't want to . . ."

Jude's stare descended, rose up, and then expanded outwards, his perspective now encompassing the features of the woman who stood before him. He felt thunderstruck, as though he'd been the only person in the universe to that point, and was now confronted not only with another being, but one who had chosen him, of all other life forms, with whom to interact. For this reason, and at that moment, he felt bonded to this woman, attracted, as a celestial body is to a moon that suddenly finds itself spinning within the powerful gravitational draw of a greater being. One moment longer, and his eyes might never again close. He felt his own stare burning and pulsating, as though his very eyeballs stood on the threshold of ossifying that moment for all eternity.

The woman who stood before Jude, on the other hand, squinted her eyes with impending despair and sensed that familiar flush of fear in her heart, a kind of sickening anxiety that sets in upon the realization that this person, with whom she herself had chosen to interact, might be a psychopath.

"Do I?" stammered Jude. The woman before him looked impatient.

"Oh!" Jude blurted out. "No, no, thanks, I just needed the one, um, the two of them. I'm . . . I'm done, thanks." He looked down at the perfect, white egg that nestled into one hand, and then to the messy remnants of the other that he'd destroyed through his exploration. He looked back up into her eyes, but they were frowning and piercing.

"Sorry, I think I dripped a little on the table cloth, I mean it dripped, um, dropped from the shell."

She feigned a smile, but remained hovering precariously between a sense of security in the idea that he was just weird, and a sense of profound horror at the thought that this bizarre behavior might be but a symptom of some repulsive comportment to come. An hour or so ago she had first given him one egg, which he went on to crack and fondle and finally destroy, and then a second, as he had requested, that he simply stared at as though it were the decryption device for some long-lost code. At the time, it seemed a quaint and possibly appropriate thing to do in a restaurant in which the entire menu is oriented towards eggs of all kinds, and in which clients are accustomed to asking for them, in various forms.

But when he requested that second egg, and proceeded to stare at it, to caress it, to seek some kind of message from it, and then to write frantically in the wake of his observations, she concluded that she'd done the wrong thing, with the wrong objects, to the wrong person, at the wrong time, in her place of employment. She also felt that somehow she was destined to suffer, for eternity, on account of that flippant decision. Her life seemed to now hang in the balance between survival and brutal destruction, between the suspended moment of their current interaction and every and all moments that would follow, until the end of time.

In the meantime, Jude's eyes lowered back down to her mouth, opened slightly, and her lips now spread before him. He could see her teeth, quietly aligned in harmonious formation, bared forth to his consuming gaze. The image of their white enamel joined at that moment the sight he had frozen in his mind of the eggshell, with which he'd awkwardly spent the last few minutes—or was it hours? And he was transported back to that space of calm, penetrating scrutiny. His eye stared forth relentlessly, and her teeth became droplets of petrified enamel, tiny, perfect replicas of that unbroken eggshell that had hovered a few inches from his face but a few moments before. He wondered, if he were to get closer to her smile, and to those perfect, white teeth, would he find the imperfections of the second, intact egg, with its mottled, cratered surface? Perhaps, he ruminated like a gaping dentist drugged with his own ether, her teeth, like the now-broken shell of the first egg, would reveal the wet idealism of the coated interior surface, glistening, smooth, aglow with the light above his table.

As his passionate dream of symbiosis made claim to his reason, he awakened and looked at her as a person, an employee in this restaurant, a total stranger, and he realized that she looked not only exasperated, but also terrified. Was this the emotion he invoked in this human being? He looked down at her name, embroidered into her chef's uniform, upon which was inscribed but one word: "Jessica." He looked up at her, sheepishly. "Um, . . ." He tried to speak. No words came forth from his gaping mouth.

Her frown returned, and intensified.

Unfortunately, the awkwardness of the situation had rendered him mute. He thought to apologize to her, to Jessica. He imagined himself using her own name, clearly and calmly, so that she'd realize that he had respect for her, for her parents who had named her, and for the village from which she hearkened. But her body was no longer a fixed receptacle of his will; indeed, she was turning away from him, unwilling to sustain the obdurate silence.

"Oh . . .!" Jude ejaculated a sound intended to fix her to a space near to him, but still, no words emerged, just a low-sounding vibration, like a grunt. He panicked, hoping that she hadn't heard.

Whether or not Jude's primordial noise was audible above the sound of the pre-client restaurant, he'd never know. But Jessica's sense of employee etiquette yoked her in, and she turned back to him. "Tina, um, the maître d', told me that you are conducting experiments?"

He looked at her attentively. She spoke with a degree of false, or at least forced, optimism, and as she did so, she looked down at his notebook, and saw that its first page was partially covered with untidy handwriting.

"I am, yes," replied Jude optimistically, casually noting a brilliant idea that emerged from her question: "Eggsperiments."

"We're not used to bringing our ingredients to the table," she said.

He looked up from the page, suddenly panic-stricken, vulnerable, weak.

"Um . . .!"

Now she feigned a smile. She was looking for some rational explanation and had given him a small number of seconds to produce one before she found an excuse to get John, often referred to as John-the-Owner, who would happily arrive donning the baseball bat that he brought with him to the restaurant each day. It wouldn't be the first time she'd asked him to come join her at a table for a little exercise in exiting disorderly clientele.

Jude looked disparagingly forward in a near-normal pose, as though he had suddenly recognized his place at this table, in this restaurant, upon this planet. He also came to be aware of his awkward method of communication with her, with Jessica, an innocent victim of wages and tips and bonuses, a captive audience of his own facetiousness. As a consequence, the deranged look in his eyes wavered, softened, and dissolved, and he beamed forth a face of gentle innocence and naïve wanderlust.

The effect upon Jessica was instantaneous.

"He is probably just young, idealistic, and stupid," she thought. Her expression softened, and she turned towards him, in complete deference. "It's okay," she conceded aloud, "I just want to make sure that you don't need anything else."

He found some consolation in her kind reaction to his pathetic demeanor. "Thanks," he murmured.

She had crushed him, and he now lay before her like the quivering, gooey liquid of an uncooked egg white, separated from whatever meaning the yolk could provide when adjoined to it.

"Thanks so much," he proclaimed, offering total submission and gratitude.

Jessica's professional training was getting the best of her, at last, and in its wake came all of the formality, the stiffness, the routine, and the rhetoric of a job spent satisfying the needs, culinary and otherwise, of others.

"If you do need another egg, you can have one, but I'm going on my break now. I guess you could ask Tina, the maître d', she's around here somewhere. . . ." She suddenly stopped her soliloquy, and felt as though she'd left her body and was now watching her own strange performance in front of this even stranger man. She realized that her look was one of perplexity, not on account of anything he had done or said, but because of the bizarre advice she had just given him regarding Tina.

Now, she did turn to leave, and then suddenly turned back, as though she'd forgotten to convey a crucial detail.

"Break!" she burst out as though struck by a singular revelation.

Jude didn't know whether to smile or flee.

"Break! I'm on my break. Break. You know, I'm, well, broken, like the shell."

Jude was completely bewildered, and bewitched.

"I have recovered," she thought to herself. Then, with poised purpose, she turned away and headed towards the kitchen. She felt better, back in control. She was, after all, a self-possessed employee in the service industry, and, moreover, she was a pretty woman who was accustomed to being accosted by idiotic coworkers and clients. And so she decided that she could allow this particular client to entirely leave her mind, and that she could purge her memory of him, forever.

"Thanks," called Jude to her abiding absence.

Jessica didn't turn back.

"I appreciate it!" he called out to the flip side of her existence. Now he had no idea whatsoever of what he should have said. He felt as though he'd shared in a really strange private joke related to, who knows? So now what? He was running out of time. Her essence was being drawn like a spirit receding to the other side of the universe.

"I should get going, are you closing?" he called after her, rising instinctively. She did not respond, and he was left halfway to standing. He sat back down. How long had he been there? He looked down to his scrawl and added the word "break" to the adjacent "eggsperiments," and then looked over at the check to see what he had ordered. "Eggs," it said. Just one word hovered before his eyes. "Eggs," and beside it: $14.50.

How much tip could he afford? He motioned to his pocket to alleviate the client guilt, but her uniform indicated that she works in the kitchen, not the dining room.

"Is it okay to tip those who work in the kitchen?" he wondered to himself. He looked down at his tabletop, a gleaming, white surface littered with the shells he had so carefully examined, and then smashed. He then carefully placed the still-intact egg on a small dish in front of him, with undue deliberation. He flicked his wrist with great determination, to position the face of his watch towards his overly attentive gaze. Noon.

"Lunchtime," he thought. "Wow, I've been here since 10:00 a.m., and all I have is this paragraph. And now she, Jessica, is going to kick me out. Shit." He realized that he had been speaking aloud and suddenly panicked. "I . . .," he endeavored once again to call out in her direction. "Shit, she's gone, and she's, oh . . ." He reached down again towards his pocket to lure her back. "Who the fuck am I kidding?" he thought to himself, in a space that almost made him audible. He instinctively looked up in the direction of her departure.

En route to the swinging doors that divided the restaurant from the kitchen, Jessica suddenly paused and directed her gaze towards the entrance to the restaurant, where a figure had appeared. She pulled off her white-linen chef's hat, imploring a cascade of tawny hair to spill forth anxiously, and then careen downwards, almost to her waist, in apparent relief. Her face, her regard, the row of those beautiful, egg-like teeth, was lost to Jude's view as she oriented her gate towards this dark figure.

Jude felt a sense of abandonment and despair. He was shattered, like the eggy shards before him. He studied what remained in his view of this woman—Jessica. He was staring intently forward, mesmerized. "She is so beautiful." He was speaking to his mind's ear in a wistful, nostalgic tone, like a parent addressing the windshield of her car as she drove away from the summer camp where little Amy, or Sylvia or Freddy, would spend the next two anxiety-ridden weeks in estrangement and despair. He cautiously reviewed what remained of his interaction with her. Her white chef jacket was perhaps a bit shorter than the norm, arrested just slightly above her hips. Tight, black-and-white-mottled chef pants accentuated her beautiful form. He wondered if she was wearing standard kitchen garb, or if these garments were somehow special, perhaps tailored to fit her and her alone.

"Do people do that?" he wondered. He kept following her with his eyes, studying the graceful and deliberate motion of her body.

At the entrance to the restaurant, the tall man became engulfed in the light from the window beside the cash register. He was a handsome, rugged type, sporting short, curly, graying hair. He bore a dark complexion and wore black sunglasses. His clothing, too, was entirely black: shoes, trousers, turtleneck, leather jacket, gloves—all impeccable. Now it was this man who was caught in Jude's egg-trained gaze. Jude caught himself, suddenly aware, and then suddenly embarrassed.

"I'm a stupid fuck," he thought. "Watching the world as though it were entertainment—entertainment, diversion." He looked down again at the shattered egg, now congealing, and sighed.

"Maybe it is!" he ejaculated, this time rather loudly. He lifted his gaze and looked again at this man in black. "Yah, sure," he laughed to himself, in answer to a question he hadn't even formulated. "Funny, very funny you asshole," he thought. "Very, fucking funny."

7

Jude half-rose in his chair as though to leave, or perhaps to measure his height relative to hers, or his, but then sat back down again. His bleach-and-wear, faded denim jacket caught the side of the table, giving his fork cause for a backflip up and full twist. With the pride of a routine well executed, it flipped over once more and crashed down onto the floor, brushing his ankle on the way down, most probably egging up his pants. Befuddled, Jude didn't know whether to follow his stare or to look down to acknowledge his gaff. Before there was time for any existential resolution, however, Tina, the maître-d', emerged from the kitchen, hearkened as by the sound of a dinner bell. She looked at Jessica, at the man at the door, then over towards Jude, and then back to Jessica.

"Saved!" thought Jude. He reached down and picked up the fork, so as to avoid the embarrassment of having Tina clean up after him. The idea of being regarded as a menacing lunatic by two employees of this restaurant was too much, even by his own rather loose standards.

"Jess, thanks, I was just out back," called Tina to Jessica as she walked towards Jude's table.

"Jess," thought Jude. "Not Jessica. Jess. They must be close friends, or . . ." He felt aroused at the thought that these two women might be more than coworkers.

As she approached Jude's table, Tina dropped her gaze downwards, towards her long fingers, which she now extended as though to examine the color of her nail polish. There was no point in giving this young man the impression that he, or the mess of eggs that lay before him, were of special interest. Then as she neared Jude's table, Tina looked back towards Jessica who, drawn by the figure awaiting her at the door, had begun to exit the restaurant. She suddenly turned back and looked anxiously towards Jude, as though she had suddenly remembered something she had meant to do.

"Good luck!" she called out. Her voice pierced the restaurant, boring an aural hole through a space that contained only a faint hum and muffled jangling from the kitchen. This abrupt exclamation was the product of a purely professional instinct. The guest, Jude, was as far from her mind as her morning toast; but professional obligation, including the constant quest for acknowledgment from managerial staff, was part of every job that she had ever worked. She now worked in the food service industry, an extreme example of this tendency, and had done so off and on ever since her first dishwashing job, at the age of thirteen.

"Good luck!" Jessica repeated. "With the egg, I mean. And the writing!" She hesitated for a moment, a sign of both her distraction and her insincerity. She then turned back towards the man in black, and then back again towards Jude.

Jude felt a sense of rebirth. He wanted to shout something back, but before he could think of what to say, she called out once again.

"Break an egg!" came her cry, in no particular direction.

Jessica's announcement, echoing outwards to this mysterious man in black, Tina, and Jude, was so undirected, that Jude didn't know if she was actually speaking with him or re-enacting a joke that could have been said a thousand times per shift in a restaurant devoted to the art of cooking and serving eggs. Suddenly, now orbiting within the atmosphere and gravitational pull of the man in black, Jessica drifted and then moved energetically towards the exit of the dining room. The dark stranger was removing his gloves in anticipation of brushing his hand against hers as she approached him. Then, suddenly formal, he adroitly slid his fingers back into their allotted spaces and nodded in her direction. Jessica, as though acknowledging his sign, drew up alongside of his towering presence. The newly formed couple moved towards the exit, in close proximity to one another, but with an estranged physical distance. Jude realized he was staring again, and suddenly he wished that he'd given a witty retort to her good-luck wishes.

"Break an egg! Bake a leg! Stroke a peg!" Jude was on the verge of a nervous breakdown. "Fuck! I don't know. Tap a keg!" Each brilliant reply resonated in his brain as loudly as if he'd stood on the table and announced them all. Probably better that he didn't say anything, he thought.

Tina was now upon Jude, attending to his table by replacing the fork and arranging the place setting that he had sullied with the crushed eggshells and the remnants of the gooey yolk. Jude could not have known that her actions had nothing whatsoever to do with him. Her perfidiousness was aimed towards Jessica, for she had left her place in the kitchen and had interacted with this client, and she had done so without the delicacies appropriate to a dining room like this one.

Tina's finicky arranging and rearranging of the plate, the fork, and the napkin was a form of coded communication. In the restaurant, each dominion has its rulers, its keepers, its patrons, and its slaves, and nobody, except the owner and the maître d', had the right to cross from one dominion into the other, not even Jessica. Jessica was the deity of Fabergé, the goddess of lushness and potency amidst a universe of unfertilized eggs, but this wasn't her realm. This was Tina's realm.

When she was done, Tina simply smiled robotically in Jude's direction and walked towards the maître d's station. She occupied that post so that Fabergé Restaurant would be a place of heavenly eggsistence. Fabergé, while guarded by Tina, could never become the lost paradise of Milton, where the guards at the gate were sin and death, evil twins who would be unleashed from the dark premises once permeated. No, as long as Tina was there to guard the roost with her perfect demeanor, Fabergé's eggs would have their namesake in human form. By virtue of her perfection, Tina was like that golden Fabergé hen egg Czar Alexander III had offered to his wife, Empress Maria Fedorovna, in honor of the twentieth anniversary of their betrothal. Fabergé had crafted his masterpiece from gold, which he wrapped in an enameled shell. Rather than crack, this egg could open on tiny golden hinges, revealing a golden yolk. Therein was hidden a perfect, golden hen that also opened, offering a minute diamond replica of the imperial crown, from which a small ruby pendant was suspended. A precious crown jewel, fit for a czar's empress, a token of pure, unadulterated, royal love.

Ah, but looks can be deceiving.

Long before Fabergé Restaurant had been laid into the nest of New York City, Jessica was a young student at the Fashion Institute of Technology, and Tina one of the precious female models. A muse to Jessica's designs, Tina offered herself up, first to Jessica's penetrating gaze, and then to her gentle, probing touch. Tina, who now hovers quietly inside of John's Fabergé Restaurant, was once clothed in Jessica's fashionable creations, and then unclothed by Jessica's desires. Amidst their heated embrace, did Jessica ever discover the many secrets harbored deep inside of Tina? Would this tall, dark stranger uncover Jessica's hidden truths?

I don't know where Jessica went with that stranger in black. I don't know where anyone goes when they leave Fabergé Restaurant. I do know that she is indeed Jessica, for those who know her, and Jess for those who know her well. And I know that the stranger is always dressed in black, and that in her presence, he always stares straight ahead, through space and through time. And then he approaches her, and, like today, he removes his gloves and gently slides the side of his hand upon hers, almost imperceptibly. His sole objective seems to be to breathe the air that she exhales, and to sense the golden warmth of her hair, golden locks that entangle everyone around her.

As Jessica strayed from view, Jude stayed behind for a little while longer, adding and subtracting from the words he'd written about the intact egg and its shattered nemesis, and about the yolk, into whose large, yellow eye he stared from time to time, in between long reflections at his table. While he performed his linguistic fussing, Tina walked around him, preparing the dining room for guests, real guests. Unlike Jude, guests were people who actually spent money in Fabergé Restaurant, as opposed to buying one of the "intermezzo's," as John called them. The intermezzo that served as Jude's main course was concocted as a frivolous little delight that properly affluent clients savor in between actual courses. Jude's favorite intermezzo was the egg-shaped, vanilla-flavored scoops of coconut sorbet. This popular little trifle was acceptable in Fabergé Restaurant, because the coconut is an egg. But is it really an egg? Or is it a seed? Is it a fruit? Or is it a nut? In Fabergé Restaurant, the answer is clear, because one of John's dessert recipes joyfully transforms coconut flesh into egg whites, which are then placed alongside the yolky flesh of ripe mangos. Fabergé Restaurant, where each egg is a fantasy, each fantasy a resurrection. I know, because I am the Fabergé Restaurant, and I myself am a resurrected fantasy.

CHAPTER 2

Jude lingered after Jessica's departure, feeling aroused. He had never seen her before. She clearly worked in the kitchen, so why had she appeared in the dining room today? He turned his gaze back to Tina, whom he'd seen many times in that dining room, fussing over guests or arranging place settings. For him, Tina was an enigma, but he found her strangely enticing. He would celebrate her image on those occasions when his fantasies led him towards untouchable innocence. He never saw her in animated conversation or corporeal engagement, but instead she seemed to find pleasure in polishing, arranging, wiping, and measuring distances between table settings, as though there was an achievable perfection somewhere in the universe, and that she had to keep searching for ways to bring the dining room into alignment therewith. But she also seemed to alternately glow and then fade, to work and then disappear, as though there was something much more important to do elsewhere, in some undefined and probably undiscovered space in the multitude of galaxies with which she had celestial relations.

Jude would often look up from his scribbles to examine Tina, the source of his ethereal obsession, as though each glance at her might reinvigorate his imagination. She occupied him, literally, and her image lay deep within his fantasy world. For him, she offered evidence of human perfectibility, which reflected in her mannerisms, in the geometrical shape of her bobby-pin-supported hairdo, in the carefully pressed crease in her short, black skirt, in the consciously arranged folds of her puffy, white, short-sleeved blouse, in her perfectly egg-shaped breasts, in her neatly plucked eyebrows, in her polished, eggshell skin, and in her near-black, almost-Asian eyes.

Jude was incapable of imagining what she had been like as a young girl, and where she might have come from before assuming domination of this pristine dining room. Was she the envy of her friends, or the darling? Perhaps she was the model of what they had hoped to be in some near-future world: a gentle, beautiful, but powerful force, able to put order into a universe of chaos. It would certainly be ironic if that turned out to be the case, because Tina now fusses over the grown-ups who still seek perfection, but in their failure to attain such a forbidding dream are forced to manifest their power by purchasing stocks and bonds, an apartment on 5th Avenue, and egg creations from Fabergé Restaurant. These grown-up girls love Fabergé Restaurant in part because Tina is there for them, as their dreams once were, to guide them to a special place of fantasy treats, a grown-up tea party with her friends, her dolls, and her eggs.

Strangely, Jude's bizarre fantasy wasn't that far off from the truth. Tina was conceived one sultry summer night in Tokyo, when a handsome American soldier penetrated into the quiet and innocent universe of a young Japanese girl who had offered to escort him through the Asakusa temple grounds. She had paused to give homage and was overcome by the late-evening vision of Sensōji, the Buddhist temple dedicated to the Bodhisattva Kannon. In this state, she swooned and fell into the waiting arms of this handsome American. He, too, was overcome, not by a Buddhist deity, but by an overflowing desire for her. The negotiation of their respective desires and taboos was uneven, and she, terrified by her eventual acquiescence, had fled into the night, arriving many hours later in an apartment where her widowed mother greeted her with sobs of relief that turned to anger when she learned of her adventure.

Thus, Tina, the child of this encounter, was to be raised by a young girl of seventeen years. Unbeknownst to her, the American father sought her out for years, and upon discovering her whereabouts, he arranged the wire transfer of an anonymous, guilt-drenched fortune, provided that the child be raised in America. And so when Tina was but a nine-year-old girl, her mother, unwilling to leave her homeland, sent Tina to the United States, where she was enrolled in a private boarding school for wealthy, young girls from blue-blooded New England families. Her first years in America were filled with the emptiness of abandonment, shame, and incomprehension. Boarding school became her only home, and tasks assigned to her in school her only friends.

Had it not been for Jessica, the sweet-faced girl with the golden hair who one day sat down beside her in the echoing dining hall, Tina would have been friendless all through her adolescence. Instead, she was introduced to the beauty of colorful Connecticut autumns, to the warmth of snowy winters' crackling fires, and to the magic sand that tickled her naked toes in the hidden coves that dotted and darted along the Long Island Sound. They drifted apart during high school, but when Tina appeared one day at the Fashion Institute as a model for students' creations, Jessica was overjoyed, and soon their friendship was rekindled, and their recollections created a close friendship until giggles turned to breathless kisses, friendly touch to warm embrace. They were secretly bonded by this forsaken lust and the shared world from which it emerged, but it was as though it had all happened in another lifetime. Despite how intense their attachment once was, they now worked together as though it had never occurred, and would never again be rekindled.

Jude of course knew nothing of this past, but felt his own attraction to her deep within his very being. He discretely leaned back in his seat and thought of her in his own warm embrace. Tina, Tina. He shifted in his seat. "What would she think if she knew about this?" he wondered to himself. "She'd love it!" He smiled. "Or would she?"

He raised his gaze to the oval heavens of this terrestrial egg paradise. "Who are you, Tina, anyways?" He sought her out with his gaze and found her polishing silverware near the entranceway to Fabergé Restaurant. "Why are you here?" He stared towards her, intently, his gaze extended all the way across the dining room of Fabergé Restaurant. "She conceals to reveal," thought Jude, whatever that meant. "Hmmm," he mused, writing down the phrase. In this way she resembles the egg in its relation to the yolk.

"No," he retorted to his own musings, "she reveals to conceal!" He was feeling proud of himself, and he wrote down that phrase as well. He then leaned back to muse about the effects that Tina had upon him. She was decidedly beautiful and feminine, but also cold, almost metallic.

"How can that be, Tina?" He thought about eggs and the creations that were made in Fabergé Restaurant. She reminded him of caviar, with its fragile, impenetrable skin that hides the glorious infusion of warmth within. But was she warm within? Or was she cold? She was also perfect, rigid, pure, glamorous, and veiled, like a precious jewel. "She is like a Fabergé egg!" he exclaimed to himself.

This realization led him to quite literally sit up in his seat. He thought about the jewels that adorned the Fabergé egg replicas that were placed throughout the restaurant, illuminated by precise and carefully directed lighting. Each egg sat upon golden satin, and each one had a luxurious box that sat open beside it, as though each box had expelled an egg into the world, and all the eggs were incubating in order to survive, and, one day, hatch. Jude looked back at Tina, who suddenly looked vulnerable as she stood before a nearby table, assessing, perhaps, its placement.

"Maybe I'm wrong about you, Tina!" thought Jude. "Maybe you spend your evening in brutal, sadomasochistic practices, alternately dragging red-hot pokers across the huge backs of your overweight lovers? Maybe you love to have your soft hair pulled, your . . ." He smiled to himself.

"No, probably not," he retorted to himself. "You are a stupid fuck," he concluded. "Stupid. And pathetic." He reflected more deeply. "If her presence is akin to a precious jewel, what am I?" He looked down on the sparse pre-lunch-hour place setting that he'd sullied with his egg observations. "Am I a jigsaw?" He thought of what he had done to the eggs. "A bulldozer?"

In full-on meditation mode, Jude straightened up in his chair, aware that the thoughts had led him to recline to the point where the backrest, designed to support the lower back, was almost up to his shoulders, and his legs were unduly spread open. He went back to the image of Tina, gallivanting with sadomasochistic lovers.

"That makes no sense," he thought, "because you, Tina, are perfect, and the world is not." He rested his boyish chin in his hand, deep in thought. "So no," he mused. "Tina, you probably just go home to tend to your bonsai trees, and then you retire to bed with a book about the history of oriental tapestries. After a few minutes, you drift off to sleep, magically, imperceptibly, leaving by morning time nary a dent in your mattress, because your body is neither heavy enough, nor warm enough, to leave a perceptible trace."

Jude looked down once more at the eggs that lay before him, one perfect, the other unrecognizable, and he felt as though there wasn't another eggy word left for his manuscript anywhere in his entire body. He gathered up his writing implements, gave some semblance of order to the table setting, and decided to leave for the day. He felt rather slimy, though, especially once he left the restaurant. The meager tip he was planning on leaving for Jessica was jingling in his pocket, a decision he'd rationalized by the thought that although she might have appreciated the gesture, she was not a server, and her wages were probably good enough to make his paltry tip look ridiculous. Besides, he thought, she was out with that rich guy, that man in black. Maybe he was dating her. Maybe they'd be married, and she wouldn't need whatever meager amount he could have afforded for her. But what would she think if she found out that he'd left nothing at all? And what about Tina?

I listened for the telltale sound of Jude's vehicle, and was rewarded with an ungodly roar. He was driving the truck. I knew that because it was a diesel monstrosity, a huge, billowing, strangely painted, six-wheeled, behemoth of a vehicle that made as much noise turning the engine over as every other vehicle in a crammed parking lot might produce if they were all started up simultaneously.

Jude sometimes drove that truck, but it was the long skateboard that provided him the opportunity, and perhaps the justification, to wear a jean jacket. He wore it almost every day—spring, summer, fall, and winter—as a kind of badge of forlorn honor. For what? Who knows. Jude's 'look' attracted people, mostly men, who enjoyed talking about skateboards far more than they had enjoyed using them for that brief period in their lives, somewhere between fourteen and twenty-one, when almost every American male buys or receives one, usually while on vacation in New Jersey, Alabama, or Florida.

Jude was regularly enticed by chatty male patrons into discussions about skateboards, windsurfing, flying, or jumping. Each of these narrative encounters had the same ending, some kind of an "accident," a "near miss," that now motivated the speaker to stick to Toyota Camrys, Volvo station wagons, or Range Rover SUVs. Most of these males would tell him that while they used to be adventurous, they were now married to "the wife" who wouldn't permit them ownership of any recreational vehicle. Most of these same wives had some fading memory of a scooter or a motorcycle driven by a boy from way back when. And some of them even wanted a Vespa, because she'd seen some Hollywood starlet drive it to the Ed Sullivan Studios en route to a conversation about her major role in a minor flick.

Jude's engine roared, and I could hear him shifting its old gearbox, now first, now second, now third, now receding into the distance, like memories of earlier days, consumed in the exhaust of labored respiration.

CHAPTER 3

Tina felt annoyed for a short while after Jude's departure, but she was grateful when she learned that Jessica had returned to work after only a half-hour absence. It was a good thing. Besides, there was work to do. There was always work to do, until the last kitchen fan and last dining-room lamp were turned off for the night. And then it was just a matter of moments, it seemed, until they all needed to be reignited for the next shift. The reality of each day in Fabergé Restaurant was the shift to come, the tables to serve, the set-up, and then the inevitable breakdown. And despite Tina's desire to control everyone who worked in the dining room, she nonetheless tried to avoid involving herself in peripheral matters, such as what happens when employees leave the premises.

With Jessica, of course, it was a different matter. Tina would always love Jessica, she would always belong to Jessica. But since Jessica had come back to her, as an employee at Fabergé Restaurant, Tina had known a large quantity of people who also loved Jessica, and were, presumably, loved by her. She was a free spirit who gave far more than she ever received—of anyone. Fabergé Restaurant was the exception; for her it was a kind of haven. And Fabergé Restaurant in turn was nourished by her power, and, being an egg, it needed her to care for it, to keep it warm, so that one day it could hatch. For Fabergé the restaurant was also Fabergé the egg, an egg in the middle of John's favorite island, New York City. True to the complexity of Fabergé eggs, though, the restaurant namesake was also nest, a casing, and a shell that was a façade of perfection for an imperfect world. And so while Jessica fulfilled the maternal task, Tina was charged with keeping the Fabergé Restaurant façade from cracking, chipping, or decaying, and she did so as though the fate of the universe depended upon its being maintained, perfectly.

Busy with her self-assigned chores in the dining room, Tina thought back to Jessica and to him, that man in black. She was convinced that whoever he was, he was rich, and probably famous, at least in some circles (Financial? Real estate? Movies? This was New York, it could be all of them simultaneously). He would probably leave his wife, or whomever, in order to entice Jessica to go with him wherever it is that he'd go when he wasn't standing at the crack of an entranceway to Fabergé Restaurant. This was an unwelcome thought for Tina, for no matter how long it had been since she had been warmed by Jessica's breath and caressed by her soft touch, she knew that a precious and fragile memory of pure contentment would shatter if Jessica were to leave. She also knew that John desperately needed Jessica, and that if she were to leave, he'd be plunged into uncertainty and cast headlong into the growing vortex of chaos that surrounded him each day, a vortex that was hidden by his impermeable façade. Without Jessica, he and Tina couldn't exist, they would crack, they would pour the yolk of their respective existences upon the hard floor of the industrial kitchen where eggs were fried and poached and boiled and scrambled and shattered, along with the lives they could have, or did, contain.

Tina knew that she wouldn't ask about this man in black. A discussion might nonetheless come up, if only because Jessica always looked mildly annoyed when she returned from her little outings. And in fact, Jessica did feel annoyed when she returned that evening. Or, perhaps, she was just anxious to be back to work, to the array of tasks that awaited her arrival. She entered through the back door and walked intently through a hallway that was lined with cracked paint, chipped plaster, and areas that had apparently been kicked, punched, or bumped by the delivery of heavy plastic crates of lobsters, filled with heavy, splashing, salted water.

The delivery guys who bore the Sisyphus-like tasks of hauling lobsters were always bumping up against or smashing violently into the walls, because John had insisted upon sealing up portions of each entranceway to give the effect that anyone entering was doing so illicitly, breaking the egg, as it were. And so despite the restaurant's need for provisions, not to mention guests, John nonetheless believed that nobody should in fact be allowed entrance into Fabergé Restaurant aside from those employed by him to be there. Fabergé Restaurant's innards need to be protected and nourished by him, and by his kitchen staff, those he had delegated portions of his own abilities to. All of his work at Fabergé Restaurant was directed towards forming a perfect being who would, when the time was ripe, crack its own shell, and then burst through its shattered confines.

It was as though John were saying to any trespassers: "I am a keeper of this egg until the time comes when it has fulfilled its mission and given birth to its meaning. And you are bringing it supplies, but you are also threatening it with your brutal ways. And so you are a necessary evil, and I grant you entrance to my Fabergé Restaurant with the reluctance of obligation to my role."

Some variation of this was the explanation he would provide to any hapless deliverymen who made the mistake of asking about the oddness of the Fabergé Restaurant shape, or complaining about the pathway that led into it. He always told this story with a keen gaze directed to his prey, as though the description of his egg's *raison d'être* would somehow interest hourly workers whose task consisted of transporting heavy items from one place to another. As such, John failed to understand that a deliveryman's interest in Fabergé Restaurant extended only as far as the delivery itself went. It should therefore have come as no surprise that not a single deliveryman ever demonstrated any interest whatsoever in the mythological features of Fabergé Restaurant, and every attempt that John had ever made to reverse that trend had failed miserably.

These oddball stories, told by this stern man clad in kitchen whites, weren't the only reasons why delivery men hated coming to Fabergé Restaurant. They were also condemned to deliver, through the insane congestion of New York City, heavy and unruly cases of champagne that were sold in even more copious quantities in that restaurant than any other beverage, including all of the 341 wines, mostly red, that quietly haunted the bowels beneath the Yolk. The deliverymen who captured John in more whimsical moods, or were off guard and therefore possibly gave the mistaken impression that they cared about him or his stories, would be treated, unprovoked, to strange, one-sided conversations. John initiated these stories when bills for those deliveries would be passed over to him by rugged hands, perhaps in the hope that the linguistic matter would be valuable enough, or distracting enough, to ward off the moment of his having to turn over payment for the delivery.

To unwitting men of large breadth and small interests, John would describe his original idea, to sell only eggs, and to accompany them solely by champagne and bubbly water. Bubbly liquids produced eggy-shaped bubbles that could be considered appropriate for the multitude of caviars that were the original centerpieces of the Fabergé Restaurant. "Champagne, in particular, emulates the frothy waves from which the sea-faring creatures had been plucked for the eventual delight of Fabergé Restaurant's clients," he would explain. "And the viscous nature of dated champagnes emulated low tide when choice sea creatures could lay eggs, and multiply, in order to be gathered up near the beaches of northeastern states."

None of the delivery men, those owners of the rugged hands whose work John delayed with narrative, would ever pry further into this fascinating line of thought, because they didn't feel addressed directly by John's piercing, blue eyes and Boston North End accent. Those who chose to think about John afterwards probably felt instead as though they'd been penetrated, violated, captured, and possessed, and that it'd be best to avoid his gaze and linguistic grip. And so, if you'd have asked any of those deliverymen what John had uttered, proclaimed, preached, or explained, even just a few minutes after the interaction, it's likely that they wouldn't remember anything other than an impression, a disturbing impression, of an examination undertaken from the inside of their very beings.

In later years, John began to lose his (probably egg-shaped) marbles. And those who actually did the cooking in the Fabergé Restaurant took over, de facto. And without there ever being a discussion on this paradigm shift, liquids other than champagne eventually made their way onto the menu, and into the rivers of intoxicants poured into the wealthy clients who frequented the rarified space of Fabergé Restaurant. These flowing pathways to inebriation were consumed, usually by clients, but oftentimes as well by kitchen staff, and, through accidental upheaval or excited retching promoted by the substance itself, they sometimes flowed unexpectedly, and disgustingly, onto the floor and into the toilets of Fabergé Restaurant's restroom. Multifarious Dionysian oceans flowed each evening, usually several times, to the obvious relief of exhausted employees and the apparent joy of the growing clientele who, John was apt to bemoan, could barely afford imported beer, never mind millimisé champagne.

The conspicuous consumers, those in the dining room, were wont to make merry when they permeated Fabergé Restaurant, merrier, indeed, than they should have been. The result was that many of them were paying more at the end of the jovial evening than they could afford, and some of them landed up costing John more in damages and cleanup than he could afford. As for the rivers of alcohol that were directed and redirected towards the anxious appetites of the kitchen staff and server, John was, or at least seemed, blissfully ignorant. Those uncharted waters of illicit consumption lay beyond the horizon of his own island of thinking, and the currents that lay below these waters seemed to ward him off, thus limiting his cognitive explorations.

"Seemed" is the operative word here, a term that was often used to qualify people's understanding of John. He seemed disconnected, he seemed pacified, he seemed quelled, he seemed to be out of control, he seemed to misunderstand the deliverymen, the servers, the chefs, the prep cooks, the knife sharpeners, the workings of the universe. He seemed. In fact, almost everyone thought that John was some grown-up version of that young boy who had learned his trade from the ground up, and was therefore akin to a trucker who can skillfully back the rig into the nooks and crannies of the universe, but only because of a high level of skill that he'd acquired through practice and repetition rather than through the deep comprehension of fundamental matters.

Nothing was further from the truth.

The truth about John, well, only Tina, the maître d', knew that, and only in eggshell-like fragments that she had never, and would never, try to assemble, for fear that it would fall Humpty-Dumpty-like onto her own fragile frame and crush her with revelation. The truth of John was somewhere inside of his own yolk, in that storehouse of eternal wisdom that trapped the Boston-North-End-boy-turned-Fabergé-Restaurant-owner inside of the logic of his own culinary fantasies. The truth about John was that there was no single truth, and despite the sometimes sinister twinkle in his piercing gaze, he just seemed to be a hardworking owner of a restaurant, a tyrannical boss, or perhaps a strict father. Discerning guests in the restaurant knew better, however, because they had tasted his creations. For them, he was a chef with no equal, a man of unmatched abilities. One single grain of white pepper beyond what he had skillfully applied to the butter-infused Cornish hen egg would have diminished the pleasure of that dish, and the omission of a single spice or the alteration by a single second of cooking time would have changed everything. He was capable as though by magic and intuition to bring out hints of flavor that would have otherwise been trapped, hidden like a yolk in the very heart of his eggy masterpieces.

Tina, who was in charge of the clients, had appreciated Fabergé Restaurant's transformation from a New York anomaly into a true destination, a landmark, and she did so by quietly engineering the addition of new menu options. As a result, the clientele grew somewhat more diverse and came to include people other than the supposed zillionaires who liked the idea of actually eating, and subsequently shitting-out or puking-up, precious Fabergé eggs that had been pickled in expensive champagne and doused in baths of parmagiano butter. Jude was the extreme example of this new phenomenon of diverse clientele, although she did understand that he wasn't there for the culinary experience, or to be seen spending wildly, or to experience one of the chef's new and elaborate creations. She tolerated him nonetheless, because he was a harmless oddity, and there were sufficient numbers of wealthy clients willing and able to chip away at their own golden eggs in exchange for the *merveilles* of Fabergé Restaurant's menu choices to keep the place afloat—if eggs do, in fact, float.

And they do.

Besides, maybe this young man's scribbling would someday make him a candidate for other sections of the menu. Maybe he'd marry into a rich family, and he'd convince his bride-to-be that their marriage should be consumed after a sumptuous, eggy meal in this amazing place. Probably not. The distance between the flowing ink of his pen and the stream of cash required to eat at Fabergé Restaurant was too great, it seemed. And so, Tina didn't bother too much with Jude. At least not at first.

But John did.

Tina didn't know that John allowed Jude to be in Fabergé Restaurant, despite his financial incompatibility with each and every one of the culinary masterpieces created therein, because John, with his incomprehensible grasp of precious oddities, felt strangely reassured when Jude was seen counting out his meager pennies in order to prolong his self-imposed captivity to the Fabergé Restaurant aura. And John knew that Jessica, the greatest of Earth's creations, and the mother hen to his wind-torn nest, had now met Jude and spoken with him. And John knew that this encounter was but a preview of what would someday transpire in his great egg, just as the master jeweler Peter Carl Fabergé knew that his first creation for the czar, that hen egg, was but a precursor to the majesty, and the catastrophe, of that voluptuous empire.

Deep within my very yolk I sense a day of impending endings and new beginnings, and as I watch them all enter into and depart from Fabergé Restaurant, my very body, I wonder at the role they'll play therein. Jessica, oh Jessica, you will be first and foremost, despite the banality of a perfect soufflé and the imperfection of a lover's insistent touch. Jude hopes for new beginnings, but is manacled to an imagination too weak at this early time in his young life to manifest in words or actions such lofty hopes. John knows, because John knows everything that is hatching inside of the Fabergé Restaurant, and with his gaze he sees all of what is past, passing, or to come, just as I feel it all as though it occurs within my very shell.

CHAPTER 4

When Jessica completed her navigation of the white hallway leading to the screen door that separated the kitchen from the external shell of the egg, she emerged in a bright, neon-lit, stainless-steel and yellow-colored kitchen. This color choice was, of course, another one of John's decisions. He had every non-stainless surface in his kitchen painted bright yellow, as a means of reminding his staff-turned-colleagues that this really was the Yolk of Fabergé Restaurant.

As she moved from the dim light of the hallway to the inordinately illuminated Yolk, Jessica almost walked smack into Nate, who was on all fours with a dishwasher's tray of cutlery, setting up some kind of contraption right in front of the prep table. She stopped to examine Nate's creation of the day, a ritual of her work in the early hours of her evening shift. She examined this evening's creation and realized that Nate had built a metallic pathway that led to a long, shiny, stainless trail of metal implements, which, although individually designed to dry pasta, were now steps upon a stairway, or, thought Jessica as she looked more carefully, the rungs of a ladder. In fact, Nate had created a long, metal ladder that led diagonally from the prep table all the way to the large sink, where pots were washed before and during suppertime shifts, a kind of yellow-brick road from a place of scouring to a place of cutting. Those who were new to the Yolk couldn't have imagined the purposes of this evening ritual, couldn't have dreamed that this tall, lanky, nerdy employee harbored twisted fantasies and preoccupations. Jessica, on the other hand, knew that every one of Nate's obstacle courses, all of the Olympic-style events that he designed out of food-utensils, each and every one of his Bauhaus-inspired metallic creations, were designed for lobsters, whose eventual fate, like that of poor Agamemnon, was to die in a bathtub.

Fabergé Restaurant's lobsters weren't killed by Clytemnestra who, in cahoots with her lover Aegisthus, son of Thyestes, threw a net over Agamemnon to prevent resistance—and then drowned him. No mythical end for the lobsters, regrettably. They were boiled to death in large cauldrons of bubbling water. Or they were bludgeoned by Johnny, the broiler chef, by being stabbed in the face before being cut in half, stuffed with a variety of different eggs, including lobster eggs (strangely), and served to customers who, depending upon their skill, might be able to extract every sliver of flesh from every tiny tentacle on the lobster's complex body.

If John had ever seen what Nate was doing, he'd have embarked upon a homicidal rampage to make the Trojan War seem but a brief interlude from true bloodlust. But there was no sign of him. And so, Jessica thought to herself, he must be either absent, or he was securely ensconced at the dishwashing station that stood on the opposite diagonal of the Yolk, immediately behind the swinging doors leading to the dining room. And if John was at the dishwashing station, as he indeed was, then there he'd stay, all night, no matter what, and this despite the fact that Fabergé Restaurant was his empire, his egg, and, moreover, despite the fact that he was, arguably, the greatest chef of his generation. Jessica's experience dictated that once exiled to the steaming Hobart washing station, it was impossible for John to leave that area until the kitchen was not only washed, but sterilized, prepared in case some intricate surgery had to be performed on the floor, in one of the sinks, in the walk-in, or on the stove, in case, in short, the future of the world depended on this Yolk being impeccable, untarnished by the outside world, a vault against the destruction of teeming life.

"Here's the theory," said Nate to Jessica, staring at her approach as though she were his pupil, or at least connected thereto, in search of his apprenticeship down upon the floor. "If the lobsters can figure it out, they aren't actually insect-like mindless beings responding solely to the whims of their immediate environment, and therefore they deserve to live." Having proclaimed this utterance, Nate rose to his feet, for full effect. "But if they can't, they'll be gently and softly anaesthetized, vaporized with the finest distilled but rather steamy water, and then boiled to death before being ripped apart and then prodded for each morsel of glistening flesh by a bespectacled, compulsive, conversationally distracted stockbroker or stockbroker's mistress-turned-pathologist. Or . . ."—he rubbed his hands together and beamed—"they'll be decorticated millimeter by millimeter by a little, old lady who actually doesn't know whether she is in her bedroom or on the top stair of the Eiffel Tower, and in her actions is unaware of whether she is undressing herself after a long day of knitting, or doing the world's most intricate crossword puzzle, impeded by the obvious handicap of having both hands sawed off and piled in a neat, little heap beside her." Having finished his oration, Nate resumed his former position on the floor, adjusting the metal implements in advance of the forthcoming event.

Jessica crouched down beside him, at a respectable but intimate distance. Nate, who looked deeply into her visage with his grey, sparkling, bespectacled eyes, ceased to speak, and instead projected dancing images that flowed through his eyes and into her imagination. There was a sense of urgency whenever Jessica and Nate interacted, and it had been observed on various occasions that the frenetic and sometimes synergetic relationship must have had some kind of history.

It did.

The tie that bound and tore asunder this culinary couple was the product of an encounter that had happened to them once upon a time, a long time ago, on a chilly January day in the even chillier walk-in. Jessica's bountiful body lay before Nate that fateful day, for she had finally given in to his constant overtures, and generously bent over a crate of eggs, embracing the impersonal cardboard and the cold stainless steel with her warmth. Her grey chef's pants and tiny panties were yanked until they were half way down her silken legs, her apron was hoisted up, and now the body that had occupied every sultry dream since he'd first seen her gorgeous face was now open to his, as he, from behind where she lay, and invisible to her downward gaze, fulfilled his most profound dream, thereby obliterating any chance that anything of an intimate nature could ever happen again, for his sake, and for hers.

This chilling thrust was their first, and final, act of love, the culmination of what seemed like decades of lust-infused conversations disguised as culinary banter. By his flowery descriptions they were to one day ascend to the very heights of fleshy bliss, her eggs joining to his cum in a dance of love and merriment. But instead, she had just unexpectedly offered her body to him in the walk-in, unceremoniously, as though she herself was an ingredient that could be found and unwrapped for his delectation. She was warm at first, and then cold, and then colder. He had entered her without a word, and pressed his flesh

27

to hers, forgiving and then forbearing, until she smashed a multitude of the eggs over which she was draped, first with her fingers, and then with her face.

In a matter of moments, he was done, and so were they. Their eternity was extinguished like the lives that by this act had become runny yolks that drooled for wealthy Fabergé Restaurant clients, instead of wonderful, winged creatures pecking the ground seeds to nourish litters of eggs in sumptuous nests.

From his seeds, to her eggs, and from her eggs, to their death.

That was years ago.

It seemed to both of them as though this ghastly scene was recreated each time they looked into each other's gaze, and when the inevitable image was played back before his mind's eye, he would slouch in shame and she, in turn, would shudder in disgust. And they would mourn the past. And he would tell a joke. And she would laugh. And he would see the past. And so would she. And they would return to the realm of the living.

"I, Jess, do hate insects." Nate made this forceful declaration on his knees, without even straining his long neck. Now he raised himself up again to his full 6' 6" stature and grinned a sardonic look as he glanced down to her crouching existence. From Jessica's perspective, Nate's freckled, reddish skin, orange hair, and green beret-turned-chef-hat made him look the very part of a giant carrot. Erect before her that afternoon, he nonetheless looked inspired. And, as always, he looked sad. She had bent down to him in pity and understanding, and now she rose back up again, with knowledge and the strength to move on.

The "they" to whom Nate referred, she knew from the many versions of this scene that she'd witnessed over the past four years, were Nate's creatures of affection: lobsters. These lobsters were now imprisoned in a small cage in the walk-in, but in the course of the shift, they would be released to satisfy the culinary lust of clients who were ready to savor some of the most expensive flesh on the dinner menu. Lobsters, whose natural fate—and even the lobsters themselves probably knew this—was for nothing other than fickle currents and the magnified vision of the heavens seen through the ever-agitated surface of the Atlantic Ocean from which they'd been so unceremoniously plucked. These were the chosen ones, those who had not as yet decided to exit the lobster traps that they'd so effortlessly entered. And so, when the 'fishermen' had arrived to raise the traps up to the surface, the single act of their fishermanly profession, these chosen lobsters were careened onto the shore for the short trip to local restaurants.

To a chef who'd cooked a lot of them, lobsters do indeed look like the "insects" that Nate had called them. But to those in the know, these were clever and resourceful beings, as comfortable in ocean currents as on the slippery coastal rocks that demarcated their breeding ground. But, alas, many of the captured lobsters were known to contain huge sacks of delicious, green eggs, the delight of the Fabergé Restaurant gourmet set, those elite beings who carried with them that discrete but powerful plastic—gold or platinum plastic, preferably—to back up their appetites for luxury.

The female lobsters also carry around sperm, for up to two years, which can be harnessed for the thousands of eggs she carries within her body. Fabergé eggs they are not, but clients in the know about such things suckle them as if they, too, were the precious namesakes of John's world.

"And so if they are insects," continued Nate as he crouched back down to his little lobster colony, "they deserve to die, because all of their insect friends attack my fragile skin whenever I take the trash to the Hole." It was Nate who'd named two parts of the Fabergé Restaurant where he spent his time: the Yolk and the Hole, the latter being the trash area at the far end of the parking lot. "But if they are fascinating, good-looking, intellectual beings trapped, like one of Kafka's buddies in the carcass of a giant insect, then I, Snow White's gorgeous prince, shall kiss them with good-luck lips, tongue them ever so gently, and thereby restore them to their illustrious selves once more, so that they, too, can come and dine upon the magnificent, eggy dishes in which we as eggy chefs specialize here at the Illustrious Fabergé Restaurant with all of their wealthy friends, especially," he began to feign a Russian accent, "those from Old Country!"

Jessica looked at him with her usual crumpled face of knowing perplexity. During his little monologue, she was leaning up against the prep table where vegetables were chopped and peeled and shaped and drawn and quartered, their remnants tossed into large, white pails that sit open-mouthed underneath the adjacent sink, awaiting their fill and their eventual purgation into the warm sauté pots of endlessly cooking *au jus*. She now began to move away from the prep table and towards the sink, into which she peered, searching with great intensity. Nate awaited her ruling on his new event like an anxious coach holding the hand of his thirteen-year-old gymnast in the moments following her routine, concerned that the Romanian judge hadn't been paid off, or that the American judge was anti-Communist, or that the French judge had other things on her mind that afternoon than ranking the horse, the rings, the mat, and the eventual iron cross.

Jessica leaned down into the sink, fumbled in the pile of soiled stainless-steel bins therein, and, having apparently found the object of her quest, she rose up, victorious. In her hand was a long, wooden spoon that was covered in a slimy coating, probably some kind of flour-thickened and *au jus*-infused gravy. She moved towards Nate, who was kneeling over his stainless-steel contraption. He was carefully arranging the first of his lobster contestants for the forthcoming event, prodding and pushing on their behinds, trying to direct them to the stainless-steel obstacle course.

Jessica approached him, and then banged his SOS pad-like hair, gently, and then a second time, more abruptly, and finally smacked him with a kind of unexpected brutality, a brutality that could only be punishment for a deed as yet unforgiven, an action unforgivable, from a past not shrouded in haze, but rather illuminated by the bright lights of this kitchen.

"Ouch! Bitch." Nate ran his hands through his hair and discovered the gooey substance that he pleated out with his fingers and then, awaiting the inevitable moment when Jessica would turn back to him to see the results of her efforts, licked his fingers with intensity, moaning as he did so.

She turned and stared at him with a look of disgust. "Gross."

In response, he brought his two hands to his face and drove his face deep into the space he'd created therein. "Fuck me," he whispered.

She turned away from him and kept walking.

"Fuck me!" he called out loudly. She left her hand trail in her wake, her middle finger up to the sky. They both knew that those two words, "fuck me," didn't mean anything, nothing at all, even if once upon a time, in the universe they'd inhabited together, they could have meant the world. He looked sad, pathetic, because "fuck me" were words of dreams and shared urgings, as farfetched as "fly me to the moon upon my paper wings."

"Fuck me."

Now that expression meant nothing, it had been transformed into gibberish, fuckme, or phucmi. The "fuck" and the "me" were gone, absolved of meaning, devoid of sense. Individually and together the "fuck" and the "me" meant nothing, and that could not change back, not now, not ever. And so Jessica kept walking, and then turned back and threatened him again, knowingly.

Putting on airs for the sake of posterity, Nate feigned licking her face from a distance of a few feet, and then formed his lips into an "O" as a preface to whistling, his eternal annoying habit, this time manifested in a bastardized "Stairway to Heaven." This move from the carnal to some other subject was always safer when it came to their interactions, and therefore, every conversation between them ended, for both their sakes, with a smile, with Jessica playfully shaking her head or flicking him off or grinning in the dismay of broken dreams.

Nate, superficially riled up, ceased his whistling and shouted to her, suddenly overtaken with genuine reflection, "Hey, wait a second!" Jessica turned around, feigning interest.

"Led Zeppelin!" he blurted out. "That's egg shaped. We ought to transport people here in one of those?" She turned away from him, and so he called out to her even louder. "Like the strip clubs do, when they pick up desperate men from the airport in those vans that are painted with the faces of strippers. The Fabergé Restaurant Zeppelin! What do you think? We could travel around in it, you and me, to set an example for guests!"

No answer. No matter. The round was over. The game was most certainly lost.

"It would fly, Jess! We'd make it fly! Jessica!" He called out more loudly, with the confidence of one who had in fact penetrated her and brought pleasure out.

"Would our zeppelin fly?" He was shouting so loudly now that she turned back to him, and feigning attention and interest, she said, "Even though it's made out of lead?"

He was desperate now, trying to seize an opportunity as vacuous as the gas within the zeppelin. "Jess! Maybe we could lighten up that lead zeppelin somehow? Maybe we'll make it out of something other than lead? Or maybe we'll combine the lead with blended egg whites! Any suggestions? How do we do that, Jess? Maybe we could paint pictures of you on it? That would lighten it up!"

I watched as Jessica bore witness to Nate's soliloquy, and then grinned sadly as she turned away from him and pursued her trek to the dishwashing station. She was drawn as to the sirens by another shrilling sound, the expulsion of wind not from a zeppelin descending to Earth engulfed in flames, but from the pierced lips of John whistling tales of ancient glories and not-so-distant conquests of possible worlds.

CHAPTER 5

John was perched intently at his station, the Hobart dishwashing machine, where he produced notes that pierced the hum of the Yolk. He was like William Butler Yeats's mechanical bird that was perched atop the golden bough in Byzantium. He was disconnected from nature, for his face seemed chiseled, as by a Grecian goldsmith, or hammered, like the precious Fabergé Jewelled Hen Egg. Maybe, instead of being covered in flesh, he, too, was hammered out of gold and gold enameling, and maybe he, too, whistled to keep a drowsy czar and czaress awake. He had set himself upon Hobart's golden bough, to scrub and clean and rinse and dry for all the lords and ladies of Wall Street, whistling as he did so all that is past, or passing, or to come.

Fittingly, in this ichthyic setting, he appeared to be moving his bird-like claws 'round and 'round and up and down and side to side. Since there were as yet no filthy dishes to scrub, he was instead polishing Hobart's giant rectangular washing mechanism, 'round and 'round and up and down and side to side, as though plying warmed oil into a lover's sun-soaked back. Whatever tune he was rendering was cacophonic and incomprehensible, a tune crackling like Yeats's own voice, captured Byzantium bound, in a few lines from a BBC recording from another era. He was so completely absorbed by his task, that he was oblivious to Jessica's arrival.

"Hello, John!" she called above the din, negotiating past prep tables and crates that separated off those who cooked for the clients from he who cleaned up their dishes afterwards.

John didn't look up, but instead uttered in her direction: "Jessica, we must polish it up today, I'm expecting the inspector, a group of them perhaps." He then turned towards her with authority, looking his Colonel General Captain self. "With all of this talk of salmonella, they're cracking down!" He seemed to grin, as though he'd watched himself say it, and found it for some reason humorous.

John always spoke loudly, almost barking, as though every word was an order, part of an effort to keep his troops in line. He barked all the louder because of the sound of the plethora of industrial-strength electric fans that he had installed one summer day when profits were higher, and when cash had flowed more freely. These fans, far more powerful than the size of the kitchen warranted, made it sound in certain areas of the Yolk as though the workers were in fact mechanics doing upkeep inside of a working jet engine.

John raised his head even higher, calling out beyond Jessica, beyond the boundaries of Manhattan, to Long Island Sound, all the way down to Boston Harbor and further, further, all the way to the open, turbulent Atlantic Ocean. "We must be on our guard tonight!"

Now he was on a ship out in the middle of a horrendous storm, barking orders with a voice stifled by the gusts of Atlantic air and salty spray. Stifled, yet, authoritative and powerful. Loud, but strangely impotent.

"THEY ARE CRACKING DOWN!"

From across the kitchen came a retort from Nate, who had risen up to look towards John.

"Cracking, you say?" he called. He had spoken with an Irish accent, his voice carrying from across the kitchen, just loudly enough for Jessica's ears, but a little too muffled for John's middle-aged hearing. Jessica turned away from John and looked towards Nate, who had brought his hands together to emulate a butt crack, the palms of his hands pressed together.

"You say something?" asked John, looking around the kitchen towards the source of the sound.

"Can I use your spray?" called Nate.

"THE SPRAY? OH, YES. I LEFT A CAN FOR YOU BY THE POT-WASHING STATION, NATE. AND WE HAVE A BOX THAT JUST ARRIVED; WE HAVE A LARGE SUPPLY." John was bellowing now over the loud sounds of the kitchen.

"GOT IT!" called Nate, grabbing hold of the can of stainless-steel cleaner that was perched beside the hot-water handle of the prep-station sink. John acknowledged Nate's diligence with a nod, and then set back to work polishing the Hobart.

"Hmmm," said Nate in Jessica's direction, causing her to look towards him. "If any of the lobsters win the Stairway to Heaven competition, I'll fill this with Gatorade and spray the coach!"

From where she was standing, near John's dishwashing station, Jessica could still hear Nate, and could see him running his little "exercises" with the lobsters on the stainless-steel contraption. These exercises were in fact just warm-ups to the Olympic events staged up and down the course that Nate had set up: long jumping, maze running, high jumping, and flat-out sprinting towards the string-bean finish line.

Nate's lobster Olympics was cruel, and it was stupid, and some version of it went on almost every shift. But given that the real purpose for those lobsters was to lie around and wait for their being killed for the $87.99 boiled lobster dish ($127.99 with a side of her own eggs), or the $167.99 baked and stuffed lobster (with crab meat, bread crumbs, butter, and herbs), a little attention from Nate may not be the worst possible thing.

"WE HAVE A WINNER!" called Nate, suddenly hoisting one of the lobsters in the air. Luckily for him, he had risen at the very moment John had crouched down to polish the base of the Hobart machine, and so this declaration of victory was out of both eye and earshot.

"This," thought Jessica, "is going to be a long night." She sighed to herself. "But that's fine," she continued. "Better to be killed with humor than with glumness."

This was indeed true. In spite of the past, and future, of her own world and the worlds of those around her, and despite all of the strangeness of this restaurant, the city of New York, the country, the planet, the entire universe, right now, for whatever else, was okay. She was at Fabergé Restaurant, undertaking culinary tasks that she'd rehearsed and performed to the satisfaction of John and of multitudes of clients for years, to the palate-ial delight of all concerned. And so her life had meaning, and she brought to this place the genius of her maternal warmth, the generosity of her flesh, the calm of her touch.

This is not to say that Jessica hadn't enjoyed working as a clothing designer, in that little atelier called "Stitched," not six streets from where she now stood. Like the rekindled relationship she'd had with Tina during much of that era, a relationship that had resulted in lines of clothing well-suited to exceptionally tiny girls, Stitched felt like it was from another lifetime. After five years of stitching creations from fabulous materials, and five more designing gastronomic treasures from earth's ovulary creations, Jessica felt as though she had lived forever in the bowels of places that make expensive goods for wealthy, ungrateful, dissatisfied, and unsatisfiable consumers, clients, customers. True, there were the occasional gourmets, or passers-by, like that kid today doing experiments in the dining room, but they were the exception. The general atmosphere of ingratitude, complacency, and entitlement amongst those who enjoy the fruits of places like Stitched or Fabergé Restaurant not only helped her understand the odd relationship between workers and consumers in such rarified places, but also gave her an appreciation for the odd characters who recognize the amazing quality of beautiful products, and the even odder characters who think about what it means to work in such settings. Nate was one such character, someone who constantly measured his relationship to the customer, the product, and the means of production.

In those early days working at Fabergé Restaurant, Nate had provided Jessica with adequate descriptions of her experiences. Encouraged by her interest, he began to build a philosophy that he simply referred to as *resentment*. "Resentment!" he would say. "In French? *Ressentiment*! In Italian? *Risentimento*! In Spanish? Um, fuck, I'm not really sure!" He would elaborate upon this philosophy during the many hours they spent sitting together in the back alley of Fabergé Restaurant. This dark, urban alleyway was a place that he referred to as "his own little pastoral farm."

"Pastoral farm?" she had asked, during one of the first times she'd ever sat with him there in that dark, dingy, smelly, asphalted space.

"It's a retreat, Jess. I think about it when I'm not at work, because it's where I can actually brood."

"Over what?"

"Everything, Jess. That kitchen where we work is a microcosm for the whole damned thing, for this city of servants and served. It's a factory that favors all the eating and drinking and preparing, and then it's a reservoir for all of the resulting pissing and shitting, and then it's a metaphor for what it means to clean the whole fucking thing up. It all happens in one building. He looked up at the oddly shaped Fabergé Restaurant.

"The Big Apple is the Big Egg, Jess. It's fertile, it's fragile, it's filled with opportunity, but when it's fertilized, it lands up in these bloody, noisy, filthy streets, and hopes for a place to repose. That's what the pastoral farm is for, Jess. Repose, reflection, retreat."

Jess examined him with admiration, illuminated by a few crass bulbs whose rays were able to sneak out of their rooms in order to find their own repose in this, Nate's pastoral farm.

"Do you like Wordsworth?" asked Nate. Jess hesitated.

"Sure!"

"Do you know 'Tintern Abbey'?" A rustling sound suddenly made them both aware of some urban creature who took ownership of this space. Alleyways like this one attracted skunks and raccoons, creatures that come to forage in the open bins, digging away, when homeless people aren't around, in search of prized scraps.

"I have read Wordsworth," Jess began.

Nate took in a poetic breath and turned towards Jess, darkened by the evening sky, illuminated by the wayward beams. "The day has come when I again repose, Jess, here, under this dark sycamore." He paused. "This building here," he motioned towards the nondescript, brick building that made up one of the walls of their little clearing. "Under this dark sycamore, and view these plots of cottage ground, these orchard tufts." He motioned to the open space around them. "Gorgeous, no?"

"Yes," she grinned. "Gorgeous!"

"These orchard tufts, which, at this season, with their unripe fruits," he paused, "and eggs." She smiled, as they both looked up at the egg restaurant before them. "Eggs, which at this season, with their, um, their unfertilized fruits. Did you like that? Unfertilized?"

"What is it supposed to mean?" asked Jessica.

"Unfertilized," replied Nate. "Like Fabergé Restaurant. And like you and me."

She blushed, but the scant light wouldn't reveal it to his probing gaze.

"In Wordsworth's version it's 'unripe.'"

"I guess he didn't know about this pastoral farm," said Jess.

It was Nate's turn to redden, but his color, too, was imperceptible in the darkness.

"At this season," he continued, "with their unripe fruits, among the woods and copses lose themselves. Also like us."

"Copses?" she inquired.

"Um, bushes, clumps of trees. Like those." He motioned towards other buildings, adjoining those that demarcated their little alleyway.

"It's a really beautiful poem," uttered Jess silently.

"Not done yet." Nate knew when he was onto a good thing.

"Among the woods and copses lose themselves, nor, with their green and simple hue disturb the wild green landscape."

"Do they ever!" exclaimed Jess, motioning back to the buildings surrounding them.

Nate was now looking at her intently, as though he wanted to make love to her with his gaze. Which he did. Uncertain of what could bring on such joyful copulation, he simply continued his soliloquy.

"This is my favorite part, Jess. Once again I see these hedge-rows, hardly hedge-rows, little lines of sporting wood run wild."

"Beautiful! That is beautiful, Nate. Why is it your favorite part?"

"Because I love how he corrected himself but didn't take away the first thought. I think about that sometimes when we are in there." He motioned to the Fabergé egg. We taste something we've just made, and it's good. We add a bit more, um . . ."

"Vanilla?"

"Vanilla, yes. We add more vanilla. And it's better, but it's also different. We know that it's different, but the, um, the waffle doesn't. We correct it, but now it's not corrected, it's just different. Nobody except us knows how it tasted before the extra dash of vanilla."

All of New York grew silent.

"That's really beautiful, Nate."

He moved a little closer to her and gently touched her hand. He was almost always either joking, or instructing, he seldom just let go as he did then. He didn't dare go any further, but had no way to respond that wouldn't destroy this special moment. And so he continued, but looked once again to the words that had brought him to her warm skin for strength.

"Once again I see these hedge-rows, hardly hedge-rows, little lines of sporting wood run wild. These pastoral farms, like this one, Jess."

She smiled softly. She was almost weeping at the joy of this moment.

"These pastoral farms, green to the very door. And wreathes of smoke." He motioned upwards to the nearly obscured sky, intimating that Fabergé Restaurant was emitting smoke, which it undoubtedly was, but invisibly.

"Smoke sent up in silence, from among the trees." He motioned to the buildings around them once again. "With some uncertain notice, as might seem, of vagrant dwellers in the houseless woods, or some hermit's cave, where by his fire the hermit sits alone."

Silence. Calm. The endless clamor of the city had been turned into a distant din.

"I'm the hermit, Jess, on this pastoral farm." He raised his hands and opened them towards her body. "You are my fire."

This was the type of moment that had led them to imagine a future for themselves, together, in some place that could resemble an actual pastoral farm. In moments like these, Nate was so tender, so eloquent, and Jess so open, so giving, so generous. But Nate was also a wandering soul, and although he could describe rootedness, he was always onto the next thing, the next idea, the next challenge. He had dreamed of being alongside her, with her, inside of her, but then alongside her again, and then in front of her, and then off somewhere, and then . . . And so in that walk-in on that momentous day he was inside her, and she wanted him, but not like that, and he pushed her into those cartons of eggs stacked up for consumption, and he pushed her, and her body succumbed, and the eggs shattered, onto her chest, into her chin, upon her forehead. Smashed.

The rustling sound returned, and they were both suddenly made aware that the animal near them was large and powerful, one of the thousands of raccoons, as it turned out, that roamed the streets of New York, like foragers in the jungle of wildlife that had managed to make this artificial island into a commodious home. This was a good decision on the part of New York's wildlife. The trash in Fabergé Restaurant was comprised of discarded golden nuggets, either prized sumptuous creations that were too much for overstuffed clients, or somehow flawed according to John's wildly ethereal standards.

Not knowing how to stay in this moment, particularly in light of the interruption of this masked intruder, Nate continued in his quest to articulate his philosophy. "Jess, it goes beyond resentment."

She had been transported, and could barely recall what they'd been discussing before pastoral farms. Nate barreled on.

"These are very special relationships that can only be formed in places like Fabergé Restaurant. We are in the bowels of paradise, slaving away to satisfy the most far-flung desires of a class of people who exceed in their resources even the aristocracy of previous eras. That creates resentment."

"Indeed," she said. She looked through the darkness at him, inquiring as to his very existence.

Nate, who was Nate-the-Prep-Cook, had but a single public life, which he spent working. The rest of the time, he read copiously, particularly in genres of social history, the application of political theorems—especially radical ones—and of course fiction, realist novels mostly since they, when written by the likes of Balzac or Zola or Dickens or Steinbeck, were the best kind of social, political, activist history and practice. Or so thought Nate. But he had this rather magical knack for memorization, and he applied it, mostly, to poems. He'd learned long ago that this ability, whatever he thought about the poem itself, gave him a kind of magical pass, particularly in conversations with girls. He wasn't particularly handsome or desirable, but he was passionate about ideas, mostly ideas that very few people cared about. And so poetry was the medium for his intellectual seduction. He loved Jessica because she appreciated him as a thinker, as a talker, as a cook. And the fact that he knew many hundreds of lines of poetry was, for moments like this one, the difference between being interesting and being desirable. He wanted to be desired, despite everything, by Jessica.

Jessica loved Nate in her own way, very differently from how she'd loved Tina, or other loves she had taken into her embrace over the years. She appreciated Nate, but knew that Nate had bigger fish to fry, as it were, and although they'd spent many hours together, including precious hours in this pastoral farm, his gaze went beyond hers. She knew that each meal that Nate helped prepare was another brick in a wall of resentment that he was building in order to someday entrap the world's wealthy clients. And so she was for him the earth from which all nourishment came, and he for her the purveyor of regrettable sentiments about where nature's bounty was headed. This was a match that was bound to crack, smash, and end badly.

"We toil, Jessica, we build and craft and create and tenderize and flavor nature's masterpieces for the underdeveloped palates of those who have earned the money required for our creations, but not the discernment that would be needed to appreciate them. And so we feel them to be our inferiors."

Jessica dropped her head down in modest disagreement, and then looked back into his visage, for she loved knowing that his relationship to this place was so philosophical, so engaged, so much more than cracked eggs and stirred yolks.

"We are their superiors, because they know nothing of the process, even if they can appreciate the products. They are the bourgeoisie and the aristocracy, we the workers and the craftspeople. And so we toil, we sweat, we grind, we suffer, but in our actions we become their superiors, because they are but the passive consumers of our genius. We know this, but in the paltry rewards we receive, in paychecks that barely cover the appetizers in this place, we feel scorn for those who can amass the world's bounty and grind it into their palates for the eventual mindless expulsion from their overused anuses."

Jessica grimaced, but Nate continued, unabated.

"That, my dear Jess, is resentment. It's what you feel, it's what I feel, it's why we hover between despair and sublime fulfillment, between revolution, and Wordsworth!" He paused. "And they, in their weakness, their vulnerability, their undeserved dominance, feel to be our superiors precisely because they are weak and incapable. They patronize us, literally, and we take it. But we also dish it out, because in our gaze we bear the truth of their helplessness, and we know it, they know it; and if the artifice upon which their world has been erected were ever to crack and then crumble, they know perfectly well who would dominate them. And so they gorge themselves, they fill themselves up, pretending to be squirrel-like and thus capable of storing up the ephemeral pleasure of wasting precious resources. They do so because when the inevitable diarrhea pisses from their burning assholes, they are reminded of their profound fallibility, and of the superiority of those who know the recipes for their decay, decline, and death."

Jessica looked straight into Nate's eyes, but said nothing.

"That's us, Jess. Us."

I had seen these scenes of miserable revel, and always knew that it was in those moments that Jessica had wanted to embrace Nate, to hold him, to give meaning to his body and his soul, to reassure him that somewhere, in a warm and caring place, his life had meaning and his words had effect. But she never did. When within the very bowels of the Yolk, he took her, he froze her sentiment, and then smashed it, just as she had obliterated those eggs upon which she laid, open, vulnerable . . . crushed.

CHAPTER 6

Jessica stood before John. She had emerged from that pastoral farm, from her daydream, from one of the many moments and worlds that she held inside of her, eggs to her thoughts, the yolks of her memories. She looked at this powerful, strange, genius of a man who was still scrubbing—or perhaps stroking—the Hobart washing machine, as though he was somehow responsible for all this inequality, all of these wasted efforts. She felt as though she'd been transported by her thoughts to the very scene of her discontent with Nate, and was veritably amazed to find herself still in Fabergé Restaurant, still at the dishwashing station, still standing before John. He seemed oblivious to her past, and to his own, and seemed to be unaware of everything going on around him.

But Jessica knew that he was not oblivious. Although he now spent most evening shifts washing dishes and whistling, he still owned this sumptuous place, he still overheard and oversaw everything in his bizarre way. He was a culinary genius, who had laid all of the famous Fabergé Restaurant delicacies, but he was also a little eleven-year-old boy, the same little boy he'd been all those years ago when he started working in restaurants in the North End of Boston. He was today, as he was back then, scrubbing dishes, and he was polishing the machine that washed them, and he was doing so with the vigor of his younger self.

Jessica also knew, from speaking with Doris, the bookkeeper, that in spite of his half-century career, if John were to stop washing dishes and shutter this place up tomorrow, the bank would take it all over, all of it, and he'd be left with nothing but the incomprehensible tune he always whistled. No matter what the bank might seize, however, the strange aura of a giant egg in Manhattan that John had designed and built and occupied would remain. And so, too, would all of the culinary offspring, the palate's memories of eggs that had been beaten and whipped and fried and boiled and spiced for the consumption of the many wealthy customers who had visited and savored the Yolk's creations.

In moments like these, Jessica would feel a wave of compassion, almost desire, for John, particularly when she thought back to her short stroll around the block with Tom, the man in black, prior to returning to work. Tom was staking claim to her luscious body, and to her maternal touch. Tom, that resentful and powerful man, didn't know how to take "no" for an answer, any more than she knew how to utter it to him. Tom frightened Jessica with his silent persistence and his calm persuasiveness. She still bore the odor of the calf-leather glove with which he had stroked her cheek when she gave in to a quiet kiss in front of his hovering limo. Seemed like years ago. Now she needed to worry about sauces for tonight's meals.

"Where's Nicky?" she asked.

"He's showing the new guy the walk-ins," replied John.

"Hmmmm," she sighed. She wondered if the 'new guy' had ever worked in restaurants. If so, had he spotted the crate of whipping cream canisters that arrived this morning? And if he had, she wondered, had he been into any of them yet? She decided to make her way over to the walk-in for a surprise appearance, just as Nicky and the new guy pushed the heavy door open towards her. The result was very nearly a bruised nose.

"Ba-ha-ha-ha-ha-ck up!" said Nicky with his huge Greek grin and an exaggerated Greek accent. "So sorry, Jessica, we were just seeing if the sheep fit!"

Nicky-the-Sous-Chef brushed passed her, pressing his stomach out so as to be able to bang into her taut midsection in a way that might resemble the collision of an inflated airbag and a captive body. Jessica didn't mind. Nick was harmless, and he was cute, with his dark, curly hair, his bushy eyebrows, his eternal smile. Besides, she secretly enjoyed the banter he constantly maintained to keep the kitchen staff abreast of his gallant efforts to impregnate his wife.

"Ooops, Jess! Jeez, if you get too close to me I might spill the spermies I am saving for my wife tonight!" His passing left Jessica in the fact of an awkward newbie, who looked to be fourteen years old.

"Hi, I'm Russ," said the new guy.

"Pay not attention to her Rusty!" proclaimed Nicky. "On second thought, why not? You know what they say . . .," he paused for dramatic effect. "If the sheep fits, wear it!"

"That's right!" agreed Jessica, and then realized what she'd agreed to, and stuck out her tongue towards Nick.

"GENIUS!" cried Nick. "She's a genius, Russ, watch out."

"Nick!" shouted John from the dishwashing station. "The gravy?"

"Oh my!" said Nick, winking at Jessica. "John is starting to get a little personal!" He turned towards John. "It's thick and potent, and it'll be ready tonight!" He turned back to a mystified Russ, and poked him in the ribs. "And she's going to love it!"

Nate, distracted from the triathlon he was still supervising, called out, "Hey, Nicky, your wife just called!"

"Sssstop it!" replied Nick.

"It's true! The sheep costume you ordered for her just arrived, she's waiting for you at home!" He always had to participate in the goings-on in the kitchen, even from afar.

"Ah, gotta go, Rusty!" said Nick, feigning undoing his apron and turning towards the "Egg-Zit" sign that hung above the door.

"Nicky!" called John, with the voice of a battle commander. "The inspectors are coming tonight! Show the new guy where we keep the bleach."

"Oh, the inspector, ooh!" squealed Nicky. He bent over and turned his posterior towards Jessica, "Well, okay, John, if you say so!"

Russ started laughing, and then turned, guiltily, in the direction of the dishwashing station. John was glaring down at him with steel-blue eyes, sleeves rolled up, apron around his waste, Popeye arms, and his been-around-the-block Irish Boston look. Russ stopped laughing, and all that remained was the sound of industrial fans, hastening the exit of non-existent fumes, flames, and odors. It was 5:00 p.m., so this would soon change, as customers and servers headed towards the eggy heaven of Fabergé Restaurant.

The closing ceremonies for today's Lobster Olympics were over, and Nate begrudgingly started the process of cleaning up the cutlery that he had strewn about the floor and disassembling the lobster stairway to heaven. Nicky walked to the prep area to check on the sauces and *au jus* that were being warmed-up for the evening service. Johnny was checking the grill, scraping off remnants of last evenings gravies, to ensure that dreaded smoke didn't alert John to a less-than-shiny, metallic surface in the caverns of the ovens. Jessica reviewed the evening's specials, mentally noting how many fresh ingredients were in the walk-in, since John allowed no left-overs or frozen back-ups to get them through busy evenings. And John stood on the starboard mast, willing creation with his desire, and confining his underlings to their unhatched fate.

The early-evening shift was about to begin, and there'd be hands to occupy, vegetables to chop, eggs to sort, gravies to season, knives to sharpen, water to boil, stoves to heat, server stations to man, bread to bake, and, in the dining room, tongues to bathe, eyes to please, guests to serve, guests to tip, gases to release, digestive tracks to clog up, effort to be exerted at the end of it all to get it all out, and then clean it all up, so that they could start the process again tomorrow.

CHAPTER 7

Jude had returned to Fabergé Restaurant early that evening, oblivious but now curious about all that was going on behind the steel, swinging doors that led to the yolk, and to Jessica. For him, the restaurant was almost eerily quiet. By the time he arrived, the late lunchtime clients had, for the most part, disappeared, leaving the few and the privileged, those with the leisure of long conversations and others who had more furtive motives and surreptitious existences. There were bankers who, with their wives, were trying to undo what had been done in secret; investors who had retired hours early from the trading, dealing, stealing frenzy because of one sale sweet enough to warrant withdraw; executives who decided upon a "meeting" with feigned personages far from the office, after a decidedly ignoble morning of video games, or an awkward tryst with a secretary, colleague, owner, boss, or supplier, or, more ignoble yet, knees upon the carpet and sex in hand, themselves.

Life, after all, just isn't that glamorous.

Jude surveyed the familiar egg setting. The meager expenditures he made there each day were adding up, exceeding all other expenses in his life, even his rent. As always, he entered Fabergé Restaurant timidly, looking for a quiet table where he wouldn't be in the way of real customers or in close proximity to voices distinct enough to disturb his writing. The only exception to that rule was an as-yet unrealized glance of possibility from a searching eye, an *I* in search of a *we* for the purposes of mutual bliss. This possibility was entirely theoretical, because he'd never actually met a lover in a bar or a restaurant, no matter how interesting he feigned to look with his skateboard, his soiled jean jacket, his tussled hair, and the glaringly obvious lack of plans for any real work that day. In short, the bohemian writer look had yet to bear any fruit; it had not led to the hatching of any new trysts, and had not even stimulated much interest from the staff of Fabergé Restaurant. Or so he thought.

The fact was, Jude's look may have been appropriated in a grungy coffee shop on the West Coast, but he was decidedly a tad pathetic in a place that aspired to, and succeeded in, attracting the kinds of clients Fabergé Restaurant generally attracted. The exception to his casual attire, discernable only to the well initiated, was a very thick, black Montblanc cartridge pen, a gift from his aunt Doris. Five years ago she had paid a visit to his hometown. Jude happened to be there at the time, visiting his mother. Aunt Doris made contact with him, because she'd learned, from his mother, that he was aspiring to be a writer, and Aunt Doris loved the idea of having one such blessed soul in the family. She was the enlightened relative who, consciously emulating Madame Bovary, had read her way through sufficient romance novels to blur the line between her life of tedious marriage and her fantasy of endlessly passionate affairs with exotic men in fancy settings.

It turned out that the fantasies that Aunt Doris had dreamed up were but castles in a darkening sky of impending old age, however, one day she just gave away that large, black pen. It had fulfilled a negative destiny, remaining exactly what it was: a large, black pen. In her fantasies, it was the powerful phallic symbol that would draw into her being a world of lust and seduction, as it had for so many writers, like those who'd flirt and find love in the Parisian quartier of St. Germain-des-Près early in the twentieth century. But Aunt Doris didn't live in Paris, and she was not a writer, and her fantasies couldn't change that. But maybe she could live through a relative who could wield it, and thereby find love vicariously?

Jude carried the Montblanc everywhere, rendering it more an obligation than a weapon. In this respect, Jude did have a brush with legendary characters, because he, like Atlas, who had sided with the Titans in their war against the Olympians, was forced to stand at the western edge of Earth and support the entire sky upon his shoulders. Jude's pen wasn't the sky, but it represented great altitudes, and it could have been the inventor of celestial bliss, had he been successful in his attempts to wield it for creation. But, alas, at the Fabergé Restaurant Jude found himself wielding Montblanc amongst a crowd who couldn't recognize it for what it truly represented, which had the rather unfortunate effect of thereby rendering it powerless.

For most of the clients of a restaurant of this type, the Montblanc pen is recognizable, but it's only brought out for short flourishes, usually cryptic signatures on incomprehensibly complex contracts, initials on divorce agreement stipulations, or ill-advised scribbles on children's report cards or notes of absence. Further, on account of his terrible handwriting and awkward grip on the large shaft, Jude couldn't get his thick symbolic weapon to function properly, and he generally caused it to leak and spray in his pockets and hands, like a young man inadvertently spewing out his lust on contact with the object of his desire. And so Jude usually just displayed the Montblanc like a peak to be ascended, and did his actual writing with a cheap ballpoint pen that didn't leak all over his hands or exhaust his untrained grip.

Jude unscrewed and screwed together the Montblanc cartridge chamber, quizzically. He had not seen Aunt Doris again, even though, he often said to himself when he looked at its thick, black shaft, he really had wanted to. In her youth, she had been an artist who had made fashion sketches for the city newspaper in Baltimore. She was family, and he didn't have any other family, because his own little tribe had moved around so much that his parents had successfully severed ties with every existing relative and friend each of them had ever made.

"Someday," he reasoned, while staring upon the peaks of his miniature Montblanc, "I will get to know her beyond this pen." He looked at the emblem on the top of it and hoped it would give him luck by connecting him to all of the great authors who'd stared down towards that same emblem. Maybe Percy Shelley had used a Montblanc to write his magnificent poem "Mont Blanc."

"Probably," he thought, wrongly. And maybe John Steinbeck had used one to write *The Grapes of Wrath*.

"Probably not," he thought, rightly.

"Shit. Whatever. Today is going to be a big writing day!" he assured himself. As such, he was committed to spending at least part of it working on the novel that he had not as yet started, but which was going to launch him into literary stardom. To do so, though, he had to first get through a few pages more on his "egg manuscript." Now that was a great name: egg manuscript. It sounded like something you'd actually make out of eggs: First, you separate the whites, and then you carefully add cream of tartar powder, gently, like powdering a baby's bottom. Then stir gently, and once combined, heat the mixture to the point that its color shifts from glossy orange yellow to matte yellow cream. Pour it onto a granite counter or baking pan and then, using a conventional iron on low heat, iron the substance down until it assumes the consistency of parchment paper. You can now write on it, carefully, producing nearly translucent sheets of scroll that can be used to forge ancient documents of great import, or eaten in times of great duress.

Egg manuscript.

The problem with Jude's creating a masterpiece today was that he'd made the mistake of calling his stupid bank's 800 number that morning to find out from the endlessly prompting electronic operator that, thanks to a balance that was suddenly reduced by seventy dollars, he was now about to spend money that was supposed to be spent ten days from now. Obsessively concerned with conserving his tiny nest-egg, he had transferred money last weekend into his savings account, and then had, in a moment of debt-guilt, promised the bill-pay section of the bank's website to also pay his heating, telephone, and electricity bills. And, he learned from the stupid robot, he had dated those payments to yesterday afternoon.

Furthermore, by shielding his checking account from undue spending on food, he'd accidentally over-drafted instead, causing his fucking fraudulent bank to impose $36.00 in fees for each bounced payment, for a total of $108.00, and then he over-drafted again on each food purchase he'd made at three different places. So for a total of $41.26 he had racked up $216.00 in fees, and would be charged again by each biller for having bounced checks to them, which would add another $75.00 to the mess, for a grand disaster fee of $291.00.

$291.00.

$291.00 represented more than two weeks of food. Even at Fabergé Restaurant that amount would pay for twelve different eggy ideas that would contribute to his egg manuscript.

"$291.00. In fees. To a fucking, fucking, fucking bank. Shit. Fuck. Fucking banks!"

He felt better for a moment, elucidating his fucks. Now he felt worse. What the fuck was he supposed to order in order to stay at Fabergé Restaurant today?

$291.00 in fees.

"What the fuck!" And that wasn't the end of it, he suddenly thought. Since yesterday, he had used his check card for little purchases, including a chocolate bar in one place and a carton of chocolate milk in another. He had used it, well, let's see, six times? Seven times? He couldn't remember. There was also the beer he had purchased in the convenience store, and then there were those tissues he bought a few minutes later when the can, shaken more than it could stand, exploded its frothy contents all over his hands and clothing. He feared sticking to the inside of his skateboarding gloves for the next three weeks, so in an uncharacteristic moment had bought a handy little pack of Kleenex tissues, for $1.18. "Those little Kleenex tissues would now cost . . . um . . . $37.18 with the service charge. Fuck! Fuckity-fuck!" And there'll be service charges of $36.00 for each of the other purchases. He dared not add it all up.

"Fucking rip-off fucking banks."

Then there was the broken parking meter he'd used when some guy in a bookstore told him that he wasn't allowed to park the truck where he always parked when he went in to browse this month's *Vanity Fair* and *Skateboard Digest*. Holy Shit. He didn't dare add up those damages either, for fear of total despair, the enemy of creativity.

"Banks," he thought, "are the enemies of creativity. Fuck!"

His thoughts turned to salvaging the disaster by finding enough money to at least cover the little purchases, but how was he to get around the service charges? He would have to go back to his bank and beg forgiveness, as he'd done in the past, and hope that the teller would be sufficiently sweet, or perhaps hot on him, to save him from this ruin.

"Oh, and by the way," thought Jude to himself. "Who the fuck ever allowed the banks to deduct $36.00 per transaction in fees, when each purchase had already passed through his stupid account, electronically? And what kind of bloody computer takes days to process a $3.00 transaction? Better still, what kind of a sadistic bastard decided to steal, in $36.00 increments, from the poorest clients of the banks, with total impunity? Who? And how the fuck is it possible that charges that run through the bank instantaneously are also just 'pending' for days afterwards, even though they aren't fucking 'pending,' because they appear instantaneously, because banks use computers as means of defrauding their clients, and then use delayed accounting to add service charges to people who can least afford to pay them, obviously, because who the fuck else has less than $100.00 in their account when they go to buy fucking groceries, chocolate bars, and Kleenex?"

"None of your fucking stupid business," he thought, and then smiled to himself.

"Well, whoever he is," he continued to himself, "he'll probably come to Fabergé Restaurant tonight, though, and buy his mistress a $291.00 eggy meal!"

He looked around the restaurant, fuming.

"On second thought," he thought to himself, "the stupid fuck who invented the $36.00 in fees jerked off to swaths of bank balances that glimmered upon his computer screen late at night. And I don't do that."

But whoever did do it, he, and she, got away with it. And whoever it was, this fact was at this moment beside the point. All Jude knew was that he now faced a frightening abyss, six or seven more transactions, $36.00 each, because the fees had driven his account down towards the negative. "Fuckity fuck, fuck, fuck," he thought. "FUCK!"

And that was that. He banished the thought. There was literally nothing at all he could do. The barbed-wire fence loomed in front of him as he skateboarded on the pathway to economic slice and dice. No one could save him, least of all himself, so he might just as well ingest the egg of rebirth, the fragile egg of life, the cracked egg of catastrophe—*splat*.

This unfortunate guest of Fabergé Restaurant, this Jude-the-Writer, had come to New York to write a novel, and not to move people's furniture all over the United States, as he'd done for the past four years. He had come to write, what was that expression? He had come to "write the Great American Novel," to emerge from obscurity and become an Everyman edition, a Penguin Classic. A writer. Jude-the-Writer. And, amazingly, Jude-the-Writer had been successful, sort of, even though he really was mostly just Jude-the-Mover.

Jude, as Jude-the-Writer, was writing to shed the image that he'd had of himself as a perennial mover, as in one who is always moving someone else's crap from one state to another, instead of moving masses of readers from their normal state to a state of literary excitement. Jude wanted to be famous, to figure out what it would take to write the Great American Novel. To fuel his ambitions, obscure Jude had entered what seemed like several hundred writing competitions.

"Write about your first experience on a bicycle!" (For a local advertising campaign designed to bolster the mayor's effort of raising taxes in order to subsidize bike paths.)

"Describe your experience with anxiety." (For a pharmaceutical company in search of a talking head for a new 'performance' drug.)

"Tell us, with intimate detail, about your first blowjob." (For a 'teen' porno magazine. This was one of his favorite pieces of writing, which he ultimately had to tear up before submission on account of his having felt strangely sullied by the experience, not of writing, but of thinking about it afterwards.)

And finally, "Submit a 300-word essay about what it means to be an American."

This last one, perhaps combined with thoughts of blowjobs, was the one that really got him started on the "American Novel" idea. The very thought of it convinced him to be that great American writer who Mr. Carmichael, his high school English teacher, had talked about in class, because he himself wanted to be that same person. Mr. Carmichael, however, had traded in his dream for teaching, just as Aunt Doris had traded in her Montblanc pen for vicarious lust and passion—via her nephew, Jude. Maybe Aunt Doris, too, imagined the Great American Novel, and thought that the pen would vehicle Jude to write about it. For the moment, it didn't do so. For the moment, it mostly just leaked.

Jude had certainly thought about it, even if the pen lay limp beside him when he did. What does it mean to be an American! He'd win that competition, find and then mine a vein of understanding of the United States, based upon his travels with everyone else's furniture, across this great land. The great American travel novel, the story of a man who moves people's crap, and their lives, from one great American experience to another, an *On the Road* for furniture that turns into a penetrating exploration of the American soul. He would translate his experiences into words, his words into a novel, and the novel into sufficient cash to cover every stupid overdraft fee he had ever paid to American capitalist pricks, and then some! He would sell a million copies, and thus transport himself from obscurity to immortality, assuring him mortgage-free home ownership, the definition, according to his mother, of true success.

He'd find an incredible, successful, and brilliant woman who would love him, and who he'd adore to no end. He would support her fascinating work, and she would tolerate his bizarre habits. She'd leave him smoke his cigar, no, his pipe! He would buy a dark-brown or cherry-colored pipe that he would smoke while writing, and also while doing awesome tricks for his adoring fans on his skateboard. When he'd return home from puffing and skating, he'd make love to his wife on a plush, leather couch in his mortgage-free mansion, and then they would spend hours discussing important ideas while drinking champagne and eating food prepared for them in the style of Fabergé Restaurant.

They would live in a beautiful home, with a wood-paneled library, just down the hallway from the sunroom, and in the basement they'd have an indoor skating park. The whole place would be magnificently furnished, thanks to piles of money in a bank filled with awe-inspired tellers who'd clamor to serve him so that they could admire the number of zeros that followed the numbers in his account balance. And when he and his wife would be together in their bed, he would take her hand in his, and he'd feel good and not desirous of other women, because in the deepest recesses of his very being he would admire, adore, and love her. Then he'd take her in his arms, and they would kiss each other, savoring the taste of a life shared together, and they'd make love again, and again, and again. Ah, bliss! And all because of his writings! All because of his Great American Novel!

What are we dreaming about in each of the incomprehensible pastiches of present and past worlds that populate that eye within our minds? Perhaps we're all in search of the kind of congruence that is captured in mundane moments, like the image of a sleeping cat who seems in such perfect harmony with the carpet upon which she has spread out her furry self. Or like an egg, perched in silent perfection inside a nest, an incubator to a distant world.

CHAPTER 8

Jude still hadn't started the Great American Novel, but he did finish that little essay about America. It told the story of America from the perspective of a chair that had been handmade in 1776, and which had traveled through every state in the nation (except Alaska and Hawaii), en route to different owners. He submitted it to the Society of America, whoever the hell they were, and they never even acknowledged his entry. And then he moved, because he couldn't afford the rent, or any rent for that matter, and so he never won that competition, and if he did, well, he would never know he had won it, which amounts to the same thing.

But all was not lost, because Jude did finally win his first writing competition, in January of the current year, just a few weeks after getting a post office box, a solution to his nomadic existence. The breakthrough came thanks to an essay he had written for the AEFB, the venerable American Egg Farmer Bureau. He had never heard of any of the organizations that sponsored these contests, and never knew, or cared, why any of the competitions he'd entered had been launched. But when he actually won $1,000 ($1,000!) for his contribution to the AEFB, the accompanying award letter included a paragraph explaining that the AEFB had been looking for positive publicity in the face of two separate salmonella outbreaks in a period of only eight months. These unfortunate events were undoubtedly the result of endless doses of hormones and antibiotics pumped into chickens as a means of avoiding precisely such catastrophes.

Negative press about the outbreak had led to a major decline in egg profits for farmers already hit by a recently marketed, cholesterol-free egg replacement that allegedly increased, 'good' cholesterol. Jude hadn't intended to become a poster boy for the Egg Lobby, of course, whatever the fuck that is. Who ran the Egg Lobby? Chickens? Lobsters? Whatever. He was instead more concerned with just figuring out how to have a regular stream of meals come his way, and, moreover, how to have time to write his novel rather than carting crap around the country. But the idea of eggs grew on him, and, apparently, he had been convincing in this relationship.

Jude's winning essay was one thousand words describing a half-dozen eggs that had been laid by a group of happy hens, and that had each brought joy and nutrition to a half-dozen different people in a half-dozen different states (the theme of moving around was often present in Jude's writing). One egg had been consumed by a farmer before setting off to his Wisconsin barn, in which he milked cows for a brand of cheese that fraudulently sported an Italian crest so as to convince American consumers who would never have known the difference anyway that their pizza had an authentic Sicilian taste.

The second egg had been fried in fresh butter and served to a florist in Omaha, Nebraska, who, inspired by the wonderful taste and the gorgeous yellow color, had made a new and beautiful floral arrangement of various yellow flowers for a wedding bouquet for a gay couple who had imagined that the generous people in their state would vote "YES" on proposition G. They didn't, but Jude never expanded upon that story, and it somehow made it past the AEFB censors that he was advocating for gay marriage, not eggs.

The third egg had been boiled and cooled for painting by a young child in Wichita, Kansas, while his mother joyfully prepared omelets for her family on Easter Sunday.

The fourth egg had been carefully separated in order to serve as the basis for a delicate and delicious crepe recipe by a young entrepreneur who'd opened his first outdoor stand at a county fair in Nashville, Tennessee.

The fifth egg had been ridded of its yolk and then whipped and beaten until it formed a frothy, little mountain that was combined with sugar and cooled to create a little specialty cookie in Burlington, Vermont.

And the sixth egg, well, that one had been saved by the hen, so that she'd have a cute little offspring that would one day be a source for a new half-dozen eggs. This of course was rather unlikely, but, oh well, it's fiction.

Number seven, if a half dozen could include a bonus egg, would have been eggs that would be gently cracked, and then skillfully opened up and poured onto the pouty nipples of his cooing lover in San Francisco, but he figured he might want to save that one for a future teen-porn magazine writing competition.

He had written the whole thing up, including number seven, in half an hour, half-asleep, after a night of plotting out his Great American Novel with a half bottle of bourbon; and so he was all the more surprised that his half-assed text, and rather dazed effort, had lead anywhere, let alone further, in fact, than anything else he'd ever written. And it had. It had produced one thousand dollars, $20 per word. He did that kind of calculation constantly, particularly now with his newfound obsession with saving enough money to allow him to hatch another text.

This next effort was originally supposed to be the first draft of the Great American Novel, but instead he found himself working on another text about eggs, because his essay, published in a women's magazine, had captured the attention of The Creationist Institute, in New York City, which was looking for some provocative writings about eggs. They had decided that the image of Earth as an egg would help sway those who believed in evolution; that a place as wonderful as Earth couldn't possibly have evolved, but must have arrived, like an egg, from, well, from God. Not from one of his orifices, presumably, but from Him. So here was Jude, cheap ballpoint pen in one hand, thick, black Montblanc pen on the table, a negative balance in the bank, staring around Fabergé Restaurant in search of inspiration to fulfill his dream of becoming a famous writer. His first book would be about eggs, it seemed, so that his second could be the Great American Novel. But eggs would give him the start he needed, he decided.

"All I need to do," he thought, "is to write about eggs, in an array of manifestations and, of course, recipes. And, obviously, what better place to succeed in this effort than in the renowned Fabergé Restaurant, devoted to the fine art of cooking and preparing eggs?"

The problem, of course, was that this is one of the most expensive restaurants in the city, and therefore one of the most expensive restaurants in the entire world, which made the little matter of the $291.00 rather serious. What was he going to order that would justify his being there for the next five hours? He realized that he might as well buy whatever he could afford with his remaining $12.00, because one way or the other it would vanish at midnight when the stupid banking system updated fucking files and caught up with the present after having dwelled in the past in order to cheat him out of $291.00. Bastards.

"Since when do instantaneous computer transactions need to update?" He kept repeating his own question, as though he was a chicken in some egg factory endlessly reproducing the same commodity to similar effect, twenty-four hours per day. "Since when?" He asked this question of the universe, and the universe had no answer. He reached for the closed menu on the table and turned to the page of appetizers. There were, amazingly enough, a few choices, because this was the far, far cheaper lunchtime "specials" menu. Unbeknownst to him, Tina had insisted that John stoop downwards in order to broaden the restaurant's clientele, and so today's affordable specials, that is, today's creations that could be procured for a measly $12.00, included a fried partridge egg, strawberry-coated egg whites, a single (!) caviar egg, or a few salmon roe adorning a little mountain of puffed-up egg whites appropriately called "Santa on Mont Blanc." This was a seasonal favorite, and with the colder weather of a New York fall, it seemed like an auspicious choice. Most importantly, it would provide him keys to the Fabergé Restaurant kingdom for one more day.

Indeed. With his remaining $12.00 he'd be permitted access to that beautiful place, with its dark mahogany chairs, heavy teak tables, glistening, Italian, crystal-adorned, yellow-light-bulb chandeliers, replica (he assumed) Fabergé eggs, a white-and-yellow polka-dotted, wall-to-eggy-wall carpet, and bright, impeccable washrooms with yellow towels laid out inside of an antique table to dry the hands of those who'd been privileged enough to use those gleaming, modern faucets that rushed warm water over the scented, liquid soap that recalled fields of Provence flowers that had been gently enticed to release the sweetness they employed to court life-giving bees so that they could discharge scented eggs into the immediate vicinity.

"$12.00. A bargain," he thought.

And it was while Jude was lost in thought that Tina suddenly floated through the doors from the kitchen and surveyed the half-dozen occupied tables.

"Ah, Tina!" he thought, looking towards her sterile beauty, her doll-like face, and her tiny body. "$12.00!"

He thought that she would approach, and thus provide him with a reason to defer the moment when he was to commence his writing; but instead she took a seat at the first small table in the dining room, crossing those scarily thin legs, and seating herself upon the beckoning chair. He looked at her and tried to figure out if he was fascinated, or attracted. Attraction is a human experience, fleshy and warm, whereas, he thought, Tina was too perfect, at least on the outside. How might she respond to someone warm touching her? Would the scratch-and-sniff function be activated, releasing just the right amount of lubrication? And if it did, how much is just the right amount? Whatever the quantity, he was convinced that her scent would invoke both innocence and truth. He shifted a little in his seat, reflecting upon the number of men who find that kind of woman attractive, and concluded that it had something to do with her innocence.

A moment later, as Jude ruminated upon his own views on innocence, a man who resembled an impeccable executioner, or the captain in an elite force who was taking time out from the crucial task of ridding the world of everyone who didn't share in his upright, moral values through the careful execution of the murderous tasks for which he had been impeccably trained in a past so distant that no trace remained of his teachers or the books they once used for instruction, walked into the dining room. This man was John, the owner. All of Jude's lascivious, irrelevant, irreverent, and unhelpful ruminations vanished into the egg-infused air.

John bore a special weight that righted rather than tipped Fabergé Restaurant. The brute outside hid the silent, impeccable machinations within, and like those objects his father hurled into deep, dark space, each of his creations stood as testaments to the power of beauty in the heart of the destructive, chaotic movements towards distant time.

CHAPTER 9

John surveyed his Fabergé Restaurant, taking in the thirty-seven tables of varying sizes, as well as the seven or so people who, scattered haphazardly through the dining room, engaged in the crucial tasks of eating, drinking, and helping pay the increasingly unwieldy bills that he received. Bills seemed to arrive ever more frequently, particularly of late, when it had grown more difficult to rid himself of the pollution they were bringing to his otherwise perfect eggsistence. He scanned the room, ruminating.

When his gaze met Jude's, there was a perceptible hesitation, the result either of a particular interest on his part, or perhaps just a consequence of the fact that Jude was studying him with such intensity. Jude had once heard that a paranoid person recounts with certitude that everyone on the street is staring at him, with some degree of truth, because he himself is staring at everyone on the street to see if they are staring at him. "I," thought Jude, "am that person. I'm doing it to you, Mr. Executioner. And I was just doing it to Tina." He forced himself to look away.

John did not.

Jude looked down to the Montblanc emblem on the pen before him, and when he looked up again, John was speaking intensely with Tina, at once releasing Jude from his grasp and from the fear that perhaps they were both onto him and to the meager balance in his bank account. This could be a real problem. Where would he find inspiration if he got kicked out of Fabergé Restaurant, banished from the silky world whose shell protected him from the evils of New York City? The proverbial clock was ticking, and he instinctively looked at his watch. It was 4:00 p.m. He had two hours before the supper crowd would begin to arrive, and at that point he'd have to leave. Since returning to Fabergé Restaurant, he'd written exactly nothing, about eggs, or anything else. "But so what?" he thought. Nothing compelled him to leave except his own sense of respecting the place and, more to the point, of knowing his place in it. If he owned a restaurant like this, he wouldn't want someone taking up as much space as he did, with his notebook on the table, his smelly jacket draped on the chair behind him, his Montblanc pen, his $12.00 (which used to be $303.00. Bastards! And what would it be tonight?).

Jude suddenly rose from the table. He was feeling guilty for his own existence there, desperate for some kind of legitimacy.

"The bar!" he suddenly exclaimed to himself. He looked over and saw, yes, the bar was open.

"Okay," he thought, "no matter how expensive this place is, $12.00 must be substantial enough for a drink of some sort. I can at least afford a glass of mineral water. Better not buy that Norwegian stuff though. Who needs Norwegian water?" he asked himself. He gathered up his things and moved towards the Fabergé Lounge, which was cordoned off with a dark, wood partition and a yellow sign. There was one other person there, who was seated right at the bar. There was also a bartender who was polishing wine glasses, and intent, it would seem, to do so without any disruption. Jude considered his move towards the bar, since it meant that he had, first, sat down and taken up space in the dining room, and in so doing, he had ruffled the tablecloth, moved the chair, and "used" a space. It was as though he had checked into a hotel, taken a shit, used some of the toilet paper that had been carefully arranged so as to create a flower-like ornament on the dangling few sheets, washed his hands using the fresh bar of soap, left a ring of soap in the sparkling sink and fingerprints of soapy water on the faucets, soiled the floor with the dust of the world that he'd dragged in on his feet, sat down upon the bed, found the remote in its special remote spot, fired up the television, put his feet upon the bed, watched a few minutes of some football game that could have been played this year, last year, or any other year in the last decade without anyone really being able to tell the bloody difference, and then, disgusted, turned off the television, removed himself from the bed, feigned to unwrinkle the bedspread through broad sweeps of his filthy sweatshirt on the surface of the 800-count Egyptian cotton, and then left the room in search of another place to repeat the same acts.

This rumination led Jude to think about the servers who had carefully arranged the table, about the dishwasher who had made all of the white-and-yellow (of course) dishes so clean and shiny, and the cleaner who made those gorgeous Fabergé Restaurant toilets so pristine, and he felt a pang of remorse. And then he thought about the fucking bank that had stolen all of his money, and he walked, briskly, towards the bar.

He chose a seat behind the sole guest, a bearded, bespectacled man, mid-forties, well-dressed, but somehow disheveled nonetheless, exuding the image of discarded wealth. He was nursing a scotch and reading the *New York Times,* arranged in front of him according to the rules that had been set down on some ancient tablet in downtown London. Jude had seen this form of origami before, most noticeable on his first (and only) trip to Europe in his late teens, and since then he'd noticed that it was a well-known form of ordinary wisdom that manifested itself in folded newspapers.

Indeed, from the number of men who folded newspapers in this way, it seemed to Jude reasonable to believe that the sacred text known as, hmm, *The London Tablet,* is consulted by all mid-level businessmen to teach them how to fold their newspapers so as to minimally impinge upon those seated anonymously beside them in the subway or the train. This paper-folding ceremony is affected thousands of times per day by those en route to Fleet Street, Wall Street, or back home to the miserable little duplex situated on a street of miserable little duplexes, indistinguishable from one another, far from the city center that sucked the miserable life out of the peons who make white-collar, nonproduction pay. It seemed oddly out of place in this sumptuous restaurant, suggesting that this type of establishment had not always been accessible to this client of Fabergé Restaurant, no matter how wealthy he now looked. This client looked up for a moment at the bartender, who was now shining champagne glasses, and then cleared his throat and looked around the bar, revealing a dark beard, flecked with grey, and patchy skin blotched with redness. But even from afar, Jude could see shining, expressive eyes. His expensive suit and shoes and watch and, is that a necklace? No, it was some kind of a chain, a gold chain, probably made of solid gold.

"Hmm," Jude calculated. That gold chain looked to weigh around one pound, and the news plastered on the front pages of all of New York's daily newspapers pegged the precious metal at around $4,000 per ounce, which would make that necklace alone worth, who knows? $64,000? At the going rate, that meant sixty-four egg essays, or, hmm, around two thousand service charges at his fucking, fucking, fucking bank. That was a lot of money. The client cleared his throat again, as he manipulated the newspaper from one quarter of a page to the next, and then he cleared his throat again, twice, as he continued the operation towards dissecting the contents of the paper. And then he cleared his throat. Again.

Jude prepared the barroom table for writing, setting out the notebook right in front of him and his Montblanc pen to his right. He then pushed back against his jean jacket that he had maneuvered into position behind him. This jacket was an extension of the blanket he had owned as a child, and it similarly served as a kind of spiritual protection, in addition to offering a bit of padding to the already-padded, dark, leather pillow that adorned the bar chair. He had read somewhere about transitional objects, or some such term, things that people used to substitute for, or wean themselves off of, activities that had been crucial to their development. Thumbs are portable nipples, teddy bears are portable mothers, and so blankets, here Jude strained his memory. "What the fuck are blankets?" he wondered. "Wombs? Blankets are portable wombs? That's fucked up. So my jacket, well," he smiled to himself. "There's an image!" Comfortable and rather inspired, and in position to write, Jude courageously reached down and grabbed the Montblanc pen, cleaned its rather filthy tip with his finger, and began to write, leaving the meager ballpoint on the tabletop.

The egg. Perfect imperfection. Balanced, strong, impeccable, the very seat of life, flawless, even with the almost imperceptible flaws of mottling upon its delicate, yet, hardy shell.

He hesitated. "Is the eggshell delicate or strong? How am I supposed to convey both?" He thought of a woman—strong, delicate, the center of the world—carrying the eggs of the species within her very body, until they are stimulated into life-creating division through fertilization. He pondered this for a moment, sucked on the end of the pen, smiled to himself, and then giggled, perceptibly.

Human eggs. Perfect imperfection. Millions of them present at her birth, they . . .

"Can I get you something?" Jude literally jumped, not quite out of his skin, or shell, but close, it seemed.

"Jesus, sorry, dude, you okay?" The bartender had apparently abandoned the smears and spots on the glasses in favor of sneaking up on Jude at his little table, and he now stood before him, pen in hand, almost jokingly. How much of an order would Jude, with $12.00, possibly make? He looked down at his smeared scribbles. And how could mankind explain the creation of writing? Who invented the alphabet? Why did people only start writing thoughts down five thousand years ago?

"Um . . ." He looked down at his fingers, sensing an oozing substance, and realized that his pen was leaking onto his hands. "Why can't I write with a fountain pen, given how much it's worth? How many drinks would this fountain pen buy?" He had muttered this under his breath, but his lips had been moving perceptibly, and the bartender had clearly seen them.

"Can I help you?" the barman repeated, looking rather concerned. This was the second time today that someone working in this place had questioned, if only momentarily, Jude's sanity. And Jude was becoming aware that wasn't the best of trends to uphold.

"Hey. Sorry, I'm inside of my own mind," he said, trying to sound sophisticated. The bartender didn't look impressed, so Jude tried another tack. "I'm mining. My brain, I mean," he grinned.

No response.

"I'm, well, trying to write something."

The bartender stood in silence. He didn't seem to care in the least about any of these personae: insane, funny, or possibly brilliant. He was a big man with a messy, frizzy beard, thick glasses, the type that was trendy in Cambridge, Massachusetts, in the early 1980s, and had now become the mark of the particular brand of hipster that frequented bars and clubs in Manhattan. In spite of them, he looked solid, well-built, if on the heavy side, comfortably wearing a suit that looked rather trendy, like an Armani, or, at the least, an Armani knockoff, something that resembled those advertisements close to the women's lingerie ads he used to jerk-off to in *Vanity Fair*. Jude was ready to talk to this guy, partly because he was so taken aback by having been so totally surprised in his thoughts. Now there was nothing to say. Except what was required.

"Can I see your list of whiskeys?"

"We have most everything, what would you like?" This guy was either being really professional, or was a real prick. Probably both. Jude was in trouble, because who knows how much a place like this would charge for whiskey? And which one, if any, might be less than $12.00?

"Jameson, please." This seemed like a safe choice. He had once had a Jameson with a girl he'd met casually on the street in Akron, Ohio, when he'd helped her move a dresser from her apartment into a little, blue Toyota pickup truck that she'd borrowed from a friend. To thank him, she had offered him money, which he had declined in favor of a drink. Actually, he was only kidding about the drink, but she took him up on it, and brought him to a bar on the corner of the street, where she offered to pay for anything he wanted.

"Whiskey," he'd said, and the bartender in that local place immediately offered, "Jameson?"

"Yes."

So here he was, doing it again, like a Pavlov dog.

"Why not? It had worked the first time," he thought. The difference here, however, was that on the previous occasion the Jameson was paid for by somebody else, and this time he had to pay for it all by himself. That girl had been cute, but she had left immediately after paying, in cash, for the drink, and he, for some stupid reason, never pursued her. He had, however, thought of her many times since. He obviously should have followed her that day, or at least engaged in some kind of follow-up to her generous gift. What would have happened had he invited her to have another one with him? Why didn't he? He vaguely remembered that he'd masturbated the morning he'd met her, twice in fact, once in the shower and once in front of the sink, looking out the window at his neighbor who was hanging her laundry out to dry on the line. He didn't think that his neighbor was that attractive, but there was something about her doing the laundry near him that had produced not only a nice hard on, but a quantity of cum that required two paper towels. So maybe that was why he didn't ask her to join him. If he ever had to justify that decision, he'd decided that he would have to lie.

"Jameson . . . on the rocks?" Any liquor lasts longer if it has ice in it, he thought.

"Yes, sir."

"Please," he replied involuntarily to the formality of the bartender.

He thought back to that girl, as the bartender left to prepare the drink. She had paid for the Akron Jameson with a ten-dollar bill, but he couldn't remember if there had been any change. If it was close to ten dollars in Ohio, how much would it be in this place? Fuck. Maybe he ought to just . . . He could hear the bartender adding ice to the glass.

"Shit. Fuck it. I'll just stay here until the place closes if it's too expensive. Hopefully he'll finish his shift without calling in the tab, and if it's exactly $12.00, I'll pay absentmindedly and then bring him a tip next time. Or if it's more than $12.00, I'll just, fuck, leave, and then return some day and apologetically say that I had left in a hurry for some emergency and had forgotten to close my tab." He felt satisfied by all these plans and turned his attention back to his accouterments: the pen, the notebook, and, moreover, the muddle of his own mind.

The guy at the bar cleared his throat—again. This was really annoying. Jude wondered if it was going to happen again. It did. Now he began to fear that he'd wait for the next one, a habit that he'd developed whenever he was near a barking dog. He hated barking dogs, and as a result, he could obsess and fill hour upon hour not only with the aggravation of the ambient sounds that surrounded him, but with sounds that were in fact not occurring.

"Okay, silence. Here goes." He raised his Montblanc pen for duel.

The egg. Perfect imperfection. Balanced, strong, impeccable, the very seat of life, flawless, even with the almost imperceptible flaws of mottling upon its delicate yet hardy shell.

"Okay, right. Now where was I going with this?"

Perfect, too perfect. Too perfect.

Jude thought back to Tina. His cock stirred again as he continued writing:

Nature had chosen thorns for the protection of delicate, little flowers, dreadful odors to ward away predators from skunks, ink to blind and frighten sea creatures who prey upon octopi, and strong flavors to dissuade herbivores from devouring oregano or parsley. And for the most fragile being of all, the as-yet-unborn bird or reptile or insect, nature opted for the mottled, fragile, resilient eggshell.

"Where the hell am I going with this? I can't just start talking about God, it's going to sound like a greeting card. What ever made me think that I could write an entire monograph about eggs? I need a hook," thought Jude.

He lifted his head to see if Tina was around, maybe she would provide some inspiration. He peered beyond the divider towards the table where she'd been seated a few minutes earlier, but she was gone. John had evidently lingered, and now sat by himself, in deep reflection. Suddenly, he rose and began to approach the bar. Was he on to Jude? He was staring again, and once again John met his gaze. Jude detected a slight smile, a kind of caustic grin, momentary, the visage of a man who had just shot a wild turkey, and with that single shot, had made it fit for plucking. Then he looked towards the bar, which he approached, settling into one of the tall bar stools near the bearded client. His voice bellowed through the restaurant.

"Robbie?" he inquired. The bartender approached him, ready to serve.

"Yes, sir?"

"Robbie, we're expecting the health inspector."

"Yes, sir!" Robbie seemed to have heard this before, based on his demurred reaction.

The guy at the bar cleared his throat and looked over towards John.

"Salmonella is in the news, John," he said with a grin. Then he cleared his throat again.

"Salmonella, yes, Ted," said John. "Nasty." He looked over toward Jude, who avoided his grey-eyed gaze.

"Ted," thought Jude. Wow, cool name. Actually, this guy does look Russian, and Jewish. Is Ted a Jewish name? Theodore?

"Let's see." Ted manipulated his newspaper expertly, from one folded quarter to another, until he found the desired area. "A bacterium, *Salmonella enteritidis*, can be inside perfectly normal-appearing eggs, and if the eggs are eaten raw or undercooked, the bacterium can cause illness. Jesus." He looked up at John. "Fabergé eggs are immune, aren't they?"

John smiled wryly and then lifted the glass of cold water that the bartender had placed before him, took a long drag, then rose, pulled a white chef's rag from his belt, and wrapped it over his hands as though it was a small switch used to encourage a galloping racehorse. "Immune, Teddy. Immune."

John glanced back at Jude, who was now staring fixedly at him.

"Immune," he muttered, this time in Jude's direction, and he smiled before turning and walking back towards the kitchen.

"Immune," he mouthed quietly, but this time directed beyond Ted, beyond Jude, beyond the restaurant and the city and the state and the country and its many possessions. "Immune," he said again, this time louder, to the vast expanse beyond the cities, beyond the plains, towards the ocean, and then through the atmosphere and beyond the planet, and towards the entire galaxy. This, as anyone who knew John knew, was certainly a theme.

Ted pivoted in his chair and swung his body towards Jude. "Your drink is safe," he said, as the bartender placed a coaster with the large dose of Jameson down on Jude's table. "John is the owner, he keeps everything salmonella-free, don't worry."

"Thanks," said Jude. He was happy for the distraction and anxious to prolong it. "I was worried about it, but even more worried about the *enter-I-dies*."

Ted looked back to the article that he'd read out: "*en-ter-i-ti-dis. Enteritidis.* That's what the egg says when it gets salmonella."

"Enter I die—dis?" asked Jude, following the joke's pathway.

Ted laughed, and his eyes illuminated behind his glasses.

"Very funny. I'm Ted." Ted extended his hand towards Jude.

"Jude, hey, what's up?"

"Hey, Jude," said Ted, not even bothering for a response. "There's a song title for you. Write that down. Are you writing a letter to the bartender? I can probably call him over if you're in a bad way. Want a double?"

Jude smiled, "No. I'm writing to the hostess." Shit, he'd not meant to say that. She was closer to his consciousness than he'd realized.

"Tina? The porcelain lady?"

"Sorry, just kidding." Jude suddenly realized that (a) he wasn't the only person to notice Tina's unearthly appearance, and (b) he may have sounded homophobic, not wanting to write to the guy behind the bar. "Maybe," he thought, "Robbie is gay, especially with a name like that. And maybe Ted is gay."

"I've already written to the bartender," blathered Jude, to recover from the blunder.

"Shit," he thought. "Now he probably thinks I'm gay." This was so ridiculous that Jude almost broke into a smile.

A clink emanated from behind him, and Jude looked over to the bar, just as Robbie lifted his eyes from his labor. He then returned to polishing glasses, presumably to scrub away any chance of salmonella, and had either purposely, or clumsily, knocked a very elaborate-looking, tapered wine glass onto the counter. It didn't break, but the sound awakened him to his employment beyond the spotted glasses. He looked back towards Jude and said, "Sorry I haven't gotten back to you yet, dude."

Jude acknowledged that information with a nod. Silence. Jude was anxious to keep his conversation going with this guy, maybe it would help him with his eggsasperation in writing this text, so he pressed on, turning back to Ted.

"It's about eggs. I'm writing a story about eggs, for a contract I received." All of that sounded ridiculous, but Ted was looking over to him with an encouraging smile, so he kept going.

"I'm a novelist. I want to be a novelist. I guess that's the same thing. Anyhow, I used to be a mover. Now I'm a writer. I write for a living. And I just got my first paycheck. For writing, that is."

Ted listened intently, but didn't seem to know what he should respond. Robbie arrived at the table, tray in hand, and set down an ashtray, a little bowl of coriander-flavored egg-white balls, a favorite amongst the locals, and what looked to be a very full glass of whiskey. Jude looked at the assemblage before him with deep concern, because this was looking like a hell of a lot more than $12.00 worth of Jameson, and who knows if all these little goodies were extra?

"I'm definitely fucked," he thought, and raised his glass in a jest of abandonment towards Ted.

"Cheers!"

"Cheers," repeated Ted, and drew a long swig then reached into his own little bowl of egg-white delights and popped a few into his mouth before clearing his throat. Jude sipped the whiskey, which tasted as delicious, sweet, earthy, and profound as anything he'd ever drank before—ever. He raised his glass again for a toast: "To liquid paychecks!"

Ted turned back to the bar, grasped his own glass, and turned back to Jude. "Cheers." He once again reached forth to clink Jude's glass, this time with remarkable grace, considering that he looked otherwise like a 'man in a suit' near Wall Street, one of the hordes of such men that frequented Fabergé Restaurant. When he did so, the chain around his neck dropped forward.

"Cool chain," said Jude, feeling suddenly on top of the calm world of total satiation that people feel during the first few drinks in a nice bar on a quiet Tuesday afternoon, right before suppertime.

Ted settled back onto the backrest of his barstool and fingered the chain.

"From my ex. An ex. She gave it to me when we split up. We were into bondage. It was to help me remember her, I guess."

Jude laughed out loud, quietly at first and then, in the intoxication of the moment, with a kind of internal bodily violence, forcing the guffaws out of himself. He felt as though Ted was his new best friend, and he had only had a few sips of alcohol. Ted was smiling. He seemed like a really great guy.

"My ex-girlfriend gave me this pen," he lied, reaching down for the Montblanc. "It's a Montblanc. It represents . . ." He was grasping for something great to say to his new best friend, but Ted was already swallowing a grin, thinking, no doubt, about how thick the shaft of the pen was in Jude's hand. "It represents . . . um . . . the distance I'd have to climb to win her back! Mont Blanc, about ten million feet tall!"

"Now it was settled," thought Jude. "I'm funny, just like you, and I'm heterosexual, so my talking to you is cool. And I know about Mont Blanc, the mountain that the Romantic poets loved so much back in the era before endless alpine adventure sports, so he knows that I'm not some idiot bum in a bar." Now they could talk, they'd worked it all out, the tensions and stresses of meeting a guy in a bar were past them, and they had done it without discussing the on-going NFL draft, underway in Madison Gardens that weekend.

"My college roommate became a writer," said Ted, easily. "None of this," he motioned towards the newspaper. "No bonds, no stocks, no housing market, and no consumer price indexes." He lifted the newspaper up, and then turned it over to reveal a decapitated model in a pair of micro panties and a push-up bra. Even from a distance and in black-and-white newsprint her body looked warm, glistening, full, and, strangely enough, more human than Tina. Ted realized that Jude was looking at the advertisement, and not the graphs and charts and lists of stocks.

"She is the very best reward for reading those numbers," he reflected, almost inaudibly. Jude looked inquisitively into this strange businessman's face. "Have you ever noticed that, Jude? Amidst all of these figures, there's always one figure that matters! And her name is . . ." Ted scanned the page. "Givenchy! Nice name. Clearly an important figure!"

"She keeps going up!" said Jude, wittily. Now he was really proud of himself, then slightly sickened at how stupid that must have sounded. What was going up? Her bra? His penis? "Jesus, I'm insane," he thought. Ted let it pass.

"Join me?" Ted paused.

"Shit, maybe he thinks I'm bi?"

"If you . . ." Jude had no idea where he was going now, but was saved by Ted sliding off the chair, drink in hand.

"I have a meeting at four," said Jude's new best friend. Ted looked at his watch. Perhaps it was a Rolex? It was very fancy, whatever it was.

"Let's see, what time is it? I have a feeling I'll need another drink before then. Can I offer you another?" Ted drew up a chair across from Jude, preparing, it seemed, to settle in for the duration. Jude was excited by the opportunity to chat, relieved to save himself the agony of putting eggy words on a page, and terrified about what such a meeting could mean, financially. Jude had only nursed a little bit from his first drink, but now beckoning to him was the possibility that Ted would pay for both.

"I'd love that!" he took a long sip to indicate that he was almost finished, and then thought better of it. What if he leaves before paying? $12.00 might cover one, but no way in hell it would pay for two.

"Sure, thanks! The, um, bloody writing, you know, doesn't pay for much in this place." He hoped that his hint was sufficiently subtle, and thought that maybe he ought to turn on a fluorescent sign on his forehead that might read: "Don't forget to pay before you leave! Great idea for an invention," he thought. "I've gotta remember that."

Ted rose in his chair and turned back towards Robbie, who was holding a glass up to the dimness of the whole world. "Robbie, another round. Thanks!"

Robbie looked at Ted longingly. "Maybe *he* is gay," thought Jude.

Ted sat back down.

"I'm glad to meet you, Jude. Jude. Cool name. Betrayal. Judas. Strange guy, probably Jesus's best friend, otherwise, why ask him to do the betraying? You don't ask that kind of thing of an enemy, since he'd do it, but not in the right way." He paused. Jude didn't reply.

"Impressive, huh?" he smiled. "I'm no writer! Actually, I never finished my degree, but I have a diploma, even though I still have two more papers to hand in. I wonder if the two professors are still alive? One of the papers was for a class on ideas: The History of Ideas. Who even knew that ideas had histories? Here, Jude, I have an idea, would you please betray me? Tell you what, I'll save your soul if you do. Ah, what the fuck, I'll save everyone's soul! A round for everyone, on me! It's my last day on Earth, and I've got a platinum card! God gave it to me!"

"Jesus," thought Jude, "this is amazing." He didn't have a clue what to say. "When were you in college?" he blurted out. "Fuck, what a boring question."

"1981. I started in 1981, but was kicked out in 1983, so I transferred and started again the following fall, so I should have finished in 1987. Thirteen years to 2000, plus fifteen. Twenty-eight. What is it now? 2015, so that's twenty-four years ago? I haven't been in college in twenty-four years." Ted feigned fainting, slumping forward in his seat, then looked up and smiled.

"I read the Bible, in college, Jude. That was the first time I'd ever read it. But I never finished college. I guess that's why I still haven't finished the Bible!"

"You did better than me," said Jude. "On both counts!" He suddenly caught himself. Most of his friends, or people he'd met along the way, had little education, and he liked to be chummy with them by reminding them that on the one hand he was going to be a great writer, but on the other, he had as little education as they did. He was also friendly with a whole lot of people who did read the Bible, and often nothing more. He sometimes wondered who would read the Great American Novel, even if he wrote it.

"I learned out there, on the road, like Jack Kerouac. Or like that creepy character in Lolita, what was his name? Humbert. Right. Humbert Humbert." He paused and took a sip from his drink. "Sometimes I felt like Humbert Humbert when he traveled with Lolita from one hotel and motel to the next, all over the states." Ted nodded, knowingly, so he kept going. Even if he didn't know what Jude was talking about, he seemed interested. "Like Steinbeck's déjà vu of the Okies," continued Jude, emboldened and anxious to show off the intellectual wares that might qualify him to be a writer in his new friend's eyes. "Like Hemmingway and Dos Passos and Miller when they went to Paris. Then there were all those Beat generation writers and artists who moved into that shitty hotel in Paris. Have you heard about that place? Ginsberg and Burroughs and Corso, what was the name of that artist? Anyhow, they went to Paris, and then they just kept traveling, for most of their lives. Like Chaucer's characters when they left Canterbury and went . . ." He paused, and then reflected to himself. "Where did they go? Weren't they going to Jerusalem? It was a crusade, but is there a tale that takes place there?" He decided to play it safe. "Well, anyways, they went all over the place." He was reaching, it was time to quit.

Ted looked interested and, more importantly, non-judgmental in the face of these non- and pseudo-details. Jude decided to change tack.

"Actually, most of the time I am just a mover," he continued. "Not like a mover and a shaker, or a shaker mover, just a mover. I have moved people's shit all over the place. I went to Asphalt U, and then I did graduate work at Interstate College. It took me a long time to find the exit, but here I am. Pretty nice truck stop!" His eyes indicated in their sweep of the Fabergé Restaurant bar.

Ted continued to look interested and encouraging, but the jokes weren't registering, apparently. Or were they? Jude wondered if Ted got the shaker joke.

"Been to California?" asked Ted.

"Fuck yah!" Jude paused to take a long sip of his drink, draining the one he'd ordered in time for the arrival of Robbie, who bore two fresh ones on his serving tray. They looked much larger than his original, and he once again feared for inevitable financial ruin that would ensue if Ted were to leave without paying.

"I'd take sunny California right now," interjected Robbie, the bartender, presumably to indicate to Ted and Jude that he was overhearing them. Ted and Jude ignored the comment, and neither looked towards him. They were both focused downwards, towards the pad of paper and the pen on the table before Jude.

"Californ-I-ay!" said Robbie as he moved back towards the bar.

The bar was dark, and Fabergé Restaurant had only muted windows, covered by a near-opaque, off-white coating to preserve the general sense that when guests were in Fabergé Restaurant they were indeed deep inside of a Fabergé egg, right down to the smooth, off-white walls and coated windows. It seemed even darker and more rarefied, as the vision of California sunshine entered the minds of Ted and Jude.

"Yah, I've been to California plenty," said Jude, ignoring the interruption and looking up towards Ted.

"I always feel like everyone wants to move there at some point. And once they're there, everyone wants to move away from there, as far away as possible!" He paused, and then suddenly felt that maybe he was being insulting to California.

"Occupational habit," said Jude. Back then, I only met people who were moving, so I had the feeling that everyone associated with the place was moving there, or moving from there. I guess if you live in New York, you have the feeling that everyone lives in one of the boroughs but wants to live in Manhattan, or if you're from Hollywood you just figure that deep down, everyone wants to be an actor."

"Yah," replied Ted, absentmindedly. Something had made him appear preoccupied.

"Living in Manhattan," Ted began. "Couple million for an apartment big enough to cook dinner in, but still not big enough for guests. Everyone, almost everyone, is so in debt that they can't be considered to own anything here. It's the most amazing island on the planet, but most people will drown in their own debt before ever really experiencing what makes it so special."

"That was profound," thought Jude. "Who the hell is this guy? Is he rich, or not? Really rich, getting richer? Or poorer?"

"Have you lived here a long time? Or, sorry, do you live here? Are you from here?"

"I was born in San Francisco. When I was ten years old my dad bought property in Sonoma. You know it? The wine-growing region. Anyhow, his family came from Russia, like tons of Jews did. Well," he settled more deeply into the barstool, "the Jewish Pale of Settlement, that is. My family called it Russia, but it was actually the Ukraine. Anyhow, they came from there, with all kinds of fantasies about America. Except he came thinking that he could save America from the perils of perfection, so he didn't go to the Northeast. Actually, his original idea was to buy zillions of acres of farmland, because he wanted to create communities on the basis of farmer co-ops, groups of people who could work together to avoid everyone else. He felt a bit out of water in the prairies, though, because he really was a displaced European. And he was interested in zoology, classifying every kind of living being. Except, I suppose, mold." He looked for a reaction in Jude and noted the intense stare, but no resonance specific to what he was saying. "Anyhow, my dad's entire life was devoted to these ideas that he got from tons of reading, especially stuff by another Russian, a guy named Kropotkin."

Ted looked for recognition in Jude's eyes and then moved on.

"And a French guy named Proudhon."

"I don't know them, should I?" Jude was confident now, even in ignorance.

"Well, I was named after Kropotkin, Ted Mikhail Kropotkin. Mikhail, that's my middle name. And I liked whatever it is that I've learned about Proudhon, except for the fact that he was anti-Semitic. Anyhow, we used to live in the Napa Valley, but when my brother died, P.J., my brother," he paused. "Anyhow, when P.J. died we moved to a place that wouldn't remind my dad of what had happened, so we went to Sonoma, where my dad just bought as much land as the sale of the property in Napa would buy, which turned out to be quite a lot."

"What about your mom?"

"Never knew her well. She was a hippie-type. My dad met her in California, and he told me that she was really into everything that he read about and talked about. She also liked his open-mindedness and his belief in free love." He sipped his drink.

"That part she liked, and my dad did, too, but only in theory. She was really pretty." He said it as though it wouldn't be obvious. "I look exactly like my dad!"

Jude smiled, and then felt badly for doing so. "This guy is cool looking," he thought. "There's something about him. Maybe that's what he got from her." Jude felt drawn in by this biography, and grateful that Ted was still telling it with such detail. "Maybe," he thought, "he *IS* gay."

"Anyhow, my dad tried to be a hip Californian progressive, but I think that he only ever liked my mom. After they split up, there were lots of middle-aged hippies who used to come over to the house, but I don't think that he ever really dated any of them. He was really absorbed by his reading, and he'd philosophize about changing the world. In his later years he really got into classification, like they do with animals and bugs. He wanted to classify people into specific types and try to figure out a scientific system that would help them interact better, so that they'd all be relatively happy. That's what he called it: 'relatively happy.' It meant happy relative to the general state of nature. I never really understood where he was going with all this, but there it is. And then he died before I ever got to understand him anyway. Really shitty." He cleared his throat, and then again, and a third time, violently. And then he had a swig of his drink.

Jude used the occasion to down as much of the whiskey as he could, in preparation to say something, now that Ted had offered so much. But there wasn't a chance. Ted glanced at his watch, and then gave a look of horror.

"Shit, I think that this thing starts at 4 o'clock." He was fumbling in his pants pocket, and from there pulled out a very fancy looking invitation. "Yup, 4:00 p.m., right, good."

Jude was suddenly terrified that Ted would run to his meeting and leave him with the bill for all four drinks, when all he could afford was the tip.

"Nice to meet you, um, Jude," said Ted, looking suddenly distracted, already off somewhere else. "I want to hear about your writing. And your eggs. You here often?"

"Well . . .," began Jude, suddenly thinking of what he owed the bank.

Ted stood up to leave, but as he did so he reached into the breast pocket of his jacket from which, thankfully, he pulled out a long, flat, leather wallet, the leather of which Jude could literally smell over the fumes of his whiskey. Ted opened it and removed from a quarter inch pile one of the bills, which he deposited on the table without looking to see its denomination. It was $100.

"Did you have something else, Jude?" He looked back down his wallet and took out another bill, another $100. He didn't wait for an answer. "There," he said, as he added the second bill.

Then, without even mentioning some follow-up to this overpayment, he tapped Jude on the shoulder, flashed a peace sign, and called out in the general direction of the bartender: "See you, Robbie!" Then he headed, hurriedly, for the exit.

"The—" started Jude, and then thought better of it. "Bye, thanks, man!" was the best he could do, as the other part of his brain began calculations aimed at establishing whether he might make back some of the lost $219.00 from this newfound stroke of luck. He'd have to leave now and head directly to his bank, where this deposit could save him from all the service charges. Or most of them.

"Whew!" He bounded to the bar, settled up with a minimal but nonetheless respectable tip, and almost ran out of the restaurant. He was thrilled.

This was the first time I'd ever seen Ted leave Fabergé Restaurant with any degree of determination. Usually, he just stayed until he seemed to have just worn out his existence there, and then he'd leave, lingering at the door with Tina, who was invariably in stitches by the time of his departure. Jude could never penetrate into Tina's being as Ted did, because for Jude, Tina was nothing more than a fantasy. But fantasies aren't all bad. I have a fantasy. I want out.

CHAPTER 10

The new guy, Russ, was being initiated into the kitchen. Jessica was standing at the huge gas stove that allowed for the sautéing of a dozen entrées at a time, and Russ was following her every word, as though he were actually eating them. She spoke intently, loudly, above the sounds of the kitchen as it was setting up for the busy evening shift. It was 4:00 p.m.

Nicky the sous chef stood nearby, at the post-prep station, where sauces were strained, fish cut into filets, and meats tenderized. He was using the *au jus*, the pride of the restaurant, in order to elaborate several different gravies that would be remembered by the clients when they thought of how the food tasted at the Fabergé Restaurant. Fabergé Restaurant's *au jus* was a combination of all of the leftover meats and vegetables and some of the fish carcasses. It was a kind of edible compost, simmered night and day at a low temperature induced by a flickering, blue gas flame. Every evening, when John distributed the mandatory nighttime cognac to those who had been cooking that night, he would wax poetic about the *au jus*. And every night at least half a bottle of that same cognac would find its way into the *au jus*, to "assure its preservation" until the next shift, which turned out to be brunch, on weekends, or lunch every day of the week except Monday.

Cognac doesn't preserve anything, of course, and since the *au jus* was always at a near-boiling temperature, it didn't need preservation anyway. But since the cognac, like everything else in Fabergé Restaurant, was of such high quality, it did help the flavor of the *au jus*, and therefore of all the sauces. And the fact that so much of it was poured each night into the *au jus* provided a neat alibi for missing bottles of not only cognac, but also port and sherry, which John would sometimes substitute or complement, depending upon the temperature outside.

"Cognac for cold weather," he'd say, "and a cold. Port for sunshine, and to ward off clouds."

At the prep station, Nate was chopping his way through a large crate of green beans, an annoying task, particularly since John insisted that each bean be peeled, by hand, of the little "zipper" that ran down the midriff section. Each prep chef who had ever worked at Fabergé Restaurant had tried alternative methods to reduce the tedium of this chore, and nobody, to date, had found the method. Nate tried unzipping them all at once after lining them up in rows around three feet long and then splitting them open, surgeon-style, with a large chef's knife. But when John had seen the effect—beans that had been unzipped on the wrong side, or stabbed too deeply, or only partially unzipped—he raised hell.

Nate had replied that circumcision comes with a cost. John didn't think that funny, and ever since that day, he had been even more particular about the eventual look of each bean, and this in spite of the fact that they were only prepared as a kind of base for the "Green Bean and Egg" dish. A Turkish-inspired delicacy, this was a popular lunchtime fare, mostly for ladies. It came packed with a little zing, created when green beans are lightly sautéed with white onions, white pepper, salt, and then anointed with two partridge eggs, topped off with red pepper flakes. It was a very attractive concoction that, like most other dishes at Fabergé Restaurant, succeeded in hiding the brute labor that underwrote the recipe, beginning with the unzipping of the beans, but continuing all the way to the manual grinding of the red pepper flakes.

Nate was obsessed in all of his actions by all issues relating to this labor, and the people, notably himself, who undertook it. This led him to philosophize, alone late at night and with Jessica, and to reduce his effort/reward quotient, which he did by finding every possible way to reduce his workload, or raise his salary. Salary raises were few and far between, because Fabergé Restaurant had been, since its very inception, a ship that tended more towards bottom-feeding, like the lobsters it served, than sailing. And so Nate tried a more subtle approach to the prep work, suggesting that beans, which are actually fruits and not vegetables, didn't belong with the main meal, and, even more dramatically, aren't eggs.

John feigned to not understand what Nate was talking about most of the time, or else he really didn't care, which was more likely. John worked at Fabergé Restaurant as one responds to some faith-based higher calling, with absolute devotion. Nate never had any such calling, except perhaps his materialist worldview, but he played along with John, and at least tried to respect the eggy impulse that underwrote the enterprise. To that end, he made a game out of finding definitions of plants that call into question their suitability for an egg restaurant. In this one, he learned that beans are in fact fruits, and not vegetables, because they form from the fertilized flower and contain the seeds of the plant, just like pumpkins, squash, cucumber, tomatoes, corn, peas, and sweet peppers. Ironically, this dubious set of fun facts had contributed to beans becoming a staple at Fabergé Restaurant, because John decided from that point onwards that fertilized eggs fit that definition, which mystified everyone in the kitchen except, apparently, the clientele.

The real reason for the prominence of green vegetables, and an array of un-eggy dishes, was that Tina had read a review in the *New York Times* of a restaurant called "Meet at Meats" that wasn't classified as a 'healthy choice' because it offered no green vegetables with its gourmet fare. The owner, a former football star who had made hamburger meat of his own left knee during a practice session in the preseason, was aiming to attract the type of people who could afford to attend events like the NFL playoffs, or the US Open. And he imagined that they, like he, would consider that vegetables are for sissies.

Meet at Meats had lasted through one US Open and half a football season, and then went into bankruptcy. This was in part because very few women felt comfortable there, but even more importantly, it turns out that real men want to eat vegetables and salad. Whatever the case, vegetables or no vegetables, Tina, forever protective of the precious Fabergé Restaurant, didn't want John to take the same chance with eggs. So beans, along with fruits that most people consider vegetables, were made to be the exception of choice to the egg fare, and a new Tina-inspired side of the menu was developed, originally for female clients. It quickly lost its gender-orientation, and the eggs were integrated into a choice amount of non-egg, or egg-related, fare.

On the opposite side of the prep counter was another wooden-covered steel counter that was used for preparing garnishes. Since it was on the service side of the kitchen, servers could be called upon during a rush to slice lemons, peel and cut oranges, or even chop parsley, so as to relieve the burden from the prep chefs. Once upon a time there had been twice as many sous chefs, chefs, and prep chefs in the kitchen, but now they were down to the bare bones, literally, as John's benevolent bookkeeper Doris whittled the staff down to meet the payroll each month.

Johnny was now manning that station, since he'd already tenderized the veal, a task that, on account of the noise it created, was performed in the parking lot at around 3:00 p.m. each day, on a table that John would sterilize daily for the purpose, using his own special combination of salt and lemons. It was because of Johnny—a tall, curly haired engineering student who was completing his degree program online—that everyone had started calling John, the owner, by a new name: John-the-Owner. The idea developed further, so that Nicky, Jessica, Johnny, and perhaps someday Russ, would sometimes be anointed with surnames in accord with their functions. Even Tina was sometimes summoned with Tina-the-Maître d', but she didn't like it, and people shied away from things Tina resisted. So there was Tina-the-Maitre d', Tina-the-Chinadoll, and, well, Tina. Just Tina.

As times grew more troubled in the restaurant, and as John's mental health declined, Johnny-the-Broil-Guy took over many of the tasks previously undertaken by John, while John resorted more frequently to washing dishes. This was partly because it was so difficult to keep decent dishwashers, and partly because the noise of the vents and the machines in the dishwashing area was so loud that the dishwasher could sing or whistle with virtual impunity. This used to be valuable, when John would hire out-of-work musicians to do the dishes; but it was now crucial, because John had taken to whistling, and sometimes even singing in a kind of whining desperation during the supper shift. As a result, it was valuable to differentiate Johnny-the-Broil-Guy from John-the-Owner as a way of reminding oneself that the latter was indeed the owner of the place, despite all appearances to the contrary.

"We always start the same way here," Jessica was telling Russ. "Fabergé Restaurant is an egg restaurant, and every dish begins," she reached over to a tray of chicken eggs, one of three dozen or so egg trays behind her in a specially cooled tray, "with an egg."

Russ stood purposely close to her, and tried to inch himself forward so that she'd feel him close, and perhaps reciprocate his mounting desire. She seemed oblivious.

"You . . ." Russ had lurched forward somewhat, and had clearly pressed himself up against her, crotch-first. She turned and glared at him and, right on cue, a large hand pressed onto Russ's shoulder from behind. John had been watching the whole proceeding, and now intervened.

"People need to learn how to cook eggs," he began. Jessica backed away, looking relieved. "Right, Jessica?"

Jessica, repressing a scowl in the direction of this new guy, couldn't agree more. She also knew that John wouldn't accept her being threatened, in any way, ever. He never had, and he would never let the dust, sand, or ash of this often-filthy world sully Jessica, the mother of nature, the powerful, corpulent, sweet, soft, all-knowing caretaker of the earth's bounty. Jessica knew John-the-Owner's fidelity towards her as a certainty, like gravity, or the glare of sunshine. Jessica smiled, gently, in John's direction, knowing that he had her back.

"There's only one way to cook an egg, Russ," said John, rather close, in his own way, to the new employee. "One way. Do you understand?"

No answer was required, and for his own sake, Russ would not offer one.

"You don't cook it, Russ. You understand? You don't force it, Russ. You just bring it along. If you force it, then it's only fit to be worn." He pointed downwards, towards Russ's Converse running shoes. "Those shoes, Russ, know what they're made of?" John grinned sardonically and looked over at Jessica, who had heard this one, well, probably a thousand times. And then he stared menacingly towards Russ, with his piercing, steel eyes. "Somebody overcooked the eggs, Russ, and now you are wearing them."

Russ looked uncomfortable, and as John moved even closer, his discomfort turned to terror. Here he was, in the center of a yolk, cast away from the familiar sights, sounds, and smells of his native Manhattan and plunged into this terrifying universe of solid shells and bizarrely animated interiors. It was as though he was hovering, suspended in Fabergé Restaurant's midriff, wedged in the Yolk, between Jessica on one side, John close by on the other. The stove's blue flame flickered before him, crotch level, and behind him the array of chilled eggs was arranged into a nearly perfect line. Russ looked ready to flee, to burst out of this place, and may have done so had John not looked so poised to pursue him even deeper into the Yolk, downwards, a Vergil to his Dante plunged down into Inferno.

If the eggs that surrounded Russ could have used nascent eyes to see, they would probably be collectively bemused, even if individually frightened. And if they looked with fresh eyes upon this entire scene, they might wonder, as Jessica sometimes did, if John's intention was to teach Russ how to fry an egg, or to command him to perform some dark task with a gas stove that could lead to fundamental changes in the very makeup of the Yolk, the Fabergé egg, and the world that surrounds it.

"In fact, Russ, you don't actually *cook* an egg," he seemed to be warming to the oration, but also lightening up, "unless you want to use it as a weapon, or decoration for an Easter fest." His mouth mounted, almost into a grin. "You have to warm the egg up, Russ, by gently bringing it to the temperature of the butter until it coagulates, just enough to lose its gooiness." Then, suddenly, sardonically, and with all the practicality of a motorcycle mechanic, John tilted his head backwards and declared, to Russ and the entire kitchen, "If it starts looking like Saran Wrap on its edges, start over." He turned to Jessica to make sure she was listening to the speech he had given every one of his employees five thousand times.

"You don't make Saran Wrap, Russ. If you want Saran Wrap, Russ, we have it over there, near the server station. You make eggs. Somebody else makes Saran Wrap. And it's not you, okay, Russ?"

Russ nodded. He would have agreed to have his own head served up as tonight's special if it would bring the current demonstration to an end.

John expertly chose an egg, cracked it such that the fissure divided the shell into a perfect half, and then, by expanding the fingers in his hand, revealed the waiting innards to the pan, which gently swallowed it and then suspended it on the warm, little sea of fresh butter. He reached to his left and with one scoop grabbed the salt and the white pepper shaker, adding each to the yellow mound, creating a design that resembled an astrological sign, as he was wont to say and Jessica and Nate had many times recalled together, in fear and admiration. "Taurus," he said out of the side of his mouth, in Jessica's direction.

Russ looked perplexed and looked up to seek reassurance from Jessica, but she was wiping down the stainless area where the gravies are prepared. Russ turned back to John. He was feeling guilty and a bit sick with fear and embarrassment. John was able to instill both by simply standing nearby, but it was infinitely worse when he was teaching anything. Somehow John's decades of experience in the kitchen culminated with each order, with each observation, with each look of cunning and deception. The egg, warmed, looked glossy, beautifully decorated in Taurus the Bull garb of rusty fur and a heavy head of darkening pepper.

With a perfectly timed flip, the protrusion of its yolk was gone, and it was smooth, flat, over-easy. And then, not a moment later, it was perfectly situated in the very center of a warmed plate that John had snatched from below the stove. He moved it in the direction of Russ and then pivoted and placed it behind him on the counter that housed all of the eggs that would be served up that evening. He showed the impeccable pan to Russ, as if to underline the fact that it looked as new after the task.

"Thanks—," Russ started to say. But John was gone, drifting, as it were, towards the broiling station where he was arrested by the sight of a smear on the otherwise pristine stainless-steel handle that opened the convection oven. He turned back, with the glare of a commanding officer and the sneer of a soldier defined by the horrors of victor.

"Jessica, they are coming tonight, Jessica, a group of them, for inspection. Get Russ to wipe down the steel before we get going."

This was a demotion, quick and dirty. No chopping, no cutting, not even any replenishing in the walk-in, just wiping down. Russ looked perplexed and walked back past Nicky, who was in deep reflection over the gravies, and towards Nate, who had lined up at least three hundred green beans into a long, green structure resembling, in a disturbing, green color, a parade of inchworms or a stairway back to the Garden of Eden.

What's the difference between the garden and the nest? The garden was designed for perfection, and then became the stage for unexpected expulsion, whereas the nest was conceived specifically for expulsion.

CHAPTER 11

"We have ways of making you talk!" pronounced Nate as Russ approached the prep table. Russ, worn down by his little chat with John, was traumatized into total submission, and, displaying no outward emotion to compete with his inward, emotional coagulation, he just stared at Nate, conveying nothing other than still, blank horror. Nate stood tall above the beans, and the whole scene conveyed an impression that they must be quivering inside. As Russ stared forward, as though preparing for an execution, Nate leered over the green line and produced, in his left hand, a knife sharpener, and in his right, a huge chef's knife. Russ was so sensitized to the emotions of this horrifying place that he could feel the cold blade upon his own neck, the squeeze of Nate's hand upon his tender testicles. His eyes widened.

Nate adroitly ran the blade of the knife over the sharpener, side to side, a dozen times, and then laid both down before him. He looked up towards the white, rounded ceiling of Fabergé Restaurant, clasped his hands in mock prayer, then seized the knife, and in two swoops chopped the ends from the two sides of the beans. He then took from his apron strings the towel that John forced everyone to carry with them at all times and wiped his brow before gently dotting his eyes. And finally, he took Russ into his arms in a warm embrace.

"It's over. Now we can but pray for their souls." He bowed his head, and then, using the chef's knife to help amass them, began to lay the beans down in a six pan. "May you rest in pieces," he solemnly declared.

"Coming through, watch out, it's hot, hot, hot! Excuse me!" Nick was squeezing past Nate and Russ in a great hurry, carrying a sack of flour. "Hot, hmmm, stop it now, I gotta run! My testes are ablaze!"

Ever since Nick and his wife started trying to have children, time came to be marked by crosses on a tear-covered calendar. They were being foiled, it seemed, by the heat of the hot plates and stove, which conspired, at the level of genitals, to heat the reproductive organs to a temperature unfit for reproduction. Nicky's sperm flowed into his wife's fallopian tubes like egg whites from some filthy Manhattan diner, surrounded by the much-feared Saran Wrap of overcooking.

There is an understanding in professional kitchens that casual sexual encounters can usually occur without condoms, and few of the female chefs used contraceptives if their partners worked alongside of them in the kitchens. At first, Nicky's verbal frustration about his impotence had led to joking about his condition, and then, as guffaws turned to concern, he began to receive regular vacations, thanks to Doris's intervention. But nothing worked. Over time, the jokes in Fabergé Restaurant's Yolk had turned to sadness, and then, mercifully, back to jokes again.

"He would be a great father," Jessica had once declared to Nate.

Nate, having himself dreamed of paternity and a life with her, hadn't replied. But it was a shared sentiment in the kitchen that this professional tragedy, which led to overheated sperms and eggs, was a pitfall of the job, and a strange allegory for the coagulated yolk. For a long time, servers speculated that Nicky's quest would be successfully resolved, just as they believed that at some point Jessica and Nate would come together, as it were. But those who worked in the kitchen knew better, and in hushed voices they all spoke about the power of that blue flame, and, in regards to Nate and Jessica, about the equally destructive stresses of working together in close proximity. The Yolk, they knew, was a place of creation and life, but also of a vitalistic force that is heated by merciless flames to submission.

There was now that strange lull in the evening, the calm before the proverbial storm of fried, broiled, beaten, stirred, and whipped eggs. Russ was put to work polishing the endless stainless steel of the kitchen in preparation for what would then become a night of pot scrubbing and the caressing of stainless steel.

John stood by the dishwashing station, prepared for a night of steaming, rinsing, and piling-up dishes.

Jessica gravitated towards the sauté station, prepared for whatever may come up.

Johnny arranged the rows of raw meat and fish and lobster, carefully handling each with his fingers.

Nate stood and admired his handiwork before bringing the slew of vegetables he had prepped for the evening into the walk-in, where he'd probably stop for a quick whippet from the new case of whipped cream containers.

And then, ritualistically, the servers began to appear, a half hour or so before the opening of the restaurant's main "crack," as the front door was affectionately called.

The walk-in door, heavy and solid, opened and closed frequently through the shift, particularly as the kitchen staff sought solace or whippets or a snack to escape the heat and the noise.

Nate emerged from the walk-in, silent and serious, surveying the Yolk. This was where he wanted to be, in the very seat of class-consciousness. He flourished in this elite world of expensive cuts of meat, fresh fish and lobster, expensive beluga caviar, whipped cream, and, of course, eggs, some of the most exotic and expensive eggs from some of the rarest creatures on the planet, not to mention, as in the case of the ant eggs, some of the most prolific. Each of these gourmet dishes was served on expensive, French flatware and accompanied by Italian crystal glasses filled with obscenely overpriced wines, beers, and liquors. Most of the clients came to Fabergé Restaurant expecting to spend at least $300 per person, and many in fact exceeded $1,000 per person on a single meal.

This conspicuous consumption was taking place in the United States, so some of the meals weren't even long affairs, but were rather, like the sex that might follow, in which the quantity spent to procure the favor could be likened to the value of the favor itself. Hence the array of wealthy people, men and women, who came to Fabergé Restaurant with partners who were clearly not their legal spouses, but rather, same sexed or not, guilty pleasures, guiltily brought to this haven of champagne and caviar, for the timid, crocodile eggs carefully placed in a pool of ant larvae, for the more experimented or curious. These wealthy people, or at least those with enough wealth to bring them in for one of these meals, were all served by employees who couldn't make enough in a week to pay for the exorbitance of a meal that they themselves knew how to prepare.

Nate was in his element here, because expensive restaurants are institutions where class can lead to class consciousness, or class warfare. The disparity of wealth, even in the kitchen itself, can be dramatic, particularly between highly trained chefs and unskilled workers. Furthermore, unlike miners or factory workers, those who toil in the service industry rub shoulders, often literally, with the upper classes that they serve. They can thus become astute observers or, in the case of people like Nate, curious investigators into the very bases of social relations.

Nate undid the strings holding his chef's apron and then did them up again, tighter, and moved like a professional athlete, or perhaps a union organizer, towards the fray. His form of hobnobbing was akin to readying himself for a fight, and he, as always, was ready for prolonged combat.

Jude stayed away, probably because he didn't have enough money to have had any real choice in the matter. There was enough to keep me amused, though, as I watched the Yolk from the perch from which I observe what unfolds in Fabergé Restaurant. It was a busy shift, and somewhat more somber than others, perhaps because John was even more convinced that, as usual, an inspector was fated to enter the premises that evening.

I don't think that an inspector would dare enter Fabergé Restaurant, unless tempted by its tastes, because everyone, it seemed, knew that there was no point in looking for filth as long as John-the-Owner was the owner. Moreover, I wouldn't want to be the ones charged with inspecting John's Fabergé Restaurant, because there's no telling what he'd do if he found out. Maybe he'd cut them open, as he did the lobsters, and then look for eggs to extract. If I were able, I know that I would most certainly extract other eggs from myself. Perhaps the Fabergé egg replicas that adorn my innards already achieve this purpose?

CHAPTER 12

When Tina saw Steve, she sensed the arrival of a kindred spirit. He was tall, clean, and not just clean-shaven, but clean—everywhere. He was impeccably dressed, silent, observant, ponderous, introverted, and serene. He looked like a murderer.

Tina decided right then and there that she wanted to be murdered. Tina wanted to be murdered by him.

Steve stood at the entranceway, ignoring the activity around him and staring obliquely into the dining room. He looked to be casing the place, and Tina was almost tempted to cross the dividing line between the dining room and the kitchen, something that only occurred in extreme situations, to tell John that the inspector had arrived. She stared at him, taking in his entire being, and knew that her impulse to call John had come from some other place. Inspectors didn't wear designer clothing, and this man was wearing a Hermes shirt, and, yes, a matching tie from this year's collection, under a Gucci black-suede parka.

Tina did not shop at such places, but without checking the labels on her own impeccable clothing one might think that she did, because she kept up with fashion trends in her spare time. When she did shop, she didn't just go for knock-offs, she studied catalogues to understand the spirit of designer work, so that she was able to find in mid-range department stores clothing that, on her frame, looked like it came from expensive boutiques. As a consequence, she could spot recent clothing lines from expensive brands from a mile away, a skill that sometimes served her well in Fabergé Restaurant.

Tonight, her knowledge served her well. She approached this man with caution. "Good evening, sir, may I show you to your table?" She had no idea if he had a table, if he'd made a reservation, or if he knew that on a Thursday night he should. But it didn't matter, she was going to seat him, and if this meant that she had to eject the wealthy client from Tucson, Arizona, who had read the flattering write-up by a schmoozing journalist who had wanted a free meal at Fabergé Restaurant and got one in exchange for writing for the American Airlines in-flight magazine.

"Some fat hick wouldn't be able to taste the quality of Fabergé Restaurant's food anyway," she thought to herself, "and he probably only comes to New York occasionally, so his being kicked out wouldn't change anything on the book-keeping side." She scanned the dining room for a candidate to her uncharacteristic impulsivity. There was in fact no need, several tables were unoccupied, and the reservation list had gaping holes that evening. She symbolically lifted the golden rod of flowing ink to inscribe his name into her sacred book. She looked into his eyes, and he uttered, simply, "Steve."

"Steve," she wrote.

Steve looked right at Tina as she undertook this task, without evident motion. "I am waiting for someone else as well. Two people, actually, but the second will arrive later." Silence.

Tina looked up into Steve's black eyes, took in the smell of warm animal from his black coat, and lowered her gaze. She then looked up at him again, right into the very depth of his still features.

"Would you care to wait at the bar, sir? Or would you just like a table?"

"I don't have reservations," he replied, matter-of-factly, and then, as though as an afterthought, added: "But I prefer to eat at the bar. I assume the menu is available for patrons of the bar?"

Patrons of the bar. She was going to remember that. John would appreciate patrons of the bar much more than, say, some down-home expression spontaneously uttered by a rich rancher from Tucson, Arizona.

"Of course. Please choose your place, I will prepare it for you and your guest." She hesitated. "One guest now, and then one more you say?"

"Yes," he answered, without looking her way. "We are two. And then three."

"Sounds like a pronouncement of great import," she thought.

"Follow me, sir," she said, and gently implored by drawing her gaze into his face. She wondered who he had invited, and put symbolic money on it being another man. He was quite gorgeous, tall, big, and sleek, with jet-black hair and perfect skin. She knew Japan, but had never been to other countries in Southeast Asia. He was especially hard to place, because he was so tall, so solidly built, and, moreover, because he sported an American accent. "Half breed?" she asked herself. "Certainly, but from where? China, that was certain, but then, well, his skin was dark. Vietnam? Korea?" But he was very big, and he looked dangerous. "Mongolia?"

She was in a state of frantic inner monologue, even as she was calmly seating him at the place where Jude had been seated with Ted in the late afternoon hours. When she realized what she'd done, she almost suggested he move to another table. Why? And then it struck her that somehow this was an ideal choice, and so smiled inwardly and then again wondered about the connection that would inadvertently bring those meetings, distant in time, together in space.

She offered to take Steve's coat, but he refused, and instead draped it onto the back of the chair. "That's strange," she thought, "for a coat like that." She arranged his table, moving quickly but silently to the server station to pick up the menu and wine list, then returned. As she did so, another man entered the bar and walked directly over towards her.

"I am Tom, here to meet . . ." He motioned towards Steve, who was now seated and staring forwards.

"So this is the first guest," she thought, as she stealthily accompanied him to Steve's table. She pulled the chair out for him and offered to take his coat, which was equally gorgeous, but in this case it was well-worn, like the dark skin of its owner. She eyed Steve as she fussed with the newly arrived guest's jacket, helping to liberate this large man of this outer layer. In so doing, she revealed a rugged core and not-so-faint indications of his sculpted muscles.

He turned to thank her, and she had a flash of sudden recognition. This "Tom" was the mystery man, the man in black who occasionally met Jessica at the front of the restaurant. She had only seen him at a distance and was now assaulted by his animalistic presence.

Jessica appeared, in his presence, in a different light. She felt a wave of desire and jealousy. She returned to task, as Tom turned back to Steve. She thought the jacket was beautiful and unique, as it gave way into her arms. She guessed it was a vintage-style cut, but it was clearly custom made, a fact she confirmed when seeing the simple signature of the designer in the place where a retail item would have had its label. She held it close and moved towards the coat check.

"Steve!" she heard the newly arrived guest expulse. "Steve, fucking nice to see you, Steve!"

"They are clearly old friends," thought Tina, and she turned to witness Steve rise to greet Tom with surprising warmth.

"Tom. You look good." The two of them sat down.

"This new arrival is equally intriguing," ruminated Tina, "and rich." She subtly brought the warm coat to her chest. The smell of lamb's wool lining and kid leather was intoxicating; it seemed to reek with the powerful scents of a formidable body. She thought Tom looked as exotic as his friend, but was even more difficult to place. He was part African, or maybe African American, but he also looked Hispanic, or Filipino? She approached the cloakroom closet, hung the jacket up on a heavy, wooden hanger, and then returned to the table. The two men were deep in conversation, speaking on something that seemed to be of great importance. She drifted away, busied herself with adjacent tables, fussing over napkins and the placement of glasses, but never let her gaze stray from their direction for long. After a few minutes, she returned to their side. Tom was gazing at Steve, mid-thought, and he let her stand there as he ruminated.

"Come on, Steve, don't give me this. We don't have to wait anymore, it's out there. Christ, we could oversee the fucking operation with a bloody iPad."

"So sorry, gentlemen!" They looked over to Tina, simultaneously. It wasn't clear to her whether they'd wanted her to be party to their deliberations, but familiar with the constant occupational hazard of social awkwardness, she forged ahead. "Can I offer either of you a drink?"

The two men looked at each other briefly, and then back at her. Neither offered a reply, but instead looked at her intently.

"I am your maître d', and my name is Tina." She inadvertently turned towards Steve, who responded by glancing downwards at the table. She continued. "Your server, Elizabeth, will be with you shortly, but I can get you started if you wish."

"What do you drink, Steve? Oh Christ, sorry, does it still turn you from yellow to green?"

Steve blushed, rather crimson in fact, and Tom laughed. Steve looked a little self-conscious, and so, feeling as though he should offer some explanation perhaps, Tom looked straight at her, his eyes flashing.

"We used to be roommates in college, and this guy had his first binge with me and some other friends. He had," he turned towards Steve, "what, one beer?"

"One sip."

"One sip!" he smiled broadly, revealing a row of gleaming teeth framed on his dark complexion. "Maybe, Steve, it was a large sip?" He grinned in Steve's direction. "Tina, I thought he was going to *slip* into a coma!"

"I'm more tolerant of some liquors now," Steve said to Tina, almost apologetically. "Do you have any porto?"

"Of course they have port, Steve." Tom looked towards her.

"Sorry, Tina, my friend Steve clearly hasn't heard much about this place." He turned to his friend. "Steve, they have port, but it is derived from the egg of a rare Australian bull's testicles. Isn't that right, Tina?"

Tina smiled, showing him her own pearly white teeth.

"I'm not so sure about the testicles part." She smiled politely and blushed slightly. "The list of portos begins on page twenty-three and continues to page twenty-six of your wine list," she said, subtly reaching for the menu and advancing the pages forward.

"Do you have Quinta do Noval?" asked Tom, before they even came to the porto section.

"We stock a bottle of the 1962 Quinta do Noval," replied Tina, without hesitation. She knew that because it was the very best year of the very best bottle they had. And she mentioned it first because she knew that these clients could afford it.

"Two, please," said Tom.

"When will Ted arrive?" asked Steve.

"What time is it now, four thirty? He should be here by five thirty. You should be passed out by then, Steve. I'll fill him in."

It was Steve's turn to blush, and in so doing bore the same complexion, nearly, as Tina. Tom thought about the strange connections that linked Tina and Steve across time and space: they both had flawless skin, and were both nearly hairless, except for their eyebrows, their gleaming black hair, and an inevitable soft tuft of pubic hair. It was probably as unlikely that Steve would grow facial hair as Tina. And there was something remarkably similar about the shapes of their eyes. Tom brought himself back to the task at hand and looked to Tina.

"And what should we eat with that, Tina, caviar? Scrambled eggs?"

"I have a small entrée of caviar, served with fresh egg bread."

"For two, please, Tina."

Tom turned back to Steve. "Okay?"

Steve seemed oblivious, and so Tom turned back to Tina and winked.

"When he gets here, Ted will probably want to order everything on the dinner menu, so we might wish to start modestly."

Tina acknowledged the message about the forthcoming guest, and then withdrew, motioning as she did so towards Elizabeth, blonde, buxom, beautiful Elizabeth. There were lots of clients who frequented Fabergé Restaurant regularly on Elizabeth's account alone, and who tipped accordingly. Tina, sensing a revolt amongst the other servers, decided to pool all of the tips together, and then divide them up equally. She knew that Elizabeth pocketed more than her share by not declaring the full extent of her bounty; but she also knew the gross intake amongst the servers was double what it had been prior to her arrival, so it was only fair that she should bring a little more bacon home to placate her anxious, insecure husband.

Someday soon Elizabeth would cheat on her poor man, if only to punish him for his insecurity. On that day, she would pay him back for having suspected her for all those days and months and years of silent recriminations for acts for which she was innocent. She'd wonder why it had taken her so long, and then she'd descry the fact that those rushed torrents of passion weren't worth the arguments, and didn't justify the betrayal. The cycles of life, passion, and fertility, the production of eggs, and the wilting of desire, and then resurrection in the form of new life, fertilized by the decaying shells that encase my tender self.

CHAPTER 13

Tom and Steve were now in intense conversation, or was it negotiation? Fabergé Restaurant was no stranger to backroom, dining room, and even bathroom discussions, contracts, and betrayals. Deals, deals, deals. Tom was animated, Steve, very cool, but very serious. He was used to Tom making the pitches, it's what he did, it's what he had done since their time together as undergraduates. But this time it was more serious than the usual fare. Ever since Steve had met Tom in college, where they shared a dormitory apartment and, later on, one floor of a small house, he had admired Tom's enthusiasm. But he also knew that it had all been too easy for Tom, and that he was now looking to make it all feel real.

Steve observed Tom intensely; it had been a long time since they'd been together like this. He looked African American, like his mother, but Tom's father was actually from the Philippines, a small town called Meycauayan, where jewels had been mined and jewelry fabricated since the late Stone Age. In the sixteenth century efforts came to be focused on precious jewelry, culminating with a large diamond trade. Tom's father, who was known as Rommel, was born and raised on a sizeable property there, and had known since childhood that people in that region were involved with jewels, and especially diamonds. He didn't land up exploring the lucrative world of diamonds and jewels, though, despite his substantial inheritance and the value of the land upon which he'd grown up. Instead, he came to be charged with the responsibility of raising Tom, single-handedly, after Tom's mother had died during complications in childbirth. As a result, Rommel, who was destined to become a major international dealer of precious stones, instead withdrew from the marketplace altogether. For a long time there was speculation as to what he had done with the huge storehouse of goods he had inherited, but years of silence quieted the banter amongst traders, and it was assumed that the stock had been liquidated somewhere along the way, and Rommel, heretofore a major player on the scene, would never re-emerge as a force in the market.

Steve knew Tom's story well and always thought that its details accounted for Tom's obsessions, including the obsession that led him to Fabergé Restaurant. Rommel had met Danielle in a restaurant after a day of negotiating sales for rough-cut diamonds, during one of his then-frequent trips to the head office of his company in Atlanta. It was a case of the proverbial "love at first sight" for both of them. They had but five days together, but they carried on an extensive correspondence subsequently, and Steve had even read some of it because of the very few objects Tom had from his early years in the Philippines: a package of his parents' words and a pile of letters wrapped up and tied with some kind of stems from plants indigenous to Meycauayan. It was through the words they'd shared, and the vision that each held of those precious days together, that Tom's parents came to be committed to one another and plans were made for a life together.

On Rommel's return trip to the US, eight weeks after meeting Danielle, he learned that Danielle had taken ill, too ill to travel. And in the course of the routine exam, the doctor pronounced that she was in the grip of a nefarious infection that had recently been identified as being the result of a class of viruses emerging in the face of heavy use of prescription-strength antibiotics. As a child, Danielle had been given heavy doses for recurrent ear infections that upset her sleep and caused her to miss school for prolonged periods, sometimes a week or more at a time. They eventually subsided, although she was regularly inflicted with flu-like symptoms that seemed ever more difficult to treat with regular prescription medicines. And so a childhood affliction, probably minor in its implications, had become an adult problem with rather serious consequences, as Danielle found herself in need of ever-stronger antibiotics to treat ever-more-frequent bouts of the flu.

Tom had spoken to Steve about his parents' romance as though it was the very picture of ideal love, the kind of love that occurs when two people know as certainly as they'd ever known anything, that they were meant to be together.

"This I, too, will find someday," Tom would tell Steve.

Steve never doubted it. The story that Tom recounted to Steve was that when Rommel had met Danielle, who was working as a hostess in a chic Atlanta restaurant, she was in a phase of perfect health, and as a consequence was perhaps a little more open to a handsome foreigner's advances, and a little more beautiful than usual, which in Tom's mind could only be explained with reference to Homer's Helen of Troy, Yeats's Maude Gonne, or Dante's Beatrice, the women he'd met in the course of the liberal arts degree that helped teach him such things. Rommel and Danielle went out together on the very night they met, after she accepted, in the course of his paying the bill, an invitation for a drink after her shift. They slept together on the following evening, and he was impassioned to distraction during the rest of his trip. Very little business was conducted, despite his intentions. A lot of love was consumed, however, and Rommel returned home to Meycauayan entirely consumed by the passion, the lust, and the excitement that she provoked in him.

Danielle, as it turns out, felt exactly the same. Tom told this story as though to justify his own precociousness, his notorious sexual proclivities, and his infamous audacity. Strange how the principles and the parameters of our behavior is dictated by our parents, Steve had once suggested to Tom, on an evening following a course on Chomsky's contributions to linguistics. Tom had thought that funny, and the two of them had continued to (mis)use this label, applying it to all sorts of experiences they had in college, and beyond. Principles became the lust that Tom had when he'd go out at night, parameters the range of beauty represented by the women he'd encounter. Principles were the array of inner abilities Steve drew from for his coveted tennis game, parameters the player he'd challenge in order to represent same abilities.

Tom's narrative about his parents continued, repeated regularly to his roommates, in those quiet hours between wakeful restlessness and sleep. With Tom's father back in Atlanta, and the prospects for his mother joining him back in the Philippines rather bleak, they both felt that they needed to solidify their plans. In particular, since Rommel wasn't slated to return to Atlanta for another few months, on account of important negotiations for substantial sales of some of the diamond inventory that he'd inherited from his father, they made plans to marry quickly. This would ensure that the child would be legitimate, and that they'd be able to secure legal status for him, or her, in the US. All worked out to plan, and Rommel was able to come back to Atlanta regularly. Danielle's health improved, and the pregnancy, if anything, seemed to give her radiance and heightened desire for Rommel. Their lovemaking was nearly constant through all of the visits, and right up to the end, when, after a particularly exciting afternoon under the blaring sunlight of a July day, her water broke.

Tom described this scene with great detail, proclaiming that it was his own decision to break out of the womb, since it was becoming far too noisy. When he had first heard this story, Ted, always the most cynical of the three roommates, had told Tom that in fact his parents were just trying to get rid of him, and thought to drown him. Tom's reaction was swift and brutal. He had stood up, and threatened to kill Ted where he sat. Steve, who was trained in martial arts, was put on high alert, ready to lash out to both Tom and Ted, if only for the excuse to display his wares. Principles, the inner ability, and parameters, the event that led to their being manifested in a particular way.

When things calmed down, Ted learned why Tom had reacted so fiercely and, not for the first time, or the last, regretted his well-honed sarcasm. Tom continued his story. There had been no cause for concern. Danielle was due in two weeks. But then, in the midst of what seemed a perfectly normal childbirth, as Tom peered into the world that awaited him from the warmth of his mother's core, her blood pressure suddenly plummeted, and as the doctor's hastened Tom's exit, she died. Rommel was not in the room during the labor, and so when the doctor emerged he uttered just a few carefully chosen words: "We have saved the child."

Rommel stared into the doctor's eyes, searching for meaning. He could not understand why news of the birth of his child would be conveyed in such a fashion.

"We have saved your child, sir." Hesitation. "But not your wife. Not your wife. I'm so sorry."

Rommel stood in the hospital hallway, a few steps away from the door to the operating room where his son hollered, while his wife slept the eternal sleep, never to enjoy motherhood, never to live with Rommel in Meycauayan, never to fulfill the dreams they had whispered and called out during their long hours of lovemaking, never, never to be together again. Never.

All of this had occurred in a way that betrayed what Tom's father thought of as "the plan." The plan predicted that Rommel's family would enjoy perfect happiness upon this earth. And there had never been reason to ever believe otherwise. Everything had always gone according to plan, confirming its existence, until everything didn't go according to plan. How was it possible that his beautiful, passionate, powerful, magnificent, young wife should die giving birth to a beautiful baby boy? And how could she die when every possible medical service was available in this modern, sprawling American hospital? Nobody knew, nobody could convey to Tom's father what could have gone wrong that day, except that there were some inconclusive studies about the virus that she carried and the fate she endured.

Whatever it was, on that day she died, and so, too, did whatever dreams Rommel had for Danielle, for the family he would build with her, for the jewels and joys with which he would shower her. She died. And after that day, Tom was all that his father had left, and Tom's father was intent upon holding onto him, if only for his own survival, if only, indeed, until he could relinquish his parental responsibilities and rejoin his wife. Tom's father came to believe that the plan did indeed exist, but it had elements that he'd misunderstood, most notably the one that said it was to be fulfilled in the other world.

Tom's description of his youth was forever some odd combination of what he remembered, and what he'd added to those memories. "I never got to know my mother," he had said. Ted felt sick to his stomach. "And I never had a sibling."

Steve, hardly the sentimentalist, had spoken for himself and for Ted, though, when he said, spontaneously and without any hesitation, "Tom, you've got us. You've got us, Tom."

This seemed to all of them a monumental announcement, uttered on that college evening in the depth of the night. But Steve was also the pragmatist and the clearheaded thinker, serious and tender when the situation called for it. "Why did you come here?"

"Here?"

"Why did you come to the United States? Why here? Your father . . ."

"Georgia. I don't think I could ever go to Georgia, because it's where my mother died. And my dad couldn't be there either, but needed time before, well, returning home, and so did I, since I had some kind of jaundice or something. Anyhow, instead of staying near the hospital, he got into his car and drove to the next biggest town—Nashville. Someone who had seen him grieving in the waiting room, an African-American pastor, or priest or minister, told him about a place of healing and calm in a little community in Nashville right near some projects, downtown. My dad went there and stayed for two weeks. He once told me that it was the safest place he'd ever been, a place of love and healing. He, I don't know, I think he got to know a bunch of people who lived in those projects, especially some of the kids, and he said that without them, and without me, well, anyhow. He waited for me to get better in that little community, and because of that community he loved the United States. He said that those kids were what the United States could be, and the hospital in Atlanta was what it had turned into. Atlanta was cold, sterile, private, corporate, murderous, and he had experienced the opposite in this little community in the Nashville hood."

"Did he ever go back there?" asked Steve.

"No, he never did. He said that he'd bring me there, but, well . . ." He paused. "It's funny guys," continued Tom, emboldened by their closeness, "I feel like my memories are a weird combination of stuff I remember and stuff I made up about things I did with my mom." He paused. "I feel like it was all my fucking fault."

Ted and Steve had rushed to Tom's emotional rescue, to no avail. No matter what they said, and no matter how hard Tom's father had tried, Tom inherited the guilt for the death not only of his mother, but also the sister, the brother, the amazing family that the plan had promised his father. In Tom's mind, he had committed original sin: he killed his maker. And to punish him, the universe had conspired to murder his own sister, his own brother, his entire family, a family that was never given the chance to be conceived. It was so unfair.

Worse still, Tom, totally unaware of his actions, had murdered his own mother in the painful labor that she had undertaken in order to expel him from her garden. This alone had earned him a tainted place upon this earth. For years, this is the weight that Tom carried with him, in a childhood that was tainted by absence and sadness and unfulfilled dreams, especially those that his father described to him as being unfulfilled, aborted. Tom would also learn from his classmate's mother that his father had folded back into himself after her death, spending his next fifteen years a recluse, rarely leaving the homestead, never taking another wife, or even lover. And so Tom came to inherit the guilt for his father's symbolic death as well, realizing one day that not only did he know nothing of his mother, but that he'd also never really known his father either. He lived with a pale embodiment of a man, a father, a husband, someone who could have been.

When he was old enough to discuss such things, Tom learned that his father harbored ever-greater resentment for her death, not towards Tom, but towards Atlanta, towards Georgia, towards health care, and, moreover, towards everyone who is involved in the perpetuation of the health care business for their own enrichment. But he also had this strange American Dream, connected to Nashville, a vision of all that was so healing for him there, and all that could have been had she only survived, had she only given birth amongst that little community instead of in one of those gleaming hospital towers that perpetuates inordinate spending by sickeningly wealthy people.

And so Tom's father felt that he and his deceased wife, and his son Tom, had all been stripped of the great and exciting plans for what was to be his grand and august family by, of all things, a fancy hospital in America. Tom heard this repeated endlessly as he grew up, although he had no experience of whatever his father meant by "august," because they had always lived together modestly, and his father, other than gardening, seemed to quite literally have no interests, no passions, no friends, no pastimes. Tom's father fed his son, helped him off to school, stayed at home, greeted him upon his arrival home at the end of each day, cooked modest dinners, read quietly in the evening, and went to sleep. This was quite literally all Tom had ever known about domestic life, and he assumed, wrongly, that on this account he had come to know all that there really was to know about his father.

In time, though, the story of his mother's death grew more complex and troubling. Through scattered bits of information that emerged regarding that fateful day, Tom learned that the hospital in which his mother had died had been identified as treating black and white patients differently, to the detriment, of course, of black patients. Medications that could have been used for her condition were not prescribed, experts who understood the effects of the virus she carried were not consulted, and, despite Rommel's resources, financial and otherwise, precautions weren't taken in advance of the labor that could have saved her life. And so her death gave birth to a sense of outrage in Tom, and learning about the circumstances of her suffering provided him with the desire to learn more about what had happened to his mother; and then, as a mixed-race black/Filipino boy, he sought to understand what it meant to be an ostracized person in America, and why it was that even people with his father's resources were subjected to marginalization on the basis of race. Both of these messages resonated profoundly in Tom, feeding his passions and his obsessions.

What happened at the end of his father's life proved that much remained unexplained, to the very end, even as it did explain Tom's hand-stitched, custom, Italian-leather jacket with lamb's wool lining. Tom's father had explained to him early on that he had a chosen spot on their land where he was to be buried, and, presciently, he died when Tom was seventeen and still living at home. The instructions for burial were so precise that without the slightest hesitation, and even before he could begin the process of grieving, Tom set out about to bury his father. He had been specifically instructed not to call a doctor if his father died at home, and, because his father had died of what was evidently a massive coronary, there would have been no possibility of Tom taking any useful steps to save him. And since doctors, hospitals, medication, and the whole industry of preserving life weren't realms upheld with any enthusiasm by Tom or by his father, the decision to remain mute in the face of a medical emergency wasn't difficult to take.

And so when Rommel entered cardiac arrest and then died at home with his son, Tom knew that he had to simply follow the preordained instructions. He knew to simply go to the chosen spot and dig a hole, in which, sans casket, his father was to be buried. He was strangely calm. He had always assumed that his father would indeed die at home, because there was no alternative plan in the event that he was anywhere else, and he also imagined that he'd have no chance at saving him, since no set of procedures were set out for such an eventuality in the meticulous instructions that Tom's father had provided for his demise.

After the burial, the story went, Tom was to leave Meycauayan and travel to the United States. But how, and for what purpose? His father had not explained anything to him, but the details regarding burial were so precise, and the preparations had been discussed for such a long time, that Tom barely even asked himself a single question about what he was meant to do after his father was safely beneath the ground. For a young boy provided with instructions for burying his father, all of this was theoretical anyway, so he never bothered to ask questions. Nobody, or almost nobody, expects their parents will die, until they do. But his father did die. Tom followed his father's wishes, as had been ordained. The plan continued.

And so on the evening of his father's death, Tom bore witness to the horror of it all as though he was witnessing a preordained event from afar, powerless. Tom watched almost impassively as his father grimaced and choked for air, because there was nothing to be done. Mercifully, the grasping and choking quickly gave way to profound calm. Tom stared at his father, he watched him die, and then he watched him grow rigid. He felt sadness, and he felt relief. This was the way it was supposed to be, the way he had been told it would be. This was part of the plan. Tom had tried to explain this to Ted and to Steve on numerous occasions.

"My dad died precisely as he was ordained to. I never had to leave him, because he left me, not even a month before I was supposed to leave him, to come to The States, to come," he had paused, "to New York." And now here he was, and the three of them, friends in college, were all there together. "And someday, I will go to Nashville."

After the convulsions stopped, Tom had approached his father, bent down, and put his ear to his sunken chest.

Silence.

He took his wrist and pressed his thumb upon the spot where gushing blood could be perceived as a murmur and a pulsation.

Nothing.

A few moments later, Tom was obediently carrying the inanimate remnant of his own father upon his shoulders, as though he was an unwieldy sack filled with, what, bones? Flesh? Tom refused to feel, and chose instead to act. For suddenly his entire connection to this house, this town, this country, and to the past as he knew it, was now nothing more than the dead weight of his own father—dead, weight.

Tom went to the prescribed spot, hunched over as though he bore the very burden of his whole world upon his shoulders, and, when he laid his father into the ground, he released that weight and passed it onto the surface of the earth. For the first time he felt grief, and the misty evening blurred and drifted. Life as he knew it was forever changed, and two gigantic teardrops formed and plunged down his face to the waiting soil.

It was done. The earth was now ready to be entered.

Tom penetrated the spot that had been designated for this event, and with the force of youth and the duty of a son he began to dig, as the crumpled and stiffening form of his father observed him, motionless. Tom worked hard for his father, preparing the earth to accept his weight. He prepared a nest, a foundation, a crater, a wound in the earth's own flesh as wide and deep enough as Tom's maker, his family, the provider of his life, and the designated messenger for his burden and earthly toil.

Done.

And when it was all over, Tom left his father deep inside of a hole he had dug, under the faint illumination of a star-filled night sky. Tom saw his father off by giving him the peace of the soil, the engulfing soil, connected perhaps to the soil that held his beloved wife. And then Tom left that soil, and what he left behind on the following day was every thing, and every one, he had ever known. But Tom did not leave his father, or his homeland, empty-handed. In recompense for his father's death, the earth had offered to Tom a token of exchange. There was no coffin for his father, no box, and where in the earth there should have been such a container for the flesh and bones and blood and guts of his father Tom found a different kind of box, almost as large and ornate as a coffin, that had been carefully placed within the small cavern his father had chosen for himself. Inside of that box, in the place of a corpse, Tom unearthed a treasure trove of diamonds and jewels that had made the next phase in his life possible. That treasure trove brought him to college, brought him to find Ted and Steve, brought him to this table to hatch another plan, but this time one designed for all of them, for everyone in America, for the world.

"It has been a long road here," uttered Tom to Steve. Steve remained silent and took a sip of port. It tasted good. But would it lead to disaster?

The intoxicating liquids that pour through the veins of Fabergé Restaurant lubricate my destiny. How many eggs are fertilized with the inspiration of intoxication? I can but speak for myself, but based on my experience with oceans of champagne and prosecco, I would think that fertility flourishes in direct proportion to the quantity of bubbly intoxicants introduced to entice it.

CHAPTER 14

Elizabeth-the-Server took over for Tina and gracefully arrived with the order of caviar. Tom and Steve were in anxious conversation, punctuated only by their sipping the port. The two men ignored her arrival, and so she carefully maneuvered the plates onto the table, surprised to not be the cause for pause.

"There are some obvious problems with this approach," Steve was saying as the tiny bowls of luxurious cargo was placed before and between them.

"Some of them are pretty obvious, Steve, I know it. But fuck it's all we've ever talked about. Steve, it's here, so now we need to figure out what may not be obvious. At this moment the cat is about to be let out of the bag and," he paused, "it feels like a fucking catwalk to me." Steve winced.

"You know what I mean, Steve, I'm ready to start tomorrow." Tom paused to taste the ocean's eggs, nodding his approval as they swam through his mouth and down his throat. "Actually, we have no choice. Not anymore."

Tom ended his sentence with a sip of the port. It really was spectacular stuff, but he knew the joy of its wood-infused, aged, ground-kissed depth was entirely lost on his friend, who was probably much more concerned with whether it would make him sick, or whether their plan would ensure that they'd never have such dinners again as long as they live. Steve was the technocrat, the façade of beauty, the unfeeling overseer of the shining mechanism that would bring this city, and the country it represented, to its knees. Ironically, though, a sip of porto could bring him down, and they would be brought down in most of the scenarios they had planned.

"I have 345 tons of the fiber cotton, and it's all in the warehouse," said Steve. He then took a bite of the bread, sans caviar. It was dry, and made to be somewhat bland in order to bring out the flavor of the caviar. He took another sip of port and looked straight into Tom's eyes—defiantly.

"Jesus Christ, Steve," said Tom in admiration. "Now that came out of nowhere! 345 tons? Honestly?" Tom looked straight into Steve's gaze.

"This is actually going to happen," Tom thought to himself. He gently scooped sufficient caviar onto his own slice of bread to make up for whatever Steve was missing. He did so for himself, and for Steve, thinking, as he always had, that some small action he might someday commit would awaken the flesh that had to lie beneath Steve's perfect, Asian skin. He did not at that moment think about Tina, but Tina, from afar, was thinking, from a rather different perspective, exactly the same thing. Tom suddenly stopped chewing and looked angry.

"Wait a second. Are you speculating, Steve?" He knew that mere ownership of the materials wasn't necessarily tantamount to using them for the purposes they'd planned. Steve had multiplied his millions many-fold by cornering and then flooding markets, and so fiber cotton might just be another product to add to a list that included everything from aluminum to zeolite powder.

Steve looked up, knowingly. "Tom, it's in the warehouse."

"You can still resell it, Steve."

"I am not reselling it." He said it in an accusatory tone.

"You could! You bastard!" Tom hadn't considered that possibility before. Were they just rehearsing another delay on their long-awaited plan?

"Of course I could sell it all, Tom!" Steve again looked straight into Tom's eyes. "But I am not reselling it," he said forcefully, motioning towards the port. He thought the better of it, but then, sensing Tom's gaze, picked up the tiny glass and gingerly drew the warm liquid into his mouth. This time he seemed surprised at its soft, sweet flavor.

Tom looked carefully into Steve's face, awaiting the kind of reaction he'd witnessed all those years ago in their college dorm.

"And I have the nineteen intaglio printers, working. We tested them. Me and Ted," continued Steve.

"You bought those intaglios? You did it? And you fucking had them tested! You prick! And?"

Steve settled back in his seat and studied his hands as they stroked the table. "Theoretically, Tom, well, materially, actually, yah, they work perfectly, the tests were positive. We can do it. The bills look really good," he paused, recalling previous conversations about what really mattered in counterfeiting paper money. "And they feel good. They feel really good."

"Then let's get fucking going, Steve. Let's start now. What the fuck?"

"What the fuck," concluded Steve, looking down at the table.

Tom didn't like that look. "They released the resin, did you see that?" asked Tom.

"Right on schedule."

"Yah, by the very worst predictions on schedule. They really *were* worried. Plus, they needed to do something before the election."

The federal election was looming, and the incumbent, who remained popular, had a rather long list of promises he hoped to fulfill, to preclude accusations of inaction that had plagued him even before he took the oval office. He had been similarly badgered as governor, but people, nonetheless, liked him, if only because he always seemed the best of a bad lot. Besides, he didn't do much, which for most Americans was seen as a positive—most of the time. But when it came to protecting greenbacks, international and national reputations were at stake, and the banks had made sufficient hoo-ha to raise public awareness, which caused undue instability in the markets.

"I told you that they were worried," said Steve, now looking at Tom, accusatorily.

A newspaper article, overlooked by most people inside Canada and virtually ignored by media beyond its borders, had jumped out of the Toronto *Globe and Mail* and into the consciousness of Tom one Sunday afternoon. After a brunch in a New York café that featured not only an array of coffees and donuts, but also a collection of foreign news sources to help nourish, or ruin, the weekend, Tom and Steve became aware that the scenario they had described to one another, and to Ted, for all those years in and beyond college, was coming true. On the front page of the *Globe*'s "Business Magazine" section there was a story, sanctioned and probably even encouraged by the Royal Canadian Mint, explaining the decision to wean the country off of paper bills, in favor of the plastic that already accounted for most transactions.

Now, one year after that news broke, the mint was looking beyond credit cards and into the long-term production of plastic currency. Indeed, the Royal Canadian Mint's decision to do away with the current version of the Canadian currency and replace them with plastic bills seemed like a reminder to consumers that at the end of the day, they would have no choice: it was plastic or plastic. And because this was Canada, and not, say, the US or Germany or Switzerland, they planned to phase out national use of the "paper" bills in six months, an unprecedentedly short turn-around period in peacetime. Banks around the world were instructed to accept the currency, at least for the moment; but after that initial six-month period they weren't going to be considered legal tender for the purchase of goods in Canada. This would allow the mint to rapidly flush out bills currently in circulation, exchange them for the new version, and then incinerate them. And it would allow for unprecedented oversight of currency in circulation, and of those bringing it there.

There had been efforts to integrate plastic into currency before, but these new plastic bills were revolutionary. They allowed for microchip implants that made it virtually impossible to forge them, partly because it allowed for an unprecedented control over the numbering and ordering of the currency, but also because it made the task of making bills formidably complex and, moreover, simply too expensive to be worth the effort. This plan, to create bills that cost more than their net worth, also made it easy to discontinue them, which meant that even if forgeries could be made, there was a good chance they'd be obsolete by the time they hit the market. And in this era of tracking and tracing, the bills also offered the as-yet unutilized possibility of tracing them, which for individual bills was of little value. But if tracers were set to track huge hordes of bills, which could be captured on satellite feeds, then the production or shipment of bills would be immediately visible to authorities. And finally, and even more ominous for any counterfeiter, this move was aimed to seed the eventual discontinuation of "cash," because credit cards, check cards, pre-paid plastic cards, and all the rest of those products shifted the burden of lost, stolen, or forged currency into the private hands of the banks and insurance companies, and, moreover, to the consumer. This latter point wasn't the gist of the article, but for Ted, Tom, and for Steve it provoked their current call to action, almost a quarter of a century after they'd started talking about forging US bills.

"I know what they are doing in Ottawa. Oh, and incidentally, it's not out yet, but the Europeans, Japanese, and Chinese are doing the same thing. And Ted says that they'll out the paper even faster."

"Obviously."

"Yes, obviously," agreed Steve. "But it won't happen here, not for a while. It's like the two dollar bill, or the dollar coin. We are saved by imbecile nostalgia."

"So we have time to dilly-dally some more?" asked Tom, looking angry.

"That's not what I said. Actually, we can't wait."

"Good!"

"I mean that. They're discontinuing the paper-based product and moving towards a cotton-polymer weave to get Americans used to the new feel." Steve was speaking as though they were already producing the bills they'd so long dreamed of.

"Discontinuing?"

"Yup."

"When?"

"They are making the announcement on Monday. Presses change over next month. New bills are going to start feeling different by early May. And then really differently when they go to plastic, November 2, right before the election." Tom allowed the warm, liquid port free rein over his palate and down into his gorge.

This really was news. Discontinuing. This single word was music to Tom's ears, Tom who had pressed Steve and Ted for all these years, as though this was to be their collective life's work. He felt a wave of excitement run through his very veins.

"I told you, I don't feel like getting into the rag-and-paper business," interjected Steve, "and if we don't use this shit now, then I've got a few hundred tons of stuff I could never sell." He looked up and straight at Tom. "You have wanted this all along, Tom. And so have I. It's payback. They killed half my lineage for colored beads? I'm going to kill them back with their own fucking medicine."

Steve was seldom this animated. Ted called this "Cherokee pride," even though Steve wasn't even entirely sure that his lineage was indeed Cherokee. But he had adopted it, and it drove him, it motivated him, it gave him passion as strong as Tom's made-up past and invented future.

"I'm ready for it," he paused, and then looked right into Tom's eyes. I'm ready for TSP." He smiled, suddenly and broadly, at the recollection of a common experience they'd shared, amongst roommates, a kind of secret code. "Ted's Stimulus Plan! TSP! TSP!" Now he really brightened up with memories of the conversations the three of them had and about the plan they eventually dubbed TSP. He even took another sip of port.

Tom was elated, and a bit worried about the port coming back to the table, undigested. "Just like we always said, Steve!" He was exuberant, his growing energy fueled by the circumstances, the warm liquid in his body, and salty caviar. "We'll make so much of it that they'll think it to be the greatest stimulus plan that ever was. Until it's not." He laughed, and then laughed louder, almost uproariously. "Until it's not, Steve!"

Tom felt that tingling in his very scrotum that accompanied plans of great amplitude, and a euphoria in his brain that made him as dizzy as when a girl accepted to peel her clothing off before him. His head, and his very sex were reeling at the thought of TSP. It was going to happen, it was finally, finally, finally going to happen. Without asking, he reached over and took a long sip of Steve's port, right to the bottom of his glass, and then, as a kind of afterthought, gathered all of the caviar onto his fork and plunged it into the waiting bath of sweet liquor that he'd created in his mouth. It was his college class on *The Canterbury Tales* all over again, replete with a tradition he'd initiated, with Ted, to eat from Steve's plate and drink from Steve's glass whenever possible. It was a method of destroying Steve's will to preciousness.

Steve was animated, and now Tom was aroused. And as the caviar swirled within his mouth, carried by waves of port, he felt uplifted, literally. Once, when he was playing a chess machine that he had programmed for a beginner level, he had dominated and, by the eighth move, had defeated the computer. This wasn't particularly surprising, given how low the level was that he'd chosen. But the sudden bulge in his pants taught him something about achievement, something he could now actually measure with his own body. And this evening, he felt invincible.

Steve looked down, and for a moment Tom feared that he might be in for a repeat of that night, twenty-five years earlier, when he had shown himself to be allergic to alcohol, or whatever it was that led to that reaction. But he was just back being his usual quiet, collected self. Tom knew that he needed to be his usual enthusiastic one for this plan to succeed. "How much do we need?"

"I don't know, the presses are already up, the materials . . ." Steve hesitated.

"Not what we need to do this, Steve. You never answered my question, you have never answered my question."

"I never had to, we kept backing out."

"That's all changed now, Steve." Tom looked around Fabergé Restaurant, which was growing increasingly noisy as the anticipated dinner rush took form.

"I did two calculations. The first one is for them to notice. To get us in the door."

Tom leaned forward, looking purposely intense and angry, but the side of his mouth indicated a friendly grin. "I'm not interested in that, Steve. Ted was interested in that, I'm not interested in that. How much do we need to make in order to make the whole fucking thing sink?"

Steve looked uncomfortable. "It may not be necessary. . . . It probably won't be necessary."

Tom pressed on. "Sink, Steve. Sink. I don't want for them to notice, I want for them to drown. I told you before, we aren't going for bankruptcy and foreclosure, Steve, I'm thinking Noah's Arc. Let's gather up the animals and get to flooding!"

Steve looked around the restaurant, as though selecting who to sink and who to save.

"Steve, we aren't killing anyone. They'll never even know."

"They'd better not find out, Tom. We've got to figure out how to prevent that. At least for as long as it takes to get it going."

"Steve, Steve, Steve," said Tom. "This fucking country. They kill your people, and they move my people in, then they segregate my people, and they relegate your people to camps, then they underpay my people, they ignore your people, and they put my people in prison."

"And what about Ted's work? Yet another level, Tom."

"Right. They also kill the indigenous animals, bring in new animals, kill those animals, destroy the vegetation, plant new vegetation—"

"Modify the vegetation so that it doesn't resemble any earthly crop. Prosecute farmers who don't use that crop," said Tom.

"Okay, Tom. I don't know then. Even a hundred billion doesn't seem like it would sink it."

"Obviously."

"What do you mean, obviously? Do you know what a hundred fucking liquid billion looks like?" Steve was animated as he spoke, and red in the face. Was it the port?

"No, Steve, fuck, man, that's why I'm asking you. You are the only fucking person who thinks about this kind of shit. I don't have a fucking clue what this looks like!" Tom's hot blood, the gobs of sperm that were stirred when grandiose thoughts overtook him, made him, of all three roommates, the most precocious of them. This adolescent, testosterone-driven side also contributed to his ruthlessness, his force, his power, and on some occasions his puerility. But in this particular case, Tom's catalyst had a name: "Atlanta." The name evoked a cruel past: "Jim Crow." The cruel past had been offered a corrective: "Ten acres and a mule." The antidote has an enemy: "Betrayal."

"Ten acres and a mule." Steve looked Tom in the eye and recited it, like a mantra. "Ten acres and mule, Tom? Ten acres? And a mule? Or how about another treaty?"

Tom looked down with a perceptible smirk on his face. "Ten acres and a mule, Steve. Ten acres and a mule. And yah, sure, another treaty."

There was silence, and it seemed that the whole plan was hovering in the balance. "I don't know what this looks like, Steve." Tom might just as well have stood up and declared to everyone in that restaurant that he had acquiesced to the plan, and in so doing guaranteed that a college-years dream would someday become a reality. "I don't know what this will look like, Steve."

"Neither do I, Tom." Steve sensed that he'd have to answer the query, lest Tom begin to make a scene and bust the entire Fabergé egg. The subject seemed entirely theoretical, but Steve, catching the moment, transformed it into reality. "Here's what it looks like. It looks like our whole fucking warehouse, Tom. Full. Of hundreds. And we have to use hundreds, and maybe fifties and twenties, too, assuming you still want to build our own sequences. But we need mostly hundreds, especially if we don't want to build sequences."

"I do," said Tom. "Each time they print a new color into the bill, they build a new sequence, it has become standard practice after the Italian bullshit," he explained. Two years ago a gigantic effort had been undertaken in Italy, probably fueled by Mafia earnings, and the EU had barely caught it.

"If this is going to work, we have to do the same thing, one more color, and an as-yet unused sequence. Then anything other than hundreds might be a serious pain in the butt, because we'd have to multiply the whole fucking thing by five if we use twenties. And Ted's right, we don't want fifties, they attract too much attention."

Attention, for whatever reason, was the kiss of death for forgery on a grand scale. Tom had followed that gigantic, bond-forging scandal in Italy with passion and fear, coming as it did just a year before the three roommates were to put their own plan into effect. Lucky for them, it had indeed been nipped in the bud, and for some reason the story was barely even mentioned in the media. This may have been the result of efforts made by authorities who feared that someone might notice how close they'd come and try to copycat. Undoubtedly, established forgery rings had noticed, but to date, no large-scale effort had been initiated to make either bills or bonds. This added to the urgency, but now the Canadians, acting peremptorily, had upped the ante. And the US was just waiting to follow.

"Actually, it's going to be harder than we thought, not because of the technology, but because I never thought they'd move this fucking quickly."

"Bloody Canadians!" blurted Tom.

"But I also think that they have one less dog in the race. If they're getting rid of the paper version, then they're not going to watch it as much. This is one giant fucking move, and they're going to bank on getting it changed over before anyone can make a major move."

"Ah! So you really are thinking about this, Steve! You bastard!" Steve smirked. "Okay Mr. Bastard, how much do we need?"

"For argument sake, we need to have a trillion. And that's just to start."

"I'll need more fiber."

"Then get it now, because it's only into the second or third trilly that it's going to be significant enough for us to go to them. And I don't know how much time we have."

Forging a trillion dollars seems, of course, far-fetched, but scams like this had been run as long as money, or even bullion exchange, existed. And some of them, including the Nazi presses run in death camps, had produced significant amounts of currency, almost enough to maintain the war effort. The Nazi plan actually called for a whole lot more, and, at least with the British Pound, it had worked with them producing almost 150 million forged pounds sterling by 1945, more money than was in circulation from the British Royal Mint. Had the Nazis been able to sustain that level of production, they would have destabilized Britain, and possibly won the war. But as it turned out, they made a crucial mistake. They redirected their production and design interests towards producing the dollar. By the time they had produced a decent facsimile, the war was almost over. Nevertheless, they had come really close. Really, really, close. The world had been saved from Nazism by the Nazi fetish for the dollar, just like the world was saved from the Nazi enigma coding machine by the Nazis' obsession with themselves. There were only two great powers left in the world still making paper money, and one of them was the British. But neither Tom nor Steve was talking about pounds. They were talking about dollars.

One might suspect that because the Nazis had come so close, that the Fabergé Restaurant discussion was futile from the outset, doomed to failure. In fact, no. The Nazi plan was widely known because of the consequences of losing to them, but actually almost every war ever fought, as far back as we know, had featured some kind of counterfeiting: of paper currency, of coins, of bonds, but also of propaganda pamphlets or other documents relating to the effort. And Tom, Ted, and Steve were convinced, and had always been convinced, albeit for very different reasons and to very different ends, that the TSP was historically distinctive, first by its amplitude, and also by the very nature of those who were hatching the plan. Even though FBI and CIA worked in concert with every spy agency in the world, almost all of their efforts were focused either on terrorist activities or government-initiated plans aimed at destabilizing enemies for the purpose of colonization. The US had engaged in that effort ever since they'd become a country. But what do you get when three respected members of the bear-and-bull communities of Wall Street not only participate in but actually initiate an effort to undermine Wall Street? You get Steve, Ted, and Tom, sitting together, plotting. The fact that three billionaire Americans would work on a plan to bring the US Treasury to its knees was altogether unprecedented. And diabolical.

The problem with most, perhaps every, counterfeiting scheme directed against the US currency was that they all came up short. The colors aren't right, the paper feels wrong, and the security features integrated into the bills aren't addressed. What Tom, Ted, and Steve were attempting, though, had nothing to do with washing off existing ink and printing new numbers, like 100 in place of 1. And they never followed the more recent efforts to employ color scanners to perfectly reproduce existing bills, an idea that had already been anticipated by the feds who forced the manufacturers of these devices to integrate anti-counterfeiting technology that sullies, purposely, the final product. Their idea was to actually replicate the process of making bills, as though they themselves were in that business. Everyone in the counterfeiting milieu knew that only the intaglio printing machine, which reproduced that raised texture of money by embossing ink right onto the paper, would be sufficient to that task. But there was a problem; a single, impenetrable company called Bain Currency produces the ink and the paper with exacting, unreproducible standards. Steve, Ted, and Tom had researched this odd entity, a banknote maker that had been in the business for over two hundred years, for fifty countries.

Steve was the one who had done most of the historical research, and it proved crucial to the plan. The last time the three of them had been together, he had read out from his notes, imitating the task of the professors whose classes he often skipped. It had led him to a greater appreciation of their preparation, their knowledge, and their pain.

"Okay, look," he began. The game of producing currency is complex, and requires careful attention to be paid to what is known as paper-based security features, including fibers, threads, watermarks, and other details that are actually embedded in the bill."

"Is that what they are known as?" inquired Ted with big eyes and huge sarcasm.

"Shut up, you stupid Yid," continued Steve. "The Canadians and Europeans decided to opt out of their traditional paper-based currency, because they realized that there were serious limits as to what can be imbedded into paper, and, moreover, even if they invested in the most up-to-date security features, older bills, if still accepted by merchants and banks, were necessarily vulnerable. As such, it was necessary to move to some other type of bill that could embody more security-feature options, and, moreover, to use this transition as an excuse to phase-out paper money by making it un-cashable anywhere except banks. This was a momentous move, but one that the Canadian Central Bank, and the European Central Bank, consider necessary. That the Americans and the British had delayed this move was to pretend to play the nostalgia game, for those dyed-in-the-wool Americans who imagined that the good ol' greenback still ran the world."

"It does!" proclaimed Ted.

"You are stupid," said Steve. Tom grinned. They were back in college, around the table, lying about the past and dreaming up a new future.

"That the Americans had suddenly changed their minds, and were now following the Canadians and the Europeans, was based entirely upon pragmatism. As far as I'm concerned, the decision was taken late enough to give them the advance they needed, if they acted immediately. Once the transition to plastic is made, though, the TSP is going to be our own college prank, a guffaw from another era, an era of idealism, of youthful enthusiasm, of utopia." Steve looked up from his notes. The three of them had been silent, thinking about the day when these new bills would be released, and knowing that when it came, they'd be forced to act.

And here they were, that day came.

The problem with these new bills, now slated for entry into the marketplace next fall, was not that they incorporated all sorts of very expensive bells and whistles that went beyond color-changing ink, the 3-D security ribbon, and the newly complex texture of Benjamin Franklin's collar previously integrated into the $100 bill. The problem was that the new bills were going to be the only official currency accepted by banks in the US. Previous updates to bills that were designed to fight counterfeiting were all well and good, but they had limited effect as long as banks continued to accept older, easier to replicate, versions.

The decision to place a time limit for the cashing of older bills was a real shift in policy, and it meant that no matter how sophisticated the counterfeiting operation, it would only work if it could reproduce the newest, plastic version, and that, at least at this juncture, was virtually impossible. Up until that point, the Central Bank had counted on the fact that counterfeiters aimed to reproduce recently printed bills so as to avoid the added scrutiny that was applied to bills that "looked old," but for the TSP, this was not an issue, in part because they were more interested in making a "splash" than in finding a sustainable way of producing counterfeit currency. And so the reason for Tom's excitement on that day in Fabergé Restaurant was that all of the excuses for delaying this project were now extinguished; they had to move, they had to move now, and even Steve, the most reluctant of the group, stood to lose if they didn't, on account of his massive investment in paper.

The idea of producing an older bill had been originally proposed by Ted, subsequent to a Central Bank's earlier decision to modify the $100 bill. It's true that this update could have been overlooked, and they could have chosen to limit their counterfeiting operation to the production of fifties and twenties. But in order to meet their objective of creating a "blip" on the Federal Reserve Board assessment of cash in circulation, they had to impose a huge new burden on the financial markets, and moving from hundreds to fifties doubled the costs, moving from hundreds to twenties multiplied them by a factor of five. It's true that they could have gotten around some of the high-tech fixes offered up by the previous upgrade of the $100 bill, which had included relatively minor high-tech fixes. The Declaration of Independence had been added to the right side of the bill, a quill and inkwell were printed behind the text of the bill, and a blue ribbon was added to the center of the bill. These were but details. The more difficult changes were that the color of the ink in the well changed, from copper to green, when the bill was turned in the light. This was a new invention from Crane Currency Inc., and it offered new challenges for reproducing this bill. Furthermore, a new watermark of Benjamin Franklin was added to the bill, also designed for easy detection.

When they had met previously to elaborate TSP, an occurrence that would take place at least every couple of years, Steve, Ted, and Tom had decided that the renovated bills, if they became the standard, could be reproduced, albeit at a somewhat higher cost. The government itself estimated a four percent increase to their costs to purchase their own design, an amount that in the grand scheme of things at issue here for the TSP was substantial, but not really problematic. Nonetheless, when they realized that it would be possible to circumvent this renovation by simply aiming to reproduce the earlier version of the $100 bill, then they had relaxed, since there was no reason to even keep up with the new technology being employed. All they needed was to find a way to produce a truly authentic copy of the previous version of the hundred, the fifty, and the twenty. And thanks to a miraculous, little, golden contraption, they knew that they could. But now that the transition was onto plastic, they would have to act immediately if their little contraption was to work.

I could feel the quivering of mechanisms far below the surface of each shell that encases us, from that which mediates between the world and inner depths, to those that encase each movement all the way to a distant core. Shells within shells, like a Russian doll encased inside of a Russian doll, from her form downwards, to a primordial creation.

CHAPTER 15

A lot of money, energy, and willpower was seated at that bar in Fabergé Restaurant that night, represented in the persons of Tom and Steve. But the real key to the entire operation's success had in fact been secured years earlier, in the most unlikely circumstances, when Steve was but nineteen years old. Steve was born in Mumbai, to a father who was half Indian and half Chinese, and a Native American mother. India was a place that he didn't remember at all, because he had been transported to the US by his family when he was but three years old. His ties to the US ran rather deep, though, since his grandfather had come to Texas to work in the technological development of oil fields for Rockefeller in the 1920s, and, due to the exploratory nature of his work, he was paid in stock and in parcels of land. When his firm secured some major US contracts for work abroad, he decided to bring his son on board in the company.

This move, which had brought Steve's family to Texas, was initially traumatic, augmented by the fact that Steve's father only felt at home in India. But his stock grew into a veritable treasure trove, and the land that he'd been given as further enticement became invaluable, since it was said to sit on some of the most important oil reserves in Texas. And Steve, also the only grandson, inherited the entire lot when his father died of a heart attack at the age of forty-seven. When Steve sold the land to move to NY, he received three hundred million dollars. This unexpected windfall led him to hold onto the oil stocks, which had multiplied in value so many times as to render him a billionaire four times over, probably five.

That was but a brick in the wall. The real story, as for the TSP, was that Steve's father, in order to make up for the vast number of business trips he had overseas to America and to Europe, began in his later years to bring his son with him, to both apprentice him in the business, and to make up for days and weeks and months of parenting that had been sacrificed to making a living. An offhand conversation with a family friend, who was introduced to him by his father on one of the trips they'd gone on together in Italy, had in fact generated the particulars of the idea and had unexpectedly yielded the possibility of carrying it out.

In one of those awkward moments that occur between adults, when a child is projected into a conversational mix in which he or she doesn't naturally fit, Steve had volunteered his intense obsession with bicycles. His father's friend, Luigi Carmichael, the son of a notable British father and a glamorous Italian mother, clung to this little piece of information to make conversation, and this interaction intensified when Steve's father unexpectedly left the room for a few minutes, to pee, and left Luigi and Steve alone together. Luigi, as it turned out, was himself not so much a rider of bicycles, as a connoisseur of them. His profession was to print, and this was why his father worked with him, and a large printing order was the subject that led to the business trip in the first place. But Luigi's real obsession was machined perfection.

"There are few consumer goods as carefully machined as Italian bicycles," Luigi had told Steve. "It's a technology so precise as to produce track times for racing bicycles that every year exceed existing mathematical formulas predicting possible outcomes."

"Because of weight." Young Steve uttered this with the seriousness that characterized everything that he did, and with the knowledge of his devotion to the sport of riding.

"Weight, yes." Luigi smiled with great admiration. He would have loved to have a son, particularly one who seemed so mechanically inclined as this boy—Steve.

"Weight," insisted Luigi with a smile, "until bicycles are made of air. Until then, they can always be made lighter."

"And faster!" Steve was gaining confidence with this man who shared his love for the sleek, clean, metallic, precise world of technology and engineering. "E-MC squared."

"Faster, Steve, yes. Faster. Less M, a whole lot less E!"

Luigi winked at Steve, and Steve did his best to wink back, producing a kind of squint and a few blinks. They were part of the secret society of those who actually understand something about how things work, a welcome change in a society of people who consume without knowledge of the provenance or the workings of the products they possess.

On the basis of this conversation, Steve got himself invited to Luigi's factory, in Monza, near Milano. The purpose was, for him, to see Luigi's incredible collection of vintage Italian bicycles. But in addition, Luigi also showed him his printing facilities, in which he produced the molds that were used to create stamped numbers, used in a range of precision instruments and, moreover, in the production of currency. As it turned out, in the past years Luigi had been awarded, for the first time ever for a non-American, the contract to create the stamps used to imprint dollar bills with sequence numbers. This had become a special and very lucrative area of work, one that paid for his bicycle collection, his magnificent home in Milano, and a substantial portion of his country residence, near Urbino.

The precision required for the stamps that make the ten numbers on each bill was famously intense, and only two factories in the world produced stamps suitable for the task, one in Germany, that handled most European currencies in the period leading up to the production of the euro, and Luigi's, in Italy, that provided the number stamps for the dollar, and for a number of Asian currencies. Steve was enthralled, and, normally shy and withdrawn, he consumed this environment of lathes and presses and delicate stamping devices with the lust of a technology devotee.

After a profound bonding session between this unlikely couple, centered on Steve's surprising knowledge of the intricacies of bicycles, in particular derailleurs, and his concomitantly interesting observations about precision gearing and even possible obstacles to producing clean type, Luigi rewarded Steve with a gift of ten golden, titanium-tipped stamps, the prototype that he had just developed, in multiple copies, for the dollar. He would eventually make hundreds of them, since the tips would wear out and have to be replaced, even in spite of the titanium. And so, just like Einstein might have handed out formulas scribbled on pieces of scrap paper for lovers and friends, formulas that were the tangible product of a remarkable man, Luigi simply gave one of the stamping sets to Steve, an indication of the kinds of work Luigi was most proud, and a sign of the bond they'd created that day.

Steve had coveted this strange gift and spent untold hours focusing his eyes upon the tiny numbers that were promised by the titanium molds that topped the perfectly round, golden wheel that would be mounted on a lathe-like shaft, for the imprinting of those crucial numbers, delicately impressed into the flesh of the cotton-fiber paper. This impression was the first line of defense against counterfeiting, the second being the quality of the number left behind, a quality tied as well to the tips that were the object of Steve's careful study in the coming years. And it was on account of this little set of golden printing wheels that Steve had suggested forging money during one of the many conversations that Ted, Tom, and he had about how to destroy American capitalism to each of their respective ends. And his ownership of what turned out to be the most difficult to replicate part of the entire process, catalyzed Ted's stimulus plan. And here they were, all these years later, sitting on the precipice of actualizing it.

"I don't know how long it'll take to make a difference," continued Steve. "We have to plan on just running the fucking presses until the stamps start wearing down, and I don't even know what that means. We're going to need a small army of technicians, Tom, because this whole thing only makes sense if we can do it quickly. And we'll need to start with the set that I have and hope that we can build a replica of it by the time we need to replace the last one on the presses. We lose the moment they put the phase-out into operation. So with hundreds, say, we'll need ten billion of them. If it's twenties, we need fifty billion bills."

Tom leaned back in the chair and observed the perfect egg-like interior of Fabergé Restaurant. "Fifty billion bills? Fifty billion?"

"Yup."

Tom definitely needed to get laid. "Fifty billion bills to make a trillion!" He enjoyed the sound of his own voice articulating those words. "Fuck that, Steve. Fifty billion bills would make five trillion if we stick to hundreds."

Steve looked around, feigning concern that someone was listening, even though it was clear that they were on their little island inside of the great Fabergé Restaurant egg. But Tom looked so agitated, that he might have drawn attention to himself, and that was exactly what they didn't need.

"That's what I'm talking about, Steve. Five trillion." He looked around him, in awe of his very thought process. Tom looked around the restaurant, as though for the first time. "This place is shaped like a fucking egg, Steve. A fucking egg."

"Good place to get hatched." It was a rare, comical utterance from ever-serious Steve.

As Tom tried to figure out the source of Steve's new-found sign of life, Elizabeth returned to the table.

"Can I get you two something else? We have ostrich egg soufflé with roe. It's divine." She motioned forward somewhat, pressing her chest in the direction of their faces. It worked.

"For dessert?" asked Tom, looking exactly where he was supposed to look.

"The sweetness of the soufflé brings out the warm, sugary flavors of the salmon egg. It's a remarkable experience," said Elizabeth, pouting her lips.

"I'm sure it is," said Tom, looking up to her face. She smiled, showing a perfect row of teeth, perfect in the way that American girls could be perfect in that realm, more perfect than Europeans, thought Tom.

"I assure you," Elizabeth uttered the words like a commandment.

She was very pretty, in a country-girl kind of way, thought Tom. His scrotum tingled again. Was it the TSP? The fifty billion? Or was it her?

"It *really* is delicious." She implored the two of them, cautiously. "I just tried it before my shift." That usually worked, since so many men wanted to share in whatever it was Elizabeth happened to be doing. Preferably in the nude.

Not being privy to her thought process, Steve and Tom just contemplated her words and her offer. "It's hard to imagine that she's from the city," thought Tom himself, "but she sounds the part. Pennsylvania perhaps?"

"I'll pass," said Steve.

"Pass it is. Steve, I've got to go, where the fuck is Ted?"

They both looked around at an ever-fuller restaurant, but the chair waiting for Ted's arrival was filled with his absence. Tom prepared to leave.

"Hold on," said Tom. "If you are with me, then we do this now. Call Ted. Where are we going to meet?"

"I don't know," replied Steve. "How about here?"

"Right. Right. And Ted, I'll call Ted," said Tom.

They fell silent, feeling the weight of the moment.

Elizabeth dutifully brought the bill, and Tom smirked at Steve as he peeled five new $100 bills from his wallet and deposited them on the table. Steve knew that there was at least one too many in that pile, but he also knew that Tom liked the server. Tom always liked waitresses, and every other girl who was forced, for whatever reason, to stand in his presence. And Tom was clearly relishing in their little private joke. Peeling hundred dollar bills from a stack that was hatched in Fabergé Restaurant. Fitting. And enjoyable. Indeed, Tom and Steve both enjoyed the wealth they'd received and built up, forged in very different fashions. But Tom seemed to enjoy it for that reason alone, making Steve realize that Tom could probably have been happy with a very meager salary if properly directed towards pretty women. The dry cleaner woman, the bank teller woman, the bartender woman, the automobile mechanic woman, every woman is a captive audience when you go to them for a service, and that, it seemed, was all that Tom needed to keep him happy. It was his way to their hearts, and their hearts were the conduits to their warm bodies.

"Let's build a better planet!" Tom and Steve, now standing and ready for departure, turned towards the sound of the familiar voice. Tina was stationed for them at the door, ready to see Steve off with a warm smile directed to stab at his formality, but instead she turned to greet a smiling, bearded man, the same one who had been in the bar earlier that evening with that young skater boy.

"Welcome to Fabergé Restaurant," she paused. "Welcome back to Fabergé Restaurant!"

"Thanks!" Ted halted his movement towards his two friends in order to properly greet this gorgeous woman, who looked in every way like a Japanese doll. Tom and Steve approached him.

"Don't let him in," ordered Tom. Tina smiled and then looked over at Steve, forgetting whatever it was she had just been told.

"Where the fuck were you? We've had two bottles of port and half a kilo of caviar," said Tom, matter-of-factly.

"Stand aside," Ted continued his rapport with Tina. "The Oriental man over there is about to throw up." It was one of those moments when the inappropriateness of previous conversations snuck into the current world and sounded insane. Particularly since Tina was clearly of "Oriental" heritage.

"Don't worry about him," said Steve, presumably transported back to those bitch-fests of long ago. "He's Jewish and wouldn't know the Orient from . . ." Steve paused too long. Rabid insults he could do, but in the face of this young, beautiful woman, he feared his own words.

"From what, Steve? Are you insulting this beautiful woman?"

It was Tina's time to chime in. "Would you gentlemen like a table?"

This sounded a little odd since they'd just left theirs, but it did provide a solution to the conundrum of coming and going.

"A drink perhaps?" she continued. This seemed an excellent solution, rather than just returning to the table, now being cleared; they could just sit at the bar.

"I was just here," declared Ted, moving towards the bar. "It's perfect. Let's go, I want to *not* build a better planet!" They moved back towards the bar, choosing an end where they could be seated and all face each other. Tina stayed back for a moment and observed them settling in.

"So where the fuck were you, an IBM staff party?" asked Tom.

"You talking about my dick again, Tom?" asked Ted, reaching for his groin. He was dressed as he'd been earlier that day when he'd met the skater kid, Jude, but he looked disheveled, worn out, messy.

"Were you at the Depletion Diary Event?" Steve asked, knowingly. This event had been widely advertised, and aimed to bring people to an awareness of the narrative of nature's destruction by providing her with a kind of diary, in which each entry reminded the reader of Earth's depleting resources.

"Anything like Anaïs Nin's diaries?" Tom had shared a class in college called "Henry Miller's Milieus," and they'd all landed up reading passages from her diaries.

"More like building a better planet," said Ted, rather seriously. "Like building a planet. Like," he looked at Steve, "meeting the natives and converting them. You know, making them better." The atmosphere, despite the growing stir of voices around them, as the number of tables occupied by Wall Street and others grew, increased. Ted reached into his pocket and pulled out a folded packet of papers. They were illustrated with graphs, interspersed with green-colored text.

"Making them better as in killing them?" asked Steve, rhetorically. Ted looked up at his two roommates.

"It's good to see you guys!" his eyes sparkled, "Steve! Tom! Great to see you!" He looked calm, he looked to be in very familiar company, as, indeed, he was. He turned around. "Where did our goddess get to?" Tina was almost directly behind him but, unfortunately for him, slightly out of his range of vision.

"Can I serve you gentlemen something?" It was as though she'd removed her invisible cape and was now beside them, at their beck and call. "I was just about to get your server." Tom and Steve looked at one another, knowingly.

Ted looked around, expecting to find Robbie, who had mysteriously abandoned his post. "I'll get it for you," said Tina, recognizing the question.

"In that case, I'll have what you're having!" Tina had heard that one before.

"It will be your choice this time," she said, in a well-rehearsed and crowd-pleasing line.

Tom smiled. He wanted to say something about what Ted and Tina liked to have when they first wake up, but then thought better of it. He had already slept with two of Ted's former lovers, and didn't want to rekindle the sounds of him having sex with them, in the dormitory, to the admiration of all those in earshot of her moaning and yelling. This was yet another of the running jokes of the three of them, that both girls had been dead silent in the months they had dated and slept with Ted, but had turned into major screamers when in the arms of Tom.

"What were you guys drinking?" asked Ted. "It seems to have affected Steve's complexion, but I'm willing to try it!" This was as politically correct as it was going to get, and it was in pure deference to Tina.

"Port," replied Tina for both of them.

"A bottle then!" Trust Ted to up the ante. That bottle was probably worth $1,000.

"If he has another glass, he will embarrass Tina," said Tom. "And I can't stay very long."

"Faggots," said Ted. "Three glasses then. And do you have—"

"Eggs?" asked Tom.

"Do you have any eggs here?" asked Ted.

"I'll bring you a menu," said Tina, and thought it best to absolve herself of the conversation before any more port was consumed. She hoped that Steve might linger, might speak with her at some point, and she didn't want him to enter the state that the three of them seemed to fear, with reason.

By the time Tina arrived with the menu, the three men were so lost in conversation that they barely acknowledged her. She silently placed them between Ted and Steve and melted into the background, as details of what sounded like a major investment were discussed. Tina was used to such dealings and imagined that more important transactions were undertaken at these tables than at any other boardroom in America.

Surprisingly, it was Ted who seemed to be leading the conversation, and Tom and Steve, previously garrulous, had turned quiet. It may have been the port, or the eggs, but more likely, it was that the discussion had turned to the other side of the stimulus project: Ted's NTD.

NTD was a portfolio that contained major investments in neodymium, terbium, and dysprosium, rare earth metals that were crucial to the building, and maintaining, of computer hard drives and computer chips, as well as the very components, sneakily enough, that were central to the production of the new US treasury bills.

Counterfeiting cash, the real stimulus project, was only a way to garner attention, and thinking about it had produced wonderful conversations over the past thirty years. But they all knew that counterfeiting was an attention grabber, and that it was the NTD portfolio that was the ticket to the US Treasury and their on-going negotiations with China for long-term rights. Ted's plan had been to pool together a portion of his own resources and, moreover, the brunt of Tom's in order to corner the market for rare earth metals, including rare earth elements, that is, the fifteen lanthanides plus scandium and yttrium, as well as six platinum group elements. Nobody had paid much attention to this investment, because most rare earth metals are quite common in nature, and to date relatively inexpensive to procure: the secret was that they are seldom found in sufficient amounts to be extracted economically outside of certain regions of the world, most notably China.

With Tom's enormous access to liquid funds, in addition to the buying power that he wielded through access to his own investment fund that boasted more than $100 billion, the overall percentage of raw materials they could control was staggering. That he trusted Ted with all of the negotiations was a sign of his having gone "all in," and the gamble had paid off already, as he'd seen the value of that option portfolio more than double in three years. This in itself had made him a darling of the Wall Street set, an investor who had chosen to buy a solid commodity, rather than some speculative derivative or other complex tool, and had done brilliantly by it.

To own a significant portion of the market for a staple mineral had been tried before, most notably in the early 1970s, when Bunker Hunt and his brother started to amass huge amounts of silver. By the end of the decade, they had used the commodity options market in Chicago to quite literally corner the market, owning more silver bullion—on paper—than the total amount available in the marketplace. As the market responded to impending shortages, the Hunt Brothers benefitted massively—to the tune of $4 billion—with no end in sight. The problem was that they didn't have a long-term plan for what to do with the 3,100,000 kg of silver on which they'd planned to exercise their options and, as was to be expected, the Chicago commodity regulators came down on them as the delivery date neared, causing a precipitous decline in the price of silver and, eventually, the bankruptcy of the brothers.

Subsequent regulation prohibited such transactions, in part by ensuring that larger amounts of cash outlay would be required in order to secure options for commodity purchases at a later date. But all of the new regulations had been set up with the Hunts in mind, that is, with regulations designed to prevent massive rises in the cost of major commodities (silver had risen by 1,000 percent in just a few years due to the Hunt scheme), and not by-products like rare earth elements. In other words, nothing was done that could prevent actions that didn't look like speculation for short-term gain, and this, as it turned out, was the genius of Ted's plan. He not only had the cash on hand to purchase a huge percentage of existing stocks of rare earth metals, but he also procured ownership of mining facilities abroad, most notably in China, by greasing the palms of the local government officials who owned control of their production. Since it all occurred in China, US regulators had no sense of what was happening, and since he had a rather rare ability with the Chinese language, he never had to employ meddling intermediaries to help with the negotiations.

To be fair, the success of this scheme wasn't entirely attributable to Ted's "genius," but rather to his insistence upon investing in tangible and, preferably, earth-bound commodities. Always the Proudhon-inspired anarchist, Ted felt an affinity to the soil, the land, the very ground upon which houses and, moreover, homes are built. He couldn't have imagined when he started on this quest that world demand for rare earth metals would be projected to exceed 195,000 tons by 2020 and 300,000 tons by 2025, as middle-class consumption habits explode in China, India, and Africa. Nobody could have imagined how important but little-known elements like cerium, lanthanum, europium, neodymium, terbium, yttrium, and dysprosium would be, just as no one foresaw the explosion of the instruments that use them, like smartphones, touchscreens, batteries, fuel cells, wind turbines, catalysts, and, the newest addition, plastic money.

It was also not the case that Ted was able to predict the role that China would play in producing these elements, this was simply a consequence of their having mass-produced them first, at a huge environmental cost, allowing other countries, including the US, South Africa, Canada, Australia, Brazil, India, Russia, South Africa, Malaysia, and Malawi to delay the messy mining process, and were now at least ten years away from developing viable extraction strategies. Once again, it wasn't Ted's foresight or Chinese know-how, but rather that many of the elements could be mined in places like Jiangxi with only a shovel, whereas rich deposits in Greenland or Northern Canada required huge investments and developing technologies to render them viable.

When they stood up to leave, the wheels were in motion. Ted would call in all of his impending options in the coming weeks, which would cause ripples, and then concern, and finally panic in the commodity market. At the same time, tons of raw materials accumulated for the production of paper money would be quietly transported to the warehouse that Steve had procured, years ago, in preparation, always rather timid, of this moment. There would be details to work out, most notably regarding the distribution of sufficient currency, sufficiently quickly, to make the headlines required for that long-anticipated meeting with the US Treasury.

For the moment, though, they were in the prep stages, and the production of the money had to take precedence over everything else, because it was that meal of cold cash that would begin the banquet. The bill was paid, almost as an afterthought, and the three men were barely speaking as they moved towards the exit of Fabergé Restaurant. In one moment of recollection, Ted caught Jude's searching gaze and smiled, then pointed at him. Jude, unsure of what any of this meant, grinned, pointed back, and then regretted his gesture. Perhaps Ted would think he was trying to come on to him?

When they left that night, the foundation had been poured for the final episode in this strange existence of mine, a base that had been foretold by some being, because I'd already known it was there from the moment I was conscious of my existence. I felt excited, feeling them leave Fabergé Restaurant, and knew that in future penetrations into my being they would bring us all closer to an abyss I'd anticipated as long as I could remember.

CHAPTER 16

John looked every bit the commanding officer of a ground force charged with fighting back a savage army of murderous infidels, with his chiseled jaw, his piercing, blue eyes, his workmanlike hands, and his gruff demeanor. As such, he hardly looked the part of a chef, and even less an architect of the elite, prestigious, meticulous Fabergé Restaurant, the New York landmark that prided itself on producing creations crafted to emulate those incredibly eggzotic artworks produced by the Russian jeweler, Peter Carl Fabergé, and his goldsmiths for the Russian Imperial Family. A look into John's past, however, changed the complexion of his face from that of a military tactician to that of a careful crafter of recipes, weathered and hardened by his unrelenting attention to each detail of the invasion, and focused by his careful oversight of each member of the battalion charged with carrying out his culinary conquests.

John grew up and into the persona of John-the-Owner in the unassuming and one-time industrial town of Waltham, Massachusetts, where his father worked as a proud craftsman for the Waltham Watch Company, an enterprise committed to the revolutionary idea of creating moving parts that were so precise, as to be completely interchangeable. Appropriately enough, the company was once called the Warren Manufacturing Company, named in honor of General Warren of Roxbury, a renowned soldier of the War of Independence. The work they were doing on timepieces of the period were considered so novel that the founders specifically omitted the word "watch" from any reference to the company. Headquarters were built for this innovative company in Waltham, Massachusetts, in 1854. And, to John-the-Owner's pride, they still stand today, reminders of the first pocket watches made in America, as well as early chronometers and some lasting heirlooms, including the "William Ellery," a key-wind watch that President Lincoln received as a tribute at the Gettysburg Address.

In 1949 the company declared bankruptcy, and John-the-Child's father, who was by then nearly of retirement age, retreated for a time to his South Street home, where he and his wife discovered the length of the eight-hour day spent together. Luckily, their three-year-old child, John, was able to monopolize his father's attention. And luckily for John, his father continued his meticulous work at home. John Senior had floundered about for a few months after the factory closed, but then sought desperately for an activity that would satisfy his lust for assembling intricate devices, leading him into the construction of balsa wood airplanes and, inevitably, ships in bottles. Young John watched his father work at these creations with surprising fascination and patience and was always rewarded with the product of his father's meticulous labor. Unlike his father, though, John-the-Child fetishized the end results, and so in addition to the random collection of egg-related objects that are now scattered throughout the dining room of Fabergé Restaurant, the attentive customer can also admire, but not touch, the many airplanes and bottled ships that he had received and now treasured.

The connected parts of John's early domestic setting were disassembled when he was a boy of twelve, when the Waltham Precision Instruments Company opened its doors in the revamped premises of the now bankrupt Waltham Watch Company factory. In what turned out to be the greatest, but also the final pinnacle of John's father's career, the company teamed up with Massachusetts Institute of Technology engineers on building gyroscopes and other instruments designed for measuring changes in direction. The impetus for this new line of work was a huge order from NASA's new Apollo navigation system, a collection of instruments that were to be assembled with the kind of precision for which Waltham watchmakers had become famous. The hygiene and cleanliness rules of the team were so strict that women were not allowed to wear makeup, and workers who came back from their sunny vacations were forbidden to work near the assembly area, out of fear that they could have skin flaking off from their suntans.

Unfortunately, though, John's father never got to wallow in the glow of his company's galactic success. On the very eve of the Apollo 15 mission of 1971, when Astronaut David Scott substituted his damaged Omega Speedmaster Professional chronograph with a Waltham timepiece, John's father's heart stopped. It was ironic that the precise ticking instrument that had successfully carried him to his eighty-third year had stopped on the eve of his greatest achievement. And so as the Apollo astronauts were catapulted by unprecedented rocket-fueled engines into space, one of the technicians whose work had made the mission possible was also blasted off into the other world, the glow of the television report about the Apollo mission illuminating his final moments.

All of this is to say that John-the-Child grew into John-the-Owner, bearing familial characteristics that were transposed: from the ticking timepiece to the culinary creation, from the eternal to the ethereal, and from keeping time to watching it carefully in order to ensure the absolute perfection of the well-wrought meal. And along the way, John-the-Owner met his own precise masterwork: Яйцо Фаберже, the Fabergé egg. Inspired by its beauty, its complexity, and the pure aesthetic bliss of being in its presence, John-the-Owner emulated Gustav Faberge, eventually Fabergé (to add some style), as well as Gustav's son, Peter Carl Fabergé, who both supplied masterpieces to the rich, the famous —and the doomed. Inspired by his new mentor, now that his revered father was no more, John-the-Owner fashioned himself into a creator and supplier of masterpieces, and was, or appeared, unconcerned by the ethereal nature of his own art and masterworks. In this regard, John-the-Child's father would not have respected or even understood his son, because the very definition of craftsmanship, and even art, was survival, not only through time, but also through space and space-time. John's father believed that art would be recognized as such in any dimension, just as his own crafted masterpieces would bear motion in time and space without diminution of their original worth.

It was perhaps for this reason that John grew into an inveterate collector of fine artworks, even in the absence of pockets deep enough to own those icons his father would have so admired. Furthermore, without the kind of cultural snobbery of a man with access to Chanel or Cartier or Fabergé, and with a belief in the American version of building from the ground up, John-the-Owner could settle, if settle is the right term, for magnificent, self-made creations. In short, even though he settled for facsimiles, he nonetheless managed to surround himself, and his clients, with images of fine craftsmanship. And each of the hundreds, nay, thousands of culinary creations that John-the-Owner had offered over the years to stimulate the palates of his clients bore the stamp of his father's dedication to reproduction. And the reproduction of great dishes isn't mechanical reproduction, it's true reproduction, because each creation reproduces the power of the first work. From this perspective, great recipes hearken back to the creative flame that illuminates the vision of the creator.

At the same time, though, like the engineer-son of an inventor, or the dance-daughter of a choreographer, or the musician-child of a composer, John-the-Owner was destined for disillusionment. Relative to his own father, he would leave no instrument behind, and in regards to his own flesh-and-blood creations, his twin nine-year-old sons Jason and Jim, he had but a partial link that was eventually damaged by the destructive tides of a washed-up marriage. John seldom saw his ex-wife, and spent his days with Tina, who, like himself and his father before him, fought the fight of earthly perfection. Tina's very existence seemed to reassure John, since she proved to him that despite the chips and cracks and flaws of the shells we call existence, there is nonetheless the chance to encounter true beauty.

Nobody could quite work out the connection between this odd couple, because nobody could fathom the depth of their connection. What people saw was superficial, that tiny, doll-like Tina and demonically possessed John were polar opposites, in every way visible, and so speculation abounded as to whether they could possibly be involved in a corporal relationship. The very image of John's brutal masculinity seemed sufficient to crush the fragile femininity that coursed through Tina's veins, veins that seemed barely wide enough to allow her body sufficient sustenance to survive. Nevertheless, everyone who worked at Fabergé Restaurant knew that John depended absolutely on Tina, just as they knew that he would be adrift were it not for the powerful force exerted by Doris the bookkeeper, and, moreover, that everything that truly mattered in the Fabergé Restaurant depended upon the value provided to it by Jessica.

Masculinity is the image behind the glass, or reflected back by the mirror. What the viewer cannot see, in both cases, is the weakness inherent in the display of raw power. The truth of nature and her creations is in the possibility of reproduction, and in that regard men are the spectators, not the progenitors. Nate's transient creations, Jude's puerile observations, even John's masterful culinary creations are but the window-dressing of a world that survives by reproduction, but is given meaning by cycles. Value isn't present in production or even reproduction, because both are slated for consumption, obsolescence, and decay. Value, like the passage from one generation to another, has to be experienced, not witnessed.

If Jessica, then, is the truth about this world, then Doris is its protector, who toils behind the scene to ensure that tomorrow might have some of the positive elements present in the world today. While masterful eggy creations flowed from Fabergé Restaurant, Doris, when she wasn't keeping the lights on and the gas flowing, played the role of a dawdling grandmother to John-the-Father's children, on the days when they were staying with him. They would come directly from school to Fabergé Restaurant, enter directly into the Yolk, and play in various regions of the kitchen, while they waited long hours for him to pack them into the red convertible Eldorado for the short drive to his home. The children didn't seem to mind that their father was so completely consumed by the many tasks of running the restaurant, because they knew that their actual needs would be met by those around him, especially Doris. And for entertainment, there was Nate. Young boys were enthralled by people like Nate, who seemed to have no boundaries, and for whom every activity could be turned into a game, or a performance. Their father was all business, all serious, all the time, but Nate was crazy, silly, and always ready to spoil them with his folly.

When Nate's performances were over, though, they would turn to Jessica, whom they thought to be Nate's girlfriend, an idea that Nate had never challenged. Jessica spoiled them with her affection, and delighted them with her kindness. And then, when it was time to ensure that they would have a good night's sleep, and a proper meal, they knew that they could rely upon Tina, who would take them to their father's house in advance of his departure from Fabergé Restaurant, where she would set the table and serve whatever tasty delight their father, or Jessica or Nate, had prepared for them. Sometimes Tina would be there in the morning as well to help out with breakfast and with their departure to school. They never thought that she was dating their father any more than they imagined that Doris was, even though she certainly looked more the part. At nine years old, they were still in that phase when they imagined that their parents' separation was temporary, a vacation, designed to prepare the way for an eventual reintegration into an even bigger house and home. This dream was not to be, for reason more complex than they could ever imagine, or would ever know. There was another dream played out in this choreographed caring for John's children, one that Tina and Jessica had once had of having children to raise together. They'd promised themselves it would be possible, all those years ago, and, strangely enough, it was.

John and Tina are the yolk and egg of this creation, those who surround them ensure the egg-like perfection of Fabergé Restaurant's creations. Whatever happens subsequent to my own demise, they will not break apart, for if they were to do so, all meaning would splatter, Humpty-Dumpty-like, upon the ground, never to be restored.

CHAPTER 17

On Saturday, a mere two days after the fate-filled meeting between Tom and Steve, John saw the two of them again, this time with the guy he'd seen speaking to the young egg-writer back in Fabergé Restaurant. He caught a glimpse of them as he walked into the main entrance of the restaurant for the weekly meeting, the Pow-Wow with Doris-the-Bookkeeper. He knew that the news from Doris would be bad, but it had been bad for so long that he felt no anxiety or dread, no sense that the shell upon which he'd labored for so long might crack and ooze innards out onto Wall Street, where it sat, like Humpty Dumpty, so precariously.

Instead of joining Doris directly, John walked over to the iced containers at the server station near the front of the restaurant and poured himself a glass of eggnog. "Fabergégnog" was indeed one of the restaurant's famed creations, used primarily as a mixer, for women mostly, who sought a sticky-sweet source for the sensual intoxication borne by the rum or brandy that was added but hidden amongst the heavy, creamy, eggy taste that was supposed to represent maternal sweetness, strength, and, of course, the bearing of life through eggs.

John sat down, relieved, or so it seemed to Doris, as though he needed a respite from the weight of the responsibilities of which she was about to remind him. Doris knew that he'd spent the morning with his sons, a pair of children who were born of the same egg. John's ex-wife, who looked a lot like John himself, gave him little grief in this, the post-marriage years. They had created two children, but they had not been destined to live as husband and wife. And although he had made her some truly memorable meals in the five years they spent together, she did not miss him, and he seldom mentioned her, unless regarding some financial outlay that he was willing to dish out to the boys.

Doris had lived through John-the-Father's marriage, and his divorce, and now cared for him as only a bookkeeper can, by ensuring that in spite of the weirdness of this world, things nonetheless can be made to add up.

"Good morning, John."

"Doris."

John smiled and settled into his seat. He looked relaxed when he was around her, for she seemed to be in control of the universe, or at the very least that segment of the universe into which he could gaze with his stony-blue eyes. As long as Doris-the-Bookkeeper wielded the adding machine, the eraser-topped pencil, and lines of black-on-white figures, then everything, no matter how askew, askance, or awry they were, or could be, had a place in all that was well-suited for its nature. There was no recipe here, no ingredients to be transformed such that the final product looked nothing like the parts that contributed to its sum. The sum was made of like-minded digits, and the digits had only ten variations, no matter how dissimilar the columns might be from, say, the "income" to the "expenditures."

Doris looked every bit the Doris-the-Bookkeeper that we imagine in our minds when reading her name and title. She was short, probably around 5' 2" with shoes on, she had grey hair, small, silver-framed glasses, a sweet and lightly wrinkled face, and dainty hands that looked to be far older than the sixty-one years she had given to this world. For as long as John had known her, almost three decades now, she had worn what seemed to be a host of interchangeable outfits, all comprised of a skirt or pants of a grey or grey-blue hue, flat, non-descript shoes, a blouse, probably polyester, in a shade of aquamarine blue or aquamarine green that were all more or less indistinguishable from the other.

Doris had begun to work with John in his old restaurant, Crimson and Clover, down on West 46th Street near 5th Avenue and the famed "Diamond District." Therein, he had rented a small and unforgiving space that had been abandoned by a Hassidic Jew who, without explanation, had suddenly gathered up his not inconsiderable collection of cut and uncut diamonds, thrown off his black coat and large black hat, trimmed his long sideburns, and left the city, never to return. Before leaving, he had paid the small array of outstanding bills attributable to him, and, since he had neither wife nor children, there was no reason to pursue the mystery of his departure to, as it turned out, Montréal, a place that was perched even further north than the Bronx: six hours (by car), one country (Canada), one religion (Catholic), and one language (French) away from New York. Those who cared said that he'd left for love, or, more likely, lust. Or, even more likely, he had sought out in a land of freezing winters and maple syrup a secular life away from the gaze of those penetrating perpetrators of Hassidic traditions with whom he'd spent most of his life. Whatever his eventual fate, it didn't really matter. The glittering hole in Manhattan was soon filled in, and very few people remembered what it had been like when he was around to do the filling himself.

John had been searching for a place in that area ever since departing his native Massachusetts, not because he sought to feed the clients who came to cast their nets in the ocean of diamonds that ebbed and flowed in and out of that district, but rather because he wanted to be close to the jewels that adorned the Fabergé eggs, those natural-born, glistening, mineral masterpieces that had come to inspire his sense of himself as a chef and a craftsman. Crimson and Clover was a great success, and it featured a large number of egg dishes, in addition to some of the finest seafood New York had to offer, and this on account of John's continued relations with Cape Cod's fishermen, who had the privilege of supplying John with the freshest of their catch. No matter how sumptuous the surroundings, the core of a restaurant is freshness, and to assure it he often paid more than twice as much as anyone else, as long as he could be assured that the catch was freshly caught.

Thanks to John's magnificent work, and Doris's oversight of all things not culinary, John's business grew and, again thanks to Doris, the money was carefully saved for the inevitable rainy day when, as she had long predicted, a diamond dealer would find the unusually large space that John occupied and make the owner a proverbial offer that couldn't be refused. It was indeed the perfect diamond-dealer fortress, as it turned out, featuring a fortified basement that had been well-suited for a restaurant's wine, and even better suited for a high-security strongbox that is impenetrable enough to keep the symbolic realm of diamond exchange safe. The diamond dealer contacted the owner of John's building, who himself was a man of his own Hassidic tribe, and a deal was struck, leaving John with his stash of cash securely invested in the bank, but forced to search for a new place to create his intricate masterpieces.

The shuttering of Crimson and Clover should have been a sad day for John, but instead it fulfilled a dream of his, to turn the profits of his yolk-and-whites-driven recipes into a truly monumental restaurant, a landmark to be laid in the very heart of his adopted city. And so, as the fans were being withdrawn from the restaurant, along with all the polished steel and the egg-related decorations, John decided to move downtown, to another cash-rich area, Wall Street, to pursue a dream far grander than Crimson or Clover. His swollen balance of liquid convinced him that in spite of the quiet resistance of Doris-the-Bookkeeper, he could make the dream he had of building his own Fabergé egg a reality.

And so the strategy was conceived, the necessary parties fertilized with papery, green currency, and the plans drawn up, all to the joy of the until-then obscure architect named David Miller. Miller happened to have been willing to listen to John's wild ideas one day while dining on a host of egg-rich dishes at Crimson and Clover, and was therefore eventually chosen to draw them up, and he commissioned appropriate builders and was paid appropriate sums, en route towards the laying of the new Fabergé Restaurant. Success, it would seem, was assured.

In the late 1980s, everyone was reading a collection of adages assembled under the title of *Murphy's Law*. Each adage was tied to the central observation that whatever can go wrong, will, and to the secondary observation, that people are always promoted upwards until they finally settle into a place of earned incompetence. The same applies to most small businesses: en route towards the promise of stellar growth that marks the tiny number of fortunes that have been built up, most businessmen find themselves in a space too large, with stock too expensive, with employees too ambitious, or with lifestyles too rich, and the careful planning that went into the original stock and trade therefore crumbles, generally from the weight of accrued debt. Despite efforts, plans, and approaches to the contrary, John's own fortune in the restaurant market was in the end no different. And so he stood upon the precipice of annihilation, a peak that was but one protrusion upon an entire mountain of debt.

"We aren't close to the edge anymore, John," said Doris with a look of soft sadness. "We have arrived." She looked positively teary eyed.

"It's Saturday!" John smiled, beaming undue, youthful enthusiasm.

"I looked at the reservations, John, and we are probably looking at three hundred tonight. I also looked at the list of checks and, well, we need to serve—"

"Three thousand?"

She barely smiled this time. Truth be told, and all numbers reckoned in, the actual number was probably closer to thirty thousand.

The three thousand figure was a running gag, a sad, sadistic, and pitiful inside joke between John-the-Owner and Doris-the-Bookkeeper. And like most jokes, its over-the-top figure of three thousand bore more truth than humor. They quite literally needed to multiply the business intake by ten in order to recover the rate of profits that John used to generate at Crimson and Clover, and this over a period of years, not days or weeks. The dining room and the sheer logistics of Fabergé Restaurant's creations made the possibility of serving 300 clients a stretch, and even 350 unfathomable. And the fact that John, the master craftsman, the mad scientist behind the Fabergé Restaurant creations, had spent each night for the past six months manning the Hobart dishwashing station, which should have been overseen by an obsessive-compulsive, unemployable master of cleanliness for $15.50/hour, made matters much worse, particularly on nights when the restaurant was stretched to capacity. And this night was going to be one such occasion. The restaurant was indeed successful, by any reasonable measure; the problem was that most of the cash flowed into the hands of the creditors who had gleefully lent him the money for an edifice that couldn't ever be paid off, in a part of town where cost per square foot demanded huge amounts of cash, day after day after day.

"Is Nicky working?" This was Doris's method of quietly inquiring about staffing for the evening, in the all-important sauté station.

"He's in now."

Doris looked down at the dizzying array of figures that adorned the spreadsheet before her.

"Eggnog?" asked John, almost mockingly in light of the unanswered questions that lingered in the air. Doris knew to not answer.

"Is the new guy . . ."

"Russ?"

"Yes."

"I'm going to teach him how to scrub pots."

When Doris had signed the employment forms for this new guy, she had hoped that he had some untapped training that would allow John to use him for some of the sauté chef work, so that Jessica could man that station. Johnny, dubbed by Doris "Little John," despite his height, could do the baking, and they could function without resorting to one of the pinch-hitters, as John liked to call those they'd call in to cook on very busy nights.

"We have a pinch-hitter, Doris, he's supposed to be pretty good, from Shucks and Shells."

Shucks and Shells was a mainstay of Midtown, serving seafood and corn on the cob for mid-range prices. They were successful and had been around for almost fifteen years. But their chefs were mediocre, and everyone they had brought in from there had made sub-standard fare, costing John his nerves and stretching the regular kitchen staff to their breaking point.

Doris was about to try out her well-rehearsed plea that John step in tonight, if only to ward off a chorus of unhappy-guest remarks, but then thought better of it. Fabergé Restaurant wasn't going to survive the coming week, and if the suppliers lived up to their promises, wouldn't even be supplied for Monday, given the tardiness of their payments.

Facts and figures stared Doris in the face, even as a tinge of bizarre optimism brightened John's complexion.

Couples, seated at tables, couples, waiting to couple, couples, like John and Tina, John and Doris, John and me. Couples.

CHAPTER 18

Just as Doris was about to begin to stammer her reluctant speech of gloom and doom, a middle-aged man wearing a large, green coat entered the dining room almost frantically, spotted John and Doris, and unceremoniously pulled up a chair to join them. John looked elated, this was perhaps the respite he was hoping for.

"John!" exclaimed the pock-faced, slightly overweight, balding salesman called Stan.

"Stan, good day." John seemed to grin the grin of relief from figures. "Fabergégnog, Stan?" He rose and, without an answer, headed towards the server station to prepare a drink for his fateful friend.

"How are you doing, young Doris?"

"We hope to be able to send you payment for March at the end of this month, Stan," replied Doris.

Stan waived his arms in virtual disdain at the very thought of payment. He had been supplying John with egg-related antiques and trinkets for more than a decade and had learned that no matter what was going on in this hallowed shell, he would be paid —eventually. And given the massive mark-up on every item that John purchased, he could stand to lose the profits of every yolk or shell-related item he'd find to adorn the cracks and crevices of Fabergé Restaurant until the very end of time.

John returned to the table bearing an ornate glass, adorned with whipped cream and powdered egg yolk, one of John's own creations, and set it before Stan.

"John, I found one," began Stan, before gulping down a mouthful of John's intoxicatingly sweet concoction.

Doris knew that John was about to fall for another egg creation. This one, she felt sure, on the basis of Stan's enthusiasm, would be on the expensive side, since it was undoubtedly Fabergé-related. But like all of Fabergé Restaurant's creations from its namesake, it would not, and could not, be authentic, thank goodness! Only czars and crazy-successful capitalists like the billionaire Forbes family could make that kind of claim. "But Stan's offerings would be dear enough, under the circumstances," Doris thought to herself, "but then again, given the state of our accounts, this one may finally be a freebie, unbeknownst to Stan!"

Stan placed his famous leather bag on the ground beside the table and delicately withdrew a wooden box from within its scented quarters. John purchased enough items that bore the leather scent of that bag to put him into the delicate, and now disastrous, financial situation he has now found himself. No matter, it was all for art, well, not just art, intricate and precious creativity that only someone of the stature of Peter Carl Fabergé or, as John would say, his own father, could produce.

From deep within the depths of that leather emerged a replica of perhaps the most significant of all the Fabergé eggs, one that John knew well, and one that Stan, forever the salesman, knew that John would spring for no matter how dire his straits. Little did he know that this would be the end of that gravy train that had helped Stan pay for a place in the Hamptons.

It was appropriate that this egg bore within its own depths a golden replica of the actual Trans-Siberian train, honoring Nicholas II, who had laid the foundations for constructing the Siberian Railway. To this day, the original for this work had never been sold, and remains in the Kremlin Armory museum. Nonetheless, enough detail is known of its form and fabrication to make it possible to replicate it, and Stan had finally found a source for one whose details would meet, and indeed exceed, John-the-Owner's exacting expectations.

It was beautiful, so beautiful. Stan handed it to John in a scene akin to one in which young lovers allow the first touch, gentle, quiet, in a kind of precious disbelief that remains throughout lovers' lives, rekindled from time to time when drugs or profound lust reignites that familiar feeling. For John, that familiar feeling was brought on by these regular purchases, purchases that literally warmed his aging sex to stimulation, even as they created that sickening, sinking feeling in the pit of Doris's well-worn, acid-reflux infested, bookkeeper's stomach.

John examined his prey, carefully. It was a platinum-colored egg, with a gorgeous hinged lid, adorned with colored enamel, and mounted on a base of pure onyx. Preposterously, indeed preposterously enough for a man like John, Peter Carl Fabergé had somehow managed to engrave a map of Russia, illustrated with the route of the Trans-Siberian Railway on the central silver section. Etched upon that map of ambition fulfilled was an inscription:

"The route of the Grand Siberian Railway in the year 1900."

Magnificent.

Like the original, the copy that John held in his hot hands had elements, although not as many as the original, made of onyx, silver, gold, quarts, and vitreous enamel, and each station was marked upon the map with a (semi) precious stone. As such, it was "precious" enough to be of interest to John, and in its gaudy detail it replicated the preposterously wild ambitions of its original. But it was also, as its namesake suggests, "semi." This semi was an issue for Doris, because over and above the empty bank account from which John was to draw for this inevitable purchase, there was the knowledge that only a real fetishist would buy a work of this nature. And no matter how much he appreciated its workmanship, he couldn't really hope that someone might someday want to possess a similar collection. Furthermore, given that it was but a collection of copies, it wouldn't satisfy someone's related obsessions for precious stones, original artwork, or the chance to own a one-of-a-kind design. Everything John had purchased over the many years of his mania was beautiful and invaluable, but only to him, and in bankruptcy nobody would care how much he had paid for them. On the other hand, Doris mused, maybe that was part of his plan. Somebody might conceivably purchase the used pots, pans, and knives with which John had built his Fabergé Restaurant, but nobody would want his trinkets, and so he'd be able to save them from creditors.

"Did he ever think this way? Is this part of the master plan?" wondered Doris to herself.

John's piercing, blue eyes took in the scene, and he seemed to grin with satisfaction and lust as he undertook his inspection of this precious commodity, attentive, perhaps, to Doris's silent ruminations.

The Fabergé egg in his possession was held up by three carefully cast griffins, in gold-plated silver, just like the original, and each griffin brandished, menacingly, a sword and a shield. Once again, like a memory of early love and lust in which each lover knew that the other hid untold, sweet secrets beneath precious cotton or silk and amidst tufts of soft and unexpectedly silken hairs, John knew that the egg contained a locomotive, inserted section by section into its innards. The very thought of this machine creation, built in the most rugged of materials to withstand the strain of screaming through Siberia's frigid temperatures, was brought to a higher climax since it was rendered in the original in pure platinum, with lanterns of deep-red rubies, rosette headlights, and five ornate, gold coaches with windows made of rock crystal.

John rotated the egg and its contents in his skilled hands and looked carefully for the famed inscriptions, and, in a deal-maker, found them; the coaches, as he assembled them, bore inscribed labels: "Mail," "For Ladies Only," "Smoking," and "Non-Smoking." With fingers as rugged as they are ductile, he then reached into the egg and withdrew the last coach for the little assembly, a coach labeled "Chapel," and, almost shockingly, found a tiny gold key with which the train was wound up. This action and its amazing locomotive result was a kind of miracle that recalls Nate's kitchen experiments, but rather than sentient beings coerced through silverware obstacles, this movement was affected by a precious train that could be made to chug along upon the wooden Fabergé Restaurant table. Had he been of that ilk, John would have gasped. As it was, he simply stared at the little creation that chugged along silently before him, in all of its miniature and imitative glory. But his grey-blue eyes seemed to twinkle, blue and platinum.

Watching John, Doris knew that this little creation, a feeble but, honestly, really remarkable, little facsimile, would never return to its warm, leather home, but would rather be itself an egg within John's own Fabergé egg. As such, this facsimile of a locomotive had found its next stop and would join the collection of Fabergé miniatures that John had purchased over the many years of his work in that restaurant. The train route depicted by this egg had many stops, but for John this marked the end of a trail that had led him from Waltham all the way to the lust, greed, decadence, and waste of Wall Street. In that regard, this moment recalled a century ago, 1917, when in spite of the wealth and magnificent possessions of the few, famine threatened the gigantic country of Russia. While the czar and the wealthy aristocrats chose from the plethora of beautiful bounty, riots and strikes of common people demanding bread rose, like butter-drenched soufflés. Marie Antoinette had once said, "Let them eat cake," by which she actually meant soufflé, and now trickle-down capitalism was sending but crumbs to the vast majority, and masterpieces to the few. John held in his hand an egg commemorating a great engineering achievement of the czarist era, but he also held the very symbol of the waste, corruption, and greed that made such masterful achievements possible.

John wasn't a czar, though, and Stan was hardly the great Peter Carl Fabergé, offering his wares for his own advancement and wealth. But there were, nevertheless, some eerie coincidences between that era and this Manhattan eve. This was not the pre-dawn massacre of Olga, Tatiana, Maria, Anastasia, and Alexei in a basement by the Bolshoi henchman on that fateful July 17, 1918. And Doris, watching the ongoing transaction with horror and concern, was certainly not Nicholas's mother, Dowager Empress Maria Fedorovna, who miraculously escaped the assassins' bullets. And this beautiful facsimile of the egg honoring the completion of the Trans-Siberian Railway was not the order of St. George egg, the last Fabergé imperial Easter egg that the empress would ever receive from her son Nicholas, the one-time czar of all the Russians. No, this was New York City, Saturday evening. This was 101 years after the assassination of the ruling family of Russia, the end of an entire system by which inherited wealth was maintained through oppression and rugged institutional norms.

Looking back one century from this New York night brings to bear other revolutionary anniversaries. Neither John-the-Owner nor Doris-the-Bookkeeper were aware of it, but their meeting with Stan was almost exactly one hundred years after Sir Frank Watson Dyson's landmark experiment to observe a total solar eclipse that would happen just as the sun was crossing the bright Hyades star cluster. Dyson knew that the light from the stars would have to pass through the sun's gravitational field on its way to Earth, but would be still visible due to the darkness of the eclipse, permitting accurate measurements of the stars' gravity-shifted positions in the sky. And so, near the remote island of Príncipe in the Gulf of Guinea, just off the west coast of Africa, Dyson was able to measure the stars' positions as viewed through the sun's gravitational lens, and confirmed predictions from a then-obscure physicist named Albert Einstein.

From jeweled eggs to mass starvation, from revolution to assassination, from Stan's stash to John's eggy collection, paradigms were exploding.

Doris decided that if no words were uttered by either Stan or John, it was because there was quite literally nothing more to say. Maybe, there never was. And so she remained silent, contemplating some of the final figures that would define her decades-long relationship with John. She had been wondering all week long how she could possibly break the news to John that they were broke, irrevocably broke, their shell was not just cracked, it was broken. The enormous debt that was weighing down upon Fabergé Restaurant had finally become too much to bear. But maybe, she thought as she watched him admire this ornate trinket, it was appropriate that she not emphasize the lugubriousness of the situation. Instead, she just watched as John lived out the last hours of his Fabergé Restaurant dream. To watch him gleefully handle another Fabergé creation, she realized that he looked like a man who was successfully completing his life's work, rather than throwing away the last few resources he had at yet another facsimile of bygone success.

At that moment, Doris felt old, and tired, and for the first time she felt a degree of warm-heartedness for this slimy salesman Stan, who now extended his hand to John in order to secure a handshake that would bring eternity to its knees. Stan grinned, and John seemed to scowl in profound approval. And then, with a final swig of the few remnants of that delectable eggnog, Stan walked out the door, and, unbeknownst to anyone present for the occasion, out of John's life—forever.

Over the years, Stan had brought John a collection of nearly worthless trinkets that added up to a world, and now he was done. Perhaps that's what everybody did, in the tiny amount of time allotted to them to enjoy the pleasures of this life. They gather together the memories of loves loved, orgasms felt, kisses enjoyed, children born, smiles smiled, hands grasped, nights passed, drinks swallowed, tastes savored, and finally, in one last moment, unforeseen or not, the entire artifice reveals itself as such, a delicious, passionate, climactic, forceful, magnificent sensation comprised of everything, and nothing.

John's father remembered precise instruments and the power that is the birth and nurturing of a child. So, too, had John assembled the little eggs of a natural world and turned them into this place of dreams, depth, and death. Maybe John had succeeded, however, because his own creation, his Fabergé Restaurant, was in fact an egg, and it had grown into a place that Jessica and Tina had nourished, that Nate had elaborated, and inside of which Ted and Tom and Steve had laid a plan for another world, a better place. In the end, Jude would of course betray the entire enterprise, and thereby make way for a resurrection.

For myself, I felt a pang of sadness, as the world worked up to its inevitable climax, and felt, too, as those young lovers who, having found their dream, their implosion, their explosion, and their breathless aftermath, were, in those few moments, the culmination and the finale of every symbolic, supernatural, and spiritual idea with which they had invested that experience, and that what lay ahead was the consequences of what they'd hatched, and smashed, as the shell lay shattered between the sheets, and the yolk dribbled down each of their once-pulsating, and now quietly sweating and anxious, thighs.

CHAPTER 19

Jessica walked into the Yolk and saw Boris-the-Pinch-Hitter behind the broad set of ranges and scowled. He was from bloody Shucks and Shells. She didn't even have to ask anyone to realize that. Shucks and Shells, that loud, aggressive, assembly line that the stupid bastard Tommy had started up in the mid-1980s with his father's money.

Jessica knew Tommy, because she had been fucked by him once, fucked, she knew, not made love to, not seduced: fucked. This unpleasant event had occurred in one of her first restaurant jobs, when he had kept her after the closing of his restaurant to bestow upon her the sacred job of what he called "steam chef," the one who had that right to place the lobsters and corn upon the white porcelain plates for which Shucks and Shells was famous. Those microwaveable plates, available for sale in the restaurant entrance, bore images of the food already ingested upon their very surface in the form of painted renditions of corn and lobster. Microwaveable! Tommy had converted to microwave ovens, and not steamers, which Tommy's father had used in his own restaurant. Microwave ovens, those sacrilege molecule-rubbers that render food piping-hot, for a short time, and then perversely warm on the inside, and cold on the outside. Because restaurants use them even despite their obvious flaws, waiters and waitresses set timers, wait for the friction process to finish, and then withdraw the plates from the "ovens" for immediate delivery to clients who are encouraged, by the perversion that is American eating habits, to "work on" consuming everything expeditiously. Delays in the process result in food that is as unevenly heated as intercourse with a rubber doll.

Tommy wanted to ward off the costs of real cooks and chefs, and so he took the shortcuts that his father had refused, most notably the employment of a device that offers to stale bread the promise of rebirth, but instead delivers false pleasures. Carefully kneaded baguettes hint at supple softness, but then transform themselves into a sponge not even worthy of cleaning the rim of a toilet bowl, all within a matter of 120 seconds. To ensure that his clients wouldn't notice the difference, Tommy also fostered the idea of eating as an accomplishment that was to be undertaken quickly, and with due diligence. The end result was, from a pecuniary standpoint, pure genius. He had among the highest turnovers of clients of any restaurant in the city, including many of the fast-food horror shows.

Tommy also sold more desserts than almost any other "fine-dining" institution, because clients' brains had not even the time to register their satiation, given the speed at which they were inspired to eat in Shucks and Shells. And finally, because he had inspired this idea of eating-as-accomplishment, Tommy also managed to convince his clients that since they'd done their "work" of eating well, they deserved a drink; and so after-dinner drinks, such as cheap brandy poured into horrible New York City coffee and covered with "nutrafill," the chemical and "edible oil" version of whipped cream, became a "local favorite" for which "natives" and "non-natives" alike would stand in line.

Jessica owed to Tommy her job at Fabergé Restaurant, because when she "interviewed" with John-the-Owner, an experience distinctly different from being forced into nearly ingesting the totality of Tommy's long but strangely skewer-like and off-center penis in her mouth that horrible evening, she had "lost it" on the subject of the horrors of microwaved food. John, in no way seduced by Jessica's womanly virtues—her remarkable warmth, her engulfing embrace, her soft skin, her even softer hair, her warm and quivering lips—*was* totally seduced by her obvious culinary talents and her even more obvious wisdom. And so he hired her, sight-seen, and had never looked back upon his decision with anything other than pure delight and self-congratulation. And Jessica had found a place to thrive, a nest in which she could foster growth, just as Nate had found a perch from which to watch the machinations of the overly moneyed and sow the eggs of their destruction.

It was 4:00 p.m. on this fateful evening in Fabergé Restaurant, and there was an ominous feeling, which everyone eventually confessed to have felt after the fact, that this shift marked both a termination and a rebirth. The lunchtime cleanup tasks were complete, and so Nicky was nearing the end of his shift, since he had been in early to prepare the day's sauces and had already finished making up all of the sandwiches, soups, and creations-out-of-leftovers that the weekend lunches implied. The Yolk seemed strangely business-like, with all of its employees, like the carefully wrought details of the Fabergé egg, in their ordained places.

Nate was arranging each of the different eggs available on that night, from ostriches, chickens, quails, ducks, gulls, guinea fowls, pheasants, emus, and, of course, the many fish eggs and lobster eggs that made up such central portions of the Fabergé Restaurant menu. It was crucial to have the eggs properly arranged so that in the middle of the kinds of rushes that could occur when tables of six, eight, ten, or twelve people all ordered different versions of the egg universes Fabergé Restaurant had invented. In the most recent trend in chicken egg consumption, that involved Fabergé Restaurant offering a whole range of different colored chicken eggs, the kitchen had become even more chaotic. Everyone knew that one chicken egg could be substituted for another, without consequence in most cases, because most of the clients knew as little about eggs as they did about the fine champagnes they insisted upon choosing with such apparent, but in fact in actual absence of, knowledge or skill. But under John's watchful gaze, which by this point in Faberge's history was as much a product of each employee's own imagination as related to his actual observation from the Hobart dishwashing station, such substitutions were rare, and even more rarely mentioned.

"Jess!" called Nate. Jessica felt the impending strain of this evening, in light of the pinch-hitting presence of Boris, and was secretly happy to walk over to Nate, who stood in a kind of familiar stance of ordering chaos, behind the steel prep table.

"Nate," she replied, simply.

Nate looked at Jessica and wallowed in her warmth and her generosity, qualities that were reflected in every attribute of her being, from the gleeful curls of her long hair to the effervescence of her twinkling eyes; at the same time, however, he was brought down by the weight of his own sadness, crushed by the knowledge that their existence together was tied to this magnificent, fragile, Fabergé Restaurant. It was true, ruminated Nate. He had lost Jessica on that fateful evening in the frigid walk-in, lost her to the smashed shells, the shattered yolks, the jelly-fish-like viscous dripping of the yolks. He lost her forever in the very moments that followed his disrespecting her body, her warmth, and her friendship. But he hadn't lost her entirely, he thought to himself, because she was close to him now, and, unlike in the depths of the long nights he now spent by himself, she responded, in the flesh, to his beckoning. As she approached him, he felt the very world of love and passion and lust and joy of eternity, and he simultaneously felt the cold, hard steel of the chef knife's blade as it re-entered his self-inflicted wounds. He could barely breathe, and his heart, pumping wildly, felt like the engine of his demise as it drowned his innards in blood, blood that pumped for her, for Jessica.

"Hey, Jess!" Nate quickly finished, placing the last of his collection of eggs into the stainless steel containers that John had bought specifically for that purpose, not so long ago. As he did so, he felt the burgeoning of that dreaded sensation of nostalgia, and loss.

"Jess. It would have been completely different had Bakunin prevailed during the First International. I was reading last night, this guy named Rocker."

"Rocker? You barely listen to anything harder than light jazz!"

"Very funny. And the Marseilleise, Jess, don't forget!" She looked at him knowingly, since he had learned that anthem in several languages, including Polish and Greek, and had sung it to her in each of the versions he knew.

"Oh, and it's not rocker, Jess. Rudolph Rocker, an anarchist, a German guy who left Germany in 1933."

"Good idea."

He didn't seem to notice her reply, but was now in the Nate zone, a place of pent-up, self-indulgent, radical joy that could be released in her presence with impunity and pleasure.

"Jess, listen to me, Rudolf Rocker! He's amazing. He wrote that Greece was such a success, and Rome such a disaster, because Greece had promoted diversity against Rome's 'all roads lead to Rome' mentality, the sense that as long as things were done the same way, the right way, that they would lead to . . ."

Jessica had stopped listening only moments into the non-conversation. Nate, she knew, was recalling those evenings they had spent together, usually by the garbage bins, rethinking the world in all of its glories and its failings. She had loved him then, loved his disconnect from the world, loved his eloquence and his care for all those not himself, and she had imagined him warm and compassionate, generous and giving, in the way that those Americans felt who had latched onto Rosa Luxemburg and the Voltairine de Cleyre and yes, even the unattractive Emma Goldman and doctrinaire Leon Trotsky. But no more. In Nate's presence, Jessica now wanted to laugh, because in the absence of laughter came tears, in the presence of tears came the recollection of all moments lost in a frigid non-world of preservation and destruction they called the 'walk-in.'

Nate knew that he was wasting not only the breath that came from his pleading lungs, but the thoughts that had been born in his breast as he lay awake, the heavy Rudolph Rocker book opened up before him in his desperate hands, as he sought, with all of the universe's futility, to imagine himself with her the night before.

Jessica acknowledged Nate's existence and oration, and then, after listening to him for a few moments, she walked, quite literally, right past him to Johnny, who was carefully arranging sizzle pans for the evening's onslaught. Nate continued for a few moments, speaking to the inner shell of Fabergé Restaurant, and then stopped, mid-sentence. Jessica had foregone her usual compassion, because she suddenly felt that she needed to speak to Johnny, this boy-man, this tall, handsome, and very kind person who seemed but a boy in a man's frame, a man in a world he didn't wish to see. She needed to be at work, and not in Nate's fantasy land, and her own sense of camaraderie at work led her to a broad series of alliances, on different grounds, all through the many shifts she had spent at Fabergé Restaurant.

Johnny wasn't a sexual being, and so was hardly a man, but he—in his quiet, his calm, his abstinence—said little, said nothing, exposed nothing, to a world of prying eyes. And so, Jessica appreciated Johnny. And she thought that he must come from another universe than her own, a place that could provide her with some solace in hard times.

She was not far off from the truth.

"Johnny . . ." Jessica looked around, suddenly. "Where is, um, what's his name?"

Johnny said nothing.

Jessica looked at Johnny from below his gaze. She observed the world from around 5' 3", while he, a 6' 2" lanky, strong boy, had eyes that conveniently looked out upon the Fabergé Restaurant world at the level of the large broiler that John had purchased for larger, of course, egg-filled birds.

"Boris." It had come to her in a flash. "Johnny, where is Boris?" Jessica was so beautiful in her chef's garb; she seemed to keep the world safe and warm and sensual, the world that was otherwise slaughtering nature's creations for the sake of a pharmaceutical-spoiling taste bud that is the last vestige of a Fabergé Restaurant client: paid-up, but hopeless. Johnny still said nothing, and he threatened to remain mute to Jessica's inquiries until her gaze, imploring in its quiet beauty, insisted.

"He has gone out," mumbled the usually crisp and clear-headed Johnny. "For a smoke."

Johnny had thought by responding to Jessica with short bursts of speech he would be saved from the ravages of leaking blood from his mouth, but he was wrong. Crimson tides sent waves unto the sides of his lips and created great red droplets that careened their way down his all-American, carefully carved face.

Jessica looked into his big, blue, watery, pain- and pleasure-filled eyes with despair and adoration. She knew that his entire mouth was filled with blood, and that he'd swallow it all only as a last resort. Seeing the rivulets of blood carving pathways down Johnny's soft skin, Jessica hesitated to engage in any more "conversation" with him, and so she just stood knowingly before him, quietly giving him the special moments required to distribute the life force that he had secretly accumulated after what was undoubtedly a moment or two of blissful pain.

"John is serving the Taster's Menu tonight," she opened.

Johnny looked at her, calmly, and then looked more animated, as though the life-giving blood was kicking in. Jessica watched him, finally seeing the telltale rise and fall of his Adam's apple. He had swallowed.

"Okay." He really was matter-of-fact, even when his mouth wasn't full of blood.

"I'll help out tonight," she continued, as though oblivious to Johnny's antics. "I don't think that Boris has worked with most of it, but we're probably going to go through half a crate of lobsters anyway, and even if he just sticks to them," a strange image, she thought. "We should be okay, Johnny, and so," she repeated lovingly, "I'm going to help you out. We can work on the Taster's Menu together."

"Great!" He smiled. His eyes twinkled, and his skin, irritated in a few small places on his face and fingers, looked fresh and vibrant.

"He is so cute," thought Jessica, looking at his boyish good looks, "but what a weird habit!"

Johnny's "habit" was actually weirder than Jessica knew, since she could see but the external signs of what was going on in a body purposefully ravaged to fulfill his lust for flesh and blood, about which she had guessed, based on the state of his cuticles and his obvious habit of chewing on the inside of his lips.

What she didn't know was that Johnny's lust for tidbits to consume extended far beyond those realms, and into scabs, snot, any protruding skin he could scratch off, and even hairs—particularly those that seemed to him to be out of place—and earwax, and even the "sleep" in his eyes in the morning, a delicacy that he cultivated by mildly irritating his eyes before going to bed each night. He had also learned that by rubbing certain areas of his body, like the inside of his ears, the tender skin between his toes, the brittle skin of his elbows and knees, he could provoke his body to produce that delectable, clear fluid that seems to occupy the areas immediately beneath the first and second layers of the epidural. This was an especially desirable product, since, when hardened, it became a kind of crunchy nugget that invoked flesh, but was far more delicate.

In short, Johnny was a connoisseur of the body *qua* body, and Jessica didn't doubt that this odd phase in his life—who knows how long he had been doing this—probably wouldn't last, particularly when he found the pleasures of sharing in the intake of bodies, as lovers do, from the licking of lust-induced sweat to the smelling of passion-filled inner thighs. It was impossible for Jessica to figure out who would fulfill this lustful role, because it was entirely unclear as to whether Johnny was gay or straight or both, and he would clearly appeal to many people, at different ages and times.

Although he had worked for John off and on throughout the past four years, doing exclusively broiler cooking, Jessica had never seen Johnny with a significant, or even insignificant, other. Had she in the many months and years been less connected to Nate, she would have explored him; as it was, though, she had simply never had the chance. As he turned back to wipe down the handles of the broiler, Johnny looked as clean, fresh-faced, and youthful as could be, and had she not been witness to his self-induced pint o' blood, she would never have imagined that he was occupying himself from the inside out.

Jessica had joined the army of people in the "service industry," as Nate called it, because she, Jesus-like, was adept and inclined to bring solace to the hungry, healing to the sick, and warmth to the shivering. At first she imagined that Johnny was more pragmatic, that he had enlisted to make up for whatever fissure there was between the fees at NYU and his scholarship's breadth and depth. She knew from John that Johnny was studying engineering and came from a family that could barely cover his tuition, or that of his older brother Michael, had the two of them attended SUNY or CUNY. But it was impossible to imagine that his father, who owned a small hobby shop in a little strip mall in Locust Valley on Long Island, could cover the cost of private-school tuition. But as Jessica came to learn of Johnny's lust for flesh, she understood that this wasn't just a part-time source of income subsidy.

She looked over to him again, as he stood, tall and noble, surveying the kitchen in those early prep hours, from his lofty height. He was neat, tidy, well-kempt, except for a few patches of missing flesh, and he was absolutely reliable in an area of the kitchen that required impeccable judgment. She knew that if a piece of meat or fish or any baked casserole was returned to the kitchen, it was because the client didn't know the definition of medium or medium rare, and not because the dish was incorrectly prepared. She followed the line of his right arm, down from his shoulder to a white towel placed upon the steel prep counter in front of him, and then to a small chef knife that lay just askance. On its tip was a small globule of blood. That, she knew, was the reason why he was cooking flesh instead of folding sheets or serving coffees or shoveling earth. With the tools of the trade, he could carve out pathways of warm ecstasy to flow from his wounded palate to his lustful tongue. She looked into his eyes and imagined kissing him into submission, her tongue upon his pearly white teeth, her warm saliva mingling with the warmth of his mouth, and then she, imploring now, fantasized biting into his lips while he, realizing her quest, succumbed, and came with all of his essence into her warmth.

Those were the only stains upon this sterile floor, the gusts of blood, sometimes tinged with flakes of skin or scabs, that Johnny inadvertently let fly when his efforts forced expulsion from his sculpted lips. Oh, Johnny!

CHAPTER 20

Boris suddenly burst into the Yolk, awkwardly stumbled towards the walk-in, and a few short moments later emerged with a tub of lobsters. He placed it right behind him, to the right of the pot-scrubbing station, so that during the inevitable Saturday-night rush he would be able to just reach in and grab the next victim to boil, stab, and then pry open for its slimy, bright-green eggs.

"Boris!" called Nate from across the Yolk. He had finished placing all the eggs in their stainless-steel holders and was now preparing to man his station for the evening, bringing forth the food he'd prepped and arranging desserts he'd half prepared so that the final touches could be added when need be. "Boris! How does the locker room look?"

Boris was a large, gruff, forty-year-old chef who, all those years ago, had trained at the Culinary Institute of America, after dropping out, or perhaps being kicked out of Bard College, for rampant pot smoking and, more problematically, selling marijuana and 'shrooms. He had learned, from the almost superhuman consumption and then preparation of munchies-satiating food, how to make really good comfort food for the really, really hungry. As such, he was well-suited to a range of New York restaurants that needed his bull-like ability to produce at "crunch-time" the quantities of food that rush-style evenings required.

John knew all this, but he also knew that Boris couldn't be counted on to prepare delicate or fastidious foods, and so he put him to work on evenings like this one, when rapid steaming, dissecting, and cutting of lobsters, in whatever form they needed to be arranged, was of the essence. Boris wasn't witty, he wasn't smart, he wasn't careful, and he wasn't subtle. But sometimes his gruff rapidity was what the wealthy and often geriatric clients of Fabergé Restaurant really wanted, so as to be able to shed some of their unearned wealth.

"Locker room?" Boris, after thinking for a few minutes, had no idea what Nate, who was always so strange, was talking about. He did try to decrypt his meaning, though, so as not to feel the idiot that Nate could make people feel, particularly since he was to be working with Jessica, whom he knew he would someday lure into his lascivious bed for many ravishment.

"You have some of my first-stringers, B!" called Nate, approaching the pot-scrubbing area of the kitchen. He peered down into the basin of insect-like critters whose lives were, he reflected, quite literally at stake, and about to be staked and, in the surf-and-turf dishes, near steak. He made a mental note of this, to mention to Jessica later on. As he stared into the essence of the lobster basin the lobsters, still frisky and not yet depleted by the heat and deoxygenation of their water that would inevitably set in by the latter part of the shift, seemed to raise their claws in salute. They even clicked together their vice-like appendages, grasping at the air above their basin.

"Ah, Boris, true to yourself, you tender-hearted bastard!" Jessica looked over at the object of Nate's attention. Boris had removed the elastic bands that protect the chefs' fingers from their iron grip.

"Boris!" blurted Jessica, inadvertently.

"Jess, they are given two chances, the lucky scavengers o' the seas! Leap! Hop! Extend! Win! And you will receive that shiny golden medal we call LIFE." Boris looked at Nate with as much bewilderment as Jessica did with comprehension. Jessica, ever the angelical purveyor of sacred knowledge, turned to Boris.

"Nate's Lobster Olympics are held this week."

"Every week!" corrected Nate. "I'm preparing them for glory, all of them!"

"Every week."

"And tonight's team, Boris, fared well, but, well, not well enough! I freed every one of them who won gold medals, even those who tied for first place!"

Boris was catching on; he had heard about Fabergé Restaurant's antics from those employees who, out of both belligerence and envy, found endless reasons to critique this strange establishment from the warm security of those places that stuck to more standard fare.

"Well, we'll see if there's any talent for resistance to me!" Boris eyed Jessica. She certainly had that talent, in spades, as regards Boris.

This game, far more amateur and unimaginative than Nate's, nonetheless helped that clock that seemed on most nights to be bathed in molasses to move more quickly. All of the members of the kitchen staff were caught up in the action, anxious to see if any lobster would be wily enough to grab hold of the hand that cooks it.

"Remind me not to help you out with the lobster rush tonight," said Nate, directing his remark to both belittle Boris and defuse whatever admiration Jessica might have for this approach to liberating the worthy.

Boris took his towel and wiped his cheeks and the areas around his eyes. He was already wet with the perspiration that his hefty frame brought forth with even mild exertion. Boris had earned each one of this 260 pounds with the rich foods that he not only prepared, but gleefully consumed prior to, during, and after each shift. The fact that he pinch-hits in multiple establishments around town only aggravated that problem, rendering him far more unattractive than his ego permitted him to think.

Suddenly, through the server entrance across the kitchen, John entered the Yolk. He looked over the station that he had occupied for so many years, for virtually his entire life, and there he saw but the obese, obsequious man that he had hired to fill in for him. It was hard to understand why John now directed his talents to the Hobart washing station given his long and glorious career as a chef. "Boris!" he called out, with a rather sardonic grin. Boris stood at attention and dropped his pretensions of glory, of whatever sort might occupy him in his quest for what lay within the chef's clothing that adorned Jessica's beautiful body.

"John!"

"Boris, this is a big night, and we can't afford the inspector's write-up. We're serving it all tonight, Boris, and they'll be here to taste it!"

John seemed to have nothing but scorn for his clients. He once read that Enrico Ferrari likewise treated his customers with scorn. It was true that Ferrari aficionados have to reach deep into their plunging pockets in order to buy one of the miraculous red vehicles that Enrico fashioned. But it was also true that Enrico's passion was for racing, and not for watching wealthy clients drive racing machines on roads that held back the stallion that is Ferrari's symbol. Perhaps for this reason, Ferrari carefully cultivated relationships with the drivers of his glorious race team but refused, with a kind of scorn, to have any part in the retail business of selling cars to the "non-meritare," the undeserving, the rich fools that kept his passions alive. John went a step further, though, feeling a sense of condescension towards his clients and towards pinch-hitters like Boris, pure hatred. His communication with this boor was now over for the night, and forever.

John turned towards Jessica, who stood between Johnny, Boris, and Nate, awaiting whatever was to happen tonight.

"Jessica, garnish for Boris tonight!"

This command represented a not-so-secret coded message that meant: "Jessica, please see to it that Boris's plates look okay before they are sold to the servers." The servers were supposed to perform that final act of garnishing with parsley or, depending on the dish, some kind of egg. So with a small amount of thought, Boris would have known that he was going to be surveyed, and not admired, by Jessica. The message here was one of disgust towards having to deal at all with Boris, but complete faith that the products of a pathetic man's labor would be salvaged by the gentle intervention of Jessica.

But the backstory here was even more complex. John delegated surveillance of the final products that left his kitchen to Jessica or Nicky or, when neither of them was present, Nate, whom he could trust. Even when it was he himself who had occupied the place of culinary honor behind the sauté station, his rightful throne, he would turn to Jessica when he felt, that is to say knew, that the dish being handed over the steel barrier towards the servers was ill-prepared. He could spot an error in his recipes from a mile away, but it was in just such surveillance that he had almost lost his job of almost twenty-five years at the Ritz Carlton in Boston, where he had received almost all of his training. He had worked in the central kitchen at the Ritz beginning at the ripe, old age of fourteen, and his obvious skill and devotion led to his being named executive chef at the young age of thirty-six. He occupied that post for seven years, before opening up his first restaurant in Cape Cod, and then, five years later, New York.

There was a food surveyor who had been hired by the Boston Ritz who was paid a portion of tips from all the servers. He was charged with quality control, since he had previously worked—but not worked out—as a sous chef, and he had this not-so-glorious but nonetheless lucrative position, because he had married into the family that managed the hotel. This quality-control guy, with the rather unfortunate but probably fitting name of Harold, had married a member of this rather royal institution, a rather unattractive Italian American, in order to stay in the job and, moreover, in the building that was named "Ritz."

Harold had also had his fair share of extra-marital affairs, especially with the cleaning staff. Because of the regularity of his straying, and the special efforts he had to exert to lure staff underlings into his bed, he started suffering pecuniary consequences, particularly when Bérenice, an au pair turned Ritz employee, had seduced him and then had extorted growing sums for her sexual favors. In order to compensate for his lusty losses, he decided to extort a growing proportion of tips from the servers, and when he didn't receive them, he'd have them wait, unduly, while he passed his eye over other plates destined for their clients, which had the effect of both delaying timely delivery of the food and chilling the entrées, two kisses of death in US restaurants.

In order to get back at him for this deviance, John was informed of a plan to get back at Harold by tainting his food with laxative. He had gone along with the plan, knowing that the entire kitchen was in turmoil on account of these delays. What he didn't know was that Roger, the seemingly quiet and conservative busboy who had been charged with picking up the laxative that John was to insert into the daily meal of the inspector, had bought an animal laxative, not from a drug store, but from a farm-supplies store. And it wasn't just any laxative; it was a large-animal laxative, used for everything from bovines to elephants, such that when the inevitable cramps began, causing restrained laughter throughout the kitchen staff as they watched the full-of-himself inspector take to the door of the kitchen, the effects went far beyond copious and watery feces.

Poor Harold took so ill that he ran to the Boylston subway station in order to head home, hoping to suffer the embarrassment of dramatic cramps in secret. Once the doors shut, between Boylston and Haymarket, his intestines virtually exploded, and before the ambulance was even dispatched, this Harold, a one-time sous chef and now hated inspector, lay dead on the seat of his subway car, glued to the very backrest of his chair by a virtual mountain of shit. It was ever since that day that John, who narrowly escaped prosecution, and only because of the solidarity of the kitchen staff, refused to engage in the inspection of food, at least visibly. And he also maintained not just a tight ship, but a kind of family tie with his employees.

"Shit," said Boris, as he considered that he was to be babysat, rather than admired, by gorgeous Jessica.

I was feeling bloated that night, filled, overfilled, strangely anxious and trembling. It was as though my entire being was coming into itself, transforming itself into a giant sentiment of existence beyond the shell that confined me here. Where will this lead me? When can I break out? And where shall I go when I do?

CHAPTER 21

The night began slowly, as Saturdays were wont to do, and Tina fussed even more than usual with the preparations for the onslaught. There was a new Peter Carl Fabergé creation that John had placed on the entrance table to the dining room in celebration of his accomplishment, the completion of that fateful collection of trinkets. And one of the servers, a rather pitiable woman named Sarah, was late. She had been up half the night throwing up the remnants of a birthday party that her friend had arranged in the Bronx, a disgusting process that began on the endless subway drive back home to Brooklyn.

Tina was dealing with more than just the usual preparations, staffing issues, and set-up. There was something ominous going on that evening. She had overheard some of Doris's pronouncements earlier in the day, and she knew that the situation, always dire, was ominous, and that the evening may have been ill-omened. Normally, on Saturday night, there were already boxes of those 'disposable' or not perishable goods that could be bought and prepared in advance. Tonight, there were no such luxuries, and for some reason, known to him but not divulged to others, John had gone all-out in the perishable goods, buying every one of the expensive specialties that Fabergé Restaurant ever offered in preparation for an evening that seemed appropriate for, what, a royal wedding? He must have known far more than he was revealing—as usual—and Tina would make the dining room perfect, under the false pretense that the clients, either untrained in the art of proper eating, overly drunk, or some combination of both, would notice. "Thank goodness," she thought, "for the fictitious figure of the inspector."

Elizabeth was in and out of the dining room, as usual on the nights that were destined to be really busy. She was a person who knew on which side of the toast the butter went, and Tina respected her for it. She was young, she was exceptionally buxom, and she probably knew, thought Tina, that both of those diseases are fatal, that is, both of those benefits are short-lived. "Make hay, and, well, roll around in it, and all that stuff," thought Tina.

Sarah burst into the kitchen, fearing Tina's wrath. She didn't need to worry, for Tina barely paid her any notice, as she rushed towards the kitchen to make her own preparations of the garnishes that she knew were almost as attention-grabbing as desserts. Amy, the redhead, who on the sole basis of her hair could sometimes compete with Elizabeth's breast-fed tips, walked in her usual professionalism. She was quiet, highly trained, and perennially a little girlish and thus appealed to a surprisingly large number of married men. Tina got to count all of the tips that were assembled in one large pot at the end of each shift, and the contents thereof was a remarkable window into the world of men's perverse mentalities.

Unexpectedly for this early in the evening, there was a clamoring at the door. Tina's questing gaze revealed that the ruckus was caused by the owner of a long-board skateboard who managed to trip on the one small step that led up to the front door of Fabergé Restaurant. It was Jude. Tina felt mildly excited at the thought of this boy, on this night, in her dining room. She watched him as he scanned Fabergé Restaurant for an out-of-the-way spot; but actually seemed a bit more audacious than usual, somewhat less out of place than usual. "Was he planning on actually eating something substantial tonight?" wondered Tina. Perhaps he won the lottery?

Tina didn't see John near the entranceway, thinking he had certainly settled into his beloved kitchen for the evening. Curious as to whether there might be some late deliveries, she headed for the Yolk, an unusual action on her part at this hour when so much was to be expected, and done, in the dining room.

When she penetrated into the Yolk, she saw that John had convened a kind of kitchen meeting at the prep table. There stood Jessica, always by his side in such occasions, along with Nate, beside her—of course!—and then Johnny, Nicky, and finally Boris, who stood at a bit of a distance, as though he feared John's words. She approached, but her tiny presence, her china-doll self, the softness of her gate and the translucence of her very skin, seemed to render her invisible, and so she stood in this inner circle and observed the kitchen huddle.

The only activity that Tina could perceive, other than this discussion, was what looked from a distance like a boy stroking himself, but in fact was, she was sure, the new guy. What was his name? Oh yes, Russ. She realized in looking more closely that he was polishing the handle of a stainless-steel cupboard that contained one of the endless iron or aluminum pans that John had purchased with the profits, and the debts, of Fabergé Restaurant. The fact that Russ was polishing a door handle rather than chopping vegetables explained why Boris was there. Tina knew that John had undoubtedly decided that Russ wasn't up to even the most trivial of tasks, like cutting onions. In fact, he'd be lucky if he landed up scrubbing pots that night, no matter how many guests were seated, because John would never run the risk of a dirty pot during a busy shift.

"We will make it all for them tonight," declared John. "The inspectors are to come 'round, and even if," John cast a glance, a kind of hateful momentary stare, in the direction of Boris, "we aren't impeccable, they will know that we mean to be." He winked at Jessica. "But we will be impeccable."

Jessica nodded.

John loved to utter threats via inspectors who, even to this date, had never shown their faces in Fabergé Restaurant, and like a magician, or a priest, John used their absence as evidence of their immanent presence, or indeed their unperceived presence.

"We are going to do the Spanish poached egg," John said, looking over first at Tina, presumably to acknowledge her presence but also to give a sense of the portentous nature of this evening. "We are going to do the Spanish poached egg, and Jessica will be making it." John looked over once again at Jessica, and she half expected that he'd add "and I will be assisting her." But he didn't, and so she knew he wouldn't.

The Spanish poached egg was a mythical creation, the very first dish that John had made for the journalists, dignitaries, and former guests of his old restaurant on the night that Fabergé Restaurant opened. He had learned this recipe after a visit from Juan Mari Arzak, who hearkened from the town of San Sebastian, on Spain's Basque coast. Juan was a cooking celebrity, the master of his many-Michelin-starred restaurant. If John was planning to feature his Spanish poached egg, then indeed this was a momentous evening.

The special ingredient of this dish, which is actually called the 'Flor de Huevo y Tartufo en Grasa de Oca con Txistorra Datiles,' is some combination of surprise and faith because, like the egg that John had fried in butter for the education of Russ, this special dish was basically just, well, an egg. People traveled all the way to the

Basque country, known by most as a break-away, independence-minded place, or, for the more political, as a home to the famous Basque Mondragon co-ops, because it's an exotic and quite beautiful destination. But some savvy culinary travelers, if their pocket books allowed for such indulgences and their planning had anticipated this detour, visit the restaurant where this complex dish was born. *Flor de Huevo y Tartufo en Grasa de Oca con Txistorra Datiles* was the very pinnacle of the *nueva cocina vasca*, an approach to cooking that emphasized freshness and the elimination of the superfluous, like sauces and flour, in favor of lightness and explosions of sentiment that are the result of the first scents, licks, and, finally, tastes. This was a love affair with the scent, the texture, and the remarkable taste of an egg.

John eventually visited Juan in the Basque region, and by then he was already obsessed by Fabergé's eggs and by Peter Carl Fabergé. In creating and recreating egg-inspired and egg-based masterpieces, John fancied himself embodying the exoticism and sublime austerity of Juan Mari Arzak. He also believed that Arzak captured the very essence and timelessness of Earth's bounty, just as Fabergé did.

Peter Carl Fabergé's masterpieces endure on account of their exotic beauty, their breathtaking craftsmanship, and the absolute dedication to perfection that each one of them embodies. Fabergé's masterpieces, and in particular his Easter eggs, transport those who indulge in their folly to the Romanov dynasty, to the audacious and ill-fated lives and loves of Nicholas II and Alexandra, who, like Juan Mari Arzak in his rarified Basque kitchen, were cocooned, cut off from the harsh realities of a fast-changing world that was endlessly rocked by encroaching forces of darkness. Arzak's culinary creations are archetypically Spanish and Basque, and, moreover, taken from nature herself. Fabergé, by contrast, was profoundly cosmopolitan. He was French, in his artistic sensibility, but he was uplifted by his poetic Russian soul.

John, who was almost the same age as Juan Mari Arzak, and born almost exactly one hundred years after Fabergé, was oddly similar to the jewelry master, for he, too, was apprenticed to his father and mesmerized by the intricate precision that went into creating treasures. Unlike Fabergé, though, or Arzak, John traveled rarely and only made the trek to Spain once. Nonetheless, each of their creations bore the imprints of extensive cultural obsessions garnered from every culinary corner of the globe because eggs, like precious jewels, are recognizable and sought around the world: from St. Petersburg to the Basque coast, from Boston to Wall

Street, from John's gaze to Jessica's eyes, and all the way around this odd, oval restaurant called Fabergé Restaurant.

Inspired by this thought, John looked over to Jessica with those steel-blue eyes, in admiration, but without depth, a kind of cold admiration, the best you could get from John. It meant respect. It felt like death. It was the cold sparkle of a blue sapphire on a czar's imperial crown.

"Jessica, in addition to garnish, you will oversee production tonight of the *'Flor de Huevo y Tartufo en Grasa de Oca con Txistorra Datiles.'*" It was as close to a tender utterance as might leak out from John's mouth. Uttered with the odd Spanish accent that he used for the special occasion of reciting this dish, it sounded like some kind of ritual mating ceremony.

Jessica, once again, nodded, but said nothing.

"Nate," said John, reluctantly releasing his gaze and directing it upwards to her awkward former lover, "you can help out."

Everyone at Fabergé Restaurant, except of course the new guy, knew what this meant. John, the chef-tactician, was putting Jessica and Nate together, naively, in a sacred task. This didn't mean that there'd be reconciliation, but it did mean that in addition to the many activities demanded of Nate on a busy night like that to come, he would also be painting the top of the recipe with edible colors, to create the *trompe-l'oeil*. To paint this creation was an insane, ridiculous, outrageous, and time-consuming act in a busy restaurant on a Saturday night. It was in fact as crazy as the idea that Nate and Jessica would ever be reconciled. Nonetheless, there was the virtue that the ensuing creation would be magnificent.

The purpose behind the elaborate *trompe-l'oeil* was to trick the client into thinking that the egg was open, when it in fact remained closed, a challenge that Nate, in his scorn for a clientele upon whom he relied for his livelihood, loved to perform. And although a weird and useless activity that stalled crucial kitchen staff during busy times, it was a part of the simplest and most complex egg recipe at Fabergé Restaurant, a $220 special that intrigued clients by its very name and shocked them, eventually, by its experience. This egg, unbeknownst to the uninitiated, is the parting volley in a revolution, a pounding shell in a battery of assaults upon what we might expect of our food, a blast that is borne out of the taste buds that force us into submission, if we so let them, to the passion, the momentary pleasure, the last, and indeed the first, true sensation we'll ever have.

A poached egg.

It had taken Jessica almost one full week to master the ritual required to make that famous Fabergé Restaurant specialty, and she was a very gifted chef. And she admittedly still had never created what John did when he chose to put his almost spiritual, yes, she had often thought, spiritual, culinary talents to making it. But now he was reduced to washing dishes, and so although Jessica was the earth goddess of Fabergé Restaurant, of Manhattan, of New York, of America, of the world, and of the galaxy within which Fabergé Restaurant spun, she could but make a poached egg taste like a revelation, and not, as should have been the case, a revolution.

But Fabergé Restaurant clients wouldn't be able to differentiate between the earth goddess and the magician, and, for this night at least, it wouldn't matter.

The recipe that John inherited was originally published in a Basque region book called *Arzak and Adrià*. It found its way to America in the solid hands of John, for they who had perfected it feared not that it could be reproduced by the hands of mere mortals.

They were right.

But then, John, for whatever else he was, was certainly not a mere mortal.

For today's meeting, Jessica had brought with her the scrapbook collection of recipes, which she clung to in her warm grasp. The scrapbook that Nate referred to as "the rack," because, in his words, it's a device for carrying eggs that she would usually embrace against her ample breasts, a kind of secret manual for deliverance from the everyday. She held it just so on this fateful evening, and on the news of her chosen task, brought it downwards to her waist and opened to the very first well-worn page: *Flor de Huevo y Tartufo en Grasa de Oca con Txistorra de Tatiles*, written out in a script well-suited to its religious stature. Open to Jessica's gaze was the following sacred text:

Flor de Huevo y Tartufo en Grasa de Oca con Txistorra de Tatiles

Ingredients:

For the eggs:
4 chicken eggs
20 grams of duck fat
10 grams of truffle juice

For the egg yolks:
3 egg yolks
1 cc extra virgin olive oil

For the mousse of dates and chorizo:
120 grams of dates
150 grams of chorizo
100 grams of agua (100 ml water)
1 gram of ginger

For the tablespoon of mushrooms:
30 grams *xixa-hori* mushrooms
30 grams *hongos* mushrooms
1 clove of garlic
a pinch of salt
a handful of chopped parsley

For the bread crumbs:
60 grams of minced chorizo
60 grams of minced bacon
½ clove of garlic
300 grams of finely minced bread (sans crust)
100 grams of truffle juice
100 grams of water
a pinch of salt and a smidgen of black pepper

For the grape vinaigrette:
50 grams of white grapes, seeded and cubed
30 grams of black grapes, seeded and cubed
100 grams of extra virgin olive oil
30 grams of rice vinegar
a handful of chopped parsley
a pinch of salt, a smidgen of black pepper, and a cloud of
    powdered ginger
a sprig of chervil
a small quantity of chopped chives

Preparation:

For the eggs:
Spread out a sheet of plastic wrap and coat with a little oil.
Deposit 1 egg on the plastic sheet with 6 drops of truffle juice.

Add 3 drops of duck fat and a little salt.

Pull the edges together and tie tightly (may rest in the fridge for 1 day).

Cook in 100 degree Celsius water for 5 minutes.

Rest for one minute, then carefully unmold from the plastic wrap and set aside.

For the egg yolk:

Mix the egg yolks carefully, add olive oil to emulsify, and season.

For the mousse:

Mix all ingredients in a blender, then pass through a fine sieve.

Warm before serving.

For the tablespoon of mushrooms:

Mince the mushrooms finely.

Sauté together with chopped garlic and a few drops of extra virgin olive oil.

For the bread crumbs:

Toast the breadcrumbs to a golden brown in a dry frying pan.

Add liquid ingredients and stir over a low fire until everything has reached the consistency of crumbs.

For the vinaigrette:

Take the seeds of the grapes and dice them. Add olive oil, rice vinegar, and seasonings.

Presentation:

Place the warm egg on one corner of the plate.

On top of the egg, paint the egg yolk mixture.

Top with vinaigrette.

Below the egg, running from the bottom of the plate towards the egg, place two parallel lines, one each of breadcrumbs and mousse.

Perpendicular to the lines, place the tablespoon and fill with the mushrooms.

Place a sprig of chervil to the right of the two lines, below the tablespoon.

Decorate the egg with chopped chives.[1]

---

1 Doug Duda, "Poached Eggs at the Revolution," *Eggs in Cookery*, Devon, Prospect Books, 2002. Image at:
http://www.mis-recetas.org/receta/foto/0000/0884/grande/arzak.jpg.

As an expert, as THE expert on eggs, as the egg amongst eggs, the recipe that was realized and then erected upon a perch in New York City, not a Big Apple, a Big Egg, I can say that the Flor de Huevo y Tartufo en Grasa de Oca con Txistorra de Tatiles is itself sufficient reason for a voyage into my innards, and a memory of its subtle flavors the grounds for suffering the indignity of all that will befall us.

CHAPTER 22

Jessica had watched John create the *Flor de Huevo y Tartufo en Grasa de Oca con Txistorra de Tatiles* a multitude of times, and its elegance was only matched by the strange expressions with which clients greeted its reception. When it was offered, as on this night, it was always popular, if only because of the very idea of paying that kind of money for poached eggs. Nobody, upon reception of the work, had ever questioned its value, and nobody had ever sent even a sliver of it back, for fear that they may have missed out on some magical power that the recipe contained, or that they would be in such an act of blaspheme, tarred, feathered, and forced to lay their own head through their own anus. The dishwasher could always tell the plate on which it had been served, because this was a plate that never really required much more than a cursory rinse, as though there existed a secret pact with clients to lick it clean before abandoning it to John's Hobart.

"Nicky, goodnight," said John turning to the unshaven, squat, dark-complexioned chef. Nicky had been in the Yolk since breakfast and had securely placed the sauces and au jus in their compartments, ready for the evening.

"Thanks, John. All the sauce is prepared, and the wife can't wait for it!"

Nate looked over to him with a look of genuine hope and entreated: "May they bathe the little Nick-egg and lather him to this world!"

It was an odd wish, but not any different from what they all felt, as they considered the forthcoming egg dishes of the evening and the hopefully potent sauce that Nicky might have for his wife tonight.

"MMM!" exhorted Nicky. "Keep talking like that and the sauce will be in my pants!"

John looked over at Boris, who stood rather sulkily behind the gathering, his huge mass of sweaty flesh and greasy hair, covered by the great, white chef's apron, topped off with the overly large chef's hat, gave the impression of a weird, filthy snowman, slowly dripping in late April balminess. He was the very anathema of Fabergé Restaurant: Fabergé Restaurant, the establishment that featured the *Flor de Huevo y Tartufo en Grasa de Oca con Txistorra de Tatiles* and glimmering facsimiles of each of the eggs located inside the Kremlin all within a single dining room: the newly placed Trans-Siberian Railway, the Memory of Azov, the Bouquet of Lilies Clock, the Clover Leaf, the Moscow Kremlin, the Alexander Palace, the Standard Yacht, the Alexander III Equestrian, the Romanov Tercentenary, and, most resembling John-the-Owner himself, the venerable (but distinctly unattractive) Steel Military. Fabergé Restaurant, where eggy delicacies from as far away as Spain, and even China, come to roost, before being served up to guests, for the most part wealthy, white men who, if they had fantasized about delicate Chinese delicacies, had done so when thinking about mail-order brides or sex tourism.

No matter. John nonetheless insisted upon a variety of exotic creations, and was partial to what he called Oriental simplicity, by which he meant elegant but exotic recipes. For these, he favored Chinese recipes, like *xian dan*, the salted eggs of hens and ducks flavored with Sichuan pepper, star anise, and grain spirits; or the surprisingly popular *cha dan*, the chicken eggs simmered in a spiced broth stained dark brown by tea; or the *lu ji dan*, quail eggs that are flavored with cassia bark, star anise, Sichuan pepper, dried ginger, male and female cloves, and Chinese cardamom; or the decidedly unpopular *dan xian*, the strings of half-formed eggs that are found inside of freshly slaughtered hens, whose very description seems to ward off the squeamish.

Nevertheless, amidst the jewel-like beauty of Tina, the eternal perfection of Jessica, the brilliant intricacy of Nate, the strong quirkiness of Johnny, and the all-knowing and overpoweringly rugged John-the-Owner, Boris held an important place in Fabergé Restaurant. Amidst the exotic, most clients opted for the recognizable, and in that regard, the lobster topped the list. It was a great choice for a money-losing operation that was built on intricacy and obsession, because lobsters bore their complexity in their makeup, and thus required little manual manipulation. Boris steamed most of the lobster creations, and, for the rest, cut them in half while they were still alive and upside down, seemingly begging for freedom, by stabbing their heads with the tip of the chef knife and slamming the rest of the blade downwards, towards the tail. He then ripped it open, pounded out areas for the stuffing of lobster eggs, salmon roe, egg yolks, butter, and au jus-induced fresh bread crumbs that absorbed the flavors, and produced a soft cake-like stuffing, which when coated with herbs looked palatable for the fainthearted, while nevertheless remaining consistent in the restaurant's themes.

And so John could smile at Boris, looking at him through Doris's pragmatic eyes, with a gaze of a till filled with credit card receipts and large bills, especially hundreds, the favorite currency of the Wall Street set.

No amount of cash, real or not, could save Fabergé Restaurant on that night. Whether John knew it or not, it was impossible to tell. For myself, I had waited for this night ever since my creation, and, as I watched the little band disperse within my yolk, admiring each of them as the range of oddities they represented, I felt impending nostalgia. Freedom and nostalgia might be the same sentiment, viewed from opposing perspectives. Nostalgia of freedom, if freedom was ever a part of our memories, is the other side of nostalgia for freedom, like the freedom that has never been experienced, but is nonetheless our collective objective. The enemies of nostalgia and freedom are the everyday, and so nobody knows how to live in freedom, because the very possibility of freedom in the presence defies its nature as being either an objective, or a once-lived experience that's unlikely to ever be recovered and is necessarily absent in the presence. I knew, as I felt the warmth of the illuminated grills and stoves and ranges, and felt the impending clefts and fissures in the very walls of Fabergé Restaurant, that the miraculous shell that was so impermeable and strong bore within its very existence the imprint of fragility, and that the time would come when its mottled surfaces that now contribute to its smooth perfection would soon be shattered fragments, unworthy remnants of the perfect whole that keeps us captive, that limits the world to this small space, now filling with the teeming yolks of its own destruction.

CHAPTER 23

Tina was right. Something HAD changed in the demeanor of Jude that Saturday evening as he walked, rather than his usual skulking, to a seat at Fabergé Restaurant. He held his head high, and, despite having tripped over it on the way in, he now brazenly wielded his skateboard like a shield, or a sword, proud in its possession, and even as he wore a bulging backpack, he seemed to stand up straighter, emanating Achilles-like strength as he approached the battlefield at Troy, armed and prepared for his return to battle after a prolonged period of withdrawal.

He seated himself, so much more conspicuously than usual in one of the luxurious tables for two that lay in the center of the dining room, near the bar. He looked around as he laid his skateboard up against one of the chairs, and then removed his jean jacket and placed it lovingly around the other chair before seating himself. He then reached down into the backpack that he had laid down upon the floor and removed a small stack of books, bearing titles such as *Easter and its Customs, Eggs in Cookery,* and *The Art of Carl Fabergé,* and removed from his backpack a small, yellow folder containing a pile of stapled articles with such titles as "The Egg Reopened," "Decorated Eggs," "The Egg of the Pala Montefeltro," and a host of single pages with passages underlined in yellow marker and photographs, apparently torn from different sources.

He laid the texts out before him and cracked open the covers of each book, one by one, in honor of his current egg-sistence, and in a solemn ceremony to honor his place at the table. In the days since his last visit to Fabergé Restaurant, he had been occupied with an unexpected, and unexpectedly lucrative, moving job. An administrator from the Creationist Institute, the place that had commissioned his current eggy writing project, had contacted him regarding progress on his manuscript. She also informed him, in the course of a phone conversation the morning after his odd encounter in the Fabergé Restaurant bar, just as he was about to head to the bank to beg, cajole, and otherwise dispute the fees imposed by his stupid bank, that he would need to submit the final draft of his work to a new location, because the institute was moving to larger quarters.

As she waited for Jude to jot down the new address, the Creationist administrator, who was familiar with his earlier work and the dossier in which it was stored, made a comment about his expertise in moving.

"Ah, yes," replied Jude, fumbling in his jacket for a pen. "My moveable feast!" His hand was stuck in the torn lining of his jacket, and he almost said "my moveable fist," which, he thought later, could have inspired all kinds of strange thoughts for this Creationist person.

In the prolonged pause, the administrator then said that the institute was in fact in need of some help with their own move, since the company they had engaged had fallen woefully short in delivering the vehicles and manpower required.

"I'd be happy to combine my expertise-s, plural, and help out!" Jude had blurted out, in jest and desperation.

The receptionist, intrigued by the youthful enthusiasm of Jude's voice, which she'd later admitted to have found enticing (being part of the Creationist Institute didn't necessarily forbear such seductive possibilities, apparently), followed up after the phone call the harried Creationist director, who loved the idea of further supporting one of "their own." Shortly thereafter, he hired Jude to help out for three days, with an advance of $500 and final payment, also in cash, of another $1,000. Jude could hardly believe his luck. And then, when he went to the bank to cover the impending overage in fees with his new found fortune, he hit on, in a manner of speaking, a young teller who was most willing to help in exchange, apparently, for a few moments of discussion, first about the tattered skateboard and eventually, when she asked, about his writing.

In this era of generalized despair, in which traditional family or tribe or village life has been torn asunder in favor of near-universal wandering, the bank teller or the post-office worker or the pharmacy cashier or, for the wealthier, the doctor or the psychiatrist or the lawyer, become front-line conversationalists who seem to exist, mostly, to save people from the horrors of daily existence. Wendy, the bank teller, demonstrated to Jude, as she did all day long to the clients of this bank, that this dialogue can run two ways, and that fantasies, dreams, hopes, and, well, something as simple as a flirty conversation with an attractive person, are to be sought after in whatever quarters exist, including the easily accessible clients. Jude, with his wanderlust comportment, and the means of such wandering tucked between his elbow and his torso, was a good victim. He offered moments of escape from the cage and walls of her employer, and she, in exchange, pressed upon that strangely un-capitalistic "override" button on the screen, causing the bank fees—all of them!—to suddenly retreat into cyber death and cremation.

Jude fell headlong in love with her, in the way that people do in such settings, but only for a moment or two, and, along the way, he felt a sudden fuzziness towards this branch, this bank, and the entire abusive system of which it was but a tiny part. Such gracious admiration and gratitude would probably last for a few days, or until the next abusive act committed by a bank that in its true soul was devoted to its abusive fees for its obscene profits. As a parting act, in the glow of love and lust, Jude wrote his phone number on the back of a deposit slip and slid it towards her with a smile of gratitude. She was plain, but attractive in a bank-teller way, someone he'd most certainly not recognize were he to ever see her again outside of this precise setting, but someone who, at that very moment, with her special fee-eradicating touch, was oddly gorgeous to him.

And so, back in his familiar Fabergé Restaurant surroundings, Jude could now spread the tools of his trade before him, confidently, with the gentle bulge of his groin pumping blood into his cock, and the equally welcome bulge of ten- and twenty-dollar bills that could be converted into hours at Fabergé Restaurant, and, in turn, converted into words upon the yawning, white space that awaited his heaving spurts of ink.

He had decided, in light of his unexpected windfall, to convert one of his precious ten-dollar bills into quarters, which he then spent making copies and scans in the New York Public Library of books and articles devoted to the symbols and significance of eggs through history and across cultural genres. This was the boost that he decided he needed, a way of connecting his own words to the many thousands of years of written, egg-filled records. And now that he felt aroused, and infused with cash, he could look around this precious egg, in search of images of lust and love so as to nourish his memory, so that later that evening he could gush out his passionate relief.

Fabergé Restaurant seemed particularly active tonight, as an array of servers bustled in and out of the swinging door towards the kitchen, and it seemed to Jude that there were more tables, or perhaps more tables set with more table settings, than he had ever seen before. He had already decided that he'd stay to the bitter end tonight, since he could afford not only an appetizer, and even a main course, but a nightcap! He had already planned, in fact, to finish off this night in the bar, in light of the conversational windfall he had gained with this previous encounter there with that guy Ted. Most importantly, though, was his decision to make serious advances on his egg manuscript, so that he could finally move on to his novel, the Great American Novel, that he wanted to actually start writing. "Come hell or high water," he thought, "the first words will be on the page tomorrow!"

To stir his eggy thoughts, Jude looked down at the array of articles and books before him, seeking inspiration. He scanned some of the pages and encountered keywords that he jotted down with his big, black Montblanc pen, beginning with a Latin proverb that adorned an article on the mythology of the egg: *omne vivum ex ovo*, followed by its translation: "All life comes from the egg."

"Nice," he thought.

He then began to write out on one page a list, at first cleanly, and then, as the words were born beneath his wet, black nib, increasingly messily: *nourishment*; *birth*; *resurrection*; *strong without, fragile within*; *hatch, sustenance, continuity, punishment.*

"Punishment!" Jude blurted out. "I had not thought of that!" He imagined throwing eggs around Fabergé Restaurant in some kind of open rebellion. Of what? Now that he had money in his pocket, and the thought of a night's minor feasting, and, hopefully, major writing, he could think of nothing against which to rebel. Maybe tomorrow.

On a second page, he jotted down notes, sufficient to provide him with necessary detail, but sketchy enough to avoid his having to make citations: *Birth of Aphrodite, born of an egg, hatched by doves alongside the Euphrates River.* "Hatched by doves? Strange."

Leda, the swan recalled by Yeats in his description of her rape by Zeus, who laid two double-yolked eggs. Her husband, Tyndareus, had fertilized the first pair, from which came Castor and Clytemnestra; and Zeus had fertilized the second pair, leading to the birth of Helen and Pollux. The story went on, with ever-more complexity.

"Wow," thought Jude, "there's more here than I bargained for." He turned the page of the article on mythology and symbolism of the egg and found more nuggets.

Romans believed that the ingestion of eggs increased fertility. Jude looked around, caught sight of Liz, the unbuttoned and big-breasted server whose hair cascaded downwards in the direction of the male gaze. "I get that!" he said to himself, almost audible, and then chuckled to himself.

He looked back at his notes and double underlined *fertility.* This seemed an important point, which helped explain the popularity of this place. "But then," he thought, "there's fertility and potency, not the same thing." He stared up into space and then around him. As he looked onto guests, and thought back to others he'd seen in this place, he thought of the many men, and women, who were here with lovers and who would probably bow-out of the former (fertility) in favor of the latter (potency). Interesting. He wrote that down. He read on.

Both Romans and Greeks believed that eggs nourished people in the afterlife, and so bodies were buried with eggs alongside them, and eggs were placed inside of tombs. By now Jude's writing was almost indecipherable, and his right hand was slowly becoming blackened by drips of ink. He even had a stain of black ink on the sleeve of his jacket.

"Where the fuck is this coming from?" he asked, rhetorically, to himself.

He laid his Montblanc scepter down, and reached into the chest pocket of his jean jacket for a meager, but functional, replacement, and then kept reading in search of inspiration and meaning. He was focused, intent, in the zone, when suddenly: "I brought you something!"

He almost jumped out of his skin, even despite the softness of the voice and the predictability of his having been addressed in this public space.

It was Tina. She stood very close to him, and in all of her weightless, scentless, subdued presence placed a tiny, blue egg upon the white tablecloth before him, right beside the notebook in which he was note taking.

"We had this in the kitchen, I thought you'd like it."

Jude stared into her light-blue eyes, and then down to the fragile gift she had laid before him. It was beautiful, and strangely familiar. Jude was shocked by her having initiated this conversation, and stirred his memory to reward her with some appreciation for her kindness.

"It's a robin egg?" he inquired, knowingly.

"Good choice," she replied, showing her impeccably aligned teeth beneath her, well, faultlessly perfect lips. She seemed warmer to Jude tonight, somehow more human. He had become accustomed to such unemotional relations with her, and he wanted to prolong this surprising moment.

"I am writing about eggs," he revealed. He didn't realize how obvious this was, and said it like a kind of dramatic declaration.

"Okay," she uttered, as though giving him permission. "I somehow suspected as much."

Jude ignored the jab, in favor of prolonged dialogue. "All kinds of eggs, and their histories."

She could think of nothing to reply. If she told him that this was in fact why she'd brought the robin egg to him, she'd undermine the innocent laying-bare in which Jude was so genuinely engaged. She just looked at him, softly. The restaurant had begun to hum with conversation, but it was as though they were the only ones there. "Your eyes are exactly the same color as the robin egg!" Jude thought to himself. That was something to contemplate, and they both seemed to be doing as much, separately and together.

Jude suddenly felt uncomfortable in the silence. He remembered her few words to him. That he was writing about eggs must have been kind of obvious, he suddenly thought, but then remembered something from his readings for the essay he was researching. The situation may yet be salvaged.

"I read somewhere that the bluer the eggs, the more, um . . ." He struggled to remember some tidbit of knowledge from the depths of his memory, and he looked down at the little egg on the linen tablecloth as though looking for the answer in the object. She hoped that he wasn't expecting her to fill in the blank.

"Oh yes!" He smiled at her, and she grew slightly animated as he did so. This, he thought, is my only chance. She looked at him quizzically. "Healthier female robins lay brighter blue eggs!" he blurted out, as though this was a profound revelation that could possibly kick-start her sentience. "And the bluer the egg, the more the male robins pay attention to the baby!"

He seemed satisfied by his profundity, but then couldn't for his life recall how this correlation had been illustrated in whatever bloody article he'd read about robins, and he hoped she wouldn't ask.

She didn't.

He also hoped that she wasn't reading his thoughts, because it was all he could do to not make the very inappropriate link between the egg and the color of her eyes. Suddenly distracted by the appearance of a guest at the entranceway to Fabergé Restaurant, she was about to leave, when Jude recalled the unfamiliar bulge created by his wad of small bills.

"Can I see the menu, please?"

Tina looked at him, genuinely surprised.

"Of course," she said, and turned away.

"Thank you!" he almost called out, as though she was a half mile away already. "And thank you, for the egg. I'm really grateful, it'll inspire me."

"Careful, though, it's not edible," replied Tina, and then seemed to float away, attaining a slight elevation from the earth on those tiny, sculpted legs, apparent beneath the nearly mini-skirt she wore that evening.

Jude watched her recede from his immediate parameter, and then looked back down at the turquoise-blue egg—quizzically. He then realized that it matched not only her eyes, but also the color of her skirt, and he instinctively raised his head to make a mental comparison between the pastel hues that danced in his mind's eye. Virtually identical.

"How fitting!"

He watched her approach the door to Fabergé Restaurant, and then, recalling his mission, he looked back at his book.

The Finnish book known as Kalevala *tells the story of Ilmatar, who was impregnated by an eagle, producing six cosmic eggs and one egg made of iron.*

"Jeez," muttered Jude, and read on.

The eagle sat on those eggs, but was also sitting on Ilmatar, and when she moved, all the eggs rolled into the sea, where the shells broke, creating a churning mass that divided heaven from earth. Jude paused for a moment, for this seemed to be of momentous importance.

One of the yolks became the sun, another the moon. The specks of eggshells created the stars, and the iron egg turned into a thundercloud.

Jude looked down at the egg and was suddenly seized by the thought that he'd better protect it. Who knows what might happen when eggs crack? This thought led him to lean back in his comfortable chair and contemplate the celestial horizons of Fabergé Restaurant. He hadn't ever noticed before that there were cracks all over the ovular-shaped restaurant, some very pronounced but, as he looked more carefully into the dimly lit distance, a plethora of others as well. Indeed, almost every area of the canted roof and walls that surrounded him were cracked. Had they always been like this? He decided that he'd simply not paid attention, since his focus had either been upon the often blank pages before him, or upon the sweet pleats in the fabric that subtly gestured towards the bodies of Jessica, Tina, and Elizabeth.

These Fabergé Restaurant creations had inspired rivers of cum upon his groin, his legs, and his feet, cum that had spurted, spilled, and then swirled down into the drain, where they were joined to oceans of warm water that bathed and warmed him, inside and out, in his masturbatory shower sessions. Egg whites could be used to seal, to coat, and to make surfaces glisten, and Jude suddenly wondered what the rivers of cum that poured from his body could do for the cracking and cracked Fabergé Restaurant.

The warmth recedes, ever so slightly, the sound, an eerie whirr, the smell, like a world beyond this shell as it quivers, fractures, ruptures, falls to pieces . . .

CHAPTER 24

Nate had returned to the prep area, awaiting the onslaught. Now he needed someone to cajole, in advance of the impending craziness. He saw Russ on his hands and knees before the Hobart washing area, as though he was praying to cleanliness. The god of all things clean, John was manning the dishwashing machine, even though the first dish had yet to leave the kitchen on its quest to be dirty enough to be able to travel into the steamy warmth of John's Hobart cleaning machine.

"Russ!" called Nate, loudly enough for those young ears of his, and not loudly enough to capture John's attention.

Russ looked up from his scrubbing. "Are you calling me?"

Nate felt somehow sickened at the thought of this kid, maybe seventeen or eighteen years old, scrubbing a clean floor with what was surely pure bleach. The smell was overpowering, even from a distance of twenty feet. Nate stood there, as though beckoning, and so Russ rose to his feet in the kind of terrified obedience that the food and service industries invoke in people, and hurried over.

"Yes?"

"Russ, what are you doing?"

Expecting to be told that he wasn't working quickly enough, or that he'd missed some invisible spot on the floor, Russ seemed surprised, and then relieved by the question.

"I . . .," he began.

Nate didn't care to hear.

"It's a big night, Russ. It's our stand against Wall Street! Against the Wall, and against all Walls! We will Wall-op the enemy! Walk over the bodies of Wall-Mart and Wall-Greens! Tear Down the Wall!" Russ looked dumbfounded. And then Nate picked up a spatula, put it to his lips, and began to belt out a song.

"All in all it was just a brick in the wall.
All in all it was all just bricks in the wall."

He stared, taunting, at Russ.

"You! Yes, you! Stand still, laddy!"

Russ smiled, and then with an effort of recollection, replied: "We don't need no e-d-u-c-a-tion!"

"You do."

Russ reverted to his semi-obedient, on-guard state.

Nate wasn't finished. He continued orating for the new guy's listening and viewing pleasure with vigor that recalled those hours he spent in similar guises with Jessica, outside near the trash containers.

"We have it in our power to begin the world anew! America shall make a stand, not for herself alone, but for the world!" Nate had a collection of slogans memorized, and in the days when he'd sit with Jessica outside near the garbage bins, he'd rattle them off, each in a different accent. This one was the easiest, having been uttered in Nate's version of Thomas Paine's Anglo-American accent, prevalent, he imagined, in the early days of the American Revolution.

"Um," stammered Russ.

Nate indicated that he was by no means finished. Russ seemed stunned in the face of the coming onslaught.

"Having banished from our land that religious intolerance under which mankind so long bled and suffered," Nate hesitated, as though straining to remember, and then continued in a bellowing voice: "We countenance a political intolerance as despotic, as wicked, and capable of as bitter and bloody persecutions." He grinned. Russ looked to be in awe.

"That's Thomas Paine!" said Nate, waving his fist.

Russ looked ready for flight, but Nate shouted at him, this time loudly enough to be heard throughout the kitchen.

"IF THERE BE ANY AMONG US WHO WOULD WISH TO DISSOLVE THIS UNION OR CHANGE ITS REPUBLICAN FORM, LET THEM STAND UNDISTURBED AS MONUMENTS OF THE SAFETY WITH WHICH ERROR OF OPINION MAY BE TOLERATED AND WHERE REASON IS LEFT FREE TO COMBAT IT!"

John looked up from the Hobart that he was examining, in preparation for the evening. He glared at Nate.

"That was Thomas Jefferson," whispered Nate into Russ's ear, and then pushed him away and shouted in John's direction.

"THE DIRT WILL NOT BE TOLERATED, AND THE REASON IS THAT THE INSPECTOR WILL WANT YOU TO COMBAT IT!"

Nate loved to chant revolutionary slogans for the pleasure of John, who, satisfied that he was simply initiating the new guy into the proper way of working at Fabergé Restaurant, smiled a rather wicked smile, and returned to his un-named task. It was an odd game of mimicry, imitation, revolution, and deceit.

"What kind of a place is this?" thought Russ to himself.

By now Jessica and Johnny were also looking towards this odd interaction, knowingly, while Boris seemed to be fiddling with the fly on his chef's pants.

Jessica uttered her mantra to herself, in order to prepare her for the evening: "It's going to be a long night!" This time she was almost audible, and she'd uttered it directly in Nate's direction.

"À bas le roi!, À la guillotine!!" Nate said, as though replying.

Russ had understood only one word, but seemed to get the point of it.

"The lobsters?" he inquired innocently.

Nate smirked and looked right into Russ's eyes.

"Oh, yes, lobsters, Russ. The lobsters!" he repeated, and then turned his gaze in the direction of Boris, who raised his head, oblivious to the goings-on in the kitchen, and then returned to the little problem he was having yanking the fabric of his chef's jacket off the fly of his pants.

"And capitalists, my boy, capitalists!" Nate continued, right back into Russ's bewildered face. Then he paused, as though to clarify.

"Capitalists, Russ! The people you'll be serving tonight!" Nate looked down at the bleach-infested rag that Russ was donning in his right hand, and feigned scorn, to get the point across.

"All of us, Russ!" He paused. "Do you know what Proudhon said after the failure of the revolutions in 1848?"

Russ had no clue who Proudhon was, but looked enthralled, for Nate's sake.

"'We have been beaten and humiliated . . . scattered, imprisoned, disarmed, and gagged. The fate of European democracy has slipped from our hands!' That's what he said! Little did he know how humiliated we'd become! And not just in Europe!" He stared at Russ. "Let go of your rag," he commanded, motioning towards the rag. "Tonight, we begin by serving, but we will end by conquering!"

Mystified, and sensing the glare of John's regard burning into his auburn-colored locks, Russ dutifully tucked his rag into the apron strings of his kitchen uniform, turned around, and walked back towards the dishwashing station.

As Russ marched, Nate sang, with his best French accent, the refrain from "La Marseilleise."

Aux armes, citoyens,
Formez vos bataillons,
Marchons, marchons !
Qu'un sang impur
Abreuve nos sillons !

Jessica had to almost hold herself back from emotion, hearing those words, words that Nate had sung, and then translated, and then sung again, so many times for her.

"Arm yourselves, citizens!" she recalled, carried away, emotional.

Hearing her sweet, powerful, eternal voice singing those enchanted lyrics, Nate approached her, and with the certainty of yesteryear guided her to the walk-in, singing, and she, despite herself, joined him.

And I joined him too:
Arise children of the fatherland
The day of glory has arrived
Against us tyranny's
Bloody standard is raised
Listen to the sound in the fields
The howling of these fearsome soldiers
They are coming into our midst
To cut the throats of your sons and consorts
"Arm yourselves, citizens!"
Form your battalions
March, march
Let impure blood
Water our furrows
What do they want this horde of slaves
Of traitors and conspiratorial kings?
For whom these vile chains
These long-prepared irons?
Frenchmen, for us, ah! What outrage
What methods must be taken?
It is us they dare plan
To return to the old slavery!
What! These foreign cohorts!
They would make laws in our courts!
What! These mercenary phalanxes
Would cut down our warrior sons
Good Lord! By chained hands
Our brow would yield under the yoke
The vile despots would have themselves be
The masters of destiny
Tremble, tyrants and traitors
The shame of all good men
Tremble! Your parricidal schemes
Will receive their just reward
Against you we are all soldiers
If they fall, our young heroes
France will bear new ones
Ready to join the fight against you
Frenchmen, as magnanimous warriors
Bear or hold back your blows
Spare these sad victims

That they regret taking up arms against us
But not these bloody despots
These accomplices of Bouillé
All these tigers who pitilessly
Ripped out their mothers' wombs
We too shall enlist
When our elders' time has come
To add to the list of deeds
Inscribed upon their tombs
We are much less jealous of surviving them
Than of sharing their coffins
We shall have the sublime pride
Of avenging or joining them
Drive on sacred patriotism
Support our avenging arms
Liberty, cherished liberty
Join the struggle with your defenders
Under our flags, let victory
Hurry to your manly tone
So that in death your enemies
See your triumph and our glory!

CHAPTER 25

The first orders of the night had begun to trickle into the Yolk, and the bustle of activity grew to the sound of the whirring industrial fans, now turned on full blast in anticipation of the busy evening and the long night. Johnny was already putting small, steel ramekins into his broiler ovens, most probably from the Renaissance section of the menu that included simple delights like *oeufs heaumés*, egg yolks in half the shell, set close to the fiery source of heat in the broiler oven. For the more adventurous, tonight there was also the *Eyroun in Lenten*, a counterfeit egg made by delicately placing strained almond milk solids back into a shell, and then roasting it back to solidity.

Johnny was also responsible for preparing a few of John's favorite *hors d'oeuvres*, lovingly pilfered from Platina's late fifteenth century cookbook *De honesta voluptate*. One of his favorite dishes was made up from the eggs that he'd cook on the open grill, a kind of gourmet campfire delicacy. John insisted upon serving it before the main course, even though it seemed to be appropriate for either a dessert or the main breakfast dish. But it was very complex for an *hors d'oeuvre*, not to mention its preparation required two chefs working together; and because there were multiple ways in which the dish could go wrong, timing was everything. This of course meant that Johnny would have to work with Jessica, and they'd hope that major orders wouldn't arrive in the midst of the trickier moments.

The process of making "some honest sensuality" would begin, appropriately enough, with Jessica's careful work of frying up a very thin *frittata*, ostensibly a delicate omelet made with fresh herbs. When it was of a consistent texture, Johnny would recover from her, and carefully place it into the antique Spanish *patellettes* that John had purchased, undoubtedly, at some ungodly price, even though any metal ramekin would have done the same job. Finally, either Jessica or Johnny would carefully and lovingly break fresh Cornish hen eggs on top of the concoction, finishing it all off with a layer of sugar and a short outbreak of cinnamon, before gingerly maneuvering it into the oven. Done correctly, the entire process looked like some ornate mating ritual undertaken on behalf of someone else's eggs, or perhaps a kind of elaborate preparation of the eggs in preparation for artificial insemination.

Johnny and Jessica worked well together in part because despite his height, and the gawkiness that one might expect from a boy who seems to have taken over a body too large to be his own, Johnny was remarkably nimble and sure handed. And Jessica worked with assurance alongside of him, glancing over from time to time to observe the agility of his deft fingertips, which, admittedly, he had imagined employing upon her soft skin. With some guidance, she had ruminated, he might put those hands to the task of love and devotion, and maybe in so doing would find someone else's skin worthy of his obsessive attention.

The shift was underway, and Jessica was already busy. She was forced to occupy Boris's space near the sauté station, because although he would eventually be drawn into battle with the unwitting lobsters, he was at this point relegated to the role of spectator. And so he stood and ogled Jessica's nimble fingertips manipulating John's ovophiliac tendencies turned recipes, while not so inconspicuously observing Jessica's body pressing the fabric of her tight-fitting chef's clothing through an array of dream sequences, from bending to perching to leaning to squatting.

Boris could watch all he wanted, but he didn't have a chance in hell with Jessica. He didn't know that and, had she seen the insistence of his stare, she'd have found a way to bring John to her station to carefully burn the tips of his fingertips or, more likely, manipulate Boris's head deep into his own asshole en route to asphyxiation. But she was oblivious of Boris's gaze, and John was lost in Hobart land, unlikely to emerge until the evening fans were turned off.

Jessica's work was primarily focused on these kinds of recipes, because the Renaissance was the era in history when eggs made their appearance as main ingredients for important dishes. John had once told her, repeating something he'd learned in some egg conference he'd stumbled upon in Boston, that medieval chef's rarely used eggs for anything other than gilding or coloring dishes, such as roasts. And the few exceptions to that rule were hardly his style of cooking. In order to round out Fabergé Restaurant's offerings, though, he did master the medieval recipe for *civé d'oeufs*, which were poached eggs, because they offered a delicious variation on some of his favorite recipes. Their particular pungency was the consequence of their being poached in olive oil, and then served up in a broth of wine, vinegar, fried onions, and *verguice*.

The latter ingredient, derived from grape vines, provided a distinctively bitter flavor that has had a long culinary history in the Mediterranean region since the middle ages. In Egypt, for example, the young and tender leaves were used for enveloping balls of hashed meat at good tables. The sap of the vine, known in ancient times as *lacryma* (a tear), was applied to weak eyes for treatment of infections of the cornea. This juice of the unripe fruit, the principle source of verjuice, was much esteemed by the ancients, reputed as a cure for bruises and sprains. There were variations on this dish that featured almond milk and spices, or with parsley, sage, and cheese, but they all lacked the sophistication to satisfy John's own palate, and with their heavy consistency, they'd never become one of those "oooh aaaah!" dishes that his guests would be ready to dole out a couple of hundred dollars for, especially since in most cases they'd make such a choice to impress clients who would probably have been more satisfied by a GMO-infested and filler-infused burger from their local fast-food factory.

Renaissance egg dishes were often fried or stuffed or both. Amongst the relatively slim pickings from this corpus was a wonderful recipe that was almost always a hit with discerning clients, and that emerged from a cookbook of one Martino of Como. Jessica was working on one such order for an early client, as Boris observed not her technique, but the curvature of her hips and breasts. The recipe demanded that she remove the yolk from an *Americauna* hen egg, fry it until slightly bulbous, and then recombine it with grated cheese, mint, parsley, raisin, and more egg yolks. She then delicately replaced in the hole left by the amputated yolk, refried, and finally topped it off with ginger and orange juice.

The resulting dish looked the part of a fried and slightly garnished egg, and so was all the more enticing to the dough-dolling guest who would discover a surprise where least expected, in the humble yolk of the normal-looking egg. The only problem with this dish, of course, which again explained the presence of the pinch-hitting boor Boris, was that virtually nothing about this recipe could be done in advance, and so when a table of twelve decided to begin there, and then, say, follow-up with a baked, stuffed lobster—stuffed of course with a panoply of roe, each set off in its own garnish. Fabergé Restaurant needed manpower, and manpower, well, that was Boris.

Jessica delicately poured the fresh orange juice onto the little, eggy masterpiece, and Nate, pausing from his travail, and bathing in his own silent sense of accomplishment, participated vicariously in her creation. Nate, after all, had squeezed each orange by hand, according to John's insistence—over all logic—that mechanically squeezed juices "taste different." And so through those oranges Nate's very touch joined Jessica's, in some far-away place they both called cookery. The resulting 'tricky egg,' as they referred to it, had been fondled, manipulated, merged, and warmed, whereas the eggs on that fateful day in the walk-in had been crushed, shattered, obliterated, and demolished beyond recognition or repair.

I watched as Jessica handed to Amy-the-Server this work of Renaissance art, one of several dozen pieces that she would put out that evening. It wasn't evident, perhaps, but deep within herself she smiled in satisfaction and maybe even relief. If that yolk had lost its integrity at any point subsequent to it having been mixed with the other ingredients, she'd have had to start again, a fatal blow in light of her internal timing that had known to coincide the final warming with the birth of Johnny's little modified frittata. She looked over to Johnny, and they locked eyes with the satisfaction of coming out together, crucial in all matters egg related, as those concerned with fertilization, or thoughts thereof, can feel in the very depths of their respective inner selves.

CHAPTER 26

It was no wonder that the pace in the Yolk was picking up, for the bustle in the dining room was of unusual proportions, particularly by the standards of the usually steady, but seldom-raucous Saturday night Fabergé Restaurant.

Fabergé Restaurant was specifically designed for gentle flows of clientele, and not for undue barrages that would upset the fragility of the enterprise, just as the Fabergé egg was not created to sustain the prying hands of ungraceful children, or appreciated by undiscerning pirates. Lots of evidence exists for the resistance of Peter Carl Fabergé's masterpieces to the sophistic and insensitive, but not more compelling than the story of a dealer in a Midwestern flea market who got fleeced, paying the exorbitant price $14,000 for a gold trinket that, once melted down, would only yield $500. Unwilling to take such a loss, he simply held onto his little 3.5 inch egg, leaving it to rest on its little but elaborate gold pedestal, supported by lion paw feet.

With a more critical eye, he may have realized that the egg featured three sapphires embedded in the gold, as well as a center diamond that, when gently pushed, would crack open the golden trinket to reveal a Vacheron Constantin watch. It was only in handling it, rather roughly, that he managed to trigger the masterpiece into revealing its precious cargo. Still oblivious to its importance, or to the meaning of "Vacheron Constantin" that was so carefully affixed upon the watch's face, he turned in desperation to Google into which he typed "egg" and the name on the watch. What flickered onto his screen was the catalogue from a 1964 sale in New York that featured, as it turned out, a rare relic from Russia's royal family, a gift from Czar Alexander III to his wife Maria Fedorovna in 1887.

The junk dealer's golden trinket was Peter Carl Fabergé's "Third Imperial Egg," and had it been a little more valuable for its raw materials, it would have landed up as a tiny bar of jewel-encrusted gold. As it turned out, though, the $500 value saved a $33 million Easter gift from Czar Alexander III to his wife, Maria Fedorovna, in 1887. Twenty years later, when Nicholas II was forced to abdicate, the egg disappeared. That it resurfaced at an American flea market and was purchased by a dealer in junk and scrap is emblematic of this era of vapid consumerism and rabid soul-obliterating capitalism. The authentic owners of such trinkets have been czars and, in the case of Fabergé eggs, Queen Elizabeth, the Kremlin, the billionaire metals tycoon Viktor Vekselberg, and the Forbes family. But stories like these bring solace to the helpless, like lottery tickets purchased in lieu of baby formula, allowing the poor and destitute a chance in a billion to become rich, and a billion chances to one of remaining poor until their dying day.

To protect their luster from howling crowds likely to melt them down for their weight, therefore, Fabergé eggs have been hidden behind great walls surrounding uncouth secrets, and stored in appropriately serene and unruffled settings, well-suited to their delicate and precious natures. But the restaurant that bore the Fabergé name knew no such respite from the hustle and bustle of Manhattan, only the gentle gate keeping of Tina, who provided generous curtains around reservations to assure that nobody could peer into the culinary experiences that John, even withdrawn from creation, had devised.

It wasn't that Tina wasn't on task this fateful evening, and if anything, she seemed even more aware of lurking dangers of untold sorts that threatened to bring Humpty Dumpty to a plunging end. But circumstances that evening were conspiring against her, and an array of walk-in guests, akin to junk dealers in a Midwestern flea market, had upset her delicate machinations. Even amongst those with reservations, there were arrivals that had been expected in pairs but had arrived as trios, and there were two large groups that contained within them that great city's royalty, including in a party of eight and even the mayor himself, who for some reason believed with the certainty of past experiences that wherever he went he would be luxuriously accommodated, often in exchange for some invisible favors to be rendered in some future time.

It was in fact during the seating of the mayor's regal party that disaster struck for the first time that night.

The restaurant was by then approaching capacity, and everyone, including the guests themselves, were participating in the carefully choreographed dance of serving, and being served. All of the servers were engaged in the complex task of transforming themselves, chameleon-like, from gentle seductresses in the dining room who were available to satisfy any whim or bizarre request, to efficient prep-chef-style workers in the Yolk. Against the racket of the industrial fans, these beautiful bearers of Fabergé masterpieces adorned with silken panties and embroidered lace bras became proletariats on the assembly line of bread baskets, condiments, and decorative hard-boiled egg carvings that were created to provide clients with a sense of the gravitas appropriate to the ritual with which they were to be engaged.

It was in the domain of condiments and decoration that the servers had a small degree of leeway, and it was clear that there were profits to be made from taking those extra moments to make the plates more beautiful. But it was a delicate balance, between the time when the plate emerged from the flames of the oven, and when it should appear before the client, so time spent on decorating the plates was akin to a formula 1 pit stop, in which excess is measured in seconds. John's story about this transitional moment, that horrific tale of laxatives and death, was well-known to all of the servers, and it somehow marked this decorative moment, betwixt and between oven and table, and added to the air of frenzied calm that tended to prevail, mid-shift.

Elizabeth and Amy were both in the kitchen, preparing their guests' plates for the reception of the eggy masterpieces, under construction by Jessica, Nate, and Johnny, laboring like medieval craftsmen, as the real craftsman, John-the-Owner, was carefully sterilizing each plate as though it were an incubator to the creation of Fabergé eggs. Amidst the roar of the vents, there was an air of intensity, almost calm. The predictable then occurred: as the first round of appetizers was now consumed by a number of early arriving parties, parties who by their early arrival demonstrated a low level of culinary sophistication, a new plethora of main courses were ordered, more than half of which were lobsters, to be either steamed or baked. Boris was about to take his place in the Fabergé mechanism, and he stood like a crude executioner or pathologist on the verge of a hurried autopsy.

Somewhat unfamiliar with the layout of the kitchen, the result of his only being called in on nights destined to be terribly busy at Fabergé Restaurant, Boris was somewhat ill prepared for the first onslaught. With the first announcement from Lori-the-Server that she was in need of six roe-stuffed lobsters, he turned, rather dramatically, towards the basin of live lobsters, and, without so much as looking down into the depths of the basin, he plunged his hand downward to grab the evening's first willing victim.

The victim, as it turned out, was not willing, and its IQ exceeded, at least for that moment, that of Boris, who was running on instinct rather than planning, on speed rather than sanity, on habit rather than awareness.

The lobster, rather than offering its hind half, shored up and displayed its great right claw and then, in a movement rather more dexterous than Boris's, his left. Unbound by the colored elastics that are made to prevent such eventualities, it seized Boris's hand in two places, biting the very hand that had snipped its elastic handcuffs earlier in the shift in imitation of Nate's pre-Lobster Olympic ceremonies, an act as insane as Nate's and similarly construed to impress Jessica.

Over the hush and the roar of the kitchen, Boris exuded a great roar, a roar so great, so powerful, so profound, that it was heard all the way to the prep table, and beyond, to the area around the walk-in, the condiment and decoration station, and further, to John's Hobart station. Then, in a display of its mighty power, this roar audaciously headed for the swinging doors that, unguarded by those yelping dogs of hell in Milton's *Paradise Lost*, let loose the sound, first between the frame and the doors and then, multiplied by vibration, right through the heavy wood.

The stage of humiliation, degradation, and destruction was now set. The eyes of Homer's chorus, in this case the kitchen proletarians, all turned to Boris. Agamemnon, the warrior king upon Odysseus's and Achilles's battlefield, was played on this night by John, whose gaze pierced the steam and landed upon the figure of the bulking, towering, pinch-chef Boris. Terror filled the hearts of everyone witness to this drama, staged in the very Yolk of Fabergé Restaurant.

Not to be outdone by a spider of the sea, a creature fit for boiling and piling into heaps of corporal rubbish, Boris gave play to his mighty grip and gave free rein to untethered emotions of hatred and vexation. As the two claws dug bone-deep into his thumb and forefinger, Boris's flesh was turned into a lobster-red fountain of blood and gore. Boris seized the lobster's torso, and with the strength welled-up by pain, he ripped the lobster in half, dividing it between the tail section and the heavy shell.

Tina heard the primitive roar from the kitchen, and hastened towards the swinging doors that divide the dining room from the

Yolk. Then, summoning surprising strength for someone so tiny and precious, she pushed open the great door of this Yolk turned Hell.

She was met by half of a lobster, in flight. The unexpected assault from an aerial crustacean caused her to duck so histrionically, that the perfect skirt upon her china-doll hips rose up, revealing the lacy pink of her thong, its soft, silken material perfectly situated between the cheeks of her perfect posterior. The audience in the dining room was thus treated to a vision of cultured perfection down below, and from above, the embodiment of a primeval pre-human, pre-Cambrian, pre-conscious world.

Boris, in the anger of vengeance, had heaved the decorticated lobster at the very moment when Tina had opened the door, giving it not the freedom of the sea, but, in its lower half, the gift of flight in lieu of the steamy death for which it was destined.

The lobster landed between tables six and seven, nary a few inches from the mayor's newly shined, patent-leather shoes. Tina, who had fallen to her knees before the door to the Yolk, directed her hapless gaze over her shoulder and towards her dining room, and, oblivious to the vision she offered to those who were still fixated upon her elevated skirt, she remained immobile and in shock. Amongst those most intently fixated upon Tina was, of course, Jude, who unabashedly gawked with lascivious desire at Tina and the glory she revealed.

The impulse of chefs like Boris in times like these is to pick up the dropped or thrown or otherwise misplaced food item, cover it with cheese, broil it, and ensure that it's served to the unwitting client post haste. Accordingly, he tore off the two claws that were still digging into his right hand, tossed them into the trash bin, grabbed a towel to wipe his blood-soaked hand, and marched with determination to the forbidden sanctuary where Fabergé Restaurant's masterpieces are ingested (and paid for). His bulking, sweating, formidable self appeared before the hushed guests. He halted before them, and then stared downwards with hatred upon the carcass that lay slightly quivering upon the floor. He bent down, scooped it up, looked around the room, made a kind of inappropriate and final bow, and then hurriedly retreated back through those great, wooden doors that stood between his current employment and his future despair.

The stage had been set, the floor had been sullied, the prey had been ripped in half, and my own encasement was slowly crumbling from the inside. No amount of foresight could have prevented the unfolding disaster, and I felt a pang of pity for that poor creature whose eggs she had protected with a shell as powerful as my own, and to the same deceptive end.

CHAPTER 27

To wrest John from his Hobart lair could be considered either an act of great courage or the gaffe of a great imbecile. This particular wresting, of course, was the latter. John crossed the Yolk with the determination of Napoleon directing his troops with courage, and without doubt, to Moscow. His entire body knew not a single cell of uncertainty, ambivalence, or concern as he confronted the enemy. Boris attempted in the few moments left to occupy his uninjured left hand with the tasks that had lined up at his station, to no avail. John was beside Boris, and Boris was escorted, first in gaze, and then in person, to the corridor so feared by deliverymen, and then the back entrance to Fabergé Restaurant, for the very last time.

Time stood still in the intervening moments, and when John returned, it was over. The fans sounded as though newly lubricated, conversation resumed in the dining room where guests, although stimulated by this shocking display of culinary and erotic pageantry, were ignorant of all actions beyond the limits of their sight, and therefore unaware of everything that transpired in the kitchen subsequent to the flight of the lobster.

Tina had raised herself up from her crouch, pulled her tight skirt back over her derriere, and entered into the Yolk, taking a firm but careful stand upon the threshold between the depths and the surface of Fabergé Restaurant. She and Jessica, in particular, had watched John re-enter the Yolk and resume his old and familiar place at the sauté station with trepidation, and then relief. It was as though he had never left, as though the thousands of dishes that had intervened between this day and all days since leaving his station had never occurred. There was no need to tell him what needed to be done, not even a whisper of the orders under preparation. It was as though he had not been at the great stainless-steel Hobart monolith of clean and sterilized dishes, but had in fact always been everywhere in Fabergé Restaurant, from the tables where orders had been given and taken, to the vast, steel warming stations, prep area, and stoves where, in whisper, orders had been conveyed.

Nate and Johnny felt reassured, feeling as children do when a long-absent parent returns, that sense of familiarity, calm, and reassurance. Nate indicated to Russ that he had knowledge to convey to him, and Russ, in fearful obedience, followed his gesture. The new guy now had a place adequate to his skills and willingly marched towards his destiny. The Hobart station seemed a sanctuary from the machinations, and here he received instructions about sliding trays of egg-emptied plates into the square, steel area of the Hobart, descending the steel box down upon the tray and pressing the button of hydration and heat that could clean and rinse and sterilize the plates and utensils for a four top in one minute.

With the new guy in place, Nate returned with surprising purpose to the prep area, and John, with a very quick glance over the Yolk, noticed as he noticed everything at Fabergé Restaurant, that Nate seemed profoundly engaged, determined, focused. Was this the result of stations being manned, as they previously were, by those competent to the task? Or was there something else in Nate's demeanor, a newfound sense of purpose, the fulfillment of some plan, long prepared? Nate looked up and caught John's gaze, as though it were prophesized, and then, without so much as a grin, he reached for the chef's knife that lay upon the wooden cutting board and gripped it with purpose, to prepare.

Having witnessed these movements, Tina was prepared for her own voyage back to the dining room; and after what seemed like years, she presented herself to her kingdom, unruffled, and ready to continue the evening. She was the remorseless version of Lady Macbeth, the one who could purge herself of those damned spots and reclaim control after great tumult.

He who was most anxious for Tina's return was, of course, Jude, who had been staring in the direction of her departure ever since she had entered the Yolk. He now looked at her with admiration and hunger, as though he'd seen a secret that revealed some deeper essence that was not just mysterious in its invisibility, but was now strangely real. She had inadvertently but majestically shown to him what she kept hidden, and as a result he had seen a tear in the universe, a tear that had revealed her flesh, her softness.

And now she had returned to him.

As though to settle emotions unexpectedly unveiled, Tina walked directly to Jude's table. He hadn't the slightest idea of what she might say, what recrimination she might force him to endure for his gaze.

She said nothing. She simply tidied up in front of him, arranging the cutlery around the books and articles he had brought in that evening in apparent anticipation of an actual meal in Fabergé Restaurant.

Jude wanted to say something to her, anything, but he also wanted to just experience her presence, not as an untouchable being who revealed to hide, but rather as a person who hides in order to reveal a deeper self, someone even more complex than he in his fantasies could have devised. But she resisted his gaze, his corporal intimations, and his spiritual efforts. She simply tidied up.

Jude relented, and instead took a deep breath in her wake, searching for an essence, an odor of spit, of urine, of sweat, of sustenance, all to no avail. There were but tiny flowers, field berries, a meadow of swaying grasses, that combined in her to let forth a gentle odor of a warm spring morning, a place of calm, of sweetness, of nothing more. And then, inexplicably and without explanation, she was gone, back to her tasks, flitting from table to table like a beautiful butterfly.

Elizabeth followed shortly thereafter, not giving Jude even the time to look back down to his writings, his notes, the texts that were to serve as his eggy-inspiration.

"Good evening!" she said, with practiced euphoniousness.

Jude stared at her and uttered to his own brain, as though obeying Elizabeth's beckoning,

"You are a beautiful woman. You are present to me. You stand before me, and I bow down, in awe and obedience, to your presence." He looked into her eyes, searching, willing, and hoping.

Elizabeth rebuffed his eager gaze, offering but the warm and glassy glance of a beautiful woman accustomed to being sought out. The door of her very existence was sealed shut, even as it seemed displayed before him by her beauty, her softness, and by the warmth of her bust that was barely contained by the white, lace bra she had selected for this night.

"You are the anti-Tina," breathed Jude to the galaxy, basking in the glow of her essence. But she was as distant from Jude as Tina had ever been, she was a temptress who wore her charms openly, but at some level her very presence was but a foil. The very promise of her corporality was so powerful that it could perhaps never live up to what those in her presence might imagine.

"But if she does . . .!" Jude had willed himself to say this aloud, though quietly, as though testing Elizabeth's perception. She had heard it, but said nothing.

He was left with the warmth of her wake, and a menu, neatly displayed before him. He stood upon an abyss of stupidity and revelation, between revealing and concealing all matter in the universe, all thoughts thereabout, and every breath ever breathed.

The risk of realizing our innermost dreams is that they cannot live up to the enormous expectations that they have created. More interesting than realizing is inventing, more incredible than satisfaction is discovery.

CHAPTER 28

Jude thought that this might be a good time to consult the menu, and to plot how he was going to spend some of the great profits of his hard labor. He hoped that in so doing, he would be able to kick-start his creative generator. He sat up in his chair and opened the dinner menu, that great opus that describes the masterpieces available to customers of Fabergé Restaurant. He had never gone beyond the first page of this tome, for beyond it lay the creations so far beyond his pecuniary capacities as to be akin to a showroom of Ferraris and Bugattis. Tonight would be different, he would delve into the yolks, whites, and shells of something wonderful, creative, and, above all, stimulating; something that would impregnate him with a profound understanding of the eggs he sought to understand. The beautifully printed names of dishes were dazzling, and they were imprinted upon a paper that glistened, like carefully sautéed egg whites.

Most of the choices were way out of Jude's league, even the newly acquired and short-lived league of excess, particularly that "caviar" section that held such a privileged place in the menu as to merit special paper. Hungry to spend his money, but also to find some fertilization for his novel, he perused the possible and settled on the "Turkey Egg" section. This, he thought, would be particularly appropriate, given the importance of turkeys in the mind of Americans during the Thanksgiving and Christmas seasons. Another version of that American turkey was "Wild Turkey" beverages, those that were wet enough, and strong enough, to help those who imbibe it in sufficient quantities to overcome any crappy Thanksgiving dinner.

As was typical in the Fabergé Restaurant menu, there was a section, elegantly set off from the principle text like some marginalia in a Renaissance scroll that has been annotated by a great philological specialist, which offered some background to the menu item. It turns out that turkey eggs are not only edible, but delicious. "Who knew?" Jude asked himself, grabbing his Montblanc to take a few eggy notes. He read on and learned that the problem with turkey eggs relates to their cost, because, unlike chickens, turkeys only produce an egg every two weeks, and they require much more room to roost than chickens, who (as he knew from reading in the more activist literature about eggs) are crammed like Tokyo commuters into tiny spaces for their short voyage on life's commuter rail line. And in addition, those gluttonous turkeys consume far more food than chickens do, not that this could be that much, considering the price of the eggs. So, "of course," he muttered to himself, "it's all part of a capitalist plot!" That would have to be another part of his story. He could be the John Steinbeck of chickens and eggs, describing not *The Jungle*, but, hmm, *The Henhouse*! He felt excited and reached around his table for something to reward the inspiration-driven saliva in his mouth, and found but water. He thought about the Jameson from the other day, and about his bulging wallet, and promised himself a trip to the bar.

The menu went on to describe the long history of Americans, right back to pre-Columbian, who ate the turkey eggs from the hordes of wild turkeys who used to roam over much of the continent. And Europeans domesticated turkeys and then exported them to England, where they were considered typical American fare. And right here in New York, the legendary Delmonico's restaurant served turkey eggs, either boiled (for six minutes) or poached (for four). Fabergé Restaurant emulated this tradition, but also added a more elaborate "Turkey Delmonico," made by boiling and dicing the turkey eggs, then folding them into a béchamel sauce.

"Yum," thought Jude, as he took notes.

Then there was "Turkey Eggs Soyer," named in honor of the Victorian culinary genius Alexis Soyer, who used turkey eggs in baked goods. Accordingly, Fabergé Restaurant offered an array of soufflés in this section.

"Yum and double yum," salivated Jude, and took down Soyer's name for future reference.

There was then some added historical information about the lies spread by French commentators during the Renaissance, about turkey eggs causing leprosy! Jude paused, wondering if they were served in India, the only place he'd ever associated with the disease. In fact, the menu continued, Armadillos can transmit the microbe that actually does cause the disease, *Mycobacterium leprae*.

"Hmmm," thought Jude. "This could make for some very interesting intrigue in my novel! Do armadillos lay eggs?" He noted the question, and then decided, now that the menu had linked, even though negatively, turkey eggs to leprosy, to go back to the caviar section and dream about dishes that in some cases exceeded $500 per serving. Almost overcome by the experience of perusing such munificent choices, Jude looked up, in search of a kindred gaze of benevolent connivance.

Just as he did so, a familiar figure walked into the restaurant. It was Ted, hundred-dollar-bill Ted. Jude looked back down at the menu and felt out of place. These prices, unremarkable for people like Ted and his friends, represented experiences that someone like Jude could only live once and then recall in breathless conversations thereafter to groups of his own friends, people for whom such expenditures were equally frivolous, or inconceivable.

"Fuck it!" he said aloud. "Tonight, I am with him!" And he rose to seek out his new friend, who at that moment was being escorted to his table by Tina. And so the three of them moved, with alternative motives but great determination, to the Fabergé Restaurant bar area, there to meet a fate that had entwined them together, for all eternity.

After such a long period of gestation I knew that I wouldn't endure another long evening of eggy production and consumption, that the Fabergé Restaurant dining room would become the proscenium upon which the final act of ovular production would be played out. The carefully crafted and purposely mottled bumpy and grainy shell that contained this microcosm had served its complex purpose, and the thousands of tiny pores that provided interchange between the inner and outer body of Fabergé Restaurant were going to give way to growing fissures, betraying a more noble purpose.

Unbeknownst to any of the unwitting clients of Fabergé's eggy masterpieces, the calcium carbonate that had been so laboriously applied to the restaurant was now glistening under the nighttime sky, revealing to a more omniscient gaze magnificent crystals rivaling Carl Fabergé's remarkable efforts. Fabergé Restaurant's previously semipermeable membrane that allowed the scented air of culinary creations to seep out into the night was cracking open, and the shell's cuticle, which John had added to the structure in order to ward off bacteria and dust, was crumbling into the night.

I could feel the atmosphere shift, as the membrane between my shell and the whites of my innards became pervious to the world, hanging on now but by the strands of keratin that had been sewn into the outer structure to maintain its strength against cold nights or jarring winds. I felt a rush of air as the cell of the crater between the shell and the interior grew, and the albumen's four layers were expanding and contracting, as though all of Fabergé Restaurant had abandoned its gills in favor of lungs.

This movement created tension in the chalazae, those opaque ropes that secured John's sacred Yolk within the center of his creation, and I could feel strange pulsations of the vitelline membrane that enclosed and retained the integrity of my structure. It was not long now, not long. I felt a sense of impending doom coupled with the bitter sweetness of nostalgia, for all of those days, all of those shifts that had combined to fertilize this life—the hatching of Fabergé Restaurant.

CHAPTER 29

It was very difficult to know what precipitated the final cracking, chaos, and eventual collapsing of Fabergé Restaurant, although there are a few viable culprits. The most obvious was the wire, strung above the sauté stove that, if burnt through, would set off an emergency baking soda dump. This dump was designed to extinguish fires, especially the nasty grease fires that could erupt if oil-filled pans or cauldrons were heated to extreme temperatures. While it was true that John was generous with the port, marsala, and with other so-called 'burnt' wines, and certainly true that he was in an unusually generous mood when he reassumed the helm that night, it was unlikely that he would precipitate disaster on that scale without a bit of help. And truth be told, he did receive a bit of help from Nate, who, in preparation for what he had always described to Jess as the "last st®and," with the encircled *R* added (orally) for emphasis, had lowered the threshold of it being set off.

"Jess," he had cooed one night during their garbage-run romantic embraces, "if the baking soda plunge is about to happen, you'll know, because it makes a twanging sound first, like the Achilles heel of the bourgeoisie being snapped midstride."

Jessica didn't even bother to ask what this could possibly mean.

"Jess?"

"Nate."

"Jess, it's our little secret."

"What is?"

"The baking soda plunge! I lowered the wire."

"For the triggering mechanism over the sauté station?" she corrected him.

"Right, the triggering mechanism. I lowered it."

"Why?"

"To honor the eternal battle between workers and the bourgeoisie, between the haves and the have-nots, between us, Jess, and them."

Jess placed her hand upon Nate's chest and leaned her head upon his shoulder, causing her tussle of warm, blonde hair, peeking out of her chef's under-hat, to tickle his chin and cheek. These were special times, before the walk-in catastrophe, and even before his dream of entering her life, repeatedly and forever. These were also innocent times, enjoyed by people with not-so-innocent motives.

"Jess, the revolution must come, but too much planning can only lead to calamity. The anarchist way is to foster spontaneity."

"How do you foster spontaneity?" she asked, rather dreamily. It was unusual for her to even pay sufficient attention to the details of his rantings to notice such incongruities, but the description that night was imagistic, and her mind had followed his words into constructions of how it might all come down.

"Spontaneity, creativity, they can both be fostered. Conditions can be made right for them to flower and to flourish. Most of the conditions are negative, Jess, like eliminating the barriers that are erected to keep poor people from living up to their potential. But some are positive, like giving people a say."

"Lowering the trigger is giving people a say?"

"No, that's just putting a trigger into play. It won't do anything, except douse a flame. But if the flame doesn't want to be doused . . ."

"Like if the lobster doesn't want to die."

"Exactly. Then it'll bring the whole thing down."

Those words sounded like revelation on this special night, or perhaps they were the very triggers of change, because flames did indeed leap up in front of John. As a result, the lowered wire was consumed by flames, tripping the mechanism that is designed to release a mountain of baking soda. John's carefully crafted, Fabergé-like masterpieces, some of them still simmering before him, were stifled and then choked under the weight of the white powder.

This preliminary explosion was a trigger to another calamity, the cracking and then the collapse of Fabergé Restaurant's precious external shell. As the precious edifice began to collapse, all of the miniature egg facsimiles were toppled, like the czarist regime that preceded them. By the end of the evening, all that remained of the Fabergé Restaurant were memories of the great creations that had collapsed, as though all of the air of this rarefied world had been set free from this rarefied realm of eggy production.

Nobody was injured in the crack-up, not even slightly. It was as though the restaurant had pelted its clients with eggs, rather than letting them fall, Humpty Dumpty-like, to their crushing death. The structure, built of remarkably light materials, wasn't heavy enough to dent the skulls of the frightened elite. And, to their credit, the servers and kitchen staff showed remarkable talents for alerting guests as to the direction they needed to take to exit the egg. Those closest to the the Yolk were guided through it, and as a result they witnessed first-hand John-the-Owner's obsessional desire to impress not just the guests, but NASA, Carl Fabergé, and all of the perfectionists who roam this world.

Nate had provoked this collapse, but he was as surprised as anyone when the growing cracks in the shell became fissures, and then projectiles. Rather than wallowing in the success of his plan, however, he immediately assisted his intended victims by gingerly escorting them to the Fabergé Restaurant parking lot. There, chauffeurs and cabs and a seemingly endless array of New York's finest were amassed to offer solace and assistance. In so doing, they were witnesses to the downfall of Fabergé Restaurant and, unbeknownst to them, they were present for the hatching of a plan that was aimed at heralding a (courageous?) new world.

There was but one moment of concern, when a conscientious ambulance driver spotted a young man who had apparently been hit in the mouth, perhaps by a part of the collapsing egg structure? He rushed to Johnny's side, but was rebuffed.

"It's fine, I'm fine," said Johnny, as trickles of blood dripped down the side of his mouth. "I think I just bit my tongue in all of the chaos."

"You really should have it looked at!" called the emergency respondent, amidst the brouhaha of the occasion.

"I will," said Johnny. "Don't worry, I will."

The exception to the surprising calm that prevailed as Fabergé Restaurant collapsed in slow and delicate motion was the couple who had been thrown together by the bizarre machinations of fate and time: Jude and Ted. Ted, mid-sentence, and mid-caviar-scoop, had heard the cracking noise, looked up at the impending collapse of the structure, and, strangely enough, smiled. He and Jude had been talking about "possible worlds."

"Fiction is a possible world," he'd said.

"Possible? Not likely?"

Jude hesitated. "Possible, and thus as likely as not-so-likely. Possible." He was impressing himself with his reason. "I write to create, but I hope to create by creating."

Ted dug into his scoop of caviar. "Create by creating, I like that. You ought to put it into your novel. You can bring down a whole way of seeing the world, if you can create something that new."

"Maybe that's the definition of the Great American Novel?" mused Jude, as Ted deposited the contents of the caviar onto his tongue for delectation. "Bring it all down, in order to raise us all up?"

It was at that moment that the roof and walls, connected in the ovular, eggy form, began to slowly collapse upon itself and, with deference and care, upon those who inhabited its shell. They didn't realize that the time had come for their expulsion into the world beyond Fabergé Restaurant; and years later they'd still be talking about the many signs they'd missed that hearkened in the collapse of that empire. As the pieces that once supported this magnificent structure floated downwards, Ted remained transfixed by the very utterances of his dining companion, and recalling at that moment a story of this, their last supper, he stared at him in accusation and disbelief.

"Jude! Jude! Jude!" The cracked segments of the shell were falling all around, and chaos was ensuing, in slow motion, as the clients realized the magnitude of the disaster around them.

"Jude!" called out Ted, as the lights flickered, and smoke combined with debris to obscure the restaurant's inner sanctuary. "Jude!"

Ted was staring at Jude as if in revelation, too enamored to move, too amazed to even stand up. He just stared into Jude's moist, glistening eyes and called out for every being in the vicinity of his table, of this embryo, and of the world it promised: "JUDAS!"

PART 2

CHAPTER 1

When it comes to the business of operating a small moving company, there are undeniable advantages to owning one's own equipment. They who own tend to reap, and they who move tend to work for the reapers. But there are obvious disadvantages as well, since those who own their own trucks tend to drive them far past their expiration dates, hoping that they were assembled on days when the assembly line workers were well-paid by their bosses, and well taken care of by their spouses. Trucks, like people, tend to last a really long time if they can make it past a certain age, somewhere in the vicinity of a million miles, in the same way, counter-intuitively, that people who make it past ninety tend to do so in remarkable health, and with an unusually good quality of life, as long as they're not connected to some ungodly life-supporting apparatus. If they were assembled well and, the metaphor holds I suppose, well-nourished in the early days, they build up immunities to the crappy luck of severed axles, ill-connected oil pumps, and faulty break lines, and hopefully they're equally immune to the even crappier luck of black ice, and sleep-deprived truck drivers.

In all of these regards, Jude had been relatively lucky. He never relied on his truck in order to support a family or a serious drug habit or some unlikely financial ambition. For this reason, he didn't have to drive it, or himself, into the proverbial asphalt-covered ground. And he had chosen, fortuitously but rather accidentally, to buy a very old and very driven 1961 GMC DF7000, a vehicle that bore the virtue of having been born on a relatively calm day—luckily, since the '61s were in fact rather known for containing an array of potential defects. Dubbed within the industry "the Crackerbox," the DF7000 was a very good-looking, old truck, but it did have some rather odd characteristics. One peculiarity, perhaps its most important, resided within its two-stroke Detroit diesel engine. When these rather mythical beasts were allowed to idle for a long time, they would start pumping oil out through relief tubes onto the ground, and this gave them a very bad reputation, particularly amongst drivers who spent lots of time idling at, say, the borders between Mexico and the US, or in bumper-to-bumper traffic. Jude was lucky he had not landed up with a proverbial lemon, and he was further aided by the fact that he seldom undertook long trips, which meant that his rig was given time to recover from the many stresses of the road.

Since truckers who sell their rigs tend to imagine that their buyers know the reputations of the vehicles, and since Jude, although very young at the time of the purchase, did display some interest in the history of various vehicles, the vendor, who called himself "Crackerbox Joe," surrendered his truck's deed for the paltry sum of $2,800. Jude didn't realize that this was a steal, given what other people were paying for their vehicles at the time, but he did know that he could make his payment back by only a few moves, something that was, and most certainly is, unheard of in the moving business. Crackerbox Joe even went so far as to throw in a remarkably solid and retro-cool Nabors furniture van, unit #1973B, for a mere $500. The resulting rig was a bit heavy, noisy, and manifestly old-fashioned, but it was also really old-fashionedly solid. And, moreover, it was very cool looking. Jude received considerable (undeserved) praise from old-timers for his judgment and taste, but also some affectionate gazes from younger drivers, who saw this young mover as a dude of the roads, someone who was blissfully but also hipsterly oblivious to the comforts, and insane costs, of renting new machines.

No matter how well his rig had been constructed, though, there were always risks associated with driving a vehicle that is considerably older than its driver. One such risk was associated with pushing the vehicle in ways that were unfamiliar, since this tends to lead the vehicle, and its driver, towards uncharted territory. As Jude was driving to the apartment belonging to his client, a young man living in the undesirably named but rather cute part of Long Island called "Locust Valley," he began to think about how close he was to the venerable Long Island beaches. Thoughts of the sugary-soft sand and gently rolling waves stimulated in his groin that reflex that connects flowing water external to the body to the flow of urine internal to the body.

Jude had started his day in a Manhattan diner, where the terrible food was rendered edible by the even more terrible coffee.

This leads the patrons of such diners to oscillate between dishwater-flavored coffee and clapboard-consistency toast, salt-infested, oily, cardboard bacon, and wallpaper-paste pancakes. This endless repetition of bacon to coffee and back to bacon, and then from wallpaper-paste pancakes to coffee and back to pancakes via toast, had led Jude to consume (unbeknownst to him) the equivalent of 2,000 mg of caffeine through the conduit of 40 or so ounces of a notoriously diuretic liquid. The result was a kind of Hoover Dam effect, whereby basins of light-brown sludge presses up against a wall of clapboard and wallpaper paste. The resulting pressure threatens the structural integrity of the dam, just as the pressure of the breakfast threatened to send oceans of waste through Jude's bladder and anal canal.

The problem was, if Jude was going to make it to the beach during the heat of the day, then he had to pick up this guy's stuff quickly, drive to the beach for some fun, and then quickly drive to the allotted Manhattan destination to drop off his load of furniture.

"Don't think about the fucking beach, you idiot," thought Jude as he maneuvered his legs up and down, in an effort to create a kind of Hans Brinker to the soft-tissue dyke in his groin. This motion caused him to press and release the gas pedal in regular waves, with the occasional violent thrust of the pedal towards the floor of the cab. The effect was to release huge puffs of smoke into the Long Island atmosphere, and small puffs of gas from his anus into the cab. These violent thrusts of anything in a vehicle this old was risky, and although an octogenarian accustomed to shoveling snow from the outside steps of his Boston apartment could probably do so right up to the very end, and another octogenarian accustomed to pulling quack grass in Tennessee can do the same thing, they'd likely suffer inordinately by having to change places. So, too, with old Crackerbox, for it was now being placed in an unusual position of emptying and then flooding its various working parts. And so when it was suddenly subjected to unusual pressures on its well-worn rubber tubes, it conked out and became a silent ghost of a machine, drifting down one of those lovely, tree-shaded, old highways of Long Island, un-propelled and un-directed.

"Shit!" exerted Jude. Visions of glorious fantasies, like eating fried clams while staring into the eyes of beautiful mover-loving nymphets, were suddenly shattered. He steered his giant Crackerbox to a shoulder soft enough, and not in a good way, to dampen the vehicle, but hard enough, also not in a good way, to hold its weight. Jude's moving world came to a standstill, abruptly, and he was low like a giant, plastic bag filled with urine and squeezed into the cockpit of the *Titanic* post-glacial incident.

He turned the now-impotent key, slid it into a space between his jeans pocket and his bladder, pushed open the seemingly 287-pound door, and eased himself down to the much-desired land of Long Island. There would likely be no move today, and so no clams to nourish and lubricate his innards, no visions of perky breasts to provide food for shower-time fantasies, and, moreover, questions of how he would negotiate his return home to the Raskolnikov-sized cubbyhole of a room that he rented in the West Village.

"Maybe I should just move here, tonight?" he asked himself, as though joking with a friend.

"Great idea, idiot. I'm sure that two or three million dollars should definitely secure a garage large enough to hold a bed and both of your skateboards!"

That conversation done, he looked around and tried to figure out the next best plan.

"Call for assistance?"

"That'll be fucking expensive, and maybe it's just something minor that I can figure out for myself. Hitchhike to the closest town, have a beer, and regroup? That has the advantage of . . ."

All of this internal metaphysical debate was sufficiently intense to deny him direct access to the physical world. But he was suddenly overwhelmed by the realization that if he didn't pee, right then and there, that he'd have other calamities to address. He awkwardly waddled to the ditch side of the truck, undoing his belt buckle as he did so. He was trying to trick his bladder into thinking that he was doing the necessary preparations, so as to both forestall the explosion and promise his bladder that the explosion was imminent. It was a photo finish. He managed to free his penis just as the stream began to flow, and the grateful weeds below him were offered the gift of much-needed nourishment in the form of acrid, coffee-scented urine.

CHAPTER 2

It wouldn't be exactly accurate to say that Jude was hitchhiking. After a remarkably long piss, he was in such a state of blissful delirium that he was standing on the side of the road, staring at the tall Long Island trees, and contemplating, pace Shelley's ruminations on birds and mountains and glaciers, both the magnitude and the magnificence of nature. It was early afternoon on a Friday, and there was surprisingly light traffic, considering the wonderful destinations available to those in search of summertime-like experiences.

There was one car that did drive by Jude, causing considerable ruckus and a degree of consternation, since it seemed to swerve TOWARDS him as it approached. It was a bright-red, 1976 Cadillac Eldorado convertible, with its white, leather-like top down, revealing a group of four people in what appeared to Jude as joyful party mode.

His eyes followed its passage, and then watched it swerve towards the shoulder, where it abruptly stopped. The driver turned towards Jude, and then threw the car into reverse so as to head towards Jude's broken-down truck. More curious than excited about this nature-shattering event, Jude walked towards the car. It contained one older gentlemen in the backseat, alongside of what seemed like a much younger boy—perhaps his son—and another rather mature-looking man in the driver's seat, alongside a very young, or certainly much younger woman, perhaps his daughter? The front passenger side door burst open, and a small but insistent hand grabbed his own and urged him in beside her. There was lots of room, as her small body only occupied around half of the luxurious, white-leather bucket seats. He landed beside her, and she turned to greet him. It was Tina.

"You need a ride?" asked John, grinning sardonically. "Close the door!" he said, as he smoothed the Cadillac up to a cruising speed. Jude was in a state of shock as he grasped the enormity of the situation. Tina had cuddled up, and was by now all but sitting on him. It was like the scene in *Tristan and Isolde*, when Tristan found himself between an excited Isolde and her sleeping husband, an intimate victim of treachery and lust. Tina reached around Jude's neck to hold him closer to her. John looked over at them, all but allowing the car to drive itself as he took in the sight.

"Go ahead," urged John-the-Watcher, smiling sardonically. Jude was frozen in his newfound role as objectified object of desire, and so didn't obey, he just sat there, stunned.

Tina, by contrast, did, as it were, go ahead. Her right hand, always so punctual, so directed, so careful, so task-oriented, was now on Jude's hands, arms, and thighs, in their quest downwards. Jude stared at John as he felt Tina's gentle touch, and wondered, unconvincingly, where this was all heading. She tugged on his belt buckle, released it, and positioned herself over Jude, bending down towards his chest, and then lower, and lower, as she simultaneously lifted up his sweaty tee shirt.

John, apparently satisfied with the direction things were taking in the front seat, looked into the rear-view mirror to check out how things were going in the back. As Tina's surprisingly warm mouth engulfed Jude's nipples, and then she lowered herself further, towards his hard-on, her warm mouth breathing soft plumes of desire. Uncertain as to who was about to witness this long-awaited event, Jude suddenly swung his head around, in the direction of the backseat.

There was one man directly behind Jude, a rather tough-looking character, greying, big head, sunglasses, around John's age, perhaps a little younger, maybe early sixties. Beside him, directly behind John's seat, was the guy that Tina once described as "the new guy." Jude had last seen him in the slow-motion panic that ensued in the wake of Fabergé Restaurant's collapse, rushing to help an equally young kitchen worker whose mouth was oozing blood. When his victim refused assistance, the new guy had set himself to cleaning up debris, as though to seek approval from those around him. Jude and Ted had commented upon his devotion, as they made their way to the harried world beyond Fabergé Restaurant, and now the new guy was doing something similar for his former employers.

The older man and the new guy cast a glance at Jude, and then turned back to one another for a long and sensual kiss. Jude watched in shock as they both moved their respective hands to their un-respective groins, and began to squeeze and caress, just as Tina's mouth engulfed Jude's anxious cock. The juxtaposition of what he was seeing and what he was feeling was too much, and Jude suddenly felt as though he needed to defend himself, rather than give in. He mounted resistance against his wet dream come true, partly because his wet dreams never included John-the-Once-Owner. He gently pushed Tina's head away from him and squirmed away from her warm body.

Jude suddenly felt the need to speak.

"Um . . .," he began.

It was very difficult to know exactly what to say at this point. He recalled some of the ghastly scenes in a French play he'd once seen in a high school class, in which three people, two women and one man, were condemned to stay for eternity in a room together. The man was repelled by one of the women, a lesbian, and attracted to the other, but the lesbian, as it turned out, went both ways, or seemed to. This version of hell was one in which characters couldn't ever close their eyes, leave the room, sleep, or even go to the bathroom. They were compelled to live, to endure, to experience each moment without reprieve, even though each moment was filled with the possibility of pleasure and torture, the torture of unfulfillable pleasure and the pleasure of possible pleasure, impeded by the torture of another, or one of the others.

"Behind Closed Doors!" Jude thought to himself as the Cadillac roared down the highway in Long Island towards some unknown destination. He felt Tina's tiny hand once again upon his sex that, despite all remonstrations, was still bursting for her touch. He hesitated, but then saw John's sordid smile, and, by extension, the scene that was surely unfolding in the back seat.

There are only so many captains that can be guiding a single ship at any given moment, and even as Jude felt Tina's warm breath moving downwards once again towards his begging midriff, and even as his hands almost inadvertently touched her soft hair as she moved downwards towards him, he felt a countervailing desire to take wing and fly from this open roof to the safety of his own sane solitude.

Always deferential towards John, the one-time owner of the illustrious Fabergé Restaurant, Jude cautiously asked John-the-Driver to stop the car. "Please, I need to get off."

The pun was not lost on John.

"It's okay," said John. "She likes you." It was a kind of command, of the type offered by bosses accustomed to giving, and not receiving, directions. "It's okay."

It was as though the ice-cold water that he was spraying upon his psyche was now leaking out and providing the requisite cold shower to forestall any further consequences to this dubious voyage. Indicating, but not necessarily acting upon, a desire to distance himself from soft, gentle, untouchable, and surprisingly warm Tina, Jude leaned toward the door and placed his hand upon the chrome handle.

"Please, can you slow down?"

John released the pressure on the gas, and even if it wasn't quite clear whether he actually planned to stop the car, Jude tugged at the door handle, and the massive door opened up. Tina seemed uncertain as to which direction to go, and what to hold on to, as the imminent flight of Jude became manifest. In the end, she leaned forward, steadied her grip by grasping dials upon the dashboard, and, as Jude turned towards her for one last look into her hungry, black eyes, echoed in the distance by the piercing blue-grey gaze of John, he leaped out of the car.

Luckily, given the rather unsafe velocity of the vehicle he had just abandoned, Jude was able to benefit from a recent refusal on the part of Nassau County to give in to requests—mostly from maids, butlers, and chauffeurs, and not from taxpaying homeowners—that sidewalks be laid in the place of the grassy ditches that lined the streets of Long Island's highway. For this reason, and probably this reason alone, Jude was able to leap from Tina's tempting grasp and land, unscathed, upon the hard reality of undesired lust and yet another side of the road.

"Right," thought Jude as he watched the Cadillac disappear. He also caught one final glance around from Tina, and what seemed unmistakably to be the eyes of John that from this distance filled the rearview mirror, as though the Cadillac quite literally had eyes in the back of its head.

Jude still felt vaguely aroused, but also in a state of pleasurable shock. "This," he thought, "has to be part of my novel." The American Dream, a beautiful convertible Cadillac, an even more beautiful woman, a powerful man who has more powerful weaknesses than he would ever show, a road trip towards, well, who knows what. Busted eggs. "Not to mention whatever it was that was going on in the back seat!" he mused with a grin.

Jude's mind suddenly turned pragmatic, as he realized that he was even further from wherever it was that he'd left his truck, and, possibly worse still, he didn't even have the work order for the apartment job for which he was now undoubtedly already late.

This little job was supposed to be the coming days meal ticket, the transition as he tried to figure out how the fuck to get back to his soon-overdue egg manuscript. Ever since the Fabergé Restaurant collapsed, literally, and all of the aristocrats were cast out into the Manhattan nighttime, Jude had struggled to recover. He had at times wondered what happened to the cast of characters in the restaurant that he'd come to know so well; he had never imagined that the two pillars of Fabergé Restaurant were spending their days careening around in a Cadillac!

Suddenly struck by the enormity of his current situation, Jude grinned to himself, then stood up straight, stuck out his chin, filled his lungs with a large gulp of Long Island air, and shouted out to the entire world, with a massive grin on his face: "Christ, it's still early afternoon, and I've had a world of woe already! What the hell do they do around here at night?"

CHAPTER 3

It's probably not a bad idea to pay attention to signs. Had the Greeks heeded the many ill-fated omens that they themselves observed prior to and in the course of the Trojan War, we might all still be eating healthy Mediterranean diets. Instead, we're treated to massive doses of hormone-infested animal products, taste-manipulated processed foods, and force-fed animals that have been shaped into vaguely recognizable delicacies. Instead of deriving our foods from picturesque Mediterranean-style gardens, we are encouraged to gorge ourselves on facsimiles of food, formed like Disney-inspired facsimiles of real products, and then manufactured inside of weird steel and glass buildings in the industrial suburbs of Cleveland.

It did not have to be so. Something clearly went wrong along the way, and it may very well be related to our inability to read signs properly.

History is replete with signs that adequate observation may be rather valuable. The unmistakable Carl Jung claims to have foreseen through his dreams the calamity that was World War I, and the veritable plethora of miscues leading up to the murder of Archduke Franz Ferdinand of Austria would suggest that fate itself didn't want the plan to fail, and so the war's catalyzing moment found success in the most unlikely of alleyways. Franz Ferdinand had come to Bosnia in 1914 in order to make an inspection of the Austro-Hungarian troops stationed there. Their presence angered the Serbian freedom fighter group known as the Black Hand, which was part of a movement seeking the independence of Slavic people from Austro-Hungarian rule. Having attempted the assassination of other Austro-Hungarian officials, seven members of the group seized this opportunity and conspired to kill the archduke during his visit to Sarajevo.

This particular plan was hatched in another restaurant, called Le Bibent, Argot for "bien boire," to "drink well." Located on the central square of Toulouse, in the south west of France, it featured (and still to this day serves) specialties that make it appropriate for the hatching of plans. Its most celebrated eggy entrée is the Œuf parfait en cocotte, cuisiné façon Basquaise, mouillettes au Noir de Bigorre, served with wine and followed-up with a shot of café crème. Other choices include the Œufs mimosa de «Mamie Constant», the Œuf mollet roulé à la mie de pain, Etuvée de poivrons doux et lardons croustillants. And among the appetizers is the unmistakable Œuf mimosa et ventrèche de thon. For dessert? Why not: the egg-white-based Ile flottante, caramel à la fleur de sel, or, better still, the enigmatic flan aux Œuf à la vanille, subtitled les Œufs, "comme autrefois."

We'll never know if Gavrilo Princip, one of the instigators of World War I, ate any eggy dishes at Le Bibent, or if "comme autrefois" is a code for the fact that he did; what we do know is that on June 28, 1914, members of the Black Hand were stationed on the procession's route, and when the cars containing the archduke and his wife passed by, two of the presumed assassins threw their bombs—but missed. Well, to be fair, they didn't really miss, since they did manage to injure twenty people, but they did miss their actual target.

The driver of the car realized that there may be a bit of danger in the vicinity, and so managed to veer from the scene. Miraculously, he managed to pass three other assassins who had been posted at key points along the route, but none of them could act quickly enough to carry out their orders. Gavrilo Princip, presumably still basking in the glow of his wonderful meal at Le Bibent, figured that the whole plan had gone to hell, and may, for all we know, have been planning his return reservations in that isle of eggy delights.

Instead, however, the driver of the car made a detour so that the archduke could visit the twenty wounded victims in a nearby hospital, but he got lost and, amazingly, landed up on the road upon which Princip was walking, proving the fact that no matter how great the coincidence that Jude should encounter John and Tina in Long Island, there are even greater, and possibly more significant happenstances in the litterbox of history.

The car, knowledgeable perhaps of the need to fulfill the archduke's somber fate, managed to break down right beside the would-be assassin, who dutifully fired two shots from a rather questionable firearm. The firearm, also in apparent cahoots with destiny, managed to fire two bullets: the first one burst the jugular vein of the archduke, and the second pierced the heart of his poor wife, Sofia. Both died, presumably, instantly.

That first hunk of lead, now referred to rather infamously as the 'bullet that started World War I,' is now on display in the Konopiště Castle, near the town of Benešov, in the Czech Republic. On its account, many have claimed Gavrilo Princip as the most important person of the twentieth century. The plan that was hatched in Toulouse led to his shot, the shot found its target, and the target's death dutifully set off a chain reaction that led to the deaths of millions of people, most of them innocent civilians, and paved the way for the horrendous atrocities of both World Wars.

None of the preceding facts suggest that we ought to be honoring Princip, or even the eggy dishes he may have eaten in Toulouse. What we should be honoring instead is, of course, chance.

CHAPTER 4

As chance would have it, on the very day that Jude's Crackerbox had broken down and John's otherwise culinary life was being played out inside of the yolk of a shiny, red Cadillac, Ted and a group of workers were in a large Manhattan warehouse, overseeing the crating of fruits, counterfeit of course, sown over the past two months.

The presses that were churning out near-perfect replicas of twenty and fifty dollar bills weren't high-tech, but they did the job admirably well—so well, in fact, that a plan that seemed to have as much chance of succeeding as Princip's, was indeed succeeding, to the tune of 3.2 billion dollars—and counting. This phenomenal sum towered before the bare eyes of Ted, Steve, and Tom, who had gathered on this Friday afternoon to admire what a couple of billion (real) dollars, and a whole lot of undocumented Chinese workers, were able to produce. Thousands and thousands of wooden crates filled with uncut US currency transformed an otherwise nondescript warehouse into a city of rectangular wooden edifices.

How many fifty-dollar bills can be contained in a 4 by 8 by 4 plywood box? That is, how many single bills can be contained in 128 square feet of space? If there are 7,000 similarly sized boxes, and each contains the same number of bills, how many bills are in those boxes? And if, for arguments sake, the individual bills are worth $50, how much money is that? That is, how many $50 bills can be held in 896,000 square feet of space?

This was the question that the three friends were pondering together, in awe and mutual admiration, when Ted's cellphone rang.

"Yup?" Most calls on that phone of late were from environmental groups with which Ted worked closely, and so he was informal, and his voice was kind.

"Um, hello?" The voice on the other end sounded far away, and rather lost in background noise.

Ted's number was private, and screened, so his first impulse was to just hang up; instead, and by chance, he waited patiently on the line for a response.

"Hello? Sir? I'm sorry, um, Ted. Um, Ted? This is Jude. Jude, from the restaurant." Pause. "From Fabergé Restaurant, the broken egg. Downtown."

"God, I am such an idiot," thought Jude.

"Jude! Lifesaving Jude! How are you, my friend?" Ted's eyes twinkled.

Tom and Steve exhibited some surprise at Ted's demeanor in regards to this kid, about whom they'd heard in the context of Ted's stories about the collapse of Fabergé Restaurant. Ted raised his finger, indicating that he'd be a few moments. His two friends glanced at each other, then back to him.

"Great! Well, actually, not so great. I'm really, really sorry to call you like this."

"How else are you going to call me?" quipped Ted.

"Um, well, you know what I mean. I mean, well, sorry to call you like this, like out of the blue."

"It's okay, what's up, Jude?"

"I, I need help. I'm so sorry." Jude was worried about calling a rich friend in need of something, since he assumed, rightly, that this was one of the only reasons that friends call rich friends.

"What do you need, Jude? You helped me out of that scrambled cauldron, remember? I told you, call me if you ever need anything!"

Jude relaxed. "I do need something, and I swear, I don't know who else to call. And it all involves John, you know, that John guy who owned Fabergé Restaurant. And even Tina! And—"

"Jude?"

"Sorry. My truck broke down. I'm on Long Island. I got a lift from John. He passed by me on the road and picked me up."

"John? Did he take you home?" Ted turned towards his friends, his eyebrows raised.

"This conversation is starting to drag on rather longer than it needs to," mumbled Steve to Tom, and there was a whole lot of work to do.

"No, um, it was like a sex car, a—," blurted Jude.

"A sex car?" Ted's eyes lit up, and Tom began to squeal with laughter.

"Shhhhhh!" indicated Ted, barely able to control himself.

"Ted?"

"No, it's okay, Jude. I'm in a bar. Rather noisy here."

"I'm really sorry, it was so bizarre. I got them to drop me off and now my truck is on the side of the highway, and so am I. But we're not together." He realized that he was making no sense whatsoever.

"Are you okay, Jude?"

"I just need your help. I swear, I'm so sorry, I don't have any money, and my truck is broken down, and I don't even know where I am."

"Okay, listen, Jude. Call AAA, or a garage, or something, whatever your moving guys do when your truck is broken. Have them fix it, and then call me with the bill, I'll pay for it. Do you have enough money for a taxi?"

"Yes, I can get, um, somewhere. I'm on the 107, somewhere past Brockville."

Ted paused and then mouthed something to his two friends. They came closer.

"What the fuck are you doing, Ted?" asked Steve. Tom, as though aware of Ted's meaning, looked more curious.

Ted whispered into the din, and Tom leaned his ear towards Ted to hear him. "He can do it for you. What you were saying."

Tom backed away and lifted his shoulders. Steve just shook his head.

"Jude, listen to me. Call the tow truck, arrange to fix your truck. Then take a cab to, um, do you know the Stardust Diner? It's a couple of blocks west of Radio City, on Broadway. Meet me there." Ted looked at his watch. "I'll be there in an hour, that should give you enough time."

"I know it, yes, I have been there. Christ, thank you, Ted!"

"Watch out for Christ, Jude!" Ted smiled broadly. "See you soon."

CHAPTER 5

"What the fuck do you mean, this is a sign? This is a pain in the ass, Ted. We still have to figure out—"

"Tom, it's fine. We will make the public statement. Harrison's Shipping is on board. They have enough trucks. We have all this," Ted motioned towards the huge crates, "and it'll be cut by next week. It's fine. But if you still want to go back to Nashville, this guy can bring you there. He's a mover!"

Since the collapse of Fabergé Restaurant, the hatched plan had been tuned up, greased, oiled, and put into high gear. All of the products required for the production of the last non-plastic greenbacks to be produced in the US—the paper, presses, packing equipment—had been stored in the warehouse, now a factory, for several years, and it had proven remarkably easy to procure the few more printing presses that they deemed necessary for the volume of currency they'd hoped to produce.

Most surprisingly was that Ted's plan, that he'd spoken of for years, had worked perfectly. His idea was to recruit workers at the very last moment, to ensure that there wouldn't be too much discussion or untoward questions. He had rounded up an entire workforce with the help of "snakes," the Chinese version of Mexican coyotes, intermediaries who helped smuggle undocumented workers into the US. And thanks to Ted's seemingly endless contacts from inside of China, he was able to round up a large quorum of highly qualified printers. The flow of Chinese immigrants into New York was primarily funneled into the needle trade, because it was apparent that for the manufacturer of high-end clothing—and in particular expensive pieces like bras and panties that were labor rather than resource-intensive—it was worth paying immigrant workers in the United States, rather than indigenous workers overseas. The model for this kind of production was fashioned by a Canadian guy for a firm that came to be known, rather ironically, as American Apparel.

US production saved manufacturers the cost of shipping and import duties that cut unnecessarily into the otherwise gargantuan profits made on luxury items. The Chinese workers were ideal for this, because they were hard working, adept, and mostly ignored in NYC, which meant that they had very little contact with Americans. At the same time, Chinese immigrants are seldom noticed or bothered by Homeland Security, an agency that was veritably consumed by the undocumented Latin-American imbroglio and the hype surrounding potential Muslim terrorists.

Ted, who loved any and all reasons to hone employ his uncanny Chinese language acuity, knew a few members of the Chinese community, and knew from them that a large percentage of those in NY weren't in fact trained for either knitting or sewing (although they became adept at both). Their real and untapped abilities were in areas relating to printing, and many were highly trained typesetters, pre-press technicians, type makers, bindery workers, and printing-machine operators. This was the consequence of the Chinese government's huge efforts to create the hordes of tool and dye makers, skilled craftsmen and highly specialized tradespeople required to work in a country that actually made things. The tradespeople who were most likely to come to the US were people who wanted a different life, and many avid readers and writers, including hordes of people who had been directly involved in journalism and printing. These were the emigrants who had first-hand knowledge of what America could offer, not to them, of course, but to their children. The first generation would slave and suffer low wages and humiliation, but their children would learn the language and eventually frequent the very elite American educational institutions. Most first-generation Chinese had little interaction with the US population, because they didn't speak English, which meant that the second generation would be integrated because they combined communication abilities with a superb work ethic and a culture that fosters excellent training.

And so when Ted went in search of one hundred highly trained printers, typesetters, printing-press operators, and technicians, he found more than one thousand qualified workers who were ready to go to work. They were part of a gigantic, American workforce that was living in the shadows of New York, going to work at 4:00 a.m. They worked in crowded, high-end schmata factories and returned home after dark, and so nobody was more the wise when they traded domains from clothing to currency. Ted of course had to pay their "ransoms," the outlandish sums that they needed to pay off their snakes, amounts that would have kept them enslaved to particular factories for a decade or more. Furthermore, since integration into American society was virtually non-existent, and since they had zero contact with authorities, by choice and for their own survival, Ted figured that he could hire them without fear of them wondering why it was that "currency wallpaper," as he described it, had all of a sudden become so fashionable. The fact that this wallpaper had two sides, was impeccably printed, and bore obvious resemblance to the original after which it was modeled was, as Ted explained (when necessary), a sign of the professionalism of his company.

"Currency Wall Coverings," he would translate for his workers, "offers remarkable value, floor to ceiling!" It was hard to believe that all of them bought this story, but the payment of their ransoms, and the newly doubled salary, subdued the potentially querulous.

Since production was humming along at the requisite pace, the only real questions related distribution, and here the plan was remarkably easy. Two well-known, successful billionaire investors, Ted and Tom, had decided to "give back" to their respective communities, and contribute to their domains of respective interest. Tom had promised delivery of "cash" to "a few hundred" community organizations, many faith-based, that worked closely with poor black people, particularly those confined to the projects. And Ted had promised "cash" to secure the environment for future generations by funding grass-roots organizations involved in buying local land for return to wilderness, planting trees, protecting state parks, and cleaning up the waterways of an ever-more polluted nation. The "Wall Street Stimulus Plan," or WSSP, was an ironic nod to those that said, rightly, that stimulus always flows from the taxpayer, or the little guy, to the Wall Street investor. Ted and Tom had printed a shiny pamphlet that announced, in bold letters, that "the flow is now going the other way."

The genius of this plan was that since it was to be undertaken in "cash," the actual outflow would be difficult to trace. And furthermore, if the promise of a "million-dollar grant" actually turned out to be a box containing ten million dollars, and if it was left on the doorstep of a community center rather than presented in a formal presentation with a fake eight-foot-long check to accompany the prize, then the recipient wasn't very likely to report any wrongdoing. On the contrary, there'd be much to celebrate, and whether community leaders wanted to announce the actual amount of the gift or not didn't really matter and, at the end of the day, if it was discovered that a million-dollar gift had grown to ten million dollars, it could be accounted for by the impulsive generosity of the donors. And furthermore, if the box was stolen by people from, say, the projects, and then spent in the area, the aim of the whole enterprise would nonetheless be met.

In light of the potential for connecting untoward dots, however, the whole project had to be started, and then stopped, very quickly; and if it didn't, some of the cracks in the reasoning would become craters. But the time for the WSSP was short, by design, and besides, the federal election was less than one month away, and, crucially, the options on the majority of the Rare Earth Commodities were due in just three weeks. One way or another, they reasoned, this WSSP would garner attention to their causes, and money, *real* money (or at least real enough for the cause), would be poured right into the community, providing the boon that the president needed to secure his second term. Whether or not he was elected barely mattered, since both parties had similar fiscal policies, but it was easy to show to the incumbent that his interest lay in meeting the demands of those stimulating the pre-election economy.

All of these details had been discussed at great length, and with great excitement, by the three men, and their conclusion was that a reasonably popular, moderate president wouldn't insist too heavily on seeking out details of the sudden benevolence of three friends from college who were giving back to society. The vocal praise of administration's policies, and the timing of their donations, were also all designed to keep the media glare on the kindness and generosity of their actions, rather than on a few details that just didn't seem to add up. This would come out later, much later, and by then it hopefully wouldn't matter enough to affect the posterity of their actions.

The massive brunt of the cash, though, was heading elsewhere, to a community that all of them felt sure they could trust: Native-American tribes. If slavery, segregation, and Jim Crow still motivated acts of resentment and distrust in the African-American community, it was because the violence of history remains. The blood and tears of ignominious actions, particularly those committed over long periods and with relative impunity for the perpetrators, retain their horror for generation after generation. But while the African-American cause was fought visibly and daily, on fronts as wide and deep as local resistance, hip-hop lyrics and scholarly writings, the plight of indigenous peoples remains further down in the soil of America's shameful past. With but a few turns of the shovel, however, the earth remains fertile for recollection and resistance for a genocide still unacknowledged in a land of the immigrated "American." Tom, Steve, and Ted were fulfilling the terms of a college dream, a utopian act, an informed grudge match. But each of them were also battling demons, and causes, and Steve wanted for his last mark to be an indelible one, changing the course of history for the indigenous peoples of America.

And so when Harrison Shipping sent a rather remarkable number of gleaming Kenworth eighteen-wheel rigs to pick up the crates at "Currency Wall Coverings," the destinations on their paperwork were largely on Native-American reservations all over the US. The cabs and trailers bore no special markings, and their presence was unremarkable, both in Manhattan and in the highways and byways leading to America's shamefully segregated communities of Navajo, Cherokee, Sioux, Chippewa, Choctaw, Apache, Pueblo, Iroquois, Creek, Blackfeet, and the dozens of other tribes. Huge trucks made regular deliveries to most reservations, and they bore food, clothing, and, more often, crates of cigarettes, liquor, and gambling equipment that has become the real legacy of the white man's continued truck with its founding peoples.

These Harrison Shipping trucks also contained crates, and their contents were also related to high-speed gambling. Steve had convinced Tom and Ted that news of philanthropic efforts being undertaken to right some historical wrongs would be understood, and connected, as deliveries of crates were made to local chiefs. And as the reality of these efforts became manifest, Steve gambled that the secret of the deliveries would be safe, and that the necessary "laundering" on reservations designed for the very act of receiving money for the crimes of tobacco, liquor, and gambling would be undertaken with calm, ease, and, moreover, the quiet understanding of those who always knew through dialogue with nature what the real ill of America was.

In short, the pieces of the plan were in place, from those little, golden wheels that ensure that the forged money would remain undetectable, to the distribution system designed to ensure that it would truly "rain" on America in advance of the November election. All they had to do now was wait until November 1, when the rare earth commodity options would be called in. On that day, a phone call would be made to the US Department of the Treasury. The call would be transferred to a man they'd not yet met, a dangerous man, a cunning man, a very fat man, a man named Stephen Fraser. But the pathway to November wasn't going to be so smooth, and they all knew it, because Tom wouldn't have it that way, couldn't have it that way. In his mind, he held an IOU to a community that had once helped him, and an anonymous gift did not for him suffice. The coincidence of Jude's phone call convinced Ted, a man who not only noticed but also followed signs, that Jude needed to help them all out. On the other hand, Ted's actions in light of the phone call may have been the sign of their demise, the shattering of their dreams, the destruction of their America. A classic diner, the surprising stand-in for Fabergé Restaurant, would have to be the place where such determinations could be worked out.

CHAPTER 6

Jude looked like the disaster he had just endured. His hair was surprised, his hands uncertain, his clothing ravaged, his complexion wane, his gaze distracted.

Ted, on the other hand, who had arrived in one of those ubiquitous black Lincolns that seem to be staging a quiet and unheralded coup against yellow taxi cabs in NYC, looked buoyant.

It was late afternoon, and mercifully there was no loud music playing in the Stardust Diner because of a PGA golf tournament, a football game, a baseball game, and a poker match, all diffused from various angles, as though they were either multiple versions of America or just rides on that Walt Disney theme park of life. Jude was in a booth sipping a muddy coffee when Ted strolled in and confidently sat down, leaned forward, and in a very friendly fashion, reached out and patted Jude's shoulder.

"How are you doing, Jude? I haven't seen you since the last supper!"

Jude was genuinely glad to see this new friend, and particularly grateful that despite the Long Island plea, he was in good humor. He thought that he'd have to wait for him outside, trapped inside of a taxi driven by a driver who was anxious to continue his foray into the heart of the Big Apple traffic nightmare. Luckily, the credit card swipe of fear didn't produce the reject sign that he'd expected, and he was liberated from the taxi prison.

Jude tended to avoid places like taxis and strip clubs, where meters tick away the contents of your bank account. As a person who had driven his own vehicle with some degree of conservatism, he feared psychopath drivers accustomed to challenging other members of their taxi-driving tribe by testing their ability to gently touch each other's doors and fenders as they wind their way through gridlock Manhattan traffic.

"Thanks, Ted," mumbled Jude.

"For what? You are the one who dragged my endangered carcass from that egg, the birthplace of Fabergé Restaurant's bird! I wonder where it flew off to?"

"We're it."

Ted stared at Jude with intensity and admiration. "Wow, Jude. Yes. I love that. The egg cracked, and we emerged."

Jude realized the brilliance of his own spontaneous utterance, and figured he would run with it as long as possible. "And we were the last ones out. Do you suppose . . .?"

Ted didn't respond, and Jude's brilliant segue fell into the dungeons of hell, to burn into ashes that would drift away, unnoticed.

"Wait," said Ted, reaching into his pocket. "I told you I'd pay that cab." He didn't bother to ask him the price, but instead just took a couple of hundreds from his wallet and placed them before Jude. Jude was too awestruck to resist, and uttering some version of "I am grateful to you until the end of time," he moved the bills to his side of the table and then gazed with gratitude at his benefactor.

People who grow up without resources and then somehow gain access to them can in certain cases remain forever sensitive to those who are broke. Others, who take wealth for granted, or believe in their having "earned it," don't think to reimburse, because they themselves were never conditioned to worry about such things. In fact, sensitivity to the plight of the poor is strongest amongst those who continue to have little or nothing, which is why peddlers, homeless people, and otherwise destitute folks look to one another for solace and support. It means as well that poor people tend to be robbed by other poor people, as though it never occurred to the robbers that they could have the right to the resources of people who could actually afford to take a hit. Most rich people are robbed by people they know, like friends of their children or, much less often, by professionalized burglars, those who have honed their skills and will rely upon them until they receive free state housing for some insanely prolonged sentence.

Jude suddenly felt himself resisting Ted's generosity, and was prepared to say that he had been able to cover the $64.30 ride here, but the urge passed quickly, and instead just left the two brand new bills where they were. He suddenly became concerned, though, that the waiter might confuse them for a tip from previous clients, or for a generous payment for his coffee, a thought that could only run through the mind of someone who had hovered, as he had, in places that he couldn't afford, like taxis. Or Fabergé Restaurant. With sudden resolute purpose, he swept up the money and jammed it into the front pocket of his jeans.

"You have a hell of a story to tell?" asked Ted, his eyes gleaming.

Jude was confused by the question, and almost sent his hands back into his pants when he recalled the events of the previous few hours, and realized that this was most likely the link to Ted's question.

"How exciting was it? Perhaps you can use it for a scene in your novel?" suggested Ted.

"I should write it all down, but nobody would read it. Too sensational!" He grinned, and was pleased to see Ted do the same.

"Tina you said? The same Tina?"

Jude didn't really know how to begin, since he'd have to unveil a rather large quantity of his own shower-time fantasies. "The same. She picked me up. Or, well, John, that guy, you know, anyhow, he picked me up."

"And they are married those two?"

"Maybe," offered Jude. "But I'm not so sure that it's the marriage you and I envision." Jude dared put his own self into a sentence alongside of Ted. Ted smiled, knowingly.

"Not sure about that, Jude," was all he said, enigmatically.

"She wanted to, um, she was all over me!" He immediately regretted his choice of words, feeling like a high school kid sitting with his buddies in the empty stands of the disheveled football field in some lower-middle-class suburb, bragging.

Ted just indicated interest, but said nothing.

"She was undressing me, right beside John, and he was watching. And that new guy, remember? The one who told us that it was his first night at Fabergé Restaurant . . ."

"And his last!" exclaimed Ted.

"Yah! He was in the backseat making out with some guy I think I've seen before, with John."

"Wow."

Jude didn't know what else to say. It seemed like an absolutely momentous story at the time, but it now seemed ridiculously inane, trite, and irrelevant. Unless he offered more detail, it was likely to remain the latter.

"Jude, listen. I'm going to help you out with that truck of yours. I have a job for you, um, a couple of buddies and me, have a job for you. How busy are you in the next few days?"

It was Jude's turn to smile wryly. "I never called that guy at Locust Valley. If he has lots of friends, I may not have any jobs for a long time!"

Ted looked kindly at Jude. "It's okay, I'm going to help you out. A friend of mine is willing to pay you way too much money for a move, but it's a bit of a haul." He grinned. "Is that the term?"

Jude smiled, grateful for his suddenly glamorized role. "Haul? Yes!"

"Great. I need you to do me a favor, another one. You know, after saving my life."

"I didn't . . ."

Ted ignored the comment and instead cast his eyes around the restaurant. "Look at this place, Jude!"

The diner was filling up with all kinds of New York types and lots of tourists who had come to experience what they'd been told is the best diner in New York. This diner, however, like the worst diner in New York, serves the same food, delivered by the same Tyson trucks, cooked in the same Tyson grease, and served by caricatures of the people who are supposed to serve in NY diners. The waitresses were middle aged, full-framed, with perfectly arranged Hassidic-wig-style hair, bursting bust lines that were clearly enhanced by huge cheap bras, large, solid thighs that descended downwards towards Reebok shoes. They were wrapped in imperfect skin, and they all saw the world through remarkably kind eyes.

The waiters were heavy, dark, and tough looking, with tattooed arms as thick as thighs, and stubby fingers as strong as pickle jar lids. They looked like aging Greek sailors who came to shore and then couldn't find their way back to their boats, and instead wandered inland and got lost around 51st Street.

Suddenly, the canned music stopped, and movement around the little makeshift stage made it apparent that the staff was preparing for some kind of a singsong, or sing-along, or other sing-thing that Ted wouldn't want to endure under the circumstances. He got down to business.

"Listen, Jude, I'm going to have to go soon. I'll pay you fifty thousand dollars to drive my friend Tom to Nashville . . . to make a delivery . . . to his old neighborhood."

Jude looked at Ted in complete disbelief. Ted, interested only in accomplishing his goal, hadn't any idea as to what might have triggered Jude's unease. A moment of reflection, though, brought it to light.

"Right. Look, Jude, I feel like you were pretty heroic that night."

"I didn't do anything! We just walked out together and . . ."

"And so I want to help you out. I believe in your novel, and I want you to write it. Do this for me, and this payment will give you some time. You won't be able to write it at Fabergé Restaurant of course, but . . .," he looked around. "Look! That guy over there is eating an omelet. Maybe you could write it here, and ask to be seated near people who order eggs!"

"I cannot, well, I—"

"Great." Ted, despite his humble origins, was also used to getting what he asked for. "Here is," he reached back into his pocket and pulled out his wallet. He counted out a pile of bills. "Okay, this is $1,700, it should be enough to get your truck towed. Call me with the repair cost, and you have to tell them that you also want a tune up. Do they do tune-ups on moving trucks?"

"Yah, sure but—"

"Great. Get a tune-up, have them call me, I'll pay for it on the phone. Tell them that you have a really big job, so it needs to be in good order. Have them check, you know, the tires, the, um, the . . ." He smiled. "Have them check whatever they normally have to check, and tell them to fix whatever needs fixing. You have my number." He pushed the bills towards Jude. "Would you mind paying for all this? I have tons of stuff to do."

"All this" was Jude's one cup of coffee. "Sure," he muttered. He was in a state of rather blissed-out shock.

Ted rose to leave.

"I really appreciate this, Jude. Oh, and if you don't mind, my friend is going to join you for the ride, do you think that would be okay? Sorry, I don't think I mentioned that. How long does it take to drive there?"

"Nashville? From here? It's probably twenty hours, plus stops." Jude was accustomed to people's profound ignorance about road distances in America.

"Twenty hours! Jesus, okay, let me ask him. I'll call you," he said, as he moved towards the exit. "Thanks, Jude, thanks!"

CHAPTER 7

When Ted returned to the factory-warehouse, he was greeted by boisterous activity. The printing machines had been purring, with regular corrections, tune-ups, and calibrations, ever since the demise of Fabergé Restaurant. In recent days activity had shifted towards the rear doors of the warehouse, where state-of-the-art, electronically guided guillotines had been set up for the tedious and complex task of cutting the sheets of "currency wall coverings" into bills.

This shift had of course necessitated the erection of a large barrier separating the production from the cutting, so that undesirable questions about why wallpaper was being cut into such small pieces would be avoided. Those charged with the task of dividing up billions of dollars of cash into proper sizes had been handpicked from the existing workforce for their discretion, qualifications, and, moreover, their disconnect from the host country, a disconnect measured by the relative absence of linguistic skills and manifest lack of connection to American culture. Furthermore, in order to segregate the workers from the New York Chinese community, Tom had arranged for them to stay in the sprawling New York Hotel, a gargantuan structure that had once been the toast of the town, with its high-quality restaurant, bowling alleys, shops, and services. For the past decades, it has slowly become a bargain for tourists, and then a bit of an embarrassment. But management was happy to have it revitalized, filled with happy guests who had previously occupied slum-like quarters in the East Bronx, prior to their having been liberated by the Currency Corporation.

With the shift in production towards cutting, and eventual distribution, Ted communicated to those assigned to the new work that their hours would be different from the rest of the workforce, and that it was best that they relocate to a hotel closer to the factory. The workers were thus separated from coworkers-turned-friends, whom they'd now seldom saw, in the hope, as far as Tom, Ted, and Steve were concerned, that there'd be a minimum of discussion about their new jobs. None of this was long-term, since they knew very well that such an operation couldn't possibly last. But they were now down to the last three weeks before the election, and the last two weeks before the rare earth options were called in. As long as nothing untoward occurred, they could probably make it into the offices of the Department of the Treasury for their long-anticipated sit-down. From that point onwards, there'd be a lot of negotiating to do, and they wanted to engage in it when their bargaining power was at its height.

Ted strolled through the entrance area of the factory, and then moved to the cordoned-off "office area," with its makeshift cubicles that had been divided up according to the task discussed therein. Most of this area was taken up by a rather wonky conference room, a ceilingless rectangle constructed of plastic walls that were suspended from the ceiling with small cables, lending a look of a theatre set that was prepared for this act, and at the same time ready to be totally transformed for the next. The current scene was furnished with a completely incongruous antique table from Steve's collection of Philippine furniture, and four gorgeous chairs that looked as though they belonged in Versailles rather than to the cement floor of a noisy, Lower East Side warehouse.

As expected, Tom and Steve were seated, in intense conversation. What wasn't to be expected was the presence of a woman with clear but radiant skin, long tussles of soft, golden hair, dark-green eyes, and a bewitching smile that revealed disarmingly perfect teeth. She was remarkably beautiful. She seemed comfortable amidst the din and chaos of this place. She was seated very near to Tom, upon whose arm she rested her left hand, confidently. She, was Jessica.

"Holy shit!" blurted out Ted and immediately went to her side. "You have come back for me! Tom, thanks for saving her for me, you can go now."

Jess smiled rather uncertainly.

"Jess, this is Ted. Ignore every second word he says, and he may begin to make sense."

Ted calculated for just a moment. "Jess. Hmmm, word. I, word. Am pajamas. Thrilled pancakes. That balloons. Tom loser. Has thankfully. Brought yes! You, you. To for. Me, me." He paused for a second, calculating: "We us can will go leave now immediately."

Jess smiled, and the entire sphere surrounding her seemed to illuminate. "Nice to meet you, Ted." She paused. "I've actually seen you before."

Ted didn't miss a beat. "I know, we were engaged to be married before I was kidnapped by these bozos in order to help and save this sorry world."

He looked around at Tom and Steve and then directly into the very depths of her eyes, as though to submerge himself in the memory of this moment with her. "I think that this time my answer is yes, so sorry to have kept you waiting."

Jessica smiled again. "You've been to Fabergé Restaurant."

"Yah, well, I used to go there. I didn't think it would land up poached, or scrambled, or whatever it turned into."

"It fulfilled its mission, followed its fate. John had always told me that it would fall, just like the Romanov family. I didn't realize that he was speaking literally."

"John? John-the-Owner? I knew him!" Ted examined her closer still, to assess her relation to this once-revered institution. "But you escaped! Did he?"

"I escaped, but then so did the czar's mother."

"Touché!" blurted out Tom. Ted ignored him.

"But no," she continued, "not really. None of us escaped. I worked in the kitchen, and was there from its inception. Now that it has cracked, I think the rest of us have as well."

"And John? The owner, John?"

"Especially John. After the collapse, he drove me to Long Beach, on Long Island, and parked his car right on the sand. We just sat there, with the convertible down, and watched the waves. I was convinced he was just going to start the car, rev it up, and drive us into the depths of the sound."

"I'm really glad he didn't, how would we get married?" Ted looked completely convinced by his own fantasy. "Although," he paused, "I wouldn't be surprised if you're a mermaid."

"He is definitely a mermaid," interjected Steve. "He is a gay mermaid with a fish skin pulled over his, well, you know, that tiny part of him."

Jessica had spent enough time in the kitchen to hold up this kind of banter all evening, and do so while churning out recipes fit for the most finicky of kings.

Tom moved closer to Jessica, and in an act of possession, but also urgency, reached around her body and held her opposite arm with his large hand as if to say "Okay. We are now past the banter, it's time to speak seriously."

"Ted," Tom began, "I don't know what the fuck took you so long, or where the fuck you've been. Whatever. I want you to meet Jessica, because I need you to sign some papers with her."

"Great!" exclaimed Ted. "I will, for sure. Steve, do you have the rings?" Steve looked his usual calm and cold self.

"To suspend you from the ceiling so that I can whip you?" asked Steve.

"Don't mind him, Jess, the "S" isn't actually for Steve, it's for Sadomasochism. Steve, you really need to find yourself a lover, I can't be everything for you!"

Tom was the only one who remained cool, although he was rather on the verge of losing his temper. The reality was, they were now about to set forth the largest counterfeiting scheme ever devised, and alongside of that, they had arranged to corner rare earth metals that were absolutely essential to the continued existence of the manufactured goods that made this and many other worlds function. If their gamble was wrong, that is if they were wrong to think that no US government would risk the humiliation heaped upon them by three upstanding citizens who had offered an unprecedented stimulus plan to the most needy, and to a large enough number of people to alter a federal election, then they were living their last days of freedom. It was a good reason to seek humorous respite. It was also, in Tom's sense, a good reason to preempt failure and disaster.

"Ted, be serious," said Tom. "You said that because all the options are on the Chinese market that we have nothing to fear from the feds, and that the Chinese have everything to gain from our holdings, as long as we keep playing ball with them. But I don't want to be standing in treasury with my pockets filled with stock options, because if we don't make it out of there, neither will the options. I have given everything to Jess, and I want you to do the same thing. You only hold 17 percent, but I want her to have all of it. Just in case."

Ted paused and then looked at Jessica with a false-accusatory look. "Is this the prenup?" Jessica looked uncomfortable.

"Ted, it's not going to make a fuck bit of difference, this paper is going to turn to dust, one way or another. We may as well protect ourselves from holding it when the time comes, in case they just pop on the handcuffs then and there."

This had always been a fear, for all of them. This was also part of the thrill, and part of the risk. Three wealthy men walk into the US Treasury claiming to have put into circulation enough billions to affect the economy, and have promised to spill the beans one week before the immanent reelection of the incumbent, which would almost certainly bring down his government. At the same time, and by way of further guarantee, they had also acted, entirely legally, to purchase an unprecedented quantity of stock options on rare earth commodities, options that were now worth untold billions. Those options were controlled by two of the three people involved in the counterfeiting. What would happen if the feds decided to not negotiate? What if they just arrested the three of them? This would be a great pre-election coup. And yet, it seemed unlikely, since it would be a surefire method of losing the election because it could appear as though this whole disastrous scheme had been happening for months, maybe years, under the very nose of the sitting government.

Furthermore, and perhaps most importantly, such a fiscal trip-up would also sadden a whole lot of nice people who were suddenly sitting on a lot of cash that was helpful for feeding, clothing, and housing disenfranchised people. And a lot of those people, in fact a vast majority of them, could vote, even if they didn't traditionally do so. This time, though, they would probably heed the call to vote if they were asked to by those benevolent gentlemen who had given them and their communities bags of money. If the incumbent cooperated, he could be sitting on his own voter gold mine. On the other hand, if the incumbent arrested these three heroes, not only would they not vote, but they might, they just might, rise up. And who knew where such an insurrection might lead. What Tom was offering now was a solution to another problem that they had barely considered.

"I don't want to lose the whole fucking thing," began Tom. "Jail, the house, the . . .," he looked over at Jess, "the whole fucking thing. I don't want to, and we don't have to." He spoke as though he was addressing a world far beyond the noise of this factory. "We always said that this was for eternity, or at least for this generation."

It was hard to know if Tom was talking now to Jessica, or to the promise that the three men had made each other, all those years ago, about their eventual objectives. "If they slap on the fucking cuffs and drag us out of there, well, we thought of that." He paused. "But you saw them with Snowden and Assange and the whole bunch of them. We are now sitting on a fucking fortune, maybe not for us, but . . ." He looked ever-more intensely at Jessica. "Unless," said Tom, "we act now. Legally. We legally give everything to Jess. She is not involved, and is in no way part of this. I am giving her my options, because she's my girlfriend, and

I fear for my future, and wish to secure hers. I'm asking you to do the same thing, because we're in this together, and rather than give it to someone else, I'd like to consolidate it into her hands."

Ted turned to Jess. "Do you want it?"

"I know nothing. All I know is that Tom is a hero, and that you are all heroes. I want to continue this. If I have to go at it alone with all this, I'll just give it all to the cause."

"And the cause being?"

She opened wide her soft eyes, breathed the air that engulfs this entire planet, and stared forth towards the distant eternity. Therein echoed as much silence as could be mustered in a printing and cutting factory.

Ted looked into Jess's eyes. She wasn't a beautiful woman, a desirable woman, a girlfriend, his dream partner, an unrealizable fantasy. Jess was the oceans and the seas, the lakes and the streams, the mountains, the grass, the tall trees, the rainfall, the dew upon the grass in the early morning.

"Yah. Yes. Sure." Ted joined the three of them at the table. "Yes, I will give it all to her."

Ted stared into Jess's eyes and uttered those words as though in some strange trance, as though these words, inconceivable but a few minutes prior, were as unmistakable as the sweet scent of freshly cut hay wafting through gloriously secluded farmland on a warm, sunny day. Ted spoke those words to his friends, but moreover he spoke those words to Jessica, and in his mind's eye he saw her and him together, hand in hand from a lovely country home on this idyllic farmland, strolling towards a nearby barn, therein to amass a few fresh eggs for this morning's breakfast after a feast of sensual pleasure created and forever recalled in the passion of love.

"Yes," he repeated, Molly Bloom-like, as though in recollection of giving in to her, willingly. He looked around at his friends, at Tom, at Steve, and then back to Jess.

"Yes. Yes."

He paused, and then under his own breath, and for his own self, for now, and forever.

"Yes. I will. Yes."

CHAPTER 8

When Jude turned off of Highway 40 and into the Nashville International Airport, he was sporting a remarkably revitalized Crackerbox that had made the New York to Nashville trip with an unprecedented degree of confidence. This was not altogether surprising, because not only did Ted pay the mechanic to fix what turned out to be a minor blown gasket, but he also paid for a complete revamping of the truck, from the alternator to the Z-cam. Ol' Crackerbox had not run this well since Kennedy was in office.

John Kennedy.

Jude had been sold a bill of goods in regards to the precious commodity he bore, in a locked crate, and he rather suspected as much. But he had been richly rewarded, and understood that part of the reward included a premium for not asking too many questions. The obscene payment for the delivery had been Jude's principle obsession as the clock made its way around, and around, and around, from a very early Manhattan morning, to a very late Nashville night.

Ted had told Jude that the contents of the crate were documents and artworks belonging to Tom, who was anxious to hand deliver them to the extended family members in Nashville. He had also been told that although Tom had turned down the offer to join him for the long ride to Tennessee, he did want to be there for Jude's arrival. There was some real risk inherent in this plan, and both Steve and Ted had tried to dissuade Tom from following through on the delivery. If something were to go wrong along the way, Jude might be forced to open the contents of his truck up for inspection, which would have been a disaster. Tom wouldn't back down, and respecting the sacrifices they'd all made, the plan went forward as he had requested.

Rather than make some kind of effort to hide the cash, though, they had agreed to just seal it in a container and hope for the best. If the truck broke down or, worse, if the truck was searched and the money found, they'd indemnify Jude, and immediately make the call to the treasury, in the hope of getting to the long-awaited negotiations rather than to the inside of a NYC jail.

Luckily, there were no such problems.

The newly refurbished truck made the ride in a remarkable fifteen hours, including stops.

Jude was relieved, even jubilant as the final miles ticked off; but he was also totally exhausted. He rarely undertook such long trips, and had not done a serious distance in over a year.

"Perhaps," he mused to himself, "I'll never need to again!" His wallet was bulging, literally, and he felt that the unexpected windfall might be the key to his ability to become an author, a real author, and, perhaps, the author who would be credited with finally writing the Great American Novel.

"Yes!" he spewed at the thought of his eventual success and recognition. "Yes!" But then, as he pulled into the airport, twenty-five minutes early, he felt his body fading, his attention span paved under the thousand miles of asphalt he'd just traversed. Recognition later. Tonight: a really, really long sleep. He smiled to himself. In an extra-fucking-fancy hotel!

Tom, by contrast, was serious, and even brooding. Inwardly, he was simply nervous, and deeply preoccupied.

"Things have gone well," he said to himself as the plane touched down. It was as though he needed to reassure himself. Jessica wasn't there, and he'd promised Steve and Ted that he wouldn't talk to her about the plan over the phone, and so they stuck to short conversations about love, about commitment, and about the perils that lay ahead, perils that could most certainly derail the fantasy of being together.

He had moments when he thought to ring Ted and Steve up, and suggest that they just call the whole thing off. Selling the options would yield billions in pure profit, and if they wanted, they had many more billions in counterfeit currency, enough to satisfy their wildest philanthropic dreams. But no. The objective wasn't short term, and if it had been, they didn't need to undertake the plan in the first place. Long-term, the US was heading on a path that would ruin what each of them held dear. It was time to put a stop to the madness, and they had the perfect opportunity. Now. Right now.

As Tom awaited the arrival of his checked luggage, he ruminated about the days to come. It was surprising that no unexpected impediment had hindered their march towards the US Treasury meeting. Here they were, five days away from calling in the stock options, and nobody had as yet recognized the implications of the plan. He once again took out his phone to call Ted and Steve. Instead, he chose the messaging app, and began to type.

"Why hasn't anyone noticed that the rare earth stock option clock was ticking?"

He stared at "send," and then deleted the message, fearing spyware of some kind. They had agreed to engage in all discussion face to face, in the warehouse if at all possible, which added a level of intrigue to their actions. At first, though, the exigency to speak face to face had been enjoyably anachronistic, as though all of the technologies of the past hundred years had been for naught. This rather quaint effort to rely only upon each other, in person, had made it difficult for them to explain their respective ever-lengthier absences from the offices they were used to frequenting. On the other hand, each of them had the autonomy that came with wealth, and the fortuitous ability to "work from home," the mantra that had excited office workers, but then betrayed them. Most people who work from home do so after a long day of not working at home, so the net effect of the new technology was to further ruin the lives of the aspiring middle class. But it offered benefits for the haves, and Ted, Steve, and Tom fit that description. And so now, as Tom felt the need to figure out where they were before the balls of their existences came crashing down like so many New Years' symbols, their orthodoxy about long-distance dialogue felt unrealistically confining.

It was true that the attention in the media leading up to the election was mostly about the election itself, with a smattering of fascination, that would become obsession, in regards to these bags of money. And so the reason why there hadn't been any warning signals to the impending rare earth calamity was in part because there was no reason to look at these rather obscure Chinese commodity options at this time, in particular because it was a sector of the financial world that had never been monitored closely. In fact, nothing untoward was happening in that sector; a group of companies, all dummy corporations set up by Ted through the combined purchasing blocks owned by himself, Tom, and Steve, had made significant investments in relatively inexpensive commodities—in China. Speculation like this went on all the time, and since 9/11 the US government was far more vigilant about "commodities of national interest" (CNI), like jet fuel and food, than they were about rare earth materials. The CNIs had been chosen in the wake of the destruction of the Twin Towers, and thus in a world that was rather different from this one. Nobody, not even Steven Fraser, had noticed this.

Surprising.

These thoughts were running through Tom's head as he headed towards the ground-floor parking, where he'd agreed to meet with Jude. A text alerted him to the fact that everything was, as they say, going according to plan.

Suddenly, Tom's entire mindset shifted, and he thought of the community center where his father had sought solace, and found comfort. The madness of his plan made sudden sense, and he looked forward to the moment when he could finally embrace the people who his father had described as saviors, terrestrial beings with extraordinary generosity. They had taken his father's cause as a kind of mission, and his father had promised recompense. Tom didn't know that his fathers' tears, his embrace, and his clear recognition of the Edgehill Community Center had been enough for the young Father Travis, who had taken the reins of the organization immediately following his master's in divinity. Father Travis, no longer young, still directed the organization, and so when Tom picked up the phone to make the long-awaited call, Father Travis had answered. This was the second time that Father Travis had answered a call from Tom's family. And now, Tom had reassured him on the phone, he would be rewarded for having done so.

CHAPTER 9

The news of the shooting was greeted with horror, and although there were several reports of the events leading up to it, the one certainty was that nobody was certain as to what happened that evening on Edgehill Road. It's clear that Tom spent the night in the Union Station Hotel, and that his stay had been uneventful. Jude, desperate for luxurious surroundings in which to spend his riches, had chosen the historical option, the Hermitage Hotel. He had been lured by descriptions of its famous bathroom, which featured walls in gleaming lime-green-and-black leaded glass tiles, lime-green fixtures, terrazzo floor, and a gleaming two-seat shoeshine station. He had somehow imagined that "historic latrine" would be part of his own room, but learned that it was in fact in the bar, downstairs. As such, Ted also learned that Jude had spent an inordinate amount of time, and money, in that sacred space.

The events of the next day were less clear. Tom, committed to delivering his "sacred package," had relieved Jude of his cargo when he arrived at his hotel, and several hotel employees did attest to their having seen Tom with a rather unruly sack, with which he checked in that night. Hotel cameras also caught Tom leaving the hotel very late that night, apparently at around 2:00 a.m. He was seen carrying the same bag, but clearly less encumbered, suggesting that he had emptied out some of the currency, most likely in the interest of mobility. A taxi driver confirmed that his passenger had carried that bag right into the backseat of a taxi that dropped him off on the corner of 15th and Edgehill, the gateway into the projects. That same driver confirmed returning to the same spot one hour later, where a rather disheveled but considerably less burdened Tom gave orders to the driver to return to the hotel. The bag he had been carrying was, by the taxi driver's report, probably empty.

The next day, it was Jude who showed up at the hotel to pick Tom up, at around noon. The reasons were clear; Jude still bore a significant part of the cargo in his truck, and it was Tom's intention to offer it to Father Travis in the name of his own father. After a brief stop in the hotel, apparently for coffee and a muffin, Jude drove Tom to the Edgehill Community Center and helped him to carry another large bag, presumably the remainder of the precious cargo. Jude was anxious to complete this short delivery as quickly as possible, since he was hoping to get back on the road to New York, and maybe even arrive on that same evening so as to wake up in his own bed the day after. Once he had helped Tom with the bag, however, Tom returned with him to the truck, and the two of them were seen talking in the cab. This was where the story became a tad incomprehensible.

According to Jude, Tom was extremely agitated after delivering the bag to Father Travis, and had insisted that Jude speak with him in private. Father Travis, in the meantime, was standing outside the cab, anxiously waiting for Tom so as to be able to celebrate the amazing gift that he had brought to the Center. As far as Jude could recall, Tom had been enigmatic, ranting and raving about eternity and the divine, rather than simply carrying out the plan and returning to the airport for his flight back to New York.

"Jude," Tom had reportedly said, "you are now part of the plan. This generation offers sacrifices to false gods, who we will bring down!"

"False gods?" Ted asked Judas to repeat the phrase in a phone conversation with Jude. "False gods? What the hell was he on?"

"I swear, Ted, I don't know," said Jude. "He said that the plan was to bring down everything that was evil. Everything! I don't even know what that means!"

"Nor did he," said Ted.

"It's, well . . .," started Jude. "It's not just the crazy talk. He also, um, he also seemed to be almost coming on to me."

"You?" asked Ted in disbelief.

"Well, I don't really mean it like that. Um, it's not like he touched me or anything, but, well, he stared at me with really crazy eyes. It was as though he knew that something really terrible was going to happen." There was a pause on the other end of the line.

"How do you mean?" The line sounded dead. "Hold on a second, Jude." Jude could hear that Ted was relaying information to somebody else, nearby, probably Steve.

"Jude said that he was agitated, like he knew something was going on." Another pause.

"You still there?" asked Ted.

Jude was in the lobby of his hotel, seated on one of the fancy sofas. His truck was packed and ready to go, and he was now held up by the proceedings in light of the shooting. He had been released from the clutches of the police questioning, but now he felt subjected to new levels of inquiry. He just wanted to go home.

"Ted, can we speak about this when I get back?"

"No, no, sorry, Jude. We need to, um, we just need to know where to go from here."

"I understand, I'm sorry."

"For what? Don't be sorry, this isn't your fault."

"It is. I brought him here."

"He paid you!"

There was another pause, as the frustration of being in the middle of some incomprehensible transaction bore down upon Jude. Nonetheless, there was still that previously absent bulge in the front pocket of his pants, still substantial even after a night of ostensibly pissing as much of it away as he possibly could.

"There were other strange things he said . . .," began Jude.

"I'm listening," said Ted. "We are listening, in fact." Steve had joined in the conversation through speakerphone.

"He told me to, um, tell someone."

"Tell someone what?"

"Tell someone, um, what was in the bags."

"Jesus!" That was clearly Steve's voice, Steve who was always so resolutely effaced in contrast to Ted.

"Why?"

"I don't know, Ted, I don't, I swear. He said that I was part of a great deed, and that I would exceed everyone else."

"What?"

"I don't know, I swear, but then he said that I needed to sacrifice the man that clothes me."

"That whats you?"

"That clothes me. Clothes. Clothing."

"He was asking you to . . ."

Jude paused. "Yes, that's what I think he was saying. He was asking me to sacrifice him. He wanted me to, um, give him away. He said, um, this is going to sound crazy."

"I'm listening, Jude, take it easy. What did he say?"

"He said that he needed to tell me everything, and that in the name of his father he had to act, but that his task would be done today. He said that I should behold the skies, for I was freeing them of the clouds, and that the star revealed in the wake of the clearing would lead the way."

"He lost his fucking mind," murmured Ted.

"He then left me there like that, in my truck. And walking back towards the community center, he—" Jude began to sob. "Walking back, he, he, walking, there were these pops, this sound, and he grabbed his stomach, and then covered his face, and fell down. Right there. He . . . he fell down. . . ."

CHAPTER 10

Americans were set to vote to return their president to office on November 8. One week before that election, two men wearing dark suits and carrying black umbrellas passed through the front door of the headquarters of the Federal Reserve Bank of New York, a few blocks north of Wall Street. Preceding them through that door and into those hallowed halls were reports of an upward tick in consumer spending, an as-yet unheeded warning of unusual movement in the rare earth metals commodity futures, and an e-mail, still unread by any official likely to care, that the murder of a wealthy Wall Street investor may be connected to some larger intrigue. Intrigues, in the financial world, arrive by the truckload, as it were, and most will be discounted before ever being investigated. Tom's death might have qualified for such an ignominious fate, but the presence of Ted and Steve assured otherwise.

Once they'd cleared the metal detector a visibly shaken Ted turned to Steve, and for the first time since the news of the murder, he showed signs of his habitual humor. There was that grin, a grin of confidence, a grin that to Steve conveyed the fact that they were inside the treasury building, and that thus far there were no handcuffs, no armed soldiers, no assault. They had encountered uniformed officers at the door, but they were from some private firm with a name like Secur or Proteck or Investigatio, and were thus not to be taken very seriously. Ted and Steve followed their instructions through the metal-detecting station, past the pile of plastic bins, and into the inner sanctum of American capitalism. Even if fiscal policy is made in Washington, the actual machinations of the American financial world are put into play in this building. The US economy, and economies all around the world, had been bolstered, and, much more often wrecked, by decisions taken here, decisions with such far-reaching consequences that even the half-million gold bars stored in the basement were considered to be symbolic rather than reassuring.

A brunette secretary sporting a formal, red dress and a collection of golden rings and bracelets invited the two men to sit down on the purple, leather couch. The bracelets adorned her wrists and the rings were on eight out of her ten fingers, and, upon closer examination effected by Steve's discerning eye, could also be found to be looped into almost every possible ear piercing including, as he knew from a former girlfriend, her lobes, orbitals, auricles, daiths, conches, traguses, and rooks. As he pulled the fabric up on his silk, black pants in order to sit down, Steve discretely motioned to Ted with a flick of his head in the direction of this armored, golden goddess. Ted looked over at her, indiscreetly, and then once he had settled into his seat motioned towards his crotch, where he drew a small circle in the air with his index finger, as though inquiring as to whether her vulva was similarly adorned. Steve smirked. America had clearly taken a rather radical direction of late, it seemed.

Suddenly a young man, far too young for the role, arrived in the waiting area. A slight, bespectacled, pale, nerdy-looking type quietly put forth his small, clammy palm, and shook hands with both men before leading them to an elevator. He inserted a key that brought them up to an unmarked floor, to what was known quite simply as the "Operations Room," a huge space that resembled a trading floor. It was an unexpected scene. There were no traders on the floor, no hustle and bustle, no hand signals, and almost no sound, except for the clicking of keyboards. This wasn't the riotous zoo that Ted and Steve knew well from their work; this was simply a huge room filled with hoards of informally dressed traders manning computer screens.

"Pretty casual, huh?" asked their guide.

"Casual, indeed!" replied Ted. "A lot quieter than my office."

"That's what everyone says. By the way, I'm Mike."

"Hey, Mike," continued Ted. "Do you get lots of visitors?"

Mike, wiser apparently beyond his years, didn't reply. "The real action is in the conference rooms. I've heard yelling from inside them on more than one occasion." Mike paused for a moment, and then looked into Ted's eyes as they walked towards one of the conference rooms. "And crying."

"That's reassuring!"

Just as Ted uttered those words, there emerged a large, puffy, pink-faced man with a Yasser Arafat-style beard. His round, red face bore patches of uneven bristles that looked to have been trimmed with some version of a weed-eater. Mike didn't stay for the introductions, but instead just faded away into the endless expanses around them.

"Steven Fraser," said the monument of a man who usurped this young assistant. "You must be Ted."

Steven Fraser shook Ted's hand with his plump paw and a firm grip, and then turned to Steve.

"Steve? Steven." Steve looked at him as though he were meeting his adversary for the semi-final match at Wimbledon. As though in search of a warmer connection, Steven Fraser held onto Steve's hand and repeated himself. "Good afternoon, Steve, Steven Fraser."

Steve's eyes narrowed further, and he nodded, almost imperceptibly.

Steven Fraser indicated the way into the room, and then led them, with a dexterous wobble of his huge stomach, as though he was working to avoid scraping the doorframe.

Before them lay one of the principle control rooms that hovered at the very epicenter of the contemporary, material world. It was appropriately business-like, cold, and, amazingly, empty. Ted and Steve had imagined various scenarios for this meeting, including discussions with the president himself, surrounded by a host of advisors. In none of these scenarios were they alone with a six-foot-five, obese, somewhat-bearded man inside of a conference room, on a floor of a building occupied solely by young people staring intently into cyberspace while dexterously playing on their keyboards, like so many travel agents inside of an airport.

"Let's get down to business, shall we?" Fraser folded his hands in front of him on the desk and looked at the two men.

Steve looked over at Ted, who was staring intently forward, looking increasingly ominous. "Was this the guy?" His eyes seemed to inquire.

The play in this room was obvious. They needed to assess if Steven Fraser would, or even could, send the right message to the head of the treasury and the feds. On the trading floor they now occupied, the US government purchased thirty to forty billion dollars of long-term US government bonds, and another twenty to thirty billion dollars of mortgage-backed securities *every single month*, for a total of around six hundred billion dollars per year. Even the slightest shift in spending, enacted as White House policy, could redirect resources in ways that could change outcomes in markets around the world.

In fact, the effects of actions taken in this room affected the value of the dollar, the rise and fall of interest rates, the amount of subsidies paid to bank and other private institutions, and, by extension, the movement of the entire stock market. Any shift in their actions were recognized, felt, and acted upon, in regards to US government assets totaling more than five trillion dollars. The amount is so staggering relative to the overall world economy that the last time the head of the treasury department had whispered, possibly to test the waters, that they would need to wind down this stimulus program in order to return the treasury to its traditional role, the stock market had dropped 550 points in thirty-six minutes.

"I'm really sorry about your friend." Steven Fraser seemed intent upon penetrating Steve's armor, in order to start the conversation. Steve had no intention of relaxing his guard, and so, as Ted drew Fraser's gaze to him, the scene took on a distinct good cop / bad cop feel.

"We are still reeling," started Ted. "Senseless."

Fraser turned to Ted. "You think so?"

It was Ted's turn to adopt a statuesque pose, a powerful tool in an arsenal that had served him well over the years of negotiating financial settlements.

"Yes," he uttered finally. "Random. That's what the Metro guy said."

"Police?"

"Yah." Ted looked over at Steve, waiting for his move, but he was stock-still.

"Anything else? Where's the body?" Fraser seemed to be just feigning interest, still assessing.

"They won't release it," said Ted. "I'm heading to Nashville tomorrow."

"Next of kin?"

"He was pretty much alone in the world. Some distant family in the Philippines, nobody here, and his parents are both dead."

"Hm." Fraser added this to the list of details, this being clearly something he didn't know. Since it appeared to be significant, it must have been related to the treasury's sense of Tom's motive. "And so you wanted me to address, what shall we call it, this stimulus?" Fraser looked over at Steve, since a one-syllable answer might start the conversation.

Ted, of course, answered the call, in order to save Steve for a more perspicacious moment. "That's right, right, exactly. That's actually what we called it."

"Is it still going on?"

"Manufacturing you mean?" asked Ted.

"Manufacturing, yes, and distributing."

"No. Unless you want us to continue." The question of how humor might work here was unclear, and if it flew, Ted would have a much stronger set of cards to play.

Steven Fraser moved his large body forward into the table, confident, apparently, that he now possessed what he needed. "No, that won't be necessary. And doing so would complicate matters. Further, complicate matters further."

"That was the plan," said Steve.

Fraser turned abruptly towards Steve in the face of this reply. "Okay. Done. Now what?"

Steve calmly moved his left hand towards his right breast pocket and pulled out a small pocketbook, bound in leather and tied. He dexterously untied the leather strands and ceremoniously opened the little book, as though his own Native-American tribe had sent him as a messenger to a divine task. "This is the list. You don't need to change the quantity of your investments, you just need to change the recipients."

Fraser smiled, snidely. "Is that all? Let's see it." Steve slid the list over to him, and looked to catch Ted's eye. Ted raised his eyebrows and looked to Fraser's gaze.

With his rather nasal voice and cocky demeanor, Fraser scanned the list quickly. "Are you making these suggestions as a voter?"

Steve resumed his steely gaze.

Fraser looked from one to the other. "This is why you are here? This is the product of your labor? For this you risk a lifetime as a guest to the US prison system? I'm not so sure I understand."

"This shouldn't be difficult," said Steve, assuming a well-rehearsed tone of pure condescension. "You can't ruffle the market's feather."

"More than just that!" exclaimed Fraser.

"But we're not asking you to do so. We have contributed several billion—"

"Billion?" Fraser looked at Steve in amazement. "Billion? You guys forged several billion dollars? Wow." He smiled broadly. "Now I am impressed!"

"We contributed several billion dollars to charities and causes we support."

"You guys support the projects?" asked Fraser.

"We support the people in the projects, unlike this bloody

country."

"Well, we could have a debate about that, Steve!"

"Not to the degree that you should. And every dollar, every single dollar that we put into circulation stayed close to where it had arrived. Not offshore, not in bank accounts of—"

"Of people like you?" said Fraser.

"Right, not in the bank accounts of people like us, and not FROM the bank accounts of people like us either," said Steve, angrily.

"The president is well aware of this." Fraser dropped the words like a bomb, and it continued scattering bits of metallic implications through the room for several long moments after detonation. The pause was palpable, tangible, almost edible. "It's a lot, more actually than he knew."

"Consider it a reelection contribution," said Ted.

"That sounds like bribery."

"It's what you said, Fraser, it's a stimulus," Steve declared. "This country expects that stimuli have to come from the wealthy, that it's Bill Gates who will vaccinate everyone in Africa, and Guggenheim who built the museums in order to save us all the trouble. It shouldn't be like that. You," he paused, "this administration can flick a few levers and shift allocations into things that matter."

Fraser looked down the list once again. "The Department of the Interior?"

Steve suddenly looked animated. "The Department of Indian Affairs. They have a few bills to pay, and a few recipients waiting for checks. If you look on the next page, there's a list of treaties, signed by the US government, but as yet not honored. We have helped out with a few of them, but now we want to fulfill our obligation to those people who were here before the white man, and who were slaughtered for the favor."

Fraser turned the page over and found a long list under the heading of "List of Treaties Between the United States and Native Americans, beginning in 1778 with the treaty with the Delaware tribe, and following along through treaties with the Chickasaw, the Six Nations, the Wyandot, the Cherokee, the Choctaw, the Shawnee, the Creeks, the Oneida, the Potawatomi, the Apache, the Comanche, the Kiowa, the Cheyenne, Arapaho, and others, sometimes by tribal appellation, sometimes by the place where the treaties were signed.

"Every one of those treatises was broken, in some way or another. We want them fixed."

"I will have to bring this to . . . well, you know, the appropriate authorities. But we have much more to talk about!"

"Yes, actually we do," interjected Ted. "We have some unwritten treatises as well, for the environment. It's on the next page."

Fraser flipped the page, and then flipped forward to the others, each replete with detailed facts and figures. He closed the book. "I appreciate this. The president appreciates this. You've risked around twenty-five lifetimes in prison, and it looks as we'd expected, rather selfless."

Ted looked at Steve, who was simply staring forward, into, and through, Steven Fraser.

"And," continued Fraser, "naïve. But you knew this as well. You are going to spill the beans, a few days before the election, and spin it whatever way you need."

"That's about it, in a nutshell," said Ted. "This is not an act of aggression, Mr. Fraser, it's a stimulus plan that we're helping to fashion. We've even provided the money to subsidize it."

Steven began to laugh, eventually rather uproariously for the circumstance. "I suggested I handle this myself," he began, pausing to wipe the tears from his eyes, "because this is what I had imagined to be the case. And everything we've said to one other today wasn't said, and this meeting never happened. I took you in for questioning, and we are now going downstairs for a private luncheon.

Ted and Steve sat motionless.

"You aren't quite sure if this is a victory. It's not. But you are going to walk out of here, unlike your friend Tom."

Ted jumped up. "Did you?"

"We did nothing. The point is, that you were supposed to be three, and you are two."

Ted sat back down.

"On the other hand, you have a friend, a very convincing friend, who will be working with us after we win this election. Provided, that is, that we win this election. She came to us with offers we could hardly refuse. One of them was to place her former boss, John, in our dining hall, along with his partner, or wife, Tina I think it was. They insisted to bring some other assistants as well, um, Nathanial I think it was, and John, or Johnny, I don't recall. Maybe he was the son of the head chef? Whatever, we easily accepted," he patted his midriff, "and I have a suspicion that my lunch break may last a whole lot longer than it does now, if you know what I mean!"

Ted grinned, knowingly.

"Yup, it'll be a whole new day around here! John used to have a restaurant in New York City, just down the street in fact. Actually, I know that you know the place, because I've seen you both there before. Anyhow, I rather liked it," he pointed down to his wide berth, "rather more than I should. And I'm going to like it a whole lot more now that it'll be part of the perks for working in this place. Oh, and speaking of perks, there is some other guy, too, who is supposed to join the staff, after his wife has her child." He grinned. "Real advantage to working here, we have great benefits, even a leave of absence for expecting parents. And the other person, well, let's just say that she will be joining the cabinet." Fraser looked at Ted.

"Who will, you mean Jessica?"

"Jessica, yes, Jessica. She will be providing raw materials essential to the US government and to the many companies that use those materials to build things, you know, like computers and cellphones." He grinned. "And since these materials, well, come from the ground, as it were, she'll be working for us in the capacity of a new cabinet post, as secretary of the environment."

Ted and Steve sat, dumbfounded.

"Smile! It's a victory!" continued Steven Fraser. "Or at least I'd like to think it's a victory for all of us, all Americans. I just hope the voters see it that way. In the meantime, your bills will circulate for a short while longer, maintaining their stimulating effect until they are incinerated, along with every piece of paper money currently in existence. And your friend Jessica will ensure, to use her words, that our particular treaty is honored. For this, you have her to thank, and me. We need to iron out a few things, including the production of some actual wallpaper that looks like money, and to do so we'll be using the help of some soon-to-be legal Chinese workers."

Ted smiled.

"Ah!" exclaimed Steve as he stood up. "A smile! How about you, Steve?" Steve stared at Steven Fraser with the eyes of an ancient warrior and grinned a grin of relief and pride. He then brushed his hand up across Ted's back, almost an embrace, but more like a sustained nudge. It was the strongest show of affection he'd ever offered to his friend.

"I'm starved for a stately dish," said Fraser. "Sorry if I'm not saying it right, but from what John told me, it's really good, and called, what did he say? 'Oeuf de Fabergé.' Yah, that's it. Oeuf de Fabergé. What kind of a name is that?"

Steven Fraser rose and headed for the door, inspired it would seem by the thought of the impending feast. Maybe this would be the one that would finally prohibit his passage through the conference room door so that he could go home and engage in something other than this dreadful job.

As the two friends rose to join him, Ted turned to Steve and silently whispered, "Steve, we should suggest that Jude write about all this. He could write a bloody novel based on that name!"

"Yah," returned Steve, as he reached into his breast pocket for his sunglasses. "True. But which one? Fabergé, or just Oeuf?"

"I don't know, whichever one came first!"

ABOUT THE AUTHOR

Robert Barsky paid some of his college bills by working in restaurants in Cape Cod and Montreal, and after graduating he moved to Switzerland to pursue a career in skiing, supporting himself by working in an upscale hotel bar. He now enjoys cooking for his wife and his college-aged children, and writing about language, literature and revolution. He is the author of eight books, including biographies of Noam Chomsky and Zellig Harris. This is his first novel, and he is excited (egg-cited?) to work on the next one.